CELESTIA

JESSICA AMMES

A catalogue record for this book is available at the British Library

ISBN: 978-1-527278-56-1

Published by Jessica Ammes

Cover: Jessica Bell

Requests to publish work from this book should be sent to
ammesjessica301@gmail.com

Thanks to my lovely family for all their support since lockdown. Special thanks go to my incredibly patient husband. Your support from the moment I began researching has been unfaltering. I had no idea where this was going but you never stopped me even though it was so hard at times. You've been amazing. You are amazing. Thank you to my parents for making me the person I am today, I never stopped loving you both even though we've had a bumpy road. Thank you to Maggie for your continued support and being part of our lovely book club with Sara.

Thank you to everyone in Joinavision. Your support has helped spur me on to the end. It's been amazing seeing how many kind people are out there, all wanting to help make the world a better place to be. I know we are creating something truly remarkable.

When asked what surprised the Dalai Lama XIV most about humanity, answered "Man! Because he sacrifices his health in order to make money. Then he sacrifices money to recuperate his health. And then he is so anxious about the future that he does not enjoy the present; the result being that he does not live in the present or the future; he lives as if he is never going to die, and then dies having never really lived."

CHAPTER ONE

STAR GRIPPED HER MOTHER BY the shoulders and looked fiercely into her large, piercing blue eyes. 'It's finally here, isn't it? Tell me it's my first Human Studies lesson today?'

Meisa laughed, though her eyes were filled with tears, and nodded. 'Look at me; I always get upset at times like this. Remember what I was like on her first day at the Centre of Learning, Mum?' she said, dabbing her tears away.

'How could I forget?' Rhea smiled. 'Just like your father.'

'I can't wait to see Lacarta and Alhena. I bet they hardly slept a wink!' Star looked at her female relatives and sprang into the air, landing high in the trees. 'It's here, everyone. It's finally here!' she shouted as she leapt from branch to branch.

'Come down from there right now!' Meisa said.

'Leave her. She's excited – just like you were,' Rhea remarked.

Star playfully stuck out her tongue at her mother and continued her antics, making wild noises as she did so. Her movement was so fluid it was nigh on impossible to keep up with her. The forest responded instantaneously; the chinuanfas chirruped, the manuanu whooped and the lameta snorted in excitement.

Meisa closed her eyes and breathed in the aroma of her tea.

Today should be filled with joy and anticipation but her heart longed for Leo to be here, to see their beloved daughter at this special time of her life. 'I miss you,' she whispered and from some far-off place she was sure Leo replied, 'I miss you too.'

Rhea reached over to her daughter and squeezed her hand. 'Are you OK, my love?'

'Not really,' she replied, watching Star leap about in the trees. 'Just because Leo died there, it doesn't mean something's going to happen to Star too.'

'Don't ever say he died,' Meisa said through gritted teeth. 'We've never had a body, have we?'

Rhea sighed. 'No, we haven't.'

'I dreamt about him again last night. This time he was screaming ...' she started sobbing. 'I tried to get to him, but these large metal doors stopped me. He had his arm outstretched, reaching for me but no matter where I went, I couldn't get any closer. It was terrible. Oh, Mum, I just know something's wrong.'

Rhea stroked her daughter's back. 'You can't keep torturing yourself. It was fourteen orbitals ago now; it's time to move on. If there's anything wrong the generals won't let them go. But if this is Star's journey you mustn't let your own fears hold her back.'

'Don't patronise me, Mother.'

'I'm not! I understand how you feel but we can't change destiny no matter how much we'd like to.' She went to stroke her daughter's hair but Meisa jerked her head away.

Meisa saw her mother wince and her heart crumpled. She moved closer and leant her head on her mother's shoulder. 'I'm sorry.'

'It's fine. I know how hard this is,' Rhea said gently as she kissed her forehead. Rhea stood up and poured them both a cup of ghuanuka tea. She passed one to Meisa and sat down next to her. They simultaneously blew on the steaming hot liquid and took a sip.

Suddenly, Star landed next to her mother, startling her. Hot tea cascaded over the cup and onto her legs.

'Be careful, will you?' she cried out.

'Stay still. You're OK.' Rhea grabbed a handful of herbs from a clay pot, some hemp cloth and placed them carefully onto the angry red marks. She held her hand firmly over the dressing, making Meisa wince in pain. After a few moments she removed the cloth, revealing skin that showed no evidence of any trauma.

'Tell me what to expect from my first lesson.' Star wriggled in between her mother and grandmother who moved along the log to make room for her.

'Well, if it's the same as mine, you'll be observing humans the same age as you. I think they call them "teenagers". Our planet orbits the sun twice as fast as theirs, so they're sixteen years old whereas you're thirty-two orbitals,' her mother stated proudly.

'Not all the boring stuff! I get it – you're eighty-four orbitals but in human terms you're forty-two years old. And Granny! Well, at one hundred and forty-six orbitals I can't even work out what that is in human years!'

'Hey!' Rhea laughed.

Star looked at the backs of her hands where her own intricate markings were starting to appear. 'I can't wait till I've got as many lines as you, Granny,' she said. 'Where's my favourite one?' She turned her grandmother's arm over, tracing her finger along the ornate markings.

'That's your mother's line,' she said, pointing to a delicate swirl. 'This tiny line coming down from your mother's is you. Every orbital you're alive, the line gets longer.'

'Have you got time for this?' interrupted Meisa. 'You don't want to be late for your first lesson, do you?' Star shook her head. 'Don't forget not to influence Lacarta or Alhena's decision.'

'I won't!'

'Studying humans isn't right for every fledgling; it can affect them badly in the long run. That goes for you too. You don't have to go ahead with this.'

Star ignored the concern in her mother's voice. 'Before our next moon I could be on my way to Earth! I mean, how mind-blowing is that?' Meisa smiled but it didn't reach her eyes. 'Stop worrying, Mum! I'll be fine,' Star said, leaning over and giving her a hug.

'We know you will be. Don't we, Meisa?' Rhea said, raising her eyebrows.

'Of course, darling,' she said brightly. 'Now go and get ready before the other two arrive!'

CHAPTER TWO

ORION CURLED OVER AND WRAPPED his hands around his legs to try and retain any heat his body had created overnight. A few bits of moss and some dried leaves provided him with scant bedding. Every inch of his body ached; the work was even more gruelling now he was all alone. His eyes sprang open as the enormity of the task dawned on him. He sat up, reached for his axe and began the monotonous chip, chip, chip that would take up his entire day. The tunnel was nearly finished but he was getting weaker by the day.

After an hour or so of working, his stomach, annoyed at being neglected, gave a low growl. He put down his axe and took a bite of the stale bread he kept in his bag. Thank Demeter he'd grabbed it from their hut the day they'd had to flee the village; it was all he had left to eat. As he ate, he thought of his Uncle Leo and felt his heart tighten. How would he ever get home now the authorities had taken him? The anger he felt inside was like lighting a fire in his belly. He put the remainder of the bread back in his bag and continued chip, chip, chipping at the rock. The tunnel wasn't finished yet and time was running out. Celestia's craft would be coming to Earth in three weeks' time and if he'd been successful in telepathically communicating with Star, she would be on it.

Orion rummaged in his bag and took out the sequente which Leo had discreetly thrown to him the day he was led away. He looked intently at the small globe and an image appeared of his mother back home, sat alone outside their hut, having her morning cup of tea. It had been two orbitals since she'd seen him; a year for him on Earth. He'd been convinced that his feelings for Mary were worth sacrificing everything he'd ever known and loved but watching his mother made him wonder if he'd made the biggest mistake of his life.

A tiny rustling noise interrupted his thoughts and he turned his head towards the sound. He extended his index finger and a bright shard of light shot out from the tip. He darted it around the tunnel but apart from two mice there was nothing to see so he lay down, the light disappearing into his finger. A little feather fluttered onto his face causing him to sneeze, just as the mice squeaked noisily and scampered further down the tunnel from where he lay. '*So many mice!*' he thought to himself. He kicked out with his foot in the hope of scaring them, then yelled out in pain when he banged his knee against the side of the tunnel.

One of the mice picked up the feather from the floor with its front paw. They both rubbed their hind legs and shape-shifted into two tiny giggling pixies.

'You're so naughty, Veruna!' Tabitha said.

Veruna, doubled up with laughter, rested one hand on Tabitha's shoulders, the other held the feather.

'Is someone there?' Orion said and a bright shard of light lit up the entire tunnel, fully exposing both pixies. With lightning reflexes, he grabbed Tabitha and held her in his hand.

'Put her down immediately!' Veruna cried out, stamping his foot.

Tabitha's little face poked out from Orion's hand; her eyes bulged in terror. 'Click your fingers!' Veruna shouted to her.

Orion stared at the tiny pixie in his hand, waiting to see what she was going to do but his firm grip meant she was unable to move her fingers. 'Who are you?' he asked. Tabitha looked up at him and trembled in his hand. 'Don't be scared. I'm not going to harm you. I only want to know who you are.'

'We're Guardians of the Underworld, Servants of Persephone!' Veruna said, stamping his foot and puffing out his chest. 'And you shouldn't be here, disturbing our world. You're lucky we've kept the Skriffter away from you – he's going to be so mad when he finds out what you're doing!'

'Who's the Skriffter?' he asked.

'He's the meanest creature that ever lived!' Veruna shouted. 'He'll eat you up for dinner if you dig into one of his tunnels.'

Orion looked alarmed. 'But I had no idea anything lived down here!'

'Well of course you didn't! We keep ourselves to ourselves; we only want a peaceful life. Where's Leo? He knows all the rules!' he said, stamping his tiny foot.

'You know Leo?'

'Everyone knows Leo! He's been working here for years!' Veruna crossed his arms and frowned. 'How do you know him?'

'I'm his nephew, Orion.'

'You're from Celestia!' Tabitha said, putting her hands up to her face.

Orion nodded. 'The problem is Leo's been taken by the authorities and I've got no idea where he is!'

'Taken?' they gasped.

'Yes! The military took him a few days ago!'

'But that means he'll miss Star when she gets here!' Tabitha said, putting her head in her hands and falling to the ground. 'After all these years of digging he's not going to see his daughter!' she wailed.

'Calm down, Tabitha! We'll help Orion find him and we'll help finish what Leo set out to do five years ago. We owe him that,' Veruna said firmly. 'Go get some of that root that'll help Orion, my sweet.' Tabitha dried her tears, clicked her fingers and was gone.

'How'd you guys do that?' Orion asked.

'Pixie secret,' he said tapping the side of his nose. 'Okay, let's get a plan together. You first,' he said crossing his arms and looking intently at Orion.

'My plan's to finish the tunnel.'

'Fantastic! Then what?'

'I hadn't really got much further than that.'

'But Leo always had a plan. I thought you were his nephew?'

'How can I have a plan when I don't even know where he is, let alone how to reach him?'

Veruna tutted. 'Not much like him in the looks department either, are you?'

'Well, I'm sorry to disappoint you.'

'Looks like it's down to me to step into your uncle's shoes then,' he tutted noisily again. 'How long till one of your craft arrives on Earth?'

'Three weeks.'

'And the reason you want Star to be on it is because …?'

'If Star's not on it I don't think there'll be a craft coming here at all. My mother always said this was her first class where they all seemed to know their path at such a young age. Human Studies tends to attract those who haven't found their direction in life. Star knows her dad worked on earth so I'm sure she'll want to find out more about this place. If *she* doesn't come, no one will, which means no craft and no way of getting Leo back if we do manage to find him. Now I've got to hope she comes here, intercept her, expect her to recognise me, as well as find out where Leo is *and* finish this tunnel! I'm never going to manage it!'

'You're not on your own anymore,' Veruna said. 'We're here now.'

'What can you do?' he said, shaking his head and frowning. 'No offence but look at you, you're tiny – no good for digging – you can't contact Star and you've got no idea where Leo is.'

At that point Tabitha reappeared with a strange, crooked root in her hands. 'Use this to find Leo,' she said, handing it to him. 'Take a bite, think of him and if he's still alive it'll take you to wherever he is. You're lucky he's your uncle – it only works with people you're related to.'

'OK,' he said slowly, taking the root from her and placing it in his bag, giving them both a dubious look. 'You promise it's safe to eat?' They both nodded. 'And it definitely can't help me find someone I'm not related to?'

'Definitely. Why?'

'I've lost someone else too.'

'Not very good at keeping hold of people, are you? Who else have you lost?'

Orion's eyes filled with tears. 'A girl I loved.'

Tabitha held her hands to her face again and gasped. 'How tragic!'

Veruna raised his eyebrows. 'Calm it with the drama, Tabitha. This one obviously feeds off it.'

'I do not!' Orion protested. 'It's this place, this world of yours that creates all the drama. I've only ever wanted a simple life!'

'Don't start pointing the finger at us, young man!' Veruna frowned and placed his fists on his hips. 'We're trying to help you, don't forget.'

'I'm sorry! I've lost everything and now I'm stuck in this rotten place with no way of ever getting home.' He put his head in his hands and rested them on his knees, emitting a few sobs.

Veruna and Tabitha looked awkwardly at each other. Tabitha signalled to Veruna to go over. 'Come, come now.' Veruna awkwardly patted Orion's ankle as he couldn't reach anything else.

'If Leo's alive we'll find him. I'm sure we'll find the girl too. But first we need to work out how to get Star here,' Veruna said, putting his hand up to his chin and stretching his index finger up to his lips.

'I've been telepathically communicating with her for some time now. Leo said he was rubbish at it, so he got me to try,' Orion said, lifting his head.

'See, you are like your uncle! Telling me you don't have a plan,' Veruna tutted.

'Just before they took Leo, he gave me this,' Orion said, showing them the sequente.

Tabitha clapped her hands in delight. 'He showed us this once! We saw Star in it, combing her lovely pink hair. Can we see her now?'

Orion shook his head. 'Unlikely. It only allows you to follow the relative you're closest to. For me, that's my mum. She's teaching Star, though, so you never know. I've got to somehow make sure Star gets to lesson three in Human Studies. That one's a trip to Earth.'

'By the time she gets here we need to have the tunnel connected to the city's underground network so you can intercept her when she has her first trip there, just like Leo planned!' Tabitha said.

Veruna took it up from there. 'You'll tell her where Leo is so she can free him while you make your way to the space compound. Star and Leo will be there waiting for you so you can board your craft and head home to your wonderful planet, Celestia!' Tabitha and Veruna clapped their hands in delight.

'You're so clever, darling!' she said, wrapping her arms around his neck and kissing him.

'Wasn't that mostly my plan in the end?' Orion asked.

'Don't be such a bad loser,' Tabitha said to Orion then turned back to Veruna, giving him another kiss. Veruna flushed with pride. 'We've been watching Leo build this tunnel for years. He was the kindest being we've ever met.'

Veruna said, 'We'll go find you something to eat and drink. Just call us whenever you need us. You're not on your own anymore!' They clicked their fingers and disappeared.

Orion looked at the funny root they'd given him and took a tentative bite. Nothing happened so he took another bite and once he felt sure it wasn't going to harm him, another. When he felt his soul lift out of his body he almost laughed in delight. The plant was enabling him to use adastral projection which he'd been taught back on Celestia!

He lay down, took a bigger bite and again it happened. His body lay still while he was able to float above it. He took a big chunk, whispered Leo's name repeatedly, and after a few moments felt a dizzying effect as his soul left his body entirely and flew above the forest towards the city at breakneck speed. Everything below him was a blur as some unseen force pulled him towards the space compound. He flew past the railway tracks that led there, into the tunnel and over officers' heads as they went about their business. He went through doors, walls and no one could see him. He had no idea where he was headed but within seconds, he found himself hurtling towards a large, metal door that had the words, STRICTLY NO ENTRY AUTHORISED PERSONNEL ONLY. He grimaced as his body hurtled through the heavy doors and then suddenly, he stopped. He looked down and what he saw made him cry out in shock. Leo, in his Celestian form, in a brightly lit windowless cell sat on a chair with his hands tied behind his back. Chains hung from the ceiling and a foul-looking toilet sat alone in one corner, a basin in another. The only sound was the steady drip, drip, drip from one of the taps. His head was bent forwards on his chest and his hair lay in matted, wet clumps around his shoulders.

'Leo, it's Orion!' he said, hovering above him. Leo grunted but didn't move. 'Leo!' he said urgently.

Slowly Leo lifted his head and his eyes widened on seeing the ghost-like image of Orion above him.

'Orion! Thank Demeter you're here,' he said urgently. 'My life-line's fading. They're going to kill me!'

'Who? Who's going to kill you?' he asked, his eyes full of fear.

Leo talked over him as he said, 'They haven't let me eat or sleep since they brought me here. He keeps asking me where it is, but I've got no idea what he's talking about!'

'What about your powers, Leo? Use them to get out of here!' Orion said, his eyes lighting up.

Leo shook his head. 'I can't use them here. I don't know why!'

'Try, Leo. You've got to try!' Orion pleaded.

'Don't you think that's what I've been trying to do ever since they caught me?'

'But how can they stop your powers? It doesn't make sense.'

'I think they've done something to me, put some kind of implant inside me or something. When they handcuffed me I felt some sort of pinch on my wrist, thought it was the cuffs. I tried shape-shifting as they marched me away but it was like everything had left me.' He paused for a moment and a tear made its solitary way down his cheek, landing on the cold hard floor. 'I'm never getting out of here.'

'Hang in there. Star's going to be here soon. We'll get you on that craft somehow.'

'I don't think I can make it till then.' He gulped back a sob.

'Don't say that! You can't give up now!'

'Why would she ever want to study these wretched beings?'

'The same reason you wanted to?'

Leo's head lolled forwards and he emitted a sob.

A voice came from the other side of the cell door. 'What are you snivelling about now, freak?'

'Orion, you've got to go!'

'You have to use your powers! They can't have stopped them forever!'

A series of clicks could be heard from the other side.

'Go – now!' Leo said urgently.

Orion pulled his soul away from Leo but not before he saw the cell door open, showing the silhouette of a man standing in the entrance pulling on a pair of black gloves. As he drew closer, Orion could make out his face. It was Melantho, the captain who Orion had worked with at the space compound! He walked around Leo until he stood behind him then leant down, saying softly into his ear, 'How we going to play it today? You going to talk to me?'

'I told you, you've got the wrong man!'

Melantho laughed cruelly. 'Don't call yourself a man, freak.' He straightened up, a pained expression on his face. 'Come on, Leo, don't make me do this. Why don't you just tell me where it is so we can stop all this nonsense?'

'How many times do I have to tell you? I don't know what you're talking about,' Leo said, his eyes darting about, his feet sliding on the concrete floor as he attempted to move away.

A vein pumped angrily on Melantho's neck. 'I've had about as much as I can take of you. You either talk to me now or YOU take us down a road I for sure don't want to go down!'

'Captain Melantho, please …'

'It's General Melantho!' he spat and walked round to face Leo, a smug look on his face.

Leo's eyes widened in shock, 'But … that's impossible. There's only one human general and that's Rigley. It's how the Committee's run ever since it began!'

A smile passed over his lips, 'Yeah well 2030 was a long time ago. Turns out the Committee wanted to even up the balance. About time, don't you think? It's obvious your kind look down on us, not allowing two humans onto your precious Committee.'

'But we've never looked down on you. We've only ever tried to protect you!'

'Protect?' Melantho laughed. 'Forcing the masses to work in jobs they loathe just to keep your precious economy going. You call that protect?'

'The economy was put in place by the Aldorians. It was nothing to do with us!'

'You've always had it in for them, haven't you?' Leo started to protest but Melantho held up his hand to silence him. 'You'll be pleased to know that my first duty within the Committee was to take a vote on whether it's about time we had two Aldorians on it.' He threw his arms into the air, 'Blow me down, turns out they've been pretty pissed off too and couldn't wait to welcome General Thuban to the team.'

'But Aldorians only look after themselves, that's why there's only ever been one of them!'

'Times have changed, Leo. Hey, maybe Aldorians have changed too? Anyway, the vote was unanimous, apart from you lot and Rigley, and he doesn't count. Way too close to you Celestians if you ask me. So, you'd better start talking to me or I'll get General Rastaban onto you!' he said bending down and grabbing a clump of Leo's hair from the top of his head.

'Please have mercy!'

'Start giving me some answers, then.' He pulled on Leo's hair, forcing him to his feet. Leo shook his head but his eyes were wide with fear. 'Have it your way,' and Melantho punched Leo hard in the stomach. 'You want to tell me now?' Melantho roared, pulling back hard on Leo's hair. Leo pursed his lips and shook his head. 'You made me do this to you, Leo! Don't ever forget that.' He let go of Leo's hair, pushing him to the ground as he did, and kicking him repeatedly in the stomach and head, saying breathlessly, 'You made me do this,' as blood spurted from Leo's nose and mouth.

Orion knew he shouldn't in case it alerted Melantho to his presence, but he couldn't watch without trying something. He uttered the ancient Celestian words which their whole culture was based on. 'Natyinahu ne haringue' – *Do no harm.* It had been a long time since he'd tried but it might work. He focused on Melantho's black gloves and transferred some of the fire in his belly onto them. Melantho screamed and stared at his hands with confusion. It wasn't much but it was all he had.

Orion felt his soul hurtling back to his tunnel as the effects of the plant wore off. When he returned to his body the pixies were there with a selection of fruit and nuts for him. They both cried out in shock when Orion told them what he'd seen.

Now that everything had changed within the Committee, Star was their only hope. His plan to return home with Leo simply had to work. He lay down, closed his eyes and focused all his energy on the female who could help them get home. 'Come to Earth, Star. Come to Earth, Star,' he repeated until he fell into a fitful sleep.

CHAPTER THREE

THE NEXT DAY ORION CONTINUED work on the tunnel. Veruna and Tabitha kept his water carrier filled and found things in the forest for him to eat. That evening he took a large bite of the root so he could visit Leo again. His body hurtled back to the space compound and the brightly lit cell where Leo sat, his bloodied head rested on his chest; his hands remained tied behind his back.

'I'm here,' Orion said softly, reaching out to try and touch him. He hovered over Leo and watched the faint rise and fall of his chest. His eyes scanned Leo's body; where had he said he'd felt that pinch? He looked at his wrists, tied behind his back, and on close inspection could see a small line of blood on his left one, about one centimetre long. They couldn't have put something inside him – could they? Leo's shape-shifting skills were renowned throughout Celestia. Escaping from here should be effortless. He thought of his own powers and shuddered at the thought of not having them. They meant everything to him, they defined him. Losing them would be unbearable.

Eventually Leo said, 'Go home, Orion. There's two Aldorians on the Committee now.' The effort of speaking wore him out and he dropped his head back down. 'Go home,' he grunted one final time.

Orion sat with him for as long as he could, gently stroking his matted hair, hoping somehow Leo could feel his ethereal touch. 'I'll be back tomorrow,' Orion said, gulping back tears. Once again, he felt his soul being drawn back to his body at breathtaking speeds. He kept his eyes closed, reliving the horror of seeing Leo in such a bad way. As he flew back down the tunnel system, he saw Veruna and Tabitha sat next to his lifeless body. His body jolted as it reconnected to its soul.

'You're back!' Tabitha cried as Orion sat upright.

'Is Leo alright?' Veruna asked.

Orion shook his head and sobbed, 'He's only just alive.'

Once he'd dried his tears Orion took out the sequente and placed it on the floor in front of him. The pixies clapped their hands in delight as the image of his mother at home appeared in the globe. They all gathered round to watch her potter about her hut, cooking her tea.

When Veruna and Tabitha had gone home, he lay down on his makeshift bed and found his mind drifting back over the events that led to him sleeping in the tunnel.

'IT'S FUNNY, MUM,' HE SAID after his second lesson in Human Studies. 'I always thought life on Celestia was so simple – maybe too simple. I pictured life being way more exciting on one of the other planets. Now I know that Celestia and all the other inhabited planets in our galaxy keep Earth safe from nuclear war, well, it's made me respect Celestia on a whole new level.'

'Getting rid of those murderous bombs was the only way we could ensure humans would never stoop so low again. We're so lucky to live on a peaceful planet,' she sighed. 'It's such a shame. There's no reason Earth can't be the same as us. At least we still have Zaurak on the Committee; he won't ever give up on humankind.'

'Has he really been a general for fifty orbitals?' His mother nodded and Orion whistled in admiration.

'He's adamant he'll only retire when Earth is running the same way as Celestia – or is at least on her way there,' she said.

'How's Arrakis getting on?'

'He and Zaurak make a good team. He's been a good replacement for Uncle Leo.'

The two sat in silence for a moment.

'Any news on Uncle Leo?'

She shook her head and said quietly, 'I think it's time to give up now.'

Orion nodded his head very slightly. 'Poor little Star – only eighteen orbitals old when she lost him.'

'Far too young to lose a parent.'

'Same age I was when Dad died.'

'I know but at least we said goodbye. I can't imagine the pain they must feel not having his body returned home. Poor Granny, losing both her boys.'

'Without a body, there's got to be a chance he's still alive. Right?'

She shook her head. 'Everyone on the craft heard the gunfire and saw him fall to the ground. I just wish we'd been given some answers; none of what they said made any sense. It still doesn't! What were they thinking, shooting at them?'

'Maybe someone on the Committee wanted rid of him?' Orion asked.

'Zaurak would have spotted something amiss if that was the case.'

The two sat quietly for a moment, their thoughts on Leo.

'Mum,' Orion asked breaking the silence, 'why do you think it got so bad on Earth?'

'I've traced it back to the introduction of money though it may well go back further. Money led humans to focus on material gains and forget about any spirituality which had been such a strong force till then. And the unfailing belief humans had in their governments. Always believing what they read,' she tutted. 'They never questioned the motives behind wars, never took the time to research for themselves – when they had the chance, that is. All their information is heavily censored now, poor things.'

'Do you think they'll ever be liberated?' he asked.

'We live in hope,' she sighed. Orion put his arm round his mother's shoulders and she drew closer to him, resting her head on his shoulder. 'I have to remind myself how lucky the galaxy is now nuclear war is no longer a threat. That really is the most important thing. If those bombs were activated there'd be a catastrophic mass extinction across the galaxy. Who knows which beings would survive – if any?'

'Those Aldorians look like they'd survive anything.'

'Must be that disgusting reptilian skin of theirs.'

They both looked at each other and shivered – the mere mention of them made their skin crawl.

'Imagine what the galaxy would be like with them in charge!' Orion said.

'Do you mind if I don't?' They sat watching the sun disappear behind the trees and waved to their neighbours as they headed to the river for their evening family swim. 'I understand that the Committee has a duty to respect every race's opinion in the galaxy but when one race is so intent on enslaving humans, is it right to allow them to have any presence at all on the Committee?'

'I guess that's the problem with our democracy, isn't it? Even when we know how ruthless they are we still include them in the decision making,' Orion said.

'And excluding them may shake their scales even more and there's one thing you don't want to see – an angry Aldorian.'

'If I ever meet one, I'm going to give them a piece of my mind,' Orion said with a determined look on his face.

'If you ever meet one, that's the last thing you'll do. You can't reason with them. They aren't like you or me.'

'Hmmm,' he said, a glazed look on his face.

'I mean it – they're not worth it! Their hero's Narcissus. I've got no idea why they're so full of themselves. You couldn't get an uglier race if you concocted an image in your head of the ugliest thing you've ever seen!' She chuckled lightly.

'Mum!' he giggled.

'Well, they are!' she said, giving him a playful nudge.

'Maybe someone needs to pull one of their long scaly tails eh?' he said, nudging her back and they both laughed.

'Am I glad we don't look like that?' she said, stroking her son's rich black hair and gazing at his face.

'I guess beauty is in the eye of the beholder and all that ...' Orion tailed off as his mother raised her eyebrow. 'Just imagine having to kiss one of them – urgh!' he said and screwed up his face.

She tipped her head back and laughed. 'Their poor females! Oh well, we've had one on the Committee for one hundred orbitals and it's worked fine. They do have incredible technical knowledge and their crafts are still the best in the galaxy. I heard their latest model has a swimming pool on it!'

Orion whistled.

'We'd only ever have to worry if there were two Aldorians on the Committee. But that'll never happen,' she said, getting up and stoking the fire.

Leo's death, four orbitals ago, had sent shockwaves through Celestia but even that couldn't deter Orion – Human Studies was his destiny. Once he'd finished Further Human Studies, he would apply to be an apprentice to the Committee. It was a long process, taking up to ten orbitals. However, as soon as he'd completed his training it would mean he would be eligible to apply to be a highly respected Celestian general when either Zaurak or Arrakis stepped down.

CHAPTER FOUR

'Lacarta! Alhena!' Star said, waving to her two best friends as they walked towards her hut with their respective families.

Alhena's family, exuding an inner sense of calm, waved back. Her loving father, Hamal, and her mother, Talitha, walked with their youngest, Estana, between them. When she saw Star, the little girl let go of their hands and ran to her, squealing with delight as Star twirled her in the air.

Lacarta's family were having an argument. Despite his father's attempts to tame a few wild strands of Lacarta's bright red hair with some of his own spittle, they kept pinging back up.

'That's gross, Dad! Get off!' Lacarta shouted, batting away his dad's hand. 'Mum, tell him!' He held his dad's wrist in a vice-like grip as his hand hovered above the stubborn strands.

'Leave him alone, Sabik!' Lacarta's mother, Vega, urged.

Sabik looked at his wife and relaxed his wrist causing Lacarta to release his grip. At that point his father smeared the spittle right across the offending lock of hair, tipped his head back and laughed whilst high-fiving Vega.

'Don't know why you put up such a fight, son. I always get it in the end.'

Star ran over and grabbed Lacarta's hand, laughing as she did. 'Come on, you! Let's get out of here.' Star, Alhena and Lacarta linked arms, turned to their families and waved goodbye.

'Dad's such a pain,' Lacarta grumbled as they walked away.

'Stop your moaning,' Star said. 'Your dad's great. You're lucky to have him.'

'Sorry, Star,' he said, squeezing her hand. 'I didn't mean to be insensitive.'

'It's fine. How's your mum today?' Star asked.

Lacarta tutted. 'She couldn't stop fussing over me all morning. I know she doesn't think I'm up to Human Studies.'

Alhena put her hand on Lacarta's shoulder. 'She worries about you, that's all.'

Lacarta shrugged her off in irritation. 'She doesn't need to. Just because my eyes aren't so good doesn't mean I shouldn't study them.'

'They've always worried about you. You're their special little boy after all,' Star said, ruffling his head boisterously.

'You're as bad as Dad!' he said, jerking his head away from her.

'I think you're incredible,' Alhena said, making them both look at her in surprise. Alhena flushed a little, not used to being the centre of attention. 'Well, you are! Mum's always telling me how determined you were to walk even though it took you way longer than me and Star.'

Star groaned. 'Here we go again. Poor little Lacarta, couldn't walk till he was six orbitals, couldn't climb a tree till he was twelve orbitals.'

'But it's not surprising when his eyesight is so bad is it? How would you feel if everything you saw was blurred? That's why Lacarta's so amazing ...'

'I am here, you know!' Lacarta interrupted. 'This is exactly what I mean. I know my eyes aren't great but that seems to bother everyone else a whole lot more than it does me.'

Alhena smiled at Lacarta, 'That's exactly why I …' and her voice tailed off.

'Yes?' Star urged her.

Alhena coughed. 'That's exactly why I think they should stop worrying about you.'

'You sure that's what you were about to say?' Star asked, crossing her arms and frowning.

Alhena nodded but couldn't meet Star's gaze. 'At least your parents don't expect you to follow the family tradition. I keep telling mine I want to keep my options open but they're adamant Human Studies is a waste of my energy,' said Alhena.

'Yeah but they know you've got to find your own path,' Star said.

'How was your mum, Star?' Lacarta asked, his eyes full of concern.

'Alright, amazingly. She can't stop me from going and hasn't wasted any breath in trying to.'

'No, but your dad did die whilst travelling to Earth! I think we'd all understand if she'd tried to talk you out of it,' Alhena said.

'I know but it was fourteen orbitals ago now. Eridamus is always telling us we can't be held back by fear.'

'You've got nothing to prove to us, Star,' Lacarta said.

'What do you mean "nothing to prove"?' Star asked, crossing her arms.

'You know – to follow in your father's footsteps. He was one hell of a being. His shape-shifting is said to have been some of the greatest Celestia has ever seen,' he replied, pursing his lips and whistling.

'I want to study humans, that's all. It's got nothing to do with "proving myself".'

Lacarta sighed. 'Sometimes you make decisions before really

thinking them through. We're your friends; we'll support you whatever you decide. We just want to make sure you don't rush into this, that you think it through before jumping headfirst.'

'This isn't something I'm jumping into – no matter what you both seem to think. I'll tell you something else,' she said, pulling them close. 'I've been having these really vivid dreams. It's like someone's calling me, telling me I have to study humans and no matter what I think, I feel like I've just got to go with it.'

'You've got to follow your heart, Star, not some crazy dream,' Alhena said.

'It's more than a dream and it's not crazy,' she said, pulling away from them. 'Anyway, I am following my heart.'

Star saw a flicker of concern pass over her friends' faces and felt herself inwardly fume. All this worry was having the opposite effect. Rather than be deterred from studying humans, their concern was actually making her want to take it as far as she possibly could. If one of Celestia's crafts was going to travel to Earth, she was going to do everything she could to be on it.

CHAPTER FIVE

IT CAME AS NO SURPRISE to everyone at the Centre of Learning that Orion excelled at Further Human Studies and after a rigorous training session, which included the long awaited lessons in shape-shifting, six orbitals after his very first lesson in HS, he was accepted onto an apprenticeship. His mother was both thrilled and devastated as it meant him living at the space compound on Earth for a whole orbital with only a couple of visits home permitted. After a tearful farewell Orion took the two sunrise flight to Earth, to settle into his new role.

Orion was under the watchful eye of Captain Melantho, one of the human officers working at the compound. His knowledge of the surveillance system was superior to anyone else's and every apprentice's first assignment was on the observation side of things.

'I don't want to talk bad of my own race,' Captain Melantho said one day in the surveillance room, 'but how did humans ever get so dull?'

'Where I come from humans aren't considered dull at all.'

'It would appear not. Remind me why it's OK for your kind to observe us but we get nothing in return?' asked the captain.

'Without us you wouldn't even be here,' Orion said, staring at the screens in front of him.

'You guys still harping on about deactivating the bombs and saving the day? Don't they teach you anything else where you come from?'

'It wasn't just us that saved the day, was it?' Orion said, clenching his fists. 'All the inhabited planets had to step in, remember?'

'And despite that happening a hundred years ago you can't help going on about it, can you?'

'You'd have obliterated yourselves if we hadn't deactivated those bombs! We'd wanted to leave you alone but the last seven thousand years you'd been heading down this route and we had no choice but to …'

Melantho held up his hand. 'Don't bore me with a history lesson. This afternoon's been tedious enough already. All this studying humans seems a bit passé to me. If I had it my way we wouldn't be living under The Committee's watchful eye and I'm not the only one who thinks that.'

'And if I had it my way you wouldn't even be working here,' Orion muttered under his breath.

'What's that?' Melantho spat.

'Sorry? Nothing. Thought I'd spotted someone drinking a beer,' he said, turning and smiling at Melantho.

'You be careful what you say to me, young man – or whatever you are. I'm your boss, don't forget.'

'There's no hierarchy where I come from,' Orion said.

'We're not on *your* planet, though, are we? If I were you, which thankfully I'm not,' he sneered, 'I'd start being a bit nicer to me. I can make your life pretty miserable if I want to.'

'You can't intimidate me, Captain. We don't operate on fear vibrations,' he said, turning back to the screens.

'I don't care what vibrations you run on,' he scoffed. 'You ETs are easier to manipulate than you believe. Check out the Plutonian generals – I've got them eating out of the palm of my hand – just like you'll be after six months on Earth. A word of advice, Orion,' he said coming over to where Orion sat and bending down with his hands behind his back. 'You don't want to get on the wrong side of me.' Captain Melantho smiled when he saw Orion involuntarily shiver. 'I'm off to get a coffee.' He turned on his heel and left the room, slamming the door behind him.

'It's egotistical men like you that got Earth into so much trouble in the first place,' Orion muttered, not wanting to admit that despite his bravado the man had got under his skin.

He turned his attention back to the cameras but nothing was happening. Maybe humans were a lot less interesting that he'd imagined, just like Melantho had said. Surveillance cameras were inside every human's house in various locations; the fridge door, the television, in their phones as well as CCTV cameras in streets and stairwells. It was 8 p.m. and the majority of people were sitting in their living rooms either on their phones, watching television or both. A few were tidying up after tea, others were laying their clothes out for the next day. Parents were reading bedtime stories, struggling to calm their children who'd being cooped up in the state-run nurseries all day. Then, out of the blue, he saw something move on one of the cameras – an arm flailing, a leg kicking. He zoomed in on the image and there she was, the most beautiful human he'd ever seen. He turned the volume up so he could hear what she was dancing to – something about a Mr Shankly. The girl held her arms above her head, twirling her wrists this way and that, her eyes closed, her hips swaying to the beat of the music. She wore a tightly fitted purple top, a short, black skirt and tights with crazy patterns on them. Her long hair hung loose and moved to the beat of the drum. A red light flashed in the corner of the screen.

Orion couldn't take his eyes off her and his heart moved in a way it hadn't since hearing music on Celestia. The red flashing light was an audio warning – this was music that shouldn't be heard on Earth. He ran a quick check on the song; it had been taken out of circulation in 2040. He was so transfixed he didn't notice the door of the surveillance room open behind him as Melantho's shadowy figure slipped in, quietly shutting the door behind him.

He looked over the apprentice's shoulder to the screen which was holding Orion's attention and a smirk crept across his lips. 'What have you found here, then?'

CHAPTER SIX

ELDER ERIDAMUS STOOD WITH HER arms folded at the entrance of the Centre of Learning and watched as her excited students gathered around the hut. Her silver hair fell to the waistband of her hemp dress and her markings snaked from her wrists up her arms and onto her neck. These lessons were going to be really tough for her but she didn't want her own experience to affect the students.

'Morning class. I do hope the dormia you collected in herbal medicine ensured a good night's sleep despite your excitement?' She looked around at a lot of shaking heads. 'No, me neither,' she smiled. 'Before we step inside is there anyone who's decided they don't want to study humans?'

A number of hands shot up and she went round the group finding out why they felt it wasn't right for them.

'I need to focus all my attention on my pequinatar so I'm ready to play at the next ceremony,' a male called Indus said.

'I don't think I'll cope well with the negative energy we've been warned about. I'm worried I'll get sick because my body's so sensitive to vibrations,' Cujam said.

She went around each being who'd put their hand up until everyone had been given the opportunity to speak. 'You've all got very good reasons not to continue with Human Studies and I'm deeply impressed you're so in-tune with your emotions.' The students looked around at each other, beaming. 'Go and see Elder Archenar who'll tell you who's going to be teaching Shape-Shifting Studies.' The group gasped in delight at one of their favourite lessons being offered instead.

'But that's not fair!' Star shouted out. 'We've been wanting to do that for ages!'

'Calm yourself, young fledgling. You'll get to learn it too but all in good time. Elder Archenar also said that he's happy to teach astrology.'

The group groaned.

'You're all named after stars so maybe you should learn a bit more about them?' A couple of non-committal murmurs could be heard. 'Don't forget, you'll see all your friends at the graduation ceremony in forty-two sunrises time. Or for those of you studying humans – in three weeks' time,' she said, smiling at those who remained seated.

The group waved goodbye to those who'd chosen not to do HS, the remaining students headed into the Centre of Learning followed by their elder who asked them to sit down.

'As you all know, today could affect each of you in different ways. Open up and talk about how you're feeling as what do trapped emotions cause?'

In unison they replied, 'Trapped emotions cause blockages, Elder Eridamus.'

'And what do blockages cause?'

'Blockages cause sickness, Elder Eridamus,' the reply came back.

She gave a slight nod, pleased all their studying was paying dividends. 'Have you kept up with your vocabulary?' She peered down at the students who nodded back. 'You won't mind me checking, then, will you? Chana, what is a television?'

Her face lit up. 'Something which tells you a vision through means of channelling and programming!'

'Perfect. Skyla, what is a mobile phone?' Skyla scrunched up her face in annoyance as she wracked her brain. Four hands shot up behind her. 'Go ahead, Star.'

'It's a small box that you talk into. You can communicate with any of your friends no matter where they are on Earth.'

An impressed, 'Wow!' went around the room.

Eridamus tested them on a few more words: fridge, microwave, dishwasher, cinema, before agreeing that they had been studying very well.

'As you know, a group of beings called the Committee oversee the smooth running of Earth. Most planets have two members of their race on the Committee. Who can tell me which planets they come from?' She looked around as the group had a moment to think before asking them to shout out the names. The group had studied well and called out, 'Celestia, Mars, Venus, Mercury, Pluto, Aldor and Earth.'

'And what are the names of the two Celestian generals?' She looked around the group and nodded to Alhena whose hand shot up.

'Arrakis and my Grandad Zaurak!'

'Correct. In fact, Zaurak is the longest standing Committee member we've ever had. Lacarta's hand shot up. 'Yes?' she asked, nodding in his direction.

'Dad told me there's only one general from Aldor and one from Earth allowed.'

'I was coming to that. That's right. Aldorians and humans don't necessarily have the best intentions of the galaxy in their hearts. They're more troublesome than most. However, we respect everyone in the galaxy, therefore it's essential the Committee has an Aldorian and an Earthling.'

'But don't they mind?'

Eridamus tutted. 'Whether they mind or not is irrelevant after what they've put us through.'

'And what was that again?' he persisted.

'War, Lacarta, war! Those Aldorians don't give a damn,' she halted, realising she was speaking in an unfamiliar way to her students. 'I'm sorry ... don't fully adhere to the Committee's ethos of protecting humans from becoming so greedy they consider war a sensible way of dealing with matters they cannot resolve.'

Next, she got them to pair up with another classmate. Star grabbed Lacarta's hand who beamed back at her. Alhena went to grab his hand too, but as always realised Star had got there first. Instead she paired up with another friend, Neroa, who lived by the river. 'Before we go does anyone have anything else to ask me?' Everyone shook their heads. 'Wonderful.' Her face lit up as she said, 'Let's begin Human Studies!'

A huge cheer rang out. The wait was finally over.

CHAPTER SEVEN

THE TWO OF THEM STARED at each other. Melantho folded his arms and raised one questioning eyebrow.

'There was an audio alert flashing on camera one-three-six-five. Seems we have a questioner here,' Orion said, his heart pounding. 'I think I may need to monitor her more closely.'

'What makes you think that?'

'I ran a check on the song she's listening to, Captain. It was taken out of circulation ninety years ago.' He turned the volume up and let Melantho listen to the dulcet tones that floated across the room.

'Good work, Orion. I'll take it from here. Can't say it'll be too hard,' he said, staring at the girl with a glint in his eye.

'Would you mind if I take this one on, Captain?'

'And why would I let you do that?' he asked.

'It would be great experience for me for a start.'

'Great experience for me too,' Melantho leered.

'But you've got enough on your plate monitoring the attractive young woman in apartment four hundred and fifty-nine, block two thousand, five hundred and ninety-three. With so many hours spent on one individual I'm sure you're building quite a portfolio of her which no doubt you'll shortly be sharing with the Committee.' A redness seeped up Melantho's neck and he opened his mouth to say something but Orion held his hand up to stop him. 'No need to thank me. We're all in this together after all. Can I confirm the hours we view footage from individual cameras are all registered?'

He saw Melantho flinch and his grin momentarily dropped before he leant down so his mouth hovered by Orion's ear.

'Have it your way – monitor this girl. Tell you what, I'll even put in a good word for you with the generals, see if we can arrange a placement for you in her office. Then I'll have front row seats when your world comes crashing down the minute she finds out what you really are. You'll soon be on your little space rocket home. We'll be able to get a decent apprentice in from one of the more financially influential planets.' He laughed maliciously as he sat down, taking a loud sip of his coffee. 'Thought you might like this too,' he said, throwing a couple of sheets of paper over to Orion. They fluttered in the air then fell onto the ground between their chairs. The girl's face stared blankly up at him. 'I spotted you observing her from the camera in the staffroom. Didn't take long to pull up her file.' As he leant down to retrieve the papers Melantho placed his black boot firmly on top of her picture.

Orion pulled hard, but when he looked up and saw Melantho's smug smile, he let go.

'She's just a girl, Melantho,' he said nonchalantly. 'I'm not a pervert.' He paused, leaving the 'unlike you' hanging unsaid. Orion's comment touched a nerve, just as he knew it would. A vein on the side of Melantho's neck pumped angrily, causing his neck to flush and he saw him clench and unclench his fists. He knew Melantho was desperate to hit him but they both knew if he touched a hair on Orion's head it would mean the end of him ever working within the space compound.

'Is there a problem?' a voice said from the doorway.

They turned to see General Arrakis staring at them, his arms folded.

'I'm not sure, Captain. Is there?' Orion asked, turning to Melantho.

Melantho lifted his foot off the papers and replied, 'Your apprentice reckons he's found a questioner. I ran a check on her and he may be right. Look,' he said picking up the papers and passing them to him.

Arrakis scanned the sheets and passed them back. 'Good job, Orion. With parents like hers it's only natural some kind of questioning has emerged. Melantho, give Orion access to all her social media sites as well. This is a good opportunity for him. It may be pertinent to organise a placement on the same floor as her for a while. It's often best to nip these in the bud early, don't you concur?'

'I certainly do. We should allow Orion to pursue this one for as long as he feels necessary,' he said, the smug look still on his face.

Arrakis looked between the two, aware that something unspoken was going on. 'Right then, carry on, Orion. We can't have too many questioning the system just yet, not when there are still so few doing it. Life could be made very difficult for her, if she doesn't conform to the unwritten rules humans adhere to. Keep up the good work,' he said to Orion as he closed the door behind him.

'You owe me one, freak,' Melantho muttered to Orion.

'I owe you nothing,' he said under his breath, stuffing the sheets into his coat pocket.

CHAPTER EIGHT

THE STUDENTS FOLLOWED THEIR ELDER round the back of the Centre of Learning. 'Any word from your son, Elder?' Lacarta asked as he ran to catch up with her.

'Not yet. He warned me it could be a long time till he's able to contact me,' she said.

'Amazing they sent him straight onto such an incredible mission after such a short time on Earth. Can you imagine having to travel so far into space you've got no idea how many orbitals it'll take to get back?' His eyes were wide with awe. 'The Committee must think so highly of him to send him out on such a long mission!'

'Yes, yes, they must,' she said distractedly. 'Here we are,' she said, coming to a standstill in front of a large tree trunk. She waited as the group gathered round. 'We've created the perfect viewing station for Human Studies but your eyes take a moment or two to adjust to the dark. Try not to bump into each other.'

'Er … Elder Eridamus?' Lacarta said raising his hand.

'Go on,' she replied.

'I know my eyes aren't great but you're stood in front of a tree.' The others around him nodded their agreement, not wanting to have been the one to point this out.

Elder Eridamus smiled at Lacarta. 'When do I ever disappoint you?' She held up her palm to the tree trunk and like a tiny fire igniting, a flicker of light grew and grew until a handle emerged within the tree trunk. 'Lesson one in Human Studies,' she said and as if the tree were made of water, she put her hand inside the trunk and pressed down on the handle. A satisfying click could be heard as a door built within the tree trunk opened. The students gasped in awe. 'Duck down and follow me.' The excited group bent their heads and filed into the dark space, emitting a few, 'Ouches,' and 'get off me's' followed by some nervous laughter.

Elder Eridamus closed the door plunging them into total darkness. She held up her index finger and a light shot out from the tip of it before rummaging around the inner wall of the tree trunk to find the object she was looking for – a large shiny silver pyramid. 'Sit down, everyone. Before we witness our first group of humans, I should explain how Earth is currently run. There is one world government that makes all the laws. Every four years humans get to vote for the next person that will rule them. In the past these people have become incredibly power-hungry and dangerous so we've come up with a way of ensuring the government doesn't repeat its mistakes. In reality it's the Committee that runs their government and their voting is irrelevant.'

'So why let them vote?' Lacarta asked.

'Because they've spent years fighting for the right to vote! It would be terribly cruel to take that away.'

'But that's crazy!' Skyla remarked.

'We know! But it's how it's been long before we came along and it never stopped them voting then. When the Committee took over, the plan was to decentralise governments returning power to local communities, but humans weren't ready for it and there was uproar. They felt powerless.'

'But they are powerless!' Junia said.

Eridamus sighed. 'Yes, but the process of voting makes them *feel* empowered so for the time being the voting system remains in place whatever we may think of it. May I also remind you that humans had become terribly detached from their planet. The economy had become their priority, not their own happiness or the safe-guarding of the environment. In order for the economy to thrive humans had been channelled for thousands of years into the belief system that it's objects, not people, that make you happy. As the population on Earth grew, she couldn't cope with the drain on her natural resources. While the economy thrived, Mother Earth died.'

'I thought it was because there was a nuclear war?' Alhena asked.

'Indeed there was – while the masses were distracted with consumerism, their governments were out of control in their pursuit of global dominance.'

'Distracted by what?' Lacarta asked.

'Television programmes, the news, celebrities and this ...' she said, uncurling her hand. The group took an intake of breath as a holographic image of a mobile phone appeared. 'The invention of the mobile phone was key to distracting humans. You were right to say that you can use this to communicate with your friends but it can also give you the news, the weather forecast, show you what's happening in your town that night, connect you to any of your peer group as well as giving you the opportunity to buy anything you like at the click of a button.'

'But still ...' Skyla said.

Eridamus gave Skyla a look that instantly quietened her. 'The problem being that instead of focusing on what their governments were doing they were too immersed in their phones to notice or care. Brave humans trying to oust the global agenda were taken prisoner, tortured and never seen again yet the masses did nothing apart from stare at their phones.'

As she spoke, she pressed a button on the side of the pyramid and a large 3D holographic image filled the room. Images of what had gone on in Earth's history flickered before their eyes: humans in prisons, headlines from newspapers, bombed-out cities, and then crowds of humans walking along busy streets, waiting at bus stops, sat in restaurants with friends – all of them staring blankly down at their phones.

'Humans allowed lines of division to separate them from their fellow beings, forgetting how connected they all are.'

'But how?' Neroa said.

'Simple – through fear. Who can tell me what happens when our bodies operate within the vibrations of fear?'

'We're easier to manipulate,' Junia said.

'Precisely. They became fearful of humans from different races, sexes, countries, ages, religions or even ones who supported a different football team to themselves. Now humans have so many laws, which they believe are there to protect them, they don't know how to behave. Break any one of those laws and you may not be able to gain access to certain things that had been simple before – housing, a bank account, it may be difficult get a job, to find friends. Communities have broken down. Humans feel isolated, frightened and helpless – too scared to connect to those around them for fear of saying the wrong thing. Spending money, drinking alcohol, eating addictive food is their only relief.'

'It sounds horrible!' Neroa said.

'The trouble is they believe they're very progressive and incredibly advanced. Yet you only have to look at the structures they used to be able to build, compared to what they've built in more recent times, to realise this is an illusion.' More 3D images appeared showing the group pyramids, circles made of giant stones, beautiful ancient palaces and then tall, ugly, concrete buildings with small windows stretching high into the sky. The group's faces turned from wonder to repulsion. 'Look at their ancient gardens compared to their fields before the Committee intervened,' she said, as more holographic images filled the room: beautiful countryside divided by hedgerows, steep hills with fields carved into them, and then pictures of vast swathes of land with tractors spraying crops, fields and fields of pigs and cows in tiny metal cages, barns crammed with chickens and lakes with gigantic cages filled with fish all struggling for space and air.

'Yet still humans convinced themselves that this was progress and that tribal communities who stayed true to Mother Earth were inferior. In a way it was almost a relief when the bombs were activated as it finally meant the other planets in the galaxy could step in. You see the galaxy has an unwritten rule that no planet must intervene with the running of another unless that one's being operated in a way that would cause irrevocable damage to the galaxy. Those bombs wouldn't just have killed almost all of the population on Earth but the toxic matter would have drifted into space and poisoned other planets too. The Committee was set up a day or two after they were activated and has been running Earth peacefully ever since. Populations have been reduced so humans can still buy whatever they want without it being detrimental to Mother Earth. The economy continues to thrive thus keeping their government happy and all the intergalactic races get to travel freely, sharing advice and technology with officials at the space centre.' She tapped the pyramid with the top of her index finger and as if it had some kind of sucking mechanism, the 3D image disappeared.

CHAPTER NINE

ORION KNEW HE SHOULDN'T PURSUE her but felt powerless to stop. That night, in the privacy of his own quarters, he read through her documents.

Her name was Mary Wright. At nineteen she was a year younger than him, had no brothers or sisters, and lived with her parents in one of the less affluent districts. Using the phone provided, he accessed her social media accounts and pictures of Mary with her friends popped up: sticking their tongues out, holding a finger up to their pouting lips, clinking their glasses as they smiled at the camera. Every picture had hundreds of 'likes' and messages such as, 'You're so beautiful, hun', 'Another great night with my besties, love ya!', 'Love this pic, 'You guys are beautiful inside and out. Love you all!'

Orion was about to give up – this seemed incredibly normal behaviour for a human. Then in amongst all these bland pictures she posted a comment. 'Rifled through some family heirlooms and found a record player!' She posted a picture of her sat smiling next to a very ancient-looking machine, holding a record with the words 'The Smiths' on it. Her next comment was, 'Finally worked out how to use it. Why don't we have music like this anymore? This band rocks!' None of the posts got any likes. She'd continued to post a variety of messages about linking processed food to numerous illnesses and finding herbs to heal instead of pills, but they became more and more intermittent and more and more down-hearted at the same time. 'I know no one will "like" this but I'm going to post it anyway.' 'Not trying to bring anyone down here, just want to say there's more out there than we think!' Then a post that sent tingles down Orion's spine. 'When are we going to WAKE THE FUCK UP?'

All posts had completely tailed off for about six months and with a little more digging he found out she'd deactivated her account during that time. Then out of the blue there were her and her two best friends in a bar, drinks in hands, smiling at the camera but something had changed. Even though she was smiling her eyes looked empty. For Orion it was confirmation she was different.

During a rare visit home as he sat watching his mother tend to the fire, Orion said, 'I've been observing the most extraordinary girl.'

'What do you mean?'

'It's probably nothing,' he said, sensing a prickle in her voice. 'It's just that most humans are either on their phones or watching television in the evening whereas this one seems to love dancing to ancient music!' he said, doing his best not to smile but failing miserably.

'Who's given you permission to monitor this human?'

'General Arrakis,' he replied confidently and his mother's shoulders visibly relaxed.

'So long as it's nothing to do with that Captain Melantho. I keep hearing from Henry he's one of the most loathsome humans he's ever met.'

'Since when did he go from General Rigley to Henry?' he said with a playful wink.

His mother flushed. 'I don't know what you mean. We've had to work together a bit more lately, that's all. You know as well as I do relationships between humans and Celestians never work out.'

'Why is that?' he asked innocently.

'Because humans operate on the lower vibrations of fear and we operate on the higher vibrations of love. You watch, after one orbital on Earth you'll come back depressed, anxious and sick. It doesn't take long for a Celestian to realise how hard life on Earth is for them –even on the rare occasions they think they've fallen in love with a human,' she tutted. 'What's this girl called?'

'Mary,' he said, lowering his eyes and smiling.

For a moment his mother was silent before saying with a start, 'Don't tell me you've got feelings for her?'

'Of course not, Mum! I haven't even met her!' He couldn't meet her eyes as he spoke. 'I only find it interesting that while everyone else watches television, she's dancing around her bedroom without a care in the world.'

His mother sat down next to him and crossed her arms. Orion edged away. 'A word of advice – don't take this any further. You could risk everything ...'

'I'm not going to "take this any further",' he said angrily. 'However, she needs to be under surveillance. Her frivolous ways could have a detrimental effect on those around her. She's very popular on social media and if her friends see her behaving differently it could make them question the system too.'

'Hmm ...' his mother said, far from convinced.

A LARGE DROP OF CONDENSATION fell onto Orion's forehead, pulling him back to the present. He reached out for Mary and his heart sank as he remembered she was no longer with him, no longer a part of his life. He had to try and find her; he couldn't just lie here waiting for her to turn up. He knew he wasn't meant to in case he got found out but he needed to try. He squeezed his eyes shut, held his breath and focused on his inner being. At first nothing happened but he felt a shift deep inside of him. He tried again and this time it worked. He shape-shifted into an eagle. The tunnel was narrow and at first the stone walls caught on his wings. He hopped a little and smashed from side to side of the tunnel, but it didn't take long before it widened and he was flying gracefully through the waterfall and out into the pitch black of night. His eyes scanned the forest for signs of life. He flew for miles, scouring every bit of forest but apart from spotting various wildlife and the odd human he recognised from the village, there was no sign of Mary. He flew to the edge of the city and rested on the high wall surrounding it. The glow from all the lights lit up the whole area, there was no pitch dark in the city. He tried flying into the city but as if it held an invisible shield a metre inside the walls, he felt his body weakening and he had no choice but to return to the wall. He rested and tried again but the same happened; it was as if some hidden vibration was affecting every cell in his body. As his eyes scanned the city he noticed the tall white masts, each placed one hundred meters apart, covering the entire space of the city as far as his eyes could see. He remembered that these masts allowed humans to operate driverless cars and trains and realised that his fragile animal cells were sensitive to them, more so than when he was in human form. He returned to the waterfall and swooped down the narrow tunnel before returning to his human self. Tears rolled down his face as he thought of never seeing Mary again. How could she disappear like that? They'd been so in love. He'd thought they were invincible.

CHAPTER TEN

'CELESTIANS REGISTERING FOR THEIR FIRST lesson of Human Studies,' Elder Eridamus said, and a 3D holographic image of a kindly faced man appeared. 'General Rigley! I expected to see General Zaurak today.'

'He told me to pass on his apologies. He's got a spot of business to take care of. I have to admit I was rather glad to step into his shoes. He's suggested I take all three classes this year so we keep things consistent.'

'What a good idea,' she said smiling.

'It's a pleasure to see so many Celestians here,' General Rigley said, casting his eye over the group. 'And congratulations on making the decision to study us. We may not be everyone's cup of tea,' the class giggled on hearing one of the human phrases they'd learnt, 'but we're alright once you get to know us.' He paused for a moment then continued. 'General Zaurak told me you all did really well in human language studies as well as excelling in understanding our concept of time which, I have to admit, we do have an obsession with. However, it's imperative you get to see how we live. Without this knowledge you're unable to understand how crucial it is that Earth is run the way the Committee's run it for the last hundred years. For the time being it's the only way that keeps the galaxy and most humans happy – but nothing is without its challenges or compromises. I hope a few of you take Further Human Studies. It's always an honour showing any being around our incredible planet.' He clicked his fingers and the group gasped as images of snow-capped mountains, huge canyons, dense jungles and vast oceans flashed in front of their eyes. 'Your elders have told me Earth is much more beautiful than Celestia because of the plate tectonics covering the surface here,' he continued. 'These have given rise to stunning natural structures. I'm aware that Celestia is incredibly beautiful too and one day I hope I will be able to visit,' he said, turning his gaze to Eridamus who lowered her eyelids as a small smile spread across her face. 'For your first lesson we thought you'd like to see humans around the same age as you. Just as you all go to your Centre of Learning, humans go to school. You'll be observing live footage from inside the classroom of one of these establishments.' The group looked around the room, their eyes full of excitement.

Elder Eridamus took over from here. 'Feel free to use your honing-in skills to explore the emotions they are experiencing. Finding out how they feel is where things get interesting, isn't it, General?'

'You have such a way with words, Elder,' he said. The pair paused as their eyes met. 'Enjoy the lesson, fledglings, and see you at the next one,' he said, waving. 'I will now connect you to the school.'

'Thank you, General.' Eridamus turned her focus back to her students. 'These humans have no idea they're being observed but you'll be able to listen to everything going on in the room. I like to think of it as a one-way semi-permeable membrane, like we learnt about in our osmosis classes. Hone-in on the energy fields of the humans you want to find out more about but be prepared to experience emotions unfamiliar to you. If getting close to them makes you feel uncomfortable, come away but continue to observe the lesson. There's plenty to learn without tapping into their energy fields.'

She paused briefly before saying, 'Ready, General?'

'Ready and waiting, Elder,' came his cheerful reply.

Elder Eridamus sat down with her students and the holographic image emerged of thirty teenage humans walking into their classroom.

Star felt her heart race with adrenalin as Human Studies began in earnest.

CHAPTER ELEVEN

IT WAS EARLY MORNING BUT despite normally seeing Leo in the evening, Orion wanted to give him the good news. He took a bite of the root and felt his soul leave his body. Leo sighed with relief when he felt Orion's presence.

'I'm still in the game,' he said softly.

'Star starts Human Studies today!'

Leo went to smile but his lips cracked and blood oozed from wounds as they reopened. 'That's great news,' he said.

'It's sickening what that man's doing to you,' Orion said, shaking his head.

'Can we talk about something nice? It's a good day today. My baby's on her way.'

'She won't be long now. What can I do to help? I feel so helpless.'

'Tell me about Mary, would you? I thought she was a wonderful human.' His words slurred as the pain of trying to talk became too much.

Orion sighed and took them back to that magical day they'd met and everything that went on after that.

IT HADN'T TAKEN LONG FOR General Arrakis to sort out the paperwork necessary for Orion to start a placement in her office. The Committee helped him create a new persona and set up all the correct social media pages in case anyone looked into him. He posted pictures of food he'd eaten, places he'd been to, including a variety of bars and managed to superimpose himself onto a few pictures with other humans, ensuring it looked like he had the right number of friends. He was given a dark-grey suit and Melantho found him some casual clothes for evenings and weekends. His name was Thomas Brown, he was twenty years old, lived in one of the more affluent districts with his parents but hadn't got the grades, which explained why he'd been given a sales role.

At last he was ready for his first day at work. The high-speed train from the compound was virtually empty. A few men and women wearing suits sat staring out of the window. After twenty minutes the train glided to a halt. The platform was spotless and deserted. He followed the others departing from the train through a door, up a set of stairs and through another door where he was met with a blast of noise. Hundreds of humans filed past him. Nearly all of them wore blue masks covering their mouths and noses. A large moving set of metal stairs delivered them to another platform where a train was arriving. Orion spotted a red-faced man trying to barge his way through the crowds. People looked angrily at him then had to stand aside for a tall man in uniform, the letters AI on the back of his black jacket, who halted him in his tracks. The officer drew a gun out as the man's panic-stricken face looked from the train to the officer. He held the gun at the man's forehead who scrunched up his eyes. An alarm sounded and the crowd started to panic, moving as far away from the two men as possible. Within seconds the officer had the man covered from head to toe in a white suit, a plastic visor covering his facial area. In an almost robotic way, he frogmarched him across the platform and the dispersing crowds and through a door labelled, 'VIRAL TESTING STATION.' The doors to the train opened and the crowds piled on, the unmasked humans fumbling around in their bags and quickly placing masks over their worried faces.

When he arrived at the towering office block, he stood in line with all the other workers as they took off their masks and queued up to the facial recognition stations. He approached the eye-level unit which checked all his details and confirmed his temperature was below thirty-six point eight degrees. Once he was given the green light to enter, he waited by the lift until Mary arrived. He held back until she was level with him, ensuring his hand brushed against hers as they squeezed into the confined space.

'Sorry,' he said, smiling at her.

'No problem,' she replied, giving him a funny look.

On departing, he tried to brush his hand against hers again but she was too quick and he found himself stroking the hand belonging to a tall, slim, dark-haired man. The look he gave Orion made him wonder whether his touch had made his day and he sharply turned away.

An unsmiling man in a dark suit waited at the office entrance. 'Thomas Brown?' he asked, stepping forwards once the workers had all filed past him.

'Yes?'

'Brian Goulding. I'm your manager.'

'Pleased to meet you,' Orion said, offering his hand for the man to shake.

'Oh, err, are we doing that? Right you are,' Brian said awkwardly, offering his elbow instead of his hand.

Orion looked momentarily confused but then lifted his elbow for Brian to bump.

'Report to me if you have any problems, or you're showing a fever or have any symptoms such as a persistent cough. This is vitally important, do you understand?' Orion nodded. 'The company is fined $30,000 if one of our staff passes on a virus to another member of the team so please make sure you abide by all the rules. You have sanitiser dotted by each door and one at your desk. Please use it every time you enter a new room and after you've spent more than fifteen minutes with someone.' Brian nodded at the silver wall unit by the reception desk, making it clear Orion was expected to use it. He placed his hands gingerly underneath. The machine whirred and a blob of white foam landed on his hands. He looked at Brian and then to the white foam.

'Go on, then,' Brian said.

Orion lifted the foam to his face and sniffed it, looking gingerly at Brian.

'Don't smell it!' Brian spat, placing his hands underneath the dispenser and rubbing the foam into his hands.

'Sorry, of course. Don't know what's got into me today. Must be nerves,' Orion said, rubbing his hands together and cursing Melantho for not prepping him more about these habits humans had. No doubt he had done it all on purpose to try and make Orion look like a fool.

Once Brian was satisfied Orion was suitably sanitised, he led him to the tiny cubicle that was going to be his workstation.

'If you sneeze, please go and wash your hands immediately then come and sterilise your area with this, here,' he said, pointing to a bottle that was hooked underneath his desk. 'Here's your headset. Listen carefully to the welcome message. It will give you all the information you need: break allowances, how you'll get paid, what the procedure is if you don't do your job correctly.' He handed Orion the headphones, being careful their hands didn't touch, then walked away, leaning over people's desks as he passed them and picking up on words they'd used incorrectly. At each sanitising unit Brian placed his hands underneath, rubbing them together as he walked. The whole office breathed a sigh of relief when he sat down at his own desk.

Orion leant back in his chair and listened to the monotonous voice in his headphones explaining how to sell insurance packages. His mind wandered as the voice droned on and he took in his soulless surroundings. All he could see was row upon row of brown wooden desks, each divided by their own plastic screen. If he sat up straight, he could just about see the tops of people's heads.

Later that morning he saw Mary head into the staffroom and followed her, copying her sanitising her hands before entering the room. Mary looked up from where she stood pouring piping hot water into her cup. 'Hey!' he said.

'Hey,' she replied, flicking the lever up, halting the flow of water.

'Can you tell me where the tea bags are, please?' he said, opening and closing the cupboard doors.

She grabbed a pot labelled 'Tea' that stood next to the hot water tap and passed it to him, raising her eyebrows. 'Not seen you here before,' she said. 'New, are you?'

'Yup, all shiny and new,' he said, smiling at her. She gave him a look that immediately drained him of any confidence he initially had. 'Sorry, I'm a bit nervous.'

'You'll be fine, don't worry. They're not so bad here – if you keep your head down.'

'And how do I do that when you work on the same floor as me? I can only see you if I lift my head up!'

Mary groaned. 'Give me strength,' she muttered, grabbing her drink before heading back to her desk. Orion inwardly kicked himself.

As he stood there feeling like a complete moron the door opened and the man whose hand he'd accidentally brushed walked in, deeply engrossed in his phone. When he saw Orion, he placed it in his back pocket.

'What's a nice boy like you doing in a shithole like this, eh?' he said as he reached over Orion's head to get a mug.

'Same as you, I guess.'

'Failed your rotten exams too?'

Orion nodded. An incessant pinging sound came from the man's pocket. 'Aren't you going to answer that?'

'Nothing that can't wait for me to have a cup of tea,' he said, filling his mug with steaming hot water and placing it on the worktop. 'Hi, I'm Robert,' he said, reaching out and shaking Orion's hand before he had the chance to offer him his elbow.

'Tommy,' he said, smiling.

'Pleased to meet you, Tommy. You should be glad you got this place to work in and not some of the others round here. Over the road, you so much as break wind during work, you're fired – accused of wasting office time since the energy it took to fart you should've put into your work.' He stood and looked at Orion's bemused face for a moment then burst into laughter. 'You're a quiet one, aren't you? We'll get on fine; I like the quiet ones.' He paused for a moment then said, 'I caught you watching that Mary.' Orion went to object but Robert put his hand up in front of Orion's face. 'Never kid a kidder. It's written all over your face. You raised the temperature of that lift so much, with your steamy stare.' He shuddered before saying, 'Ooooh, I needed a cold shower by time we reached this floor. We all did, to be honest. Poor old Mr Hitchley didn't know what to do with himself!'

Orion started to laugh. 'She does look rather lovely,' he said, lowering his eyes.

'She certainly does – no idea what she's like, before you ask. Keeps herself to herself. Well, we're Facebook friends and all that but can't say I've ever spoken to her. I try to keep my distance, to be honest – she went all weird a while ago, started posting this crazy stuff,' he said, rotating his index fingers at the sides of his head.

'Maybe she had something worth saying?' Orion said tetchily.

'No need to tell everyone, is there?' He looked at Orion's confused face and pushed him gently on his shoulder. 'Come on, when someone starts saying weird stuff it doesn't do you any favours to "like" it or comment on it, does it?'

Orion shrugged. 'I guess not.'

'I mean "they" don't like it if you say anything a little bit out of the ordinary do "they"?' he said, using his index fingers as quotation marks each time he used the word, 'they'.

'And who are "they" and what do "they" do?' Orion asked.

'Isn't that the million-dollar question? Who are "they" and what do "they" do?' he repeated, using his fingers again for the imaginary quotation marks.

'Could you stop using your fingers every time you say that word!' Orion blurted out. Robert gave him a shocked look, paused then continued. '"They ..."' he said as he went to use his index fingers then put them down by his side, 'could make life very difficult for those who start questioning the system.'

'Couldn't "they" accuse you of questioning the system just by talking like this?' Orion asked, surprised a human was well aware of the measures in place to restrict their speech.

'Friends in high places,' he said, tapping the side of his nose.

'Like who?'

'Like I'm going to tell you!' Robert said, giving him another playful shove. 'I'm only having you on. I keep myself out of trouble – most of the time. Life is way too dull if we don't push the boundaries from time to time,' he said with a glint in his eye.

Just then a voice came out of the speakers. 'Could Robert come to the office.'

'Oops, that's me in trouble again!'

'Now!' The voice on the Tannoy said, making Robert and Orion jump.

'Coming, coming – keep your knickers on!' Robert said, marching out of the room with his head held high. He turned and blew Orion a kiss before the door slammed behind him.

Orion finished making his cup of tea then headed back to his desk. He walked past Mary but she was involved in a call. She looked at him and he smiled but she shook her head in annoyance and continued talking into her mouthpiece.

'Yes, we'll get that quote over today, Mr. Henderson,' he heard her say.

'AND SHE STILL WENT OUT with you?' Another gash on Leo's lip opened as he smiled and fresh blood trickled into his mouth.

'I know! I had to work hard on my chat-up lines though! Female humans are so much harder at reading than ours! Luckily, I did my homework back at the compound. It didn't take too long before she realised, I wasn't like any man she'd ever met on Earth.' The two males chuckled softly at the irony of this sentence.

CHAPTER TWELVE

AT FIRST THE NOISE OF thirty students entering their class room had the group covering their ears: the screeching of chairs being pulled out from under desks, bags being unzipped, loud excited chatter, the dull beats of music from various devices and then the shrill sound of a bell as the clock changed to 09:00.

A man walked into the classroom and placed his bag on the larger desk at the front of the room. 'Morning! We've got plenty of work to do today so we'd better get a move on. Pass your homework to the front of the class, please.' A rustling could be heard as papers were passed to the front of the classroom.

'Today we'll be going over Venn diagrams.' An audible groan from the students. 'Yes, I know we've been over these but you've got your exams next week and they always bring them up.'

Star and her friends began to relax as the lesson settled into its own rhythm, giving them the opportunity to focus in on the energy fields of the humans. She noticed a boy at the back of the class chewing his pencil whilst looking out of the window. Opening the palms of her hands she closed her mind to the noise of the class-room and stared intently at him. She felt herself drawing closer to him and was so surprised at how well she managed to do it, she nearly broke the connection. She focused again on the boy and pulled herself even closer until she felt a tiny click as her energy field connected with his – she'd done it! Almost instantly she felt her stomach muscles tighten, her hands became clammy and her throat felt dry and scratchy. It took a moment for her to register the emotion she'd picked up on was fear.

She pulled herself away from him and honed-in on a girl at the front of the class. Another click as she connected to the girl's energy field and then the tightening of her stomach muscles, this time even worse. Star began to loathe this man who was making them all so afraid and decided to focus on him. There it was, the now very familiar feeling of fear, coming from his energy field too. She pulled away and decided to sit back and observe the interactions between teacher and pupil.

At 10.20 a.m. the bell rang, and the students pulled back their chairs, grabbed their bags and headed out of the classroom, each one slipping a mask effortlessly over their faces. The 3D picture wavered then disappeared, leaving the hut in darkness for a brief moment until Eridamus lit up the room with her index finger.

'Can you see why the general showed us this scene?' she asked.

Rigel's hand shot up. 'Is it to show us how different our places of learning are?'

'Precisely, Rigel. And how do you feel having observed theirs?'

'How lucky we are! The teacher seemed incredibly focused on what he was teaching but not whether they were listening or whether it was interesting to them,' Rigel continued. 'Did any of you manage to connect to their energy fields?' Elder asked. A few hands shot up.

'Yes, Lacarta. What did you come across?'

'Something really weird. In fact, I've probably got it wrong …'

'Go on.'

'I picked up how fearful they felt. But how can they learn if they feel like that? The teacher didn't seem that scary!'

'They're sitting exams next week. The results of these exams have an enormous impact on what jobs they can apply for. The poor things have a lot of pressure on their shoulders. Did anyone access the teacher's energy field?'

Star's hand shot up. 'He was fearful too, Elder! Why, though? He doesn't have exams to pass!'

'In a way, he does. His student's exam results reflect on him. If they're poor, his job may well be at risk but if they do well, he could be up for a pay rise.'

Skyla's hand shot up. 'What were they all putting on as they left?'

'Ah, yes. I wondered if you'd spot that,' their elder said.

'What is it?' Skyla asked.

'Humans are also very frightened of getting sick and are told to wear masks whenever they are on the move.'

'But why?' Skyla persisted.

Elder Eridamus shrugged. 'Your guess is as good as mine. They were wearing these many years before we got involved. We tried suggesting they take them down but they had become so accustomed to them they felt naked without them.'

'But why were they wearing them in the first place?' Lacarta asked.

'Ten years before we stepped in they'd had a bad run of viruses.'

'But *we* get viruses and *we* don't wear masks!'

'I know, but we're used to getting ill and we know how to heal our bodies. Humans have forgotten the power of their own bodies; how truly remarkable they are and their extraordinary healing abilities. Don't get me wrong, of course our frail will suffer worse than our young but we all do what we can to protect them by boosting their immunity. Humans took it upon themselves to protect their elders by isolating them from their young.'

'Would that mean Granny Rhea wouldn't be able to live with us?' Star asked.

Elder Eridamus smiled sadly. 'No grannies live with their families on Earth, Star. They haven't lived with them for many years. When you reach a certain age you're placed into the care of an old people's home where you stay until you pass. Family members are required to say their goodbyes the day their elders are admitted. That way they keep infection rates down. Sadly the loss for some of the elders is too much and they often pass only days later after arriving at the home.'

A melancholy settled on the room at the same time as Elder Eridamus emitted a gasp, making the light disappear and returning the room to darkness. She chuckled and held her index finger up, lighting up the room once again. Lacarta had his arms wrapped tightly round her waist, his head buried in her chest.

'You made me jump!' she laughed, wrapping her arms around him.

'We're so lucky to have you as our teacher and to live here on Celestia. I love you, Elder.'

'And I love you too, Lacarta.' The rest of the students looked on at this wonderful moment between their elder and their friend. One by one they stood up and joined the pair until the whole group was entangled in one glorious group hug.

CHAPTER THIRTEEN

ORION BECAME OBSESSED WITH MARY, wanting to find out every little bit of information he could about her. Robert and he were becoming good friends, partly due to the fact that no one else wanted to hang around with Robert for fear of getting into trouble. Orion noticed that the man behaved totally different to all the other humans, apart from the fact he too spent a lot of time on his phone, but that seemed to be part and parcel of being a human. He was also outgoing, funny and didn't seem to care what anyone thought of him. Orion wanted to know why he managed to push the boundaries but his desire to get close to Mary was more pressing so he used Robert to try and glean any tips about how he should approach her.

'I say such stupid things when I'm around her,' Orion moaned one day in the staffroom.

'Must be love, then!' Robert teased. Just then the phone in his hand beeped. He tapped in a quick reply and turned his focus back to Orion who opened his mouth to speak but the phone beeped again and again. 'Sorry, won't be a sec,' Robert said, typing quickly into his phone and placing it in his pocket.

'You're certainly very popular despite your lack of friends here,' Orion said.

Robert feigned a shocked look. 'I'll have you know I'm thought of very highly, thank you very much!' He laughed at Orion's bemused look, 'Hard as it may be for you to believe, I have plenty of friends, just not in this place, that's all.'

'I'm sorry, I didn't mean it to come out like that.'

'No offence taken which is lucky for you since you can offend pretty much anyone these days. Now, how the hell are we going to get you and the lovely Mary together?'

'You think she's lovely too?'

'Turns out we've got a bit more in common than I thought,' he said mysteriously.

Orion sighed. 'It's like she's got this wall around her. I know I've hardly spoken to her but there's something about her – as if we've met before.'

'Maybe you have?'

'No, that's impossible.'

Robert crossed his arms and tilted his head. 'Why? This city isn't that big.'

Orion hesitated. 'I know but before this job I hardly ever came in. Mum and Dad are a bit overprotective.'

'Hmmm.'

'I feel like we have a connection,' he said, avoiding Robert's questioning gaze.

'Don't we all when we fancy someone,' Robert sighed. 'Why don't you send her a friend request? Admire her from afar, it's easier that way – no one gets hurt. I can't be doing with all the mind games that go with being in a relationship.'

'But I want to talk to her face-to-face! It's so cowardly other-wise.'

'At least you keep your dignity. Nothing worse than getting your heart broken. You'll end up looking like a schmuck pining away for her. Oh god, it's mortifying,' he shivered.

'Isn't it better to risk getting hurt than not fall in love at all?'

'That's your prerogative but there's not many that would agree with you; it's way too scary to show your true feelings. Nothing worse than when you tell someone you love them before they say it to you and then they go and message all their friends saying you got too serious too quickly. One minute you're all loved up, thinking this is the one, the next you find out on social media you're no longer in a relationship and everyone knew about it before you! The humiliation.' And he shivered again.

'But why do they have to put it on social media?'

'Have you come from the dark ages? You play the game; you deal with the shame. Listen to me, what a cynic. I'm serious though, dating gets all so ...' and he waved a hand about in the air, 'messy. Dropping her a friend request is kinder to both of you. If she rejects you it's easy to move onto the next one.' He looked at Orion and said cheekily, 'Sorry, I mean *when* she rejects you. There are lots of Mary's in this city. Why tie yourself down to one when you're so young?'

'No!' Orion said angrily. 'There are not lots of Mary's out there. She's totally unique. The way she dances when she's on her own, the clothes she wears away from ...' Seeing the shocked look on Robert's face stopped him from saying more.

Just then a voice over the Tannoy system shrilled, 'Could Thomas Brown please come to the office – immediately!'

As he walked towards the misted-up door at the opposite end of the office he wondered if he'd blown his cover. Countless pairs of eyes stared up at him from their desks. Before he'd had the chance to knock, the door clicked softly open. Melantho stood at the end of a long table; a man in a dark suit sat beside him.

'What the hell do you think you're doing?' Melantho spat once the door was closed.

Orion walked over to the two men and sat down. 'I'm doing

exactly what I set out to do, surveilling those who are questioning the system. In fact, I think there maybe others in this office who we should be observing. One of the employers has a total lack of respect for the system. You're lucky he's unpopular, otherwise his complete disregard for authority sets an incredibly bad example.'

'You're talking about Robert, aren't you?' Melantho seethed and Orion nodded. 'He's no threat to the system.'

'How can you be so sure? As far as I can tell …'

'Just leave it, Thomas,' he spat. Orion went to say something but thought better of it. 'You virtually confessed you've been accessing her surveillance cameras.'

Orion bent his head. 'I'm sorry.'

Melantho walked over to where Orion sat and leant down so his mouth was next to his ear, causing Orion to shiver involuntarily. The man inhaled noisily before saying, 'If you ever put the compound under any risk again, I'll have you sent back home faster than you can say "Mary". I'm watching you … Thomas. Watching …' he paused, 'and waiting. I think of you as my little project. I've let you have wings – you need to do everything you can to make sure they don't get burnt.'

Orion smiled weakly at the other man sat round the table who smiled briefly in return.

Melantho caught the exchange of looks. 'You!' He pointed at the man who shrank into his chair. 'Don't you dare give this freak any sympathy – you hear me?' he roared at the quivering man. Melantho grabbed his phone out of his back pocket and started jabbing at it angrily. 'Just one tap, that's all it takes, Henderson! I'll have Rastaban over here in a shot!'

'No, please! I beg of you!' he said, falling to his knees and clasping his hands together in prayer.

'What's going on?' Orion said, standing up.

Like a shot Melantho turned and pointed to Orion, 'You stay

out of this!' and Orion sat back down in his chair, his eyes wide and alert but his face pale. 'Henderson needs to be kept in line. He's no different to the rest of them. Just because we use this building for observations doesn't mean he should get any special treatment.'

'Melantho, you can't speak to him like …' Orion said, slamming his fists on the table.

'Captain Melantho to you!' he screamed, glaring at Orion.

'Thomas, I'm fine,' Mr Henderson stammered. 'Captain Melantho is very good to me and my family. We've a nice house, my kids go to private school. Having …' and he paused as he searched for the correct word, 'beings like you here means we hardly have any surveillance cameras, not like all the other offices. It's suffocating working in that environment. We're really lucky. Please, Thomas, let it go.'

The man's petrified look stopped Orion from saying anything more.

CHAPTER FOURTEEN

SEEING MELANTHO YIELDING SUCH POWER over a human being concerned him enormously but his pursuit of Mary consumed him and every spare minute he had was spent thinking how he would win her over.

At the end of each working day he'd return to the compound and observe her from the security cameras whilst scrolling through her social media pages. He printed off every bit of information he found and placed it in her ever-increasing file. The other generals were deeply impressed with Orion's focus for the job. Occasionally he got invited to eat with some of his colleagues but he'd turn them down, saying he needed to continue with his research. In actual fact he was on websites giving him advice about how to approach a member of the opposite sex. It appeared that humans found this incredibly hard which gave him some hope. He observed the other men on the floor and noticed how little attention they paid to any of the women in the office. When he started chatting to them and asked them if they had girlfriends, they would show him pictures of girls on their phones they hoped to 'hook up' with. They'd confide in him that it was easier to meet girls online than engage in face-to-face conversation with them. Most of the men seemed to be slightly scared of women, unsure of what to say to them – as if they were a different species entirely. No wonder Mary had treated him with disdain – he probably came across like every other man she had met.

One day he decided to be brave and make her a cup of tea. He walked over to her desk and placed the piping hot drink on the small square mat next to her computer.

'I don't drink tea,' she said without looking up.

'It's peppermint, green tea,' he said, causing her to stop typing.

'That's about the only tea I do drink,' she said, followed by, 'Thanks'.

He shrugged and walked back to his desk with a nonchalant, ''S-okay'. Just before he sat down, he turned back to see her staring at him, her hands wrapped round the mug. They caught each other's eye and smiled. Orion sat down and did a little jig under the desk.

Later that day he requested her as a friend on her most frequented social media page. His heart fluttered in excitement as she accepted it.

That night back at the compound whilst scrolling through the pictures on her sites, a post popped up saying she was attending the opening of a new bar in town with some of the girls from work. He changed into casual clothes, had a shave and headed out.

As he entered the bar, he smiled at the doorman who wore a black face mask over his nose and mouth. He was about to pass when the man stepped in front of Orion pointing a gun directly at his head. 'What are you doing?' Orion cried out, putting his hands across his face and ducking.

'Temperature!' the man demanded.

'What?'

'I need to take your temperature!' he said, continuing to hold the gun in front of Orion.

'I'm just meeting my friend!'

'I don't care who you're meeting. You're not coming in unless you've had your temperature taken.' The man waited for Orion to stand still before aiming the gun directly at his forehead. He closed his eyes, waiting for some terrifying click or wondering if this was all a joke before hearing a little beep. 'Go on,' the man said, ushering him inside.

Mary spotted him the minute he walked in and he could tell she felt ruffled by his presence. Did her cheeks redden slightly too?

'Fancy seeing you here!' he said, composing himself after his traumatic entrance. Orion offered to buy Mary and her friends a drink which they all accepted. He returned to their table with a tray of cocktails and made polite conversation with her friends.

Mary stood back, enjoying watching him with her friends and knowing it was her he wanted to talk to. She was bored with dating men who claimed to be 'handsome, charming, affluent, funny, kind, caring,' only to find out that they knew those were the words that attracted the most girls. One date was all it usually took to discover they were anything but. Deep down she knew she was different, that she was meant for better things. This Thomas intrigued her but he needed to prove he wasn't like all the other men. She wasn't going to make it easy for him.

CHAPTER FIFTEEN

AFTER THAT FIRST NIGHT ORION and Mary began exchanging messages but whenever they arranged to meet, she'd arrive with a friend. His heart would sink as another long night of polite conversation ensued. His mind and his gaze would wander, observing other humans and their funny ways of approaching members of the opposite sex. This seemed to entail drinking so much alcohol their words became slurred and they could barely be understood. Finally, just as he'd given up all hope of ever meeting her alone, she agreed to meet him after work for a walk in the park.

When he saw her waiting at the gates on her own, he was so delighted he had to use all his willpower not to leap straight into the tree above her. He leant down and kissed her gently on the cheek, making her heart flutter in a way she hadn't experienced before.

'Hey,' he said grinning from ear to ear.

'Hey,' she smiled shyly. 'Fancy a drink? I bought wine,' she said, discreetly showing him the wine in her bag.

His face fell. He'd come so unprepared. It hadn't crossed his mind she would consider bringing something to drink. 'Errr, I'm sorry, I don't really drink on a school night,' he said, remembering the accepted excuse he'd often heard in the office.

'Me neither. I just felt tonight was …' her voice trailed off. 'Let's go for a walk, shall we?'

Orion nodded and took her hand as if it was the most normal thing in the world to do, unaware of the look of surprise on Mary's face. It was a lovely summer's evening and they had the park almost to themselves. All the over sixties were in the safety of their own homes as it was past their 6 p.m. curfew and most of the younger generation were either at home watching television, catching up on their social media pages or out in one of the bars. A number of drones patrolled the park. One of them turned to Orion and Mary and hovered over their heads. A monotone voice from above them said, 'Identification please.' Mary dropped Orion's hand immediately and pulled up her sleeve. An infra-red light shot out from the drone and scanned her lower arm. 'Mary Wright,' it said robotically. 'Medical records verified.' A green light flashed from the drone, indicating they could move on.

'Thank you!' she said pleasantly to the drone as it turned and headed towards another couple ambling along. She raised her eyebrows at Orion, 'Why'd you get off the hook? One of their special ones, are you?' she said nudging him.

'Must be,' he smiled.

They walked around a lake chatting about the office and the people who worked there. 'Robert's a nice guy,' Orion said.

'Yeah, he's great. Bit of a hero of mine to be honest,' she said, smiling.

'A hero! Why?'

Mary looked a little startled, 'Err – oh, the way he doesn't take any nonsense with the boss. He's great. I'd be way too scared to say some of the stuff he does but somehow he gets away with it.'

'He said it was 'coz he had friends in high places,' Orion offered.

'That would figure,' she said.

Orion wasn't quite sure he liked the tone in Mary's voice when she talked about Robert. 'Anyone else in the office you think is nice?'

Mary looked at him and burst into laughter. 'Fishing for compliments, eh? Well, you're no Robert, but I guess you'll do.' Orion's face dropped then she laughed again and elbowed him gently in the ribs. 'I'm kidding! Come here, you. We've got to get you to loosen up a little.' She grabbed Orion's hand and pulled him underneath the branches of a weeping willow that stood by the edges of the lake and lead him to a bench. Orion took off his socks and dangled his feet in the water. The minute his feet touched the soft mud, he felt a surge of energy course through his body. He tipped his head back, closed his eyes and breathed in deeply.

Mary watched him with interest. This wasn't the average response of a guy when she came here. Normally they'd try and get her to lie down before trying to snog the face off her.

'You coming in?' Orion asked, standing up and pulling his t-shirt off.

'What? No, you can't! We'll get caught!'

'You told me I needed to loosen up,' he laughed. 'What can they do? We're just having a swim – surely that's not illegal on Earth,' he said and jumped into the cool water.

Mary's brow furrowed momentarily then she tipped her head back and laughed. 'I guess not now you mention it!' She stripped down to her underwear and dived in too, shrieking in shock when Orion splashed her as she came up for air.

'You did that on purpose!' she cried out.

'As if!' he said, splashing her again.

'Right then.' She tried splashing him back but wasn't nearly as effective as Orion who continued to drench her. 'Alright, alright, you win!' she cried out, waving her hands in the air.

Orion dived underwater and came up next to Mary. He held her hand as they waded back to the bench. 'Here, have this to dry off,' he said, giving Mary his t-shirt. They sat under the tree and chatted, desperate to find out more about each other.

'You're so different to the person you come across as on your social media pages,' he said.

'You've been doing your homework,' she said with a wry smile. 'I hate all that stuff but if I don't do it then I don't have any mates.'

'How do you know? Where I come from our friends are friends, no matter what.'

'You must come from a different planet then,' she said and he laughed nervously. 'I guess your mates must be better than mine. I tried posting different stuff once – it didn't go well. I found these great singers from generations ago and I thought everyone would want to know about them. Turns out I was wrong. I thought my friends loved me and valued my opinion but I was wrong on that front too. I had to come off it in the end, I got so depressed. The minute I posted normal stuff I was invited out again. It's crazy.' She shook her head in disbelief.

Orion nodded sympathetically saying he felt the same. She asked him who his favourite singer was, and he froze, realising how little he knew about music on Earth. He couldn't bear any of the tunes humans were allowed to listen to which lacked any depth lyrically or musically and he made sure the radio and television were either on mute or turned off in his quarters. Then suddenly he remembered the song he'd watched her dance to the first night he'd observed her. He pictured her arms and legs moving to the beat and it came to him.

'Frankly Mr Shankly!' he almost shouted out.

She looked at him and burst into laughter. 'You mean to tell me you've heard of The Smiths? They're my favourite band! You don't happen to know David Bowie too, do you?' she asked with a raised eyebrow.

Orion nodded, realising the name sounded familiar from when he'd looked into her playlist in the data room.

'What's your favourite? Tell me it's "Space Odyssey"?' she asked, her brown eyes alive with passion.

Orion pretended to look flabbergasted and admitted that it was indeed his favourite too.

Mary couldn't believe it. After all this time of dancing alone in her bedroom, she'd finally met someone who had the same taste in music as her. She didn't care what Robert said about Tommy and where he might be from. As far as she was concerned, this guy was different to any man she'd ever met before and that could only be a good thing.

CHAPTER SIXTEEN

AFTER THE GROUP HAD EATEN and meditated, they returned to the Centre of Learning, ready to discuss what they'd witnessed.

'I found it rather boring,' Skyla said, making the group gasp on hearing this rarely used word. 'I'm sorry but I was expecting to witness something amazing! All these orbitals we've been waiting to study humans and the first lesson was plain dull! I wish I'd done adastral projection instead,' she said sulkily.

'I never said it was going to be fun, did I?' Eridamus said. 'You may believe your life here on Celestia is quite unexciting but in reality, your lives are truly extraordinary. One of the reasons we study humans is to show you that longing to see another planet may not be all it's cracked up to be.'

'Err, Elder?' Star began nervously.

'Yes?'

'I feel like I've absorbed a lot of their negative energy. I've tried releasing it using the methods we've practised but I can't seem to shake it off,' she said.

'Wonderful! I'm very proud you spoke up, Star. The only way those feelings will subside is by being totally open with us. Shout, run about, scream like a booyanic or laugh like a routeena. Do whatever you like to get those negative emotions out of your body. On occasions like this, I find I like to roar like a graffiantas ... Roooaaaaarrrrrrr!'

The students looked at their elder in utter astonishment.

'Did you just roar, Elder?' Lacarta asked.

She looked at Lacarta and laughed, 'I certainly did, young male.'

'That's hilarious,' he said with a smile.

Elder Eridamus sat up and leaning on all fours, made another loud roaring noise. This one came from deep inside her, starting more like a growl but increased steadily in volume.

The group looked at each other then back to their elder who was now moving, or more like prowling, between the students with a fierce look on her face. 'Come on, everyone. Who's going to join me?'

The group seemed unsure of what to do; not only was their elder behaving incredibly out of character but now they were expected to join in too!

'Don't be shy, now. Come on, Star. A moment ago you said you've got a lot of pent up anger inside you. Let's see how much you really have in there,' she said, patting Star playfully on the shoulder.

'But ...'

'I don't understand buts. I only speak graffiantas.'

'Err ... Grrrrr?'

'You can do better than that, I know you can. Rrrrrrr-rooooarrrr!' Eridamus began very softly before quickly increasing to a loud roar.

Star looked at her elder, the confusion in her eyes changing to acceptance. She tipped her head right back, letting her long, pink hair drape down so it touched the floor. She waited a moment and everyone watched with bated breath wondering what she was going to do next. 'Rrooooaaaarrrrr,' Star cried out with all her might, leaping onto her feet, flinging her head forwards so her face was covered with a wild mane of hair, her hands in front of her chest like a playful graffiantas.

The class fell about laughing and one by one they joined in the act, roaring and growling with all their might as they prowled around the hut.

Elder Eridamus walked to the front of the class, relieved that the tense atmosphere was broken. It had been too long since she'd let herself go. She felt someone wrap their arms around her. Knowing instinctively it was Lacarta, she wrapped her arms around him too, tipping her head back and laughing.

'I love you, Elder,' he said, looking up at her.

'I love you too, Lacarta,' she replied, tears of joy springing to the corners of her eyes.

Once the class had settled down Eridamus began on the next task ahead. 'Finally, I'd like you to split into groups and discuss the differences and similarities of school life on Earth compared to life at the Centre of Learning. I have a spot of business to attend to.'

The students moved close to their friends and began going over the lesson.

Elder Eridamus walked out of the Centre of Learning, returning to the little hidden door. The handle glowed as she held up her palm and it clicked open. Placing the pyramid back on the floor she crossed her arms and said firmly, 'General Rigley.'

The holographic image appeared of Rigley at his desk, sipping from a cup of tea. 'Ah, Elder Eridamus – I was just thinking of you.' He paused and asked, 'This is the year Leo's daughter gets to study humans isn't it?'

'It is indeed.'

Rigley leant forwards and said, 'I need to see you.'

'Why?'

In hushed tones he said, 'I happened on some documents whilst in Melantho's office the other day. He was running late as ever. The folder was labelled 'Whistle-blowers' so I thought it was going to be a file of humans that were under surveillance. Unfortunately, what I read – it's sickening.' He lowered his eyes and shook his head.

'What is it?' she urged him.

'Our suspicions were right. I can't believe it's taken me this long to pin something on him. There's been some kind undercover operation running. One of the files had Leo's name on it.'

Her hand shot up to her mouth. 'Do you think he's still alive?'

'I know he's still alive. The file had last week's date on it. It looks like after all these years they've only just found him.'

'Meisa was right! She never gave up on him.'

'I wouldn't divulge this bit of information to anyone for the time being. As far as I can tell he's in a bad way. Eridamus, we have to get him out of there.'

'What are they doing to him?' she asked.

Rigley took a deep breath. 'I can't be certain but ...' his voice tailed off. 'Do you really want to know?'

Eridamus nodded. 'I need to.'

He sighed heavily. 'I think they're running some kind of experimentation programme.'

'No! But how can they? Most races have advanced ways of escaping capture. It's only humans they can lock up.'

'I managed to look at a couple of the other files underneath his. They all had this weird barcode on them, like you get at a shopping mall.'

'What do you think it was?' she asked.

'I'm not sure. The only place I've seen that sort of thing is at the implant centre before humans start working in their jobs but these were slightly different. Had a few more digits than normal.'

'Why would they put one of them in Leo?'

'Beats me.'

'He's got no reason to imprison Leo; he's never done anything wrong.'

'I know but we've always had our concerns that Melantho was power-hungry, haven't we?'

'Power–hungry, yes, but imprisoning alien beings? Do you really think he's capable of that?'

'I've got no idea what depths he's capable of anymore.'

'What can we do?' Eridamus asked.

'I have a hunch where they're holding him but if we attempt a rescue mission, we'll need your craft here to get him aboard immediately. God knows what they'll do to him if they have much longer with him. I think we need to bring the class on Earth forwards. I'm not sure how much more Leo can take, looking at the report.'

'But what excuse can I use? We'd planned to come in twenty-eight sunrises – I mean, two weeks – to give the students time to decide whether to take the class or not. I can bring it forwards by a week, I guess? Or we could send another craft over now? They could be with you in forty-eight hours.'

Rigley shook his head. 'They've placed travel restrictions on all flights. At the moment the only craft allowed here are the ones with students on. It's all out of my control. We had a meeting about it last night and there's nothing me, Arrakis or Zaurak can say to make them change their minds. Your craft'll be the only chance we have to get Leo home.'

'This is not good. I knew that man was bad news the minute he offered me that limp hand of his to shake. Any word of my son?'

He shook his head. 'Sorry.'

'What about the girl?'

'Nowhere to be seen; it's like she disappeared into thin air. Her parents are acting like the grieving relatives when I talk to them. They told me she was really down the last time they spoke to her, that she hated living here, but when I check on the surveillance cameras, they aren't looking even the tiniest bit sad. It's really weird.'

'At least no news is good news.'

'Exactly. Let's hope they're together.'

'If they've got Leo, who's to say they haven't got him too? He's nothing like as experienced as Leo. Oh, Henry,' she said, sobbing slightly. 'I couldn't bare it if something's happened to him. We need to get word to him to get back home; it's far too dangerous for him to stay. I'll do my best to bring their lesson on Earth forwards by a week. Are you OK to carry on searching for him?'

'Of course,' he nodded.

'I think I'll have to say something about weather conditions getting poorer – a meteorite shower closing in or something.'

'Say whatever you can – just get the craft here as soon as possible.'

'I have to be careful I'm not breaking our Celestian law, 'Natyinahu ne haringue' – do no harm – by allowing our students into a potentially dangerous situation,' Eridamus pondered.

'I don't think you need to worry about that. The Committee's already broken plenty of laws looking at those documents. I have another bit of news, Eridamus.' He paused for a moment and took a deep breath. 'Melantho and General Rastaban are running such a strong campaign of fear they're lowering the vibrations of the other Committee members. Whatever I say they dismiss me, tell me I shouldn't be such a conspiracy theorist. They took a vote on whether to even out the balance and bring in another general from Aldor and Earth.' His voice rose in volume as he spoke. 'Myself, Arrakis, Zaurak and Calearo were the only generals that voted against! They promoted Thuban and Melantho straight away – they believe they'll make the Committee stronger!'

'No!' her hand shot up to her face. 'OK, I'll bring the trip forwards. It's going to be fine. We'll get Leo out of there and let's hope we can bring my son home too.'

Barely audible, he said, 'I miss you, Eridamus.'

'I miss you too, Henry,' she said softly.

He straightened his back with a start and said loudly, 'Yes, General Melantho, they really enjoyed their lesson. Thank you, Elder, and see you for the next one.'

General Rigley looked at her with an intense stare, leant forwards and pressed the button that would terminate communication between them both. His image held for a brief moment then disappeared, returning the room to darkness.

CHAPTER SEVENTEEN

ELDER ERIDAMUS STOOD IN THE dark a moment as she collected her thoughts. It was wonderful news that her brother-in-law was alive but in what state, and would they get to him in time? She hated keeping secrets from Meisa. Even though they weren't blood related she'd loved her like a younger sister the moment Leo announced they were a couple. Now Star was the only one in her class showing the emotional strength needed to study humans. If she didn't pursue HS there was a good chance no one would – meaning there'd be no craft going to Earth and no way of bringing Leo home.

She'd loathed Melantho ever since she'd first set eyes on him. His obsession with his hair, and those penetrating dark eyes gave her the creeps. How he'd managed to climb the ranks and then worm his way onto the Committee she'd never understand. She needed time to firm up her excuse as to why they needed to get to Earth sooner than planned. In the meantime, there was a lot of work to be done to rid her students of the negative energy they'd absorbed during their lesson. An idea began taking formation in her mind. She'd have to act fast though.

As she opened the door the sunlight caused her to wince momentarily. She closed her eyes, tipped her head back, cupped her hands around her mouth and made a calling noise that was so familiar to her after all these orbitals. The sound reverberated around the trees. She continued calling until, at last, her astute hearing picked up the delicate sound of fluttering wings way before she could see him. Then suddenly there he was, on the branch next to her, making soft cooing noises.

'My darling conichi.' She opened her eyes and stroked his little white chest. He tipped his bright green head back and swayed it to and fro, his orange beak in the air. 'I need your help.' The bird cocked his head, fixing his soft brown eyes on her face and cooed in response.

'Times are unsettling on Earth. We need to go sooner than planned. I have to organise a ceremony this evening. Could you alert the seniors?' The conichi cooed, nodded his head bringing a wing across his chest and bowed gracefully. With a flutter of wings, he flew off into the woods. Walking back to the main Centre of Learning she saw another elder go by.

'Elder Archernar!' she called out.

'What is it?' he said, walking over to her.

'I need to organise a ceremony.'

'That's a wonderful idea,' and his eyes lit up. 'When for?'

'Tonight.'

'But that's impo–'

'Don't say it,' she said firmly.

'You do like to keep me on my toes, Elder!' he said once he'd recovered from the shock. 'Why not be impulsive, eh? My life partner is always saying I should seize the day a bit more! Leave it with me and go and finish your lesson. Any news from your son?' he asked. She smiled but shook her head. 'You must be so proud of him. Not many get to go that deep into the galaxy on their first assignment.'

'Yes, I'm very proud of him,' she replied flatly. He hurried off with a spring in his step. Elder Eridamus felt another wave of guilt flood over her. She walked back to the Centre of Learning where the students were huddled in groups talking animatedly about the lesson they'd observed. 'Now students,' she began startling them with her sudden return, 'you've all worked really hard but I felt your energy levels plummet earlier.' The Elder paused, ready to make the next announcement. 'I've had a little chat with my conichi,' a murmur of excitement rippled round the room, 'and he's getting the woods ready for a …' and she paused again before saying, 'ceremony!'

'When for?'

'For this sunset!'

'Yes!' the group cried out.

Lacarta appeared next to Elder Eridamus almost knocking her over as he wrapped his arms around her waist. 'Thank you, Elder! I love you so much. Thank you!'

'Twice in one day, Lacarta. I am honoured! Thank you and I love you too.'

It wasn't long before the rest of the students leapt from their feet and ran to join their elder and Lacarta, all gathering into a therapeutic group hug.

CHAPTER EIGHTEEN

'GOOD MORNING,' GENERAL CALEARO, FROM Mercury, said, appearing at Orion's breakfast table one morning.

'Morning, general,' he replied.

'The Committee are very impressed with your work. They tell me you're showing a lot of promise.'

'Thank you!' he beamed.

'It's been agreed to allow you more freedom.'

'What will that entail?' Orion asked.

'We need to ascertain whether this Mary's having any influence on her family. Her father was put under the high-risk category many years ago. Even though he's sixty-nine and quite elderly, in human terms, he's a popular man within his social circles. The last thing we need is to find out there's a ripple effect emanating from Mary.'

'How would I find that out?'

'You need to meet them.'

Orion's heart fluttered and his eyes widened – this was a major step forward.

'You need to put pressure on her to introduce you to them.' General Calearo waved his arms in the air as an idea formed in his head. 'Tell her that you're falling for her, that you think it prudent to meet her family before things get too serious.'

Orion's eyes widened even more. 'What does Melantho think of this?' he asked.

'It was him that mentioned it,' Calearo replied. 'It's funny, normally Melantho goes on about how he hates us observing humans. Refers to it as being "an invasion of privacy", though he seems to bandy that phrase about as and when it suits him. Talks very highly of you, though. Says you're onto something with this Mary.'

Orion knew Melantho was hoping he'd slip up, that things would go wrong but he no longer cared what anyone thought – least of all that vile man. He just wanted to be close to Mary and gaining access to her living quarters was a major step in cementing their relationship.

The next day they arranged to meet at a bar called Sam's Place. He'd heard Robert talking about it and when he did a bit research, he found out there was no mobile phone signal once you were inside. As far as he could tell this seemed to be one of the reasons it was so popular which didn't tally with what he knew about humans.

'Tell me about your folks,' he said as they sat in a quiet corner cuddled up on one of the sofas.

'What do you want to know?' She leant forwards to reach her cocktail.

'Everything! They created you!'

'You're so funny,' she said, taking a sip of her drink and snuggling into Orion's arm that rested on the back of the sofa. 'There's not much to know. We're just the same as every other family in the block. Dad worked long hours at the distribution firm; Mum was in sales. Both retired last year. Didn't see much of them growing up but who does? Dad's getting weaker now, a bit forgetful. He tries to hide it but me and Mum know something's wrong. He's sixty-nine so he's bound to start forgetting things at his age.' Orion sat upright and nearly choked on his drink. 'He's done well to last this long to be honest. Most people pop their clogs soon after retiring. So sad, working all those years then dying just when they retire.'

'That's awful!'

'I know. But to be honest once he gets to seventy he'll be off to the old people's home anyway and I'll never see him again. Maybe it's better this way,' she said with a sigh.

'But why wouldn't you see him again?' Orion asked.

Mary turned to him. 'Well no one's allowed inside them, are they?'

'Why not?'

Mary raised her eyebrows. 'It's too risky for any of us to see them in case we infect them, isn't it? Where've you been living, eh?'

'Infection from what?' Orion said, becoming exasperated.

'From one of the many viruses we have, of course! Jeez, Tommy, it's like you live on another planet sometimes.'

'I'd love to meet them both,' he said, quickly changing the subject.

Her eyebrows raised and she sipped her drink again. 'I'll see if it can be arranged,' she replied mysteriously. 'They don't take kindly to my boyfriends though.'

'Boyfriends?' he said emphasising the 's'.

'Don't think I'm some kind of saint, Tommy!' she laughed and jabbed him in the ribs. 'You jealous or something?'

'I'm jealous of anyone who spent time with you.'

They both laughed and Mary kissed him on the lips. 'They were nothing compared to you,' she said huskily. She ran her fingers through his hair and drew him closer to her.

'Oh, Mary,' he said, kissing her. 'I can't stop thinking about you.'

She leant back a little and looked him in the eyes. 'I can't stop thinking about you, either. I've never met anyone like you before.'

'Nor me. You're so different to the girls back home.'

'What do you mean back home?' she asked, her eyes narrowing.

He kicked himself for making such a stupid mistake. 'I mean the girls that hang around the foyer.'

'No one hangs around the foyer.' She scrutinised his face for a moment but then her face softened. 'I guess I can see why they'd want to hang around for a glimpse of you, though.'

Orion breathed a sigh of relief; he hadn't blown his cover just yet.

CHAPTER NINETEEN

FINALLY, THE DAY ARRIVED WHEN Orion was invited to meet her parents. He leapt out of bed, had breakfast then went to the dressing area where he'd meet the team assigned to prepare him for the task ahead. His face fell when he opened the door and saw Melantho standing there, the usual smug look on his face.

'Aah, here he is, everyone! Allow me to introduce my little protégé,' Melantho said flamboyantly. 'Orion's come a long way since the pathetic little Celestian I first met a few months ago – the one that trembled whenever I looked at him,' he said, chuckling at Orion's obvious embarrassment. 'He's not only discovered the elusive Mary Wright who's intent on questioning the system, but the cunning little fox has managed to convince her that he's got feelings for her! Having looked at the surveillance footage of her I would say she's falling for his little act too.' He saw the look of anger cross Orion's face but carried on regardless. 'Please give the man – sorry, Orion, should we call you "man"? Or would you prefer "alien" or "ET" or "Extra-terrestrial"? I'd hate to offend you by calling you the wrong thing.'

'My name will do, Captain,' Orion said, inwardly seething.

'Of course – Orion it is. Please give Orion a round of applause for acting so,' and he forced a cough, 'professionally in his very first undercover role!' The team gave a polite clap showing it was clear they found it as excruciating as Orion. 'Kelly!' Melantho said, clicking his fingers at a friendly looking girl with a bright hair band in her hair. 'Come and do something with Orion's appearance, will you? No parent is going to give their approval for their daughter to go out with him looking like this!'

'But I'm wearing what you gave me to wear,' Orion pointed out.

'Yes, but that was six weeks ago! Times have changed; the world of fashion has moved on. Come on, get with it!'

Kelly came over and started measuring Orion around his chest, neck, arms and legs. Melantho stood and watched, enjoying how uncomfortable all this fuss was making Orion feel. Finally, he sloped off saying he was off to get a coffee.

'That man's unbearable,' Kelly said quietly whilst writing down the measurements in a pad.

'Not just me then?'

She looked at him and raised her eyebrows. 'Definitely not just you.' She lowered her voice and asked, 'Can you tell me more about where you come from? I'm sorry, I'm so nosey – I just had to ask.'

'Celestia is beautiful,' he said, glad to be able to talk about home. 'It's everything the city isn't. There's no concrete, no high-rise buildings, no cars. Just nature all around you.'

Kelly scrunched up her nose. 'Oooh, not sure if that's for me, to be honest. My mum left a dead spider in the loo the other day and I nearly fainted in shock! All those creepy crawlies wandering over you.' A shiver went down her spine at the thought. 'Yeuch!'

'It's not like that,' Orion continued. 'We're connected to every plant, insect or animal. We don't see a difference. That spider has every right to live, just as you do.'

'He should pay rent then! It's bloody exorbitant and if he's flat sharing then he needs to pay his way!' she said, laughing.

Orion couldn't help but laugh too. 'The best bit about our planet is we have no money,' he said wistfully.

'No money! How the hell does that work?' she asked.

Orion laughed. 'It works because we trade or share everything. We believe that you can't fully evolve as a being if you're distracted by money. It saves people getting greedy. We need so little anyway. We aren't like you humans – you buy an apartment and you fill it with stuff. You buy cupboards and you fill the space inside. You buy bags to fill, under bed drawers …'

'Alright, alright!' she interrupted him. 'I guess we like our things. We work hard all week; why not go out and treat yourself to something nice at the end of it?'

'But we don't feel the need to go out and treat ourselves! We don't have what you call "jobs" either.' At this, her eyes widened in alarm. 'We discover what our calling in life is then find a way of incorporating that into our day-to-day life – we don't consider it a job as we're doing what we love.'

'That would never work here,' she said matter-of-factly.

'Why not?'

'Well, there's no time to find out what your passion is. Life is fine, though. It's simple. I got lucky getting this job. I applied for a job in the military and this is where I ended up. Quite a cushy number if you ask me. Not many people get to feel the inside leg of an alien, do they?' she said with a twinkle in her eye.

'I guess not,' Orion said, smiling back.

'Right, let's get you dressed into something that will knock the socks off her, eh?'

'I don't think she wears socks,' Orion said.

Kelly raised her eyebrows and laughed.

CHAPTER TWENTY

A FEW HOURS LATER ORION looked at himself in the mirror and agreed he didn't look half bad. Kelly had dressed him in a dark blue top, jeans and brown fake-leather shoes. They also gave him a haircut and shave, splashed some foul-smelling liquid on his face and neck, and put some gel in his hair. The final touch was a top-of-the-range Bluetooth headset which was considered a necessity for anyone in his age group.

'Make sure you don't turn it on, though,' Kelly said as she placed the headset round his neck. 'Interferes with your cells or something. You lot are a bit more sensitive than us.'

They made sure he had all the correct apps and downloads on his phone to ensure he looked totally "normal" if anyone peeked a look at it.

'I think I've done a damn good job on you, even if I do say so myself,' Kelly said.

'Thanks! I hope I don't mess up in front of her parents.'

'That's where Ben comes in,' she said and in walked a guy with a headset on, talking loudly into his phone.

'Thanks, Captain. Yes, I'm here with him now. I'll get him up to scratch, don't you worry.' He paused whilst the other person spoke.

Ben mouthed, 'Melantho' to Kelly and put a hand in front of his mouth feigning a yawn which they both chuckled at. 'Yes, Captain … No, Captain. I won't let him … Yes, Captain … Sorry? Sorry, Captain. Think I must be on low battery. Gotta go!' He pressed a button on the phone and put it into his back pocket.

'He'll find you out one of these days,' Kelly said laughing.

Ben tutted. 'Well, he shouldn't be such a bore.'

'Does anyone like him?' Orion asked.

'His mother must do,' Kelly said.

Ben shook his head. 'I don't think so.'

'You are awful, Ben!' Kelly said.

'Gotta get through the day somehow, haven't we? You're meeting the lovely Mary Wright I understand?'

Orion nodded.

'I've been researching her family, likes, dislikes, phobias, allergies – all that sort of thing – and I think I should be able to give you enough information on them for you to win them over pretty easily. You've just got to listen to everything I say and behave exactly as I tell you. Her parents used to be quite rebellious but as they got older, they stopped any questioning. Life was getting quite tricky for them, you see. You might find them a little stiff, shall we say – or repressed. It's often what happens when you've once questioned the system.'

'On Celestia we're taught not to bottle our emotions up since what do trapped emotions cause?' he asked them. Two blank faces looked back at him. 'Trapped emotions cause sickness!' he said and laughed, enjoying bringing some of Celestia into the room.

'Not on Earth they don't. You only get sick from hereditary things – you know, like cancer, diabetes, heart problems.'

'We don't have them on Celestia.'

Ben raised his eyebrows at Kelly who ignored him and smiled back at Orion. 'It sounds wonderful,' she said and Orion beamed back at her.

'OK, we need to prepare you for the meal,' Ben said bringing them back to the task in hand. 'First things first,' and he thrust his hand out, towards Orion. 'Pleased to meet you, Tommy. My name's Adam.'

'I thought it was Ben?'

'It's called role playing,' he said, rolling his eyes.

'Let's try again. Pleased to meet you, Tommy. I'm Mary's dad – Adam.'

Orion put out his hand and limply shook Ben's.

'Pathetic!' Ben said immediately.

'What's pathetic?' Orion said.

'Your handshake! They're going to think you're a right drip. This is how you want to be shaking hands,' he said, gripping Orion's hand firmly and shaking it up and down.

'Right, try it again. Come over to me as if we're meeting for the first time.'

Orion tried it numerous times but each time Adam cried, 'Weedy!' 'Limp lettuce!' 'Wet blanket!' Finally, when Orion was just about to snap, Adam shouted, 'Better!' One more practise and Ben opened a door leading to a dining table where a full meal was laid out. 'Congratulations, you've passed the first test. Now, sit down, Tommy. What can I get you to drink? Brandy? Whisky? A beer maybe?'

'Water please.'

Ben tutted and shook his head. 'No, no, no. Every parent wants a drink in this situation. They're nervous, don't forget! The last thing they want is some sanctimonious youngster sat drinking water while they sit there drinking wine. You've got to make them feel at ease!'

'Aren't they meant to be making me feel at ease? That's what we do with our guests.'

'No, no, no! Well, in a way, yes, but in a way, no, if you know what I mean?'

Orion shook his head.

'Well, look at it this way – you're like a threat to them. You're potentially taking their daughter away from them and they've no idea who you are. Why should they trust you? They know nothing about you. So, you need to do your best to reassure them that you aren't some psycho intent on murdering their daughter.'

'But why would I do that? I'm meant to be falling in love with her?'

'Well, I know that and you know that but they don't know that and you need to make them know that. Know what I mean?' Orion shook his head and shrugged. 'Don't worry, you'll get there. Have a drink, you'll loosen up.' Ben passed Orion a glass of wine which he sniffed and screwed his nose up. Ben tutted and nodded at him, encouraging him to take a sip.

Orion held it to his mouth but started retching. 'I can't drink this!' he said and Ben tutted noisily again. Orion looked at him, realised he had no choice, so held his nose with one hand and put the wine glass to his lips with the other. He shut his eyes and gulped down a tiny bit of wine which he spat out with such force it sprayed over Ben's white shirt.

'What the hell are you doing?' he shouted, leaping away.

'I'm sorry! There must be something toxic in it!' he said, looking shocked.

'Of course, there's something toxic in it – it's called alcohol!'

'I'm sorry but I literally can't drink it. My body won't allow it. We don't have anything like this where I come from,' Orion said, examining the liquid. Ben raised his eyebrows and tutted noisily. 'Could you please stop making that noise! I'm doing my best, you know!'

'That's as maybe but you've got to convince this whole family you are 'normal' by end of play today. We sure have got our work cut out.'

Kelly who had been busying herself tidying the clothes away pulled out a bottle of wine from a cupboard and handed it to Ben. 'Now, Ben, you know extra-terrestrials can't handle alcohol. Let him take this; they'll be none the wiser. It's non-alcoholic,' she said as an aside to Orion who breathed a sigh of relief.

Ben looked at Kelly and reluctantly took the bottle. 'Alright then, but make sure no one else drinks it. Never tastes quite the same as the real thing. Tell them you've got an allergy to most wines so you have to be careful which ones you can drink. Before you leave, I'll give you another bottle to take tonight.' Ben poured a glass of the non-alcoholic wine for Orion who took a tentative sip. 'Now, you need to make polite conversation. Talk about the weather, what a glorious spring it's been for example. Ask them what they've been up to, what their hobbies are – all that sort of thing, OK?'

'When do I get to speak to Mary since she's the reason I'm there?'

'This is your chance to shine with her parents. Involve Mary, of course, but your focus needs to be on them. They may make it difficult for Mary to see you if they don't like you.'

'Can't Mary make up her own mind?' he asked.

Ben shook his head. 'Unlikely.'

'You're such a cynic,' Kelly said. 'Mary's different. She's falling for Tommy big time; we've all seen how she looks at him.'

'You have?' Orion asked.

'Of course! I have to say, at times you've even had me thinking you're falling for her too. The way you look at her is so convincing! I wish my boyfriend looked at me the same way,' she said wistfully.

'If he doesn't look at you that way, he's not right for you,' Orion said firmly.

'Boy, you're good!' she said, her cheeks reddening a little.

'I mean it.'

'Are they all like you where you come from?' she asked.

'Pretty much. We respect our females so much. Without them where would we be?'

'Sounds my kind of place,' she said, smiling at Orion.

'And you sound like the sort of evolved human that would thrive in that environment,' Orion replied.

'Is it Mary you like or Kelly?' Ben asked, looking between the two of them. 'I think I need to take some lessons from you; you're a bit of a babe-magnet by all accounts!'

'Well, let's see if I can win Mary over first,' Orion laughed.

CHAPTER TWENTY-ONE

ELDER ARCHERNAR HAD BEEN TRUE to his word and informed the village and the surrounding ones that a ceremony would take place tonight. The huts were alive with anticipation when the students returned home later that afternoon.

'Hi!' Star's granny said, giving her a hug as she entered their hut. 'Your mother's at the river, if you're after her?' Star nodded and headed to the river where sure enough, there she was, bathing in the clear, sparkling water. As her mother stepped out of the water Star emerged from behind a tree making her jump. Meisa ran to her and wrapped her in her cold, wet arms.

'Mum! You're freezing!' Star said, pushing her away.

'How was it?' she asked, holding Star by the shoulders and looking intently into her eyes.

'Amazing! I can't wait till the next lesson!'

Meisa forced a smile. 'That's wonderful, my love.'

'Mum, we always knew this might happen, didn't we?' Star said, looking in her mother's eyes. 'I know it's not what you want but if I don't follow my heart then it doesn't just affect me, it affects every being on Celestia.'

'Don't patronise me!' she said angrily.

Star dropped her head until a sudden burst of rage came over her, 'This is my calling, not yours, and I'm going whether you like it or not!'

Meisa looked at her beautiful daughter, full of passion and fire just like her father. 'I've already lost your father, I can't lose you as well.' She sat down on a rock and buried her head in her hands.

Star sat down next to her and put her arm around her. 'Mum, you're not going to lose me. I promise! I know Dad died whilst travelling to Earth but it was a freak accident. Nothing's going to happen to me. I just want to be closer to him even if it's only seeing his path for a few sunrises or "days" as humans call them. And in a few "days" time Humans Studies will all be over and we'll never be apart from each other again, OK?' She rubbed her mother's back, trying to comfort her. 'I miss him too,' she said softly.

'I know you do.' Meisa stood up and wiped the tears from her eyes. 'I'm sorry, you have so much of my sadness to bear. It's not fair on you.'

'It's fine. I'm proud he was my dad. I wish I'd had more time with him, that's all.'

'You and me both,' Meisa said. 'If I had it my way, I'd hold onto you forever but I know you have to go.'

'Human Studies means so much to me. All my life I've known Dad was one of the generals of the Committee. I mean, how cool is that? But I've got so few memories of him. At least now I'll be able to walk in his footsteps, see what he saw. It sounds silly but I'll feel close to him,' she said and tears hovered on her bottom eyelids.

'When did you become so grown up?' She stroked a lock of Star's hair and put it behind her ear.

'It's because I've got such a wonderful mum,' she said, wrapping her arms round Meisa and looking up into her eyes. 'And a wonderful granny too, of course!'

'Don't ever forget it,' Meisa laughed. 'Now, didn't I hear something about a ceremony tonight? How about we spend the last few rays of sunlight getting ready and go and have a wonderful time?'

Star's face lit up and she hugged her mother so tightly they both ended up laughing. She then ran into the ice-cold water, diving under when it got deep enough. She emerged a little further away and spurted water out of her mouth making a big arch, causing Meisa to laugh out loud.

Suddenly Star let out a cry and disappeared under the water. Meisa stood up in alarm. Her eyes darted over the eerily still water. As quick as she'd disappeared, she reappeared much further out in the river, flailing her arms and trying to catch her breath.

'Star! Are you OK?' Meisa called out, panic stricken.

Just then a pale-blue scaly head and a webbed hand popped up from beneath the water. Its head had large gills instead of ears, tiny slits for nostrils and sunken cheeks.

'Sorry, Meisa. Just messing about!' he called out, giving her a friendly wave. His gills at the side of his face moved in and out as he breathed.

Meisa's face relaxed and she waved back saying sternly, 'A bit too boisterous this time, Gamua!'

'Point taken, Meisa. Won't do it again!' he said cheerfully.

Star splashed the unusual creature. 'You scared the living daylights out of me, Gamua. For Venus's sake, give me some warning next time!'

'You mean like this?' Gamua popped his head back down and pulled Star back under the water, making her reappear in front of her mother. Meisa and Gamua burst into laughter at her indignant face.

'No, not like that at all! Tell me when you're going to do it next time!'

'But where's the fun in that?' Gamua asked, cocking his head to one side, his tiny ears falling flat against his head.

Splashing him purposefully, she walked out of the water and perched on a rock next to her mum to dry off.

'Must dash. More Terranians to go and annoy. Us magua's never tire of it. You're so easy to wind up,' he said, chuckling to himself.

'Wind up? You mean nearly drown! Just because you live underwater doesn't mean everyone can!'

'Don't be so ridiculous, of course you can! We've had plenty of Terranians down here for tea; you've just got to practise your breathing.' Gamua submerged his head, took a huge intake of breath, paused, then exhaled, squirting the most enormous amount of water all over Meisa and Star who shrieked in shock.

'Off you go now, Gamua,' Meisa said, putting her hands on her hips. 'That's quite enough for one day.'

'Right you are, Meisa. May you live on,' he said, waving his webbed hand to both of them.

'May you live on too, Gamua.' And with a friendly wave from the two of them, he left them to it, returning to his village under the water.

CHAPTER TWENTY-TWO

'AAAH, YOU MUST BE TOMMY,' Adam Wright said, thrusting out a hand for Orion to shake. 'Honey?' he called and an attractive woman appeared at the door, a kind smile on her face. 'This is Tommy. Tommy, meet my lovely wife, Emily. Come in. Mary's getting ready; she'll be with us in a minute.'

Adam led Orion into their apartment which was no bigger than his own quarters back at the space compound. The kitchen, lounge and dining room fitted neatly into the open-plan space. A large TV screen on the back wall took over most of the room displaying pop videos that went on noiselessly in the background.

'Sorry, the music grates on our ears so we've turned it down,' Emily said sheepishly. 'It's either that or the news which seems to be never ending.'

'It's fine. I prefer the quiet,' he said and both of them beamed at each other.

'We seem to be considered quite odd but we've got used to that, haven't we, Emily?' Adam said.

'I think we like most things nowadays, don't we, luv?' she said nervously. 'It's only because we're a bit older now we don't really like this modern pop music and at our age we don't need to listen to the news anymore. Can't go out at night now we're retired so it doesn't really matter what's going on in the world when we can stay in our little bubble up here.'

Adam continued. 'Mary likes to keep up-to-date with everything that's going on so we have an agreement that we have this music channel on in the background but on silent when we have friends round.'

'Did you say you can't go out at night?' Orion asked.

They exchanged nervous glances. 'Well, of course not. You know, it's too risky at our age,' Mary said.

Orion nodded. 'Oh yeah, because it's too dangerous.'

They visibly relaxed. 'Exactly,' Emily said. 'You never know what bug we might pick up. At our age it could kill us.'

Orion smiled at them, thinking they were joking but realising they weren't changed his smile into a concerned look. 'Good idea. I brought you these,' he said passing the wine bottles over, relieved to change the subject.

'Two bottles! You expecting a party?' Adam laughed.

'I'm allergic to most wines. Mine's that one,' he said, pointing to one of the bottles. 'It's not the nicest so I bought one for you guys that my mum recommended.'

'Oh, how lovely. Thank you, Tom,' Adam said. He opened the bottles and poured them all a glass. 'Take a seat and tell us a bit about yourself. Our Mary seems to think very highly of you.'

'Don't embarrass him, Adam!' Emily said kindly.

'Who's embarrassing him?' said Mary, appearing from her bedroom.

'Your father!'

'Leave him alone, will you?' she said, grabbing a glass of wine and sitting next to Orion on the sofa.

'What did I do?' Adam said, holding up his hands.

It didn't take long before Orion felt at ease with Mary's parents.

Adam talked about his job and how happy he was now to be retired. Emily had also retired so they were enjoying a more leisurely pace of life, away from the "rat race", but did feel a little cooped up with the restrictions on retired people that kept them indoors at times when viruses were most easily spread. However, they were just glad to still be able to live at home and not in one of the old people's homes – for the time being.

'Mary says you live in district thirty-one, Tommy? What's it like?' Emily said.

'Much the same as this one, to be honest. I guess our park's a little smaller but apart from that it's all the same shops, same facilities,' said Orion.

Adam cleared his throat. 'And what are your intentions with our Mary?' he said.

'Dad!' Mary shrieked, nearly choking on her wine. 'You can't ask him that! We've only just started dating!'

Orion beamed at her. He hadn't really considered she'd classify them as "dating". 'It's fine! Your dad loves you. He's every right to ask me and I'd like to think I'd be the same as him with our ... I mean, my daughter.' The whole room paused while they took in Orion's little error. Mary's eyes widened and she took a sip of her drink, trying to cover her smile. 'All I can say, Adam and Emily, is that you've brought up the most wonderful human I have ever met,' he said, smiling at them.

'Told you he was funny, didn't I? He's always saying things like that. Tommy, you can call me a girl or a woman, you know? You don't have to be that PC!' she said, laughing.

Orion breathed a sigh of relief but kicked himself inwardly for making such an obvious mistake. 'You never know who you'll upset anymore, do you?' he said, shrugging.

'You can't offend us, Tommy. We're only interested in getting to know you. Mary's our only child and the most important thing in our lives. We just want her to be happy.'

Mary reached for Tommy's hand and said, 'He makes me really happy.'

They both stared at each other and smiled. Adam and Emily smiled at each other too. They'd never seen their daughter so taken with someone and their hearts swelled with love. 'You remind me of us two when we were younger,' Emily said, wiping a tear from her eye.

'I told you you'd love him, didn't I?' Mary said, gazing at Orion. 'He's so different to anyone I've ever met before.' Orion's heart nearly burst.

'Oy, oy, oy, don't be too hasty,' Adam said firmly. 'You've got to win me over too, you know, and I'm not that much of a cushy number, not like these ladies! What are you like, you two?'

'Oh, Adam, come on,' Emily said, nudging him in the ribs. 'You've always been one to follow your gut. Be honest, what is that little tummy telling you?' she said, tickling his stomach.

'Stop!' he said, pushing her off and laughing. 'Oh, go on, then – I think you might be spot on.' He paused before pointing at Orion and saying, 'But don't think I'm some kind of pushover, Tom. You hurt my daughter and I'll come down on you like a ton of bricks.'

'Dad!'

'Just saying,' he said, crossing his arms.

'Understood,' Orion said. 'All I can say is I'm not a psycho wanting to murder her.'

'I should bloody hope not!' Adam said.

Looking at her parents' shocked faces Orion realised he may have said the wrong thing. Mary couldn't help but giggle.

'What I'm trying to say is I won't do anything to harm her. Now I've met you both it's no wonder she turned out so well and I'm honoured to be here tonight,' he said, dipping his head slightly.

The three of them sat there in stunned silence.

Emily nudged Adam. 'Say something,' she whispered.

Adam coughed. 'Err, thank you very much, Tom. Well said. I'm sure we'll get along fine.' He took his drink and drained every last drop of it, placing it firmly on the table. 'What?' he said, noticing they were all staring at him with big smiles on their faces. 'Anyone for a top up?' he asked, getting up to go to the kitchen.

Emily leant over to Orion and touched his elbow. 'He thinks you're great. I can tell.' She lowered her voice. 'We love Mary very much. He tries to play the stern parent but he's not very good at acting, is he, luv?'

'He's always been a soft touch,' Mary whispered, making them laugh.

'Everything all right?' Adam called.

'Yes, honey, everything's fine,' Emily replied, smiling at Orion.

CHAPTER TWENTY-THREE

THE NEXT DAY AT WORK Mary joined Orion and Robert in the staffroom while they were making their cup of tea. Mary couldn't take her eyes off Orion who kept smiling at her.

'Get a room, you two!' Robert said, fanning himself. 'For crying out loud, it's so hot in here I'm sweating like a badger!'

'But badgers don't sweat,' Orion said, a confused expression on his face.

'They would if they were in this room!' Robert replied.

'But a badger wouldn't be in this room …'

Robert put his hand up to stop Orion from going further. 'Tommy, you don't have to take everything quite so literally.' He grabbed his mug and phone, which was as usual beeping throughout their conversation, pushed the door open with his foot and headed back to his desk. Orion leant against the worktop sipping his drink while Mary made her tea.

'Your parents are wonderful,' he said.

'They think you're pretty wonderful too. I have to say, I've never seen Dad like that around anyone before. They think you're a breath of fresh air, Tommy. How did you turn out like this? I mean, you're open, funny, polite, considerate and kind!' She stopped herself from saying more. 'Listen to me, you're going to get a big head if I carry on!'

'You make it easy to be like that.' And he pulled her towards him and kissed her on the lips.

'Not here! You'll have us both fired,' she said, pulling him away.

'How about we go to Sam's Place tonight? Meet you there at eight?' she said, pushing the door open with one hand and gazing longingly back at Orion.

Orion followed her out of the staffroom and watched with a grin on his face as she almost skipped back to her desk.

That night as they sat in one of the booths at Sam's place, they talked non-stop. Despite Mary telling Orion about the lack of surveillance in the bar he turned his phone onto airplane mode and got her to do the same, something Mary was used to doing anyway, she told him. At least his phone couldn't record his conversations when it was on airplane mode. He pictured Melantho listening to all their private conversations, a smug grin on his face. 'Tell me about your parents and when am I going to meet them?' she asked.

'It's just me and Mum. Dad died a few years ago. He'd been building one of the houses in the village ...' his voice tailed off as he realised he needed to adapt the truth a little. 'Sorry, district. It's silly, me and Mum play this silly game sometimes, that we live in this cute little village where all the houses have lovely old beams and beautiful gardens and not this big tower block where we're lucky if our pot plants don't fall off the balcony and hit someone on the head below. Anyway, Dad died building one of the housing blocks four years ago. It's been me and Mum ever since.'

'I can't wait to meet her,' she said, gazing into his piercing blue eyes.

He took Mary's hand and returned her gaze. 'This may sound a bit crazy, but I think I'm falling in love with you.'

Mary stroked Tommy's hand and said softly, 'I feel the same.'

'Oh, Mary, every time I'm apart from you I miss you. I want us to be together – all the time. Not just these snatched moments here and there. I go home to my tiny apartment and lie in bed thinking about you.'

'What are you saying?' she asked.

'How would you feel about moving in with me? Well, not with me and Mum, of course – our own place, just yours and mine.'

'But how could we possibly afford to? Our jobs aren't that well paid and I've barely got any money left over at the end of every month as it is!'

'Tommy! Mary!' Robert called out to them from the bar. Grabbing his drink from the bar he came and joined them. The pair smiled weakly back but didn't invite him to sit down. 'Am I interrupting something? Lovers tiff maybe?'

'Could you give us a minute? We're trying to have a private conversation – something, it would appear, you don't know much about,' Mary said.

'Ooooh, let me guess. Tommy wants you to move in with him and have little Tommy and Mary's running about the place?' He looked between the pair and seeing their angry faces edged back to the bar. 'Sorry, guys. Think I heard someone call my name. Jerry?' he said, waving at a non-existent person at the bar. 'Yes, stay there, Jerry. I'm on my way!'

'He's so nosy!' Mary said, angry at having one of the most important conversations of her life interrupted.

'You can't help but love him, though, can you?' Orion said, smiling as he watched Robert order another drink. Just then a shifty looking man sidled across to Robert without acknowledging him. They were about to look away when Robert dropped something on the floor. The man bent down and picked it up, stuffing it in his coat pocket.

'What's going on there?' Orion said to Mary.

'Who knows,' she shrugged. 'Weren't we just saying we'd move in together?' she said, taking Tommy's hand.

'We could try, couldn't we?' A smile crept across his lips.

'It's a yes from me.'

'Really?'

'Yes! I hate being away from you too! Even Mum and Dad said they'd never seen me so happy before. Of course it's a yes! I want to be with you forever,' she said, wrapping her arms around his neck and kissing him.

'Let's not mention anything to our parents just yet,' he said when they'd got over the excitement. 'How about we spend next week flat hunting before we say anything?'

'Fine by me. Mum will only spend the week in tears anyway. She wants me to find a man and everything but she doesn't want me to leave home because she'll miss me so much. I've got to get used to being away from them though. Not that long till they have to move to the old people's home unless something happens to them before,' she said.

That night as Orion lay in his bed back at the compound he thought about his mother and everything he was about to say goodbye to. He knew he couldn't tell her the truth, that he was running away with a human. She'd never approve.

Orion knew the risks but he was sure things would be different for him and Mary. He loved Mary with every atom of his being and now he knew Mary felt the same.

CHAPTER TWENTY-FOUR

THE COMMITTEE WAS STARTING TO get frustrated by Orion's surveillance of Mary. He'd been unable to find any concrete evidence proving she was a threat to the system yet he kept making excuses as to why he had to continue to monitor her. Recorded conversations between Mary and Orion were proving hard to listen to since they would cut out frequently and the family meal had gleaned no information that made the Committee members feel any concern that her parents were questioning the system either. However, all the generals were incredibly impressed with Orion's acting skills and felt they could be put to good use in some of their other undercover operations.

Arrakis and Zaurak came and had a chat with him one day in his quarters whilst he was sat at his desk scrolling through her social media pages on his phone.

'This Mary,' Arrakis began, 'she seems alright. We don't think you need to carry on observing her.'

Orion's heart plummeted. He had to think fast. 'Funny you should say that. I was thinking the same,' he said, surprising them both. 'However, the last time we met she said she was thinking of quitting her job. She told me that her boss, Richard Henderson, is and I quote, "a right loser" and that she could do his job blindfolded. She also said she'd been speaking with a number of her colleagues who are going to try and make things very difficult for him. "Shame him into resigning" – is how she put it. That would make things difficult for us too, wouldn't it? He's one of the few humans who's fully aware of the Committee which makes it possible for you to send beings like me to the offices there, isn't that right?'

General Arrakis scratched his chin with his forefinger. 'But in all the time you've been observing her we've never heard her say that. Nor have we any evidence of her using any of the buzz words.'

'Mary's a lot smarter than you think. I've got a feeling she's aware of the buzz words. It doesn't take a genius to work out which ones to avoid.'

'What do you mean? The system's worked efficiently for many years now,' said Zaurak.

'I don't mean to speak out of turn but the system needs an update. I've been learning so much at the office and hanging around with Mary and Robert. I think I can create a system that flushes out more questioners than our current one.'

General Zaurak thought for a moment. 'I'm not sure. Melantho says he's continually updating the system.'

Orion leant back in his chair and stretched his arms behind his back clasping them at the back of his head. 'Ah, it all makes sense now. Of course, it's Melantho updating it,' he said wincing a little and sitting up straight.

'What do you mean?'

'Well, I wasn't sure who I should say this to, but I get the feeling that working on the surveillance side of things is a lot more pleasurable than he makes out – if you know what I mean?'

'Really?' Arrakis said, his eyes widening in alarm.

Orion held his hands out wide. 'It's probably nothing.'

'If you've got something to say it's better you say it,' Zaurak said.

Orion grimaced again and turned to make sure no one else could hear them. 'Maybe you should check out how many hours he spends on specific apartments. They're often the ones that just happen to belong to young attractive females.'

'Hmm, we've noticed this before but young, attractive females can question the system too, you know,' Arrakis said.

Orion shrugged. 'You're right, it's probably just me. I mean, what do I know? I've only been working closely with Melantho for a few months now. It's really nothing compared to the time you've worked with him.' He waved his hand nonchalantly. 'Ignore me. I'm sure you're right. The system's been working great all these years. Why fix something when it ain't broke. That's what they say on Earth, isn't it?' he said, turning away.

The two generals looked at each other. Arrakis leant over and said something inaudible to Zaurak who raised his eyebrows and nodded.

'Listen, Orion,' Arrakis said, 'how about you monitor her for another week. You could say something to put her off the scent about Henderson. She listens to you. He may not set the world alight but he's reliable and trustworthy. If staff start to recognise his failings it's going to be very difficult finding the right person to replace him. However, if we don't find anything else to concern us, I think we could wrap this case up. Do you agree, Zaurak?'

'Definitely. We're running a top-secret surveillance case at the moment and we need all the acting skills we can get for this one.'

'Why's that?' Orion asked.

'A famous actor's getting ready to expose some pretty high-ranking government officials for their inappropriate behaviour with some of the actors on their movies. We need someone to go undercover to get the names he's about to release so we can investigate them further before anyone else gets to him. With your acting skills we think you're the right man for the job. You may even be able to use your shape-shifting skills too,' Zaurak said.

'That sounds an amazing opportunity! I'm sure I'll be able to wrap this up by the end of the week. It'll be good to move onto something a bit more challenging.'

'You deserve it. I don't think we've ever had an apprentice act so convincingly on their first job. You'll go high places, Orion. Well done,' Arrakis said.

'Thank you, it's been an honour working on the team.'

The two generals smiled. Zaurak tipped his head slightly. 'Could you keep an eye on your phone too? We think there's a fault with it. It keeps cutting out when you're with Mary. If you need a new one just let us know.'

'How strange, I haven't noticed anything myself but thanks for letting me know.'

'We'll report back to the Committee. I'm sure they'll agree this is the most sensible route.' Arrakis went to place his palm on the hand recognition pad. Zaurak stopped him and raised his eyebrows nodding his head towards Orion. The two men turned back to Orion. 'Do you really think you can create a better system?'

'Yes, I do.'

The two generals looked at each other.

'I think it's best not to tell Melantho though,' Orion said.

'I'm not so sure,' Arrakis said. 'I don't feel comfortable going behind his back, especially as he's the one who set it up. He's got one hell of a temper.'

'Sorry, I didn't realise Melantho was in charge,' Orion said.

General Zaurak coughed and straightened his back. 'Arrakis, we've been pussyfooting around that man for too long. I've no idea how he ever came to be the one in control of the surveillance system. The next time he leaves the compound you'll have access to the surveillance programming system, Orion.'

'Should you run this by the rest of the Committee?' Orion asked.

The two generals looked at each other, their brows furrowed. Zaurak cleared his voice before saying, 'Of course – once this is all over, that is. I think it's going to be better to tell them when it's all set up; they'll probably undermine us otherwise. They seem to be doing that a lot lately. If you sort this system out, you never know, we might get back in their good books once they find out there are a lot more humans wanting to be free than they'd imagined.'

'Maybe the system Melantho set up is actually preventing them from being able to grow into fully conscious beings?' Orion said.

'There's no indication that's the case. Their bank accounts are displaying that an awful lot of money is still being spent on junk and we have huge numbers hooked on pharmaceutical drugs,' said Arrakis. 'There are still so few taking control of their own health.'

'Yes, but the fast-food outlets had their least profitable year last year,' Zaurak said.

'Wasn't that because of that nasty bug going round, though? Had to close for three months, didn't they?' Arrakis asked.

Zaurak scratched his chin. 'Maybe but we'd covered their losses for that period. It still indicates a big reduction in customers. I don't trust Melantho. It wouldn't surprise me one jot if he's making sure we don't find out if there are more waking up.'

'I think an update of the system will allow us to monitor humans a lot more closely than Melantho is currently doing. Tell you what, I'll put in an extra programme that collates numbers of humans who are reducing their consumption,' said Orion.

The generals' eyes lit up. 'That's a great idea,' Zaurak said. 'What a valuable addition to the team you're proving to be.' He came over and hugged Orion. 'Your mother will be very proud of you.'

Orion hugged the man back and smiled at Arrakis. 'Talking of my mother, I think I'm due a visit home, aren't I? I can feel my body weakening by being in this unnatural environment.'

'Yes, of course! It gets to us all at some point. You must miss her a lot.'

Orion nodded. 'She's going to be so mad at me for not getting back sooner.'

The generals laughed in agreement. 'I think General Rigley's been placating her so you probably won't be in too much trouble,' Arrakis said with a slight smile. 'Luckily there's a flight back tomorrow. You'll only have the weekend as we need you back in the office by Monday.'

'The weekend would be great, thanks.'

'No problem. Listen, we'll get there in the end. With you on the case we can really try and work with humans and not against them. Let's hope the day they become fully conscious beings isn't too far away,' Zaurak said.

'That would be wonderful,' Orion replied.

The two men smiled at him, their eyes a little watery, and left the room.

Once the door closed Orion breathed out noisily. He hated lying but he didn't really care whether humans became conscious or not and he certainly wasn't going to hang around for the day they did eventually wake up. He longed to hold Mary in his arms, watch her as she opened her eyes in the morning and gaze at her last thing at night. The opportunity to be with her was running out. He'd be moved onto a different assignment next week and may never see her again. He couldn't imagine a life without her in it. Now all he needed to do was go home and say his goodbyes before embarking on a new life here with Mary. It sounded so easy when he said it in his head but he knew this was going to be the hardest thing he'd ever have to do.

CHAPTER TWENTY-FIVE

WHEN THEY OPENED THEIR EYES the sun was setting, giving the whole village a wonderful orange glow. Beings were giving their hair a final check, brushing their clothes down and making sure their huts were tidy for their return at sunrise.

Star got up, reached her hand out to her Gran who eased onto her feet. Linking arms with Meisa, they began making their way into the woods, towards the Waterfall of Source where the ceremonies were held. They knew it would be dark when they got there but it was well worth the long walk.

The Waterfall of Source was an integral part of Celestia and it was essential that every being had access to her healing powers. The seniors came here to perform ancient rituals; they would chant, sing songs and answer questions put to them by those who were needing guidance in their lives.

Most of the villagers walked in silence, though some of the younger beings were leaping from branch to branch full of excitement. Others shape-shifted from one creature to another, leaping or jumping through the woods. The older ones were saving their energy for the long night ahead.

Star could hear the melodic sounds of their favourite song, "Har

Ji" come drifting through the forest, its gentle rhythm beckoning them to the waterfall. The singers had begun and as always, it was this song that opened the ceremony.

As they drew closer it got harder to walk without brushing another being's arm as the density of the crowd started to increase. Eventually, the forest thinned and the Waterfall of Source emerged. Stood on a ledge halfway up the rock face were the male guitarist and female singer, both dressed in matching long, white robes. The singer wore a headdress containing white and pale blue flowers and held a large crystal into which she sang; the clear quartz amplified her voice so it could be heard deep into the woods.

Pink crystals hovered and glowed in the forest, carrying the music so every being could hear her smooth tones. The duo continued playing until the numbers arriving began to dwindle. Beings were drawing in from all over Celestia. The fireflies lit up the forest, twinkling at different intervals making the effect appear truly magical. Gradually "Har Ji" got quieter and quieter and everyone found a space to sit or lie.

Star, Meisa and Rhea made sure they stuck together; it was so easy to lose each other at ceremonies. A stillness came over the crowd and everyone gazed at the Waterfall of Source which was lit up with the fireflies and crystals. The water glistened majestically.

The seniors sat in chairs that had been carved out of ancient tree trunks. They looked at each other, ever so slightly nodded, then began softly chanting their ancient Celestian words, 'Namurrahr Ghinjure Shisasanura,' over and over again. Heal, Love, Nature.

The chant spread from the front of the crowd, to the middle and then right to the back. The sound reverberated around the trees, sending vibrations that each and every being felt coursing through their body, lifting their spirits and healing any emotional disturbances. Every being had their eyes closed, some swayed gently to the natural rhythm the chant induced whereas others were motionless.

One by one the seniors ceased their chanting and the crowd followed suit.

The seniors stood up, looked at all the heads underneath them and threw their arms up into the air. A huge cheer rang out; the festivities had begun! A new group of musicians appeared to the side of them, counted 'One, two, three, four ...' and burst into song. In the blink of an eye, the crowd were up on their feet, arms in the air, dancing to the quick tempo of the music.

Rhea indicated she was going over to a log to sit with her friends. Star tapped her mother's hand and mouthed that she was going to find Lacarta and Alhena. It was incredibly hard to walk through the crowds but thankfully it didn't take them too long to find them. The families hugged each other and began dancing together, arms in the air, hips swaying to the beat.

Vega pulled Meisa over to where she was dancing. 'How did Star get on?' she asked. Seeing her best friend's eyes fill up with tears she hugged her saying, 'I'm so sorry.'

'What about Lacarta?' Meisa asked.

'Whatever he thought about it, he'll listen to Sabik and I. His father'll never let him go; it's too risky.'

The music changed and a familiar song came on that sent a flurry of excitement rippling through the crowd. The three friends joined the mass of beings who were forming a chain, one arm linked over their neighbour's shoulders. They kicked their legs to every other beat, using the weight of the other person to support them.

Star and her two friends looked down at the mass of legs and as always got the giggles. Lacarta had to focus so intently on getting the right rhythm, he had his friends in stitches watching the concentration on his face as he tried to dance in time.

When they could dance no more the three of them took themselves off to find something to drink. They found the stall offering the Situble drink, poured the pale-brown liquid down their throats and slammed the small cups down, eager to move onto the next stall.

Musicians were dotted about the outer areas of the forest, playing quietly to small groups. Craftsmen were carving bowls, spoons, musical instruments and others were offering all sorts of delicious foods, baskets, herbs and spices. A group of musicians caught their attention and they headed to a tree trunk to sit and listen to them.

'Guys, what did you think of Human Studies?' Star said.

'Yeah, good,' Lacarta said, looking at the band and tapping his foot.

'Good? Good? Is that all you can say?' Star said, slapping him on the arm.

'Maybe we should ask you the same question? What did YOU think of Human Studies?' Alhena asked, an inquisitive expression on her face.

Star raised her eyes dreamily to the sky, clasping her hands in front of her chest. 'I thought it was the most mind-blowingly awesome thing I've ever seen.'

The other two looked at each other and frowned.

'Do you really want to go down this route after everything your family's been through?' Alhena asked.

'Not you too. I've had all this from Mum. What is it with everyone? All we've ever been taught is that we've got to follow our calling, be who we are, not who others want us to be, blah, blah, blah. But when I decide to follow my path it's all, worry, worry, "Are you sure, Star? With your history, Star?" I mean, why is everyone so concerned? I can look after myself. It's been me, Mum and Granny for fourteen orbitals but all of a sudden no one seems to think I'm capable of making my own decisions!'

'Star, it's not that, you know it's not. You and your gran are all Meisa has! If something happens to you it'll destroy her,' Lacarta said, touching her knee.

Star pushed his hand away. 'She's not going to lose me! I'm studying humans, just like loads of others have before me. Why has everyone got a problem with me studying them?'

From out of the shadows her mother appeared. 'Because your dad didn't die on the craft to Earth. He was murdered when he got there and I've never been told why.'

Star's world, as she knew it, came grinding to a standstill.

CHAPTER TWENTY-SIX

As ORION GOT OFF THE spacecraft, he breathed in the scent of Celestia. It felt so good to be home. He walked leisurely to his hut. He wanted to be able to memorise every step so he could remember these moments forever. He took in the sights and smells and spent time talking to any being who stopped to ask how he was. Feeling the ground underneath his feet was like giving his body a charge of energy he'd lacked on Earth. The air was so much cleaner here and the skies bluer. Everything felt alive. He'd been doing his research, though, and he now knew there was somewhere he could go with Mary, somewhere they could be free.

He walked into his hut and there was his mother, lying on her bed meditating.

'Mum,' he whispered and her eyes fluttered open.

'Orion!' she said, leaping up and giving him a bear hug.

'I've missed you,' he laughed, hugging her back.

'It's so good to have you home! I thought you were never coming back, that you'd decided to stay on earth, make a life for yourself there!'

'Mum, stop! You mustn't worry so much. This will always be my home,' he lied.

She stroked the side of his face, gazing into his eyes. 'When do you have to go back?'

Orion bent his head. 'In two sunrises.'

His mother gasped. 'What? That can't be right! You've been there ages; you deserve more time off.'

'It's tricky, Mum. I'm on an assignment and if I don't turn up for work on Monday morning the humans in the office will get suspicious.'

'Are you still observing that girl?' she asked, trying hard to disguise the prickle in her voice.

'Yes, but not for much longer thankfully,' he said.

'And then you'll be able to come home again?'

'For sure,' he replied.

She breathed a sigh of relief. 'That's good. They're working you too hard. Even Arrakis and Zaurak come back at least once a moon to recharge. It doesn't seem right,' she said, shaking her head.

'To be honest, I've been so focused on the assignment it kind of slipped my mind. It's consumed me. I wouldn't have been much company anyway.'

'Is this Mary really such a threat?' she asked, folding her arms.

'I believe so. I've been allowed access to her family who began questioning many years ago. I've had to follow all the social connections they make and ensure those around them haven't begun questioning too.' He sat down and buried his head in his hands. 'It's been exhausting.'

She sat down next to him and put her arm around him. 'Of course, my love. It sounds like you've been doing an incredible job. I'm so proud of you. You managed to do any shape-shifting yet?' she asked with a twinkle in her eye.

Orion smiled. 'Nah. They said the next job I might though.'

She nudged him gently in the ribs. 'Fancy having a go now – just mother and son, like we used to?'

Orion smiled and nodded. 'Same as usual?'

'Of course.'

He took his mother's hand in his and they both closed their eyes and held their breath. Within an instant they had transformed into two beautiful grinfellars. They tipped their blue-beaked heads back, stretched their brightly coloured wings out and flew up and over the trees. Orion let his mother go first, following her as she glided this way and that over their beautiful land. They spotted a river below and swooped down, placing their beaks in the water as they sped over it. A group of young maguas spotted them and tried to race them, ignoring their mothers' calls to come back. Eridamus tipped one of her wings in the river and flicked it, drenching Orion, who spluttered for breath. He overtook her, showing off doing twists and turns, following the winding river until it opened out into the sea. They flew to the cliff top, enjoying the spray from the crashing waves cooling their feathers and perched on a cliff top.

'Have you ever seen anything so beautiful?' his mother asked him, one wing draped over his shoulders.

'Only once,' he said quietly but the noise of the waves was so great she didn't catch what he said.

Ginyanas leapt from the waves beneath them, playing tag with each other. Tiny boats were dotted on the horizon as beings were drawing in their nets and heading home for the night.

'Time to go home?' he asked his mum.

'I guess,' she sighed, stretching out her wings. 'Look at my feathers. The colours are paler now I'm getting older,' she said, looking from one wing to another.

'Never thought you were worried about that, Mum!'

'I'm not! Aren't they beautiful?'

Orion laughed. 'So modest!'

She laughed too. 'Come on. Time for bed.'

They flew home, back the way they'd come. When they returned to their normal bodies, Orion reached over and squeezed his mother's hand. 'That was perfect,' he said.

She smiled back at him. 'They're my favourite times with you.' Her eyes glistened in the moonlight.

The morning he was due to return to Earth he went into the woods and found the sapling of an arramanga tree in a small clearing. Using his hands, he dug around the roots and bought it back to their hut. He found his mother outside, chewing on a grefenurak leaf. 'Look what I found,' he said, sitting down next to her showing her the tiny tree.

'It's beautiful.' She reached out and touched the leaves.

He got up and dug a hole, placing the plant carefully into the empty space and refilled it with the soil until it stood firm in the ground. 'I want you to think of me every time you look at it,' he told her.

'What do you mean? This sounds like a farewell not just a "goodbye and I'll see you soon",' she said, alarm growing in her voice.

'Mum, this isn't farewell. It's just in case something happens to me, you know, like it did with Leo.'

She stood up and hugged him, breathing in his familiar smell. 'Nothing's going to happen to you, son. I won't let it.'

He knew how much she loved him; he meant everything to her and he hugged her back, not wanting to let go. He loved his mother and his planet so much but his future lay on Earth. It was the hardest thing he'd ever had to do but such was the pull he felt to be with Mary he no longer felt he had a choice.

As casually as he could he turned and waved as he headed back to the Centre of Learning for his final journey to Earth. 'See you in a couple of moons,' he called out and she waved back at him. He waved until his mother was out of sight then turned and let the tears roll down his face. It would be a few sunsets before it dawned on her.

CHAPTER TWENTY-SEVEN

'WHAT DO YOU MEAN?' Star asked, her brow furrowed. 'You told me Dad died in an accident on the craft; you said he never got there!'

'How could I tell you the truth? That there was a race out there capable of killing another being? They refused to release his body so I've never been able to lay him to rest. Why would they do that unless there is no body and he didn't die?' Tears sprang to Meisa's eyes. 'I'm so sorry. I've wanted to tell you for ages but every sunrise I prayed he'd return before I had to tell you the truth.'

Star looked at her mother, pain etched on her face. Everything felt in slow motion. She turned her head towards her two friends, saw the shock and empathy on their faces, then looked back at her mother. Meisa held out her arms and went to say something but stopped in her tracks when she saw the look on her daughter's face. Star held her gaze for a moment then turned and ran into the crowd.

'Star!' she heard her mother cry but she didn't look back. She pushed her way through the throngs of beings, arms in the air, eyes closed, dancing hypnotically to the beat of the music, caught up in their own world. She hated every one of them. She jabbed at their ribs with her elbows as she tried to make her way frantically through the dense crowd. Some yelled out in pain, others grabbed her arm and pulled her back but she shrugged them off angrily and carried on pushing through the sea of dancers with no idea as to where she was headed. Tears streamed down her face but she didn't care who stared at her. As she drew closer to the centre of the crowd, she found it harder and harder to move, bodies pressed against her, swaying, moving and grinding to the beat of the incessant, pulsating music.

She stopped pushing and gave in to the movement, swaying with the crowd as tears poured down her face. She held her hands clasped against her heart as if pleading for it all to be over, to go back to a time when it was just her, Meisa and her grandmother, with no complications. A hand clasped her right hand and moved it upwards, then another hand found her left one, linking her fingers between theirs. She opened her eyes to see a male looking intently at her. He had rich green hair and soft brown eyes. He put his hand on her cheek and she leant into it, closing her eyes as she did. He drew her into his arms and they danced together, two souls that had never met yet seemingly so familiar.

As one song drew to a close and another started the male held Star's hand and pulled her to where the crowd began to thin. She'd never been to this side of the woods before and it felt exciting to be somewhere so unfamiliar to her.

'Hey there, Procyon!' another boy with similar colourings called to them.

'Hey, Marfik!' he said, heading over to see his friend.

'Who's this?' asked Marfik.

'I'm sorry, I didn't catch your name?' asked Procyon who was still holding her hand. 'The music was too loud.'

Suddenly embarrassed at being with a total stranger Star gently pulled her hand free and looked to the ground and said, 'Oh, err, sorry I'm, err … Star.'

'Very pleased to meet you, err … Star,' he said, bowing slightly.

'Pleased to meet you too,' Star said, wondering if he was trying to be funny. Then gathering her thoughts, 'I've made a mistake. I shouldn't be here.'

She ran back towards the crowd but he was faster and grabbed her arm, pulling her back. 'I don't know what's going on, but I've only just met you. If you go back in there, I'll never find you.'

Star looked at him, unsure of what she should do. She wasn't ready to face her mother or anyone else just yet. She looked up into his eyes which had a slight twinkle to them.

'Please?' he said and gestured for her to sit down.

'I can't stay long,' she said, sitting on the ground. 'I don't even know what I'm doing here.'

'I had to stop you. I've never done anything like that before but my heart told me you needed help.'

'I'm fine, honestly. I just need some time to process something, that's all.'

'Process what?'

'I don't want to talk about it! In fact, I really should be going,' she said, getting up. He reached his hand out, grabbing her round the wrist. 'Let me go!' she demanded.

'You need to talk about it and I won't let you go until you do,' he said firmly. 'You can't go back in that crowd with all this negative energy surging through your body. It's not healthy for you or for anyone in there either. The quicker you deal with this the quicker your body can start to heal.'

Star looked at this male she'd never met before and wondered why she felt so at ease with him. She hadn't even wanted to talk to her friends about this let alone open up to a complete stranger but he was right; the whole point of the ceremony was to release all the pent-up emotion they'd absorbed from their earlier Human Studies lesson. Her body was running high on adrenalin and she knew that may spoil her chances of studying humans. They would never allow a being who couldn't process their own emotions to continue with the lessons. 'You can trust me. I'm a really good listener, aren't I, Marfik?' he said, turning to his friend.

'He sure is. I'm off to get a drink. Nice to meet you, Star, and don't forget, trapped emotions cause blockages!' Marfik said as he headed into the crowd.

The two new friends found a quiet place to sit under a tree and Star told him about the events of the sun rotation, the lesson in Human Studies and her newfound love of it, then finding out about her dad. He allowed her to talk freely and didn't interrupt once.

When she finally came to the end she stopped and looked down at her hands that had been flailing about.

'I wasn't expecting that, I have to say.' He looked at her and smiled. 'What I've taken from this is all the good!'

'What do you mean "the good"? Did you not hear me? I've been lied to all these orbitals!'

He held her by the shoulders, looked deep into her eyes and said, 'I heard everything you said. What you're forgetting is there's a chance your dad could be alive!'

Her face, which was creased up in anger, stared back at him. 'If he's alive why hasn't he come back? We can choose not to return, remember?' Star's face crumpled into tears again.

'Which Celestian you know would choose to stay on Earth if they had a young family back here? Something doesn't add up. What if he's been trying to come back and hasn't been able to? If you're as passionate about Human Studies as you say you are then you have to continue with them. You might find the answers to some of your questions on Earth.'

CHAPTER TWENTY-EIGHT

BY THE TIME ORION WAS back at the space centre he felt a lot more confident about his plan. 'Do you think I should access the surveillance database tonight, General Arrakis?' he asked the first time they were alone.

The general looked alarmed. 'Maybe we could discuss that more at the end of the week? I'm a bit snowed under at the moment.'

'The quicker I get started the quicker we can begin assessing the information coming in. The buzz words are so dated. Humans aren't stupid. They work out which ones to avoid.'

'I thought about this after we spoke. How can you be so certain?'

'Robert told me. Says he worked out pretty early on which words got him in trouble and which didn't. Said it was easy as his credit rating dropped when he mentioned certain words.'

'Robert shouldn't be speaking so openly to you about these sorts of things.'

'Why not? Isn't it my job to find out who's rebelling and whether they have any influence or not? I've been observing Robert for weeks now and unlike most humans, he doesn't care what he says yet he's untouchable. I can't figure it out.'

Arrakis looked away, avoiding meeting Orion's eyes. 'You don't need to bother yourself about that one. He's harmless. He just enjoys stirring things up a bit, that's all.'

'Too right he does. He thrives on it. What's so special about him?'

'There's nothing special about him, Orion,' he said angrily. 'Drop it will you?'

Orion realised this route was getting him nowhere. He didn't want to anger Arrakis in case it put his plan in jeopardy. 'I believe the ones who are questioning are using code words instead of the trigger words. They're managing to stay under the radar but I'm convinced there are many more questioning than we're led to believe. They don't want to have their every move watched and listened to.'

'As long as they behave themselves, they've got nothing to worry about, have they? They're only monitored if they begin questioning the system.'

'And who dictates that?'

'We do, of course!'

'That's precisely what I've been trying to tell you, though! Isn't the whole point of the Committee to guide humans into being fully conscious beings, to rid themselves of their fixation on material belongings and status and live connected to their beautiful planet? That's what we want for them, isn't it?'

'Of course, it is! Well, it is for most of us but I have to say I'm starting to worry that maybe not everyone wants that to happen.'

'There you go! Maybe the very system the Committee created, believing it a way of protecting humans and the environment, is now actually restricting their growth and inhibiting their opportunity to become fully evolved?' Orion asked.

'That has crossed my mind but according to my sources there's no evidence of humans being remotely close to that happening. They're still so obsessed with collecting "things", buying the latest gadgets, downloading the latest games. I mean look at the figures of the latest app. Nearly 400 million users – eighty percent of the population – have downloaded it already and it was only released on Friday!' He pulled out his mobile phone and opened an app called, "Me, Myself and I". 'Look,' he said showing Orion, 'it really is quite fun. You create an animated picture of yourself, your apartment and your place of work. It calculates the distances you travel anywhere – you just have to tell it whether you jogged, walked or caught public transport. You scan the barcodes of the food you eat and drink throughout the day. Every conversation is monitored via the microphone. At the end of the day everything is tallied up so you know exactly how much exercise you've done, how many calories you've consumed and how many times you laughed. The app then gives you a rating from zero to a hundred of how efficiently your body operated that day.' He showed Orion his ratings from the previous few days. 'Pretty good, eh?' he chuckled. 'I mean, look at me! Don't I look funny as a little computer-generated guy?' he said, laughing again. Orion looked back, bemused. 'The only problem is this app doesn't recognise the space compound so it's not perfect. Course they can't have this place registered on the app or everyone would know about us. I have to pretend I live in one of the blocks in district 53. It doesn't recognise any of the forests around the city either – for obvious reasons …'

'What reasons are they?' Orion interrupted.

'To protect the environment mainly but it's also easier to monitor humans when they live in cities. The trees stop the signal getting to their phones, even from the satellites they launched in the sky. I have to admit,' he said sheepishly, 'it's quite handy as it gives me a place to go to reconnect with nature whenever I can.' He paused for a moment and smiled at the device in his hand. 'Where was I? Oh yes, the results for me aren't an exact science but apart from that, I love it!' he said, chuckling again as he looked at the tiny image on the screen, its shoulders gently moving up and down as if breathing.

'Very good,' Orion said slowly, placing his hand over the phone and trying to bring the general back to the subject in hand. 'Do you normally monitor all the apps going out?'

'Good grief, no! There are far too many!' he replied.

'So why was this one so important for you to assess?' Orion asked, confused.

'Beats me. Melantho mentioned it at the last meeting and before we knew it, he had us all downloading it onto our phones. It's been quite a bonding experience funnily enough! We compare our ratings whenever we see each other. That General Rastaban is a lot fitter than you'd think!' he said, chuckling again.

'How wonderful!' Orion said brightly. 'Can I take a closer look please?' he asked, putting his hand out. Arrakis held the phone closely to his chest, a grumpy scowl on his face, and shook his head petulantly. 'General ...', Orion said as if to a child, his hand still extended. It took a moment before Arrakis met Orion's gaze – realising he meant business, he slowly placed the phone in Orion's hand. 'Thank you,' Orion said patiently, to which he got a sulky 'Humph' in reply. Orion grabbed the phone and quickly accessed the microphone, video and location services, turning them all off. 'What the hell's that man playing at?' he said, shaking the phone angrily at the general. 'For crying out loud, it's not just the masses he's been observing! He's had all your conversations recorded since you had this app. When did you download it?' he shouted.

'I'm not sure – last week sometime.'

'Before or after we talked about changing Melantho's settings on the surveillance database?' he asked, fear growing in his voice.

A hand went up to Arrakis's mouth as it slowly dawned on him. 'Before,' he replied, his head bent like a scolded child. 'What have I done?'

'Has he been in over the weekend?' Orion asked quickly.

He nodded his head. 'But I don't think he's been in the surveillance room. Let's get you there now, before he starts work.' The men pressed the button on the side of the wall and the door opened with a gentle swoosh. They walked briskly down the corridor, trying not to draw attention to themselves. They could see the door to the surveillance room further down the corridor and breathed a sigh of relief that there was no one else around to see them enter the room.

The general pressed the button on the wall and the door swooshed open. They both froze when they saw Melantho sat alone in the darkened room staring at the computer screen.

CHAPTER TWENTY-NINE

LATER THAT NIGHT, AFTER DANCING until their feet were sore, the two beings lay down and looked at the majestic sky above them. They took turns to point out the constellations above them and talked about what various stars meant to their families.

Star turned her face to look at Procyon. His brown eyes looked almost translucent from where she lay. 'Have you done Human Studies yet?' she asked him, propping her head up with her arm.

'I opted out.'

'What do you mean, you "opted out"?'

'I mean I won't be studying them! I can't see the appeal of observing another planet when I'm so happy on this one.'

'Wow, I thought everyone was as nosey as me!' Star said incredulously. 'What do you want to do then?'

'Become a carpenter. For me, the best bit about tonight is watching them. I find it mesmerising. Look over there,' he said, pointing to a man deep in thought as he carved a chair out of a large tree trunk. 'That's my dad. We spent ages searching for that log today; we only take the ones that have fallen, you see. It was so heavy we had to wait until a Trycladene heard Dad's call.' Procyon explained how the Trycladene used its muscular tail to flip the large tree trunk onto its back, rest it between its shoulder blades and neck and follow them back to their village. 'The young ones are so funny to watch!' he laughed. 'They just about get it balanced on its back only for it to roll straight over its head and land on the ground in front of them.'

'The poor things!' Star said.

'Their mother's always close by, watching them. She gives them space to try but it can take many moons for them to perfect this technique so sometimes she has to step in and help us. She's just grateful we let her young have a go. On the walk home we chat about what to make it into – a chair, a stool, a musical instrument, a beam for a house. Look …'

Star looked down as Procyon pulled out a tiny wooden spoon from the pocket of his tunic. It was the most delicate spoon she'd ever seen with markings all the way down the handle. 'It's beautiful!' she gasped.

'Thanks, I've got plenty of them back home but this is my favourite.' He paused and then held it out to Star. 'You have it.' He looked down at his feet and shuffled a few leaves away with his toes. 'That is, if you want it?'

Star was so touched she could barely speak. 'Thank you! I love it. Thank you so much!' She leant over and hugged him. Just then the music changed tempo, signalling the ceremony was coming to an end. 'We'd better go. Race you!'

They leapt onto their feet and ran into the crowd towards the Waterfall of Source. The band had been replaced by the two musicians who'd opened the ceremony and were gently strumming away on their delicate pequinatar. Indus sat watching them intently, trying to copy their movements on his instrument. The seniors stood up, raised their arms and waited for everyone to quieten down. They lowered their arms slowly and the crowd found a space to lie down. Just then the musicians began singing a very gentle, 'Om'. Some joined in, others closed their eyes and let the Om slide over them. The crystals levitating about the forest helped the noise travel effortlessly to everyone there. Eventually, the music stopped. The crowd slowly got to their feet and headed back to their villages, happy but exhausted.

Star and Procyon held hands and looked intently at each other.

'When am I going to see you again?' he asked.

'I think I need to concentrate on Human Studies for the time being but after that?'

'You gonna go for it, then?' Procyon asked.

'I have to.'

Procyon held her hands to his lips and kissed them. 'I know. Thanks for making this ceremony one of the best moments of my life,' he said, grinning from ear to ear.

Star laughed and turned to go back to the part of the forest that would lead her home, giving Procyon one final wave before he headed home too.

'See you when you get back!' he said cupping his hands and calling out to her.

'I can't wait!'

It didn't take long before she found her mother searching the crowd for her. Her face collapsed with relief when her daughter appeared next to her. They linked arms and silently walked home, the young female resting her head on her mother's shoulder. She hadn't forgotten about earlier but talking to Procyon had helped ease her anger a little.

CHAPTER THIRTY

'CAN I HELP YOU?' MELANTHO asked, crossing his arms and turning his chair to face them. 'You seem a little …' he paused, 'stressed.'

'Do we? No, not stressed – just concerned,' Arrakis began.

'What about?' Melantho had his usual sickeningly smug look on his face.

'Mary seems to have been a dead end after all,' Orion blurted out.

Melantho raised his eyebrows. 'You surprise me.'

'Yes, sorry, thought I was onto something but she's just the same as all the other humans; hooked on social media and obsessed with the latest trends. Arrakis has another assignment for me. I'll hand in my notice this morning; tell them I've got a job somewhere else. Could I access the database to update my file? Then when Richard Henderson checks out my story it'll all look above board.'

'The least Richard Henderson knows the better. Isn't that right, Melantho?' said Arrakis.

Melantho narrowed his eyes and looked at the two of them. 'Hmmm. Why would I allow you onto the system? It won't take me a minute. I was meant to look into the system over the weekend anyway,' he said, turning his chair back to the computer screen in front of him.

Orion breathed a sigh of relief. At least he hadn't checked the settings!

'Melantho!' Arrakis said, making them both look at him in alarm. 'We're in a hurry. Orion needs to be in work in forty-five minutes. It's easier if we do it ourselves.'

'I'm already here, it's no bother,' he said firmly, giving them a suspicious look.

Arrakis lowered his tone. 'Listen, Melantho, I don't want to worry you but General Rastaban was pacing up and down cursing your name when we saw him a minute ago. Had a look on his face that scared the shit out of me, pardon my French,' he coughed. 'Kept jabbing his finger at his phone, saying, "Bloody Melantho, how the hell am I meant to get a higher score if it won't register the compound!"'

Melantho got up from his chair and gathered his files together, stuffing them into his bag. 'I told him to measure the distance he walks in the compound and create a similar distance from one of the blocks to work. How many times!' He grabbed his phone and headed out the door without a backwards glance.

The minute the door swooshed shut the two breathed a sigh of relief.

'We don't have long,' Arrakis said, sitting down and frantically typing. 'You're in,' he said as a sign flashed up saying ACCESS APPROVED. 'Make sure you delete any recordings from my phone.'

'Will do, General,' Orion said as they swapped places.

'I'll keep watch.'

'Thanks.' Orion stared at the screen, scrolling through pages until he found the right one. 'I've found it,' he said and waved Arrakis away.

It didn't take long to get to the general's phone and delete all his conversations. The concerning thing was that contrary to what the general believed, he had in fact been having his telephone conversations recorded for many months. Orion wished he had all the Committee members' telephone numbers so he could check theirs as well but for the moment that wasn't possible. He would see what he could do before he left the compound. He found the page with all the buzz words, "Cartel, Government Corruption, Deep State, Space Compound, Pharmaceutical Drug Related Deaths," were a few that sprang out. He left some in but deleted the rest and replaced them with, "McDonalds, Pizza Hut, Burger King, X-box" and a few other ones just for fun. Melantho would be overwhelmed with "questioners" and it would take him months to plough through the increased numbers before checking the system's programming out. He couldn't help but smile. The door swooshed open just as he pressed EXIT on the computer.

'All done?' Arrakis said.

'Yup.'

'Let's get out of here,' he said, poking his head round the door. 'Was it easy enough to delete the recordings from my phone?' he asked as they walked briskly towards the canteen. Orion nodded and Arrakis breathed a sigh of relief. 'There's no way I'd want Melantho to hear what we said when he wasn't about.'

Orion decided not to tell Arrakis that his conversations had been recorded for much longer than he thought. He'd save that for when they weren't so hurried. If Melantho had been recording them, who else's was he recording and had he had time to listen to them all? One thing at a time though. First, he needed to have more freedom himself to be able to speak to Mary. He felt ashamed that he was putting Mary above the Committee but it wasn't his fault that Melantho held such a high position within the space compound. That blame laid squarely at the feet of the person who recruited him. His focus was to free Mary from the constraints of the system. Arrakis was right, there weren't anywhere near enough humans showing signs they were becoming fully evolved but he saw something in Mary. It wouldn't be long until they were both free from the limitations placed on them; free to grow together.

CHAPTER THIRTY-ONE

ON THE TRAIN TO WORK that morning, Orion texted Mary suggesting they go to the park for lunch. His heart fluttered when she replied immediately with a thumbs up. He got off the train and nodded at a few of the familiar faces he'd begun to recognise. When he first used the train, he thought he'd never get used to seeing people with masks over their mouths and noses. He felt desperately sad for them and tried smiling at a few of them. More often than not they'd ignore him, despite having seen him every day for weeks now. But there were some that were clearly keen to connect despite the divisive garment they wore. He was so thankful anyone working at the compound was exempt from wearing these. All he had to do instead was carry an exempt badge, in case people questioned him.

'Why are people so wary of me?' he asked Robert later that day in the staffroom while he made Mary her cup of mint tea which had quickly become part of his routine.

'Where do I start?' he said playfully. 'Maybe they're scared of you.'

'Why would they be scared? I'm just the same as them,' Orion said.

'I think we both know that's not the case,' Robert said, crossing his arms and staring at Orion who reached for a tea bag so as to avoid eye contact. 'Don't worry, your secret's safe with me.'

'I don't know what you mean,' Orion said as lightly as possible.

'Have it your way,' Robert said, reaching past Orion's head for the coffee. He leant down and whispered, 'I'll help if you need me.'

'What?' Orion stepped back and almost dropped his tea bag on the floor.

'So, how are things with the lovely Mary?' Robert asked brightly and glared at Orion as the door to the staffroom swung open and another man, Joel, walked in.

Robert nodded ever so slightly and Joel nodded back at him but both remained silent while he quietly made a coffee around them. Eventually Joel picked up his cup and headed out of the door, grabbing a packet of biscuits as he did.

'Back to Mary!' he said with a glint in his eye.

'I'm quitting,' Orion said, making Robert gasp in shock.

'Why?' he asked.

'I've got another job; reckon it's time to move on. I'm just about to tell Richard.'

'But what about Mary?'

'What about her?' Orion said as casually as he could muster and left the room, leaving an open-mouthed Robert staring at the door as it slammed shut.

As he walked past Mary, he placed her cup of tea on her desk. She looked up and smiled but he ignored her. She scowled at him in annoyance. Half an hour before their lunchbreak he strode up to the boss's door and knocked firmly then stood back until he heard, 'Come in,' from the other side. His heart sank when he saw Melantho sat next to Richard Henderson. 'Why's that man always here?' he wondered.

'Sit down, Thomas,' Richard stammered.

Orion pulled out a chair and sat down. 'Thanks for all your help,

Mr Henderson, but I've been asked to move on. Could I ask you to treat my resignation as you would do anyone else's? My next assignment is working within a company who aren't aware of our operations at the compound so no doubt they'll be looking through my employment details.'

'No problem,' Mr Henderson replied, smiling. 'Glad to be of assistance.'

'How're you going to break the news to Mary?' Melantho sneered.

'That's none of your business, Captain, if you don't mind me saying.' Orion noticed Richard wince involuntarily and shift uncomfortably in his chair.

'I'll make it my business, if you don't mind – or for that matter even if you do. It'll make for some nice evening entertainment, listening to you drop her like a sack of spuds.'

'Aah, how sweet of you, Captain. Everyone's got to have a hobby, haven't they?' he said.

As Orion walked back to his desk, he noticed Mary look at him but he avoided her gaze once again. He needed to put on the right show, to make people believe he no longer had feelings for her. It was going to be incredibly hard to pretend to finish the relationship but he wanted Melantho to hear their every word so it had to be convincing. The only way to do that was making her believe it too. As he sat down a message from Mary popped up on his screen. 'Everything OK? Don't seem yourself.'

'We need to talk,' he replied, knowing all conversations on the office's computer system would be monitored.

'Sounds serious. You're making me nervous,' she replied with the picture of a sad face next to it.

'See you at lunch,' he typed back and she returned with a smiley face. It was going to be so hard hurting Mary, but hopefully it would be enough to put Melantho off the scent and allow them to escape.

CHAPTER THIRTY-TWO

THE FOLLOWING DAY THE VILLAGE was much quieter than usual. Only the older beings got up to have their breakfast. The younger ones lay in until lunch when finally, they started emerging from their huts.

Lacarta bounced out of bed and couldn't stop talking about the night before. Alhena arrived at his door suggesting they go and see Star straight away. They found her sitting outside her hut, her hemp blanket wrapped around her head and shoulders, sipping a kiruna tea.

'Hey, Star,' they said, sitting down and putting their arms around her.

'Wanna go to the river to talk?' Alhena asked, noticing Meisa sweeping the hut very quietly, clearly desperate to try to hear what they were saying.

'I guess,' Star shrugged.

Lacarta sighed and looked at Alhena. They'd been under no illusion this was going to be easy. 'Come on, Star,' he said, standing up and holding his hand out for her. 'You need to.'

Star looked up at him for a moment before putting her cup down and taking his hand. They walked to the river in silence, their arms linked, the two girls' heads leaning on Lacarta's shoulders.

They found a strip of sand and lay down with their hands behind their heads.

'How you feeling?' Alhena asked tentatively.

Star sighed. 'I don't really know how to answer that.'

'Mum feels terrible; thinks she's let you down somehow,' Lacarta said sadly.

Star reached out and found his hand. 'Vega hasn't let me down. I love her, how could I not? She's been like a second mum to me and you're like a brother.' Star looked at him with watery eyes, 'My extra special brother.' She squeezed his hand and he returned the gesture.

He looked at her and his face crumpled. 'I love you so much. I can't bear you being angry at us.'

'I'm not angry at you guys!' Star said. 'I love you!'

Alhena leant in and put her arms round her two friends. 'I love you too,' she said.

They sat there, holding each other for a moment, feeling all their worries about their relationship with each other fade away.

'I met a forest male called Procyon last night,' Star said, sitting up.

'Now this is where things get really interesting!' Alhena said, rubbing her hands in delight. The relief she felt that her friend had met a male flooded through her veins for reasons she didn't want to admit just yet.

'Look what he gave me,' Star said, showing them the delicate spoon she'd kept in her pocket.

'It's beautiful!' Alhena said, taking Lacarta's hand so he could feel the intricate carvings.

'He made it! I love it so much. We're meeting again after Human Studies. And that's not even the most exciting part!' she said, enjoying the suspense she was creating. 'He reminded me that my father could be alive and trapped on Earth! He said he'd probably been trying to get home all these orbitals!'

Lacarta took an intake of breath. 'You mustn't get your hopes up, Star. If he's alive, why hasn't he ever tried to make contact? It's so unlikely.'

'It may be unlikely but with no body it's not impossible. You have to admit that, don't you?' The other two nodded tentatively. 'I owe it to Mum to get to the bottom of what exactly did happen to him. And that means going to planet Earth ourselves and finding out as much as we can about everything going on there.'

'Hang on! What do you mean "we"? You're not including us in your crazy scheme, are you?' Alhena said in alarm.

'Of course I am!' Star cried out. 'I can't do it without you both, can I? Anyway, it's not crazy wanting to find my dad! Lacarta, you with me?'

Lacarta began wringing his hands, gently rocking forwards and backwards. 'I don't know. This isn't my calling. Mum and Dad don't think it's right for me and I kind of agree with them.'

'Lacarta, you need to make your own decisions for once,' she said, ignoring the fact that he'd just said that. 'They don't always know what's best for you. Why does it have to be your calling? Imagine what an adventure we'd have going to Earth together!'

'Star, you mustn't push him. What about his ...?' Alhena began.

Star glared at her friend. 'Don't patronise me – or Lacarta. You need to let him make his own decisions for once.' She turned back to Lacarta and held his hand in hers. Very softy she asked, 'Come on, Lacarta. You're not going to let me go on my own, are you?'

Lacarta looked into the eyes of the best friend he'd ever had and chewed nervously on his bottom lip. He knew he couldn't let Star go without him. He was the only one who would properly look out for her – make sure she came to no harm. 'I'm in,' he said quietly.

Turning her attention to Alhena, Star raised one questioning eyebrow.

Alhena gave the slightest of nods.

'Yes! I'm going to planet Earth with my two besties!' Star said, leaping into the branches above.

CHAPTER THIRTY-THREE

IT TOOK THEM A WHILE to find somewhere quiet to sit as the park was packed with office workers on their lunchbreak, their masks sitting casually under their chins. Orion removed the coke can that remained on the bench and took Mary's hand. Her face lit up on feeling his touch. 'I have to tell you something, Mary,' he said, stroking the inside of her hand with his thumb.

'What is it?'

Orion stayed silent, searching for the words he needed.

'You're scaring me!' she said, her eyes wide and eager.

'I'm quitting my job.'

Mary tipped her head back and laughed with relief. 'That's great news! You're wasted there. Why the big drama?'

'I've got a transfer to another city,' he said.

Mary pulled her hands away from Orion's as it dawned on her. 'But when will I get to see you?'

Orion dropped his gaze. 'You won't. It's too far and they like to entertain clients in the evenings and weekends.'

'But that's ridiculous. They can't expect you to do that!'

'Financially, it's a big step up. I'll be able to send money back to mum. She's in so much debt – I don't have a choice.'

'I'll come with you!' she said brightly but tears were forming in her eyes. 'You know I hate this job. It'll be good for Mum and Dad to have the extra space too.'

'You can't,' he said, not meeting her questioning eyes. 'The job comes with accommodation but it's very basic – and only for one.'

A lone tear made its solitary journey down Mary's cheek, balancing on her jawline before plummeting onto her dress. 'But we were going to move in together. I thought we were going to get marri–' she stopped before saying more.

'I'm sorry. I can't let a relationship hold my career back,' he shrugged.

Mary stood up. 'I thought you were different,' she said, wiping the tears from her cheeks.

'Life gets serious for us all at some point, Mary. I didn't think this job would mean as much as it does to me. I can't waste this opportunity.'

'But you can throw away our relationship like it's a piece of trash, can you?' she sniffed.

Orion looked down. 'I don't have any choice.'

'You always have a choice,' she said through gritted teeth. She stood there for a moment waiting to hear his response but he looked at her, smiled weakly and shrugged. 'I thought you were like me!' she said before running through the crowds of sunbathing bodies, the toxic smell of their sun cream clinging to her nostrils and combining with her tears. She grabbed a bottle next to someone's sleeping body and screamed as she hurled it into the lake.

The man sat bolt upright in alarm. 'What the –?'

Mary screamed at him. 'Wake up, will you? Just wake the fuck up!'

'I'm sorry! It was only a catnap!' he said.

'Urghh!' she screamed, pulling at her hair. 'That's not what I meant! What's wrong with you people?' She kicked his bag and marched off through the bemused crowd.

Orion sat and stared after her. A few people looked between him and Mary's disappearing figure waiting for some explanation. He held out his hands, shrugged and smiled thinly before lying back on the grass, his arms behind his head – his heart almost bursting with joy. She'd very nearly said she thought they were going to get married! He couldn't believe it! It'd been hard seeing her so upset but he was now one hundred percent sure of her feelings towards him. He was positive she'd understand why he'd had to do this. His conversation with Robert that morning had given him an idea of how to explain the truth to her; that in order for them to be free they had to beat the system that was set up to imprison them. The only way of doing that was by leaving the confines of the city. He remembered Arrakis talking about the woods beyond the city walls and how mobile phones didn't work there. No mobile phones meant no surveillance – it was one step towards freedom. The rest he hoped would fall into place once they got there.

He ambled back to the office, trying to gather his thoughts as to how they could escape. He was sure Robert would help him, he just had to find a way of talking to him without being overheard. It was a risk confiding in a human but it was a risk well worth taking. His time with Mary was running out. He had until the end of the week before he moved onto his new job and in that time he had to convince Mary that he wasn't the prize jerk she currently thought he was and that she had to come and live in the woods with him. Melantho would be kept busy with all the extra traffic the new buzz words were creating but he had no idea when Melantho would spot there was something wrong with the system's database. The sooner he ran away with Mary the better. A week could well be too late.

CHAPTER THIRTY-FOUR

WHEN ORION ARRIVED BACK AT the office, he walked towards Mary's desk and saw her head bent and shoulders shaking. He wanted to go to her, to put his arm around her but instead strolled casually past and sat down at his desk. He typed, 'I'm sorry' and pinged it over to her. Words came up saying she was typing.

'Go to hell,' her reply came, making him wince.

At 3 p.m. he saw Robert head to the staffroom so he removed his headset and walked as casually as he could behind him, though his heart was pounding. He could risk everything by talking to Robert like this and if Robert reported him, he would never see Mary again.

'Hey,' Orion said as he opened the door.

'Hey,' Robert replied coolly, barely looking up from his phone. He waited for the door to shut before putting his phone in his pocket and shoving Orion angrily in the shoulder, pushing him into the corner of the room. 'What the hell do you think you're playing at?'

'She told you then?'

'Of course she told me! I thought you liked her?' he said, his hands on his hips glaring at Orion.

'I do like her! It's not her it's me …'

'Don't give me bullshit,' Robert scoffed. 'She deserves to know the truth. One minute you're all loved up, the next you've dumped her like a sack of taties.'

'A sack of what?' Orion smiled.

'Taties … potatoes! Stop trying to change the subject! Now give me some answers and don't you dare lie to me,' he said, pointing at Orion.

Orion held up his hands. 'People fall out of love all the time! What are you so angry about? It was you that told me there were plenty of Marys out there.'

'That's when I thought you were the same as every other guy.'

'I'm not a saint, you know! Maybe you both thought I was something I'm not.'

'Only because you put on such a bloody good act. Mary thought the world of you.'

'That's exactly why I had to finish it with her,' he said. 'I'm too young to get tied down to one woman. I'm only human after all!'

Robert went to say something but decided against it and stormed out of the door. Before it crashed back on its hinges he said, 'I can't be in the same room as you. You remind me of …' He pulled out his phone and spoke loudly into it as he shouted, 'my dad – he's a selfish twat too!' The door slammed shut behind him.

It was hard hurting these two humans he'd come to care for so much, but it'd be better for both of them in the long run. If they stood any chance of escaping the system, he needed conversations like these to be recorded to ensure the surveillance team were off the scent. No doubt Melantho would be lapping up all this drama. Trying to double cross someone so manipulative was not a task for the faint-hearted and Orion prayed he wasn't going to see through his plan.

CHAPTER THIRTY-FIVE

LATER THAT DAY, WHEN STAR had dropped Lacarta home, she knew it was time to talk to her mother. She found her sat by their hut preparing their evening meal. Meisa looked up when she heard Star approach, her eyes red from crying.

Rhea turned from where she sat hunched over washing the vegetables and breathed a sigh of relief on seeing her granddaughter.

Star sat down and put her arms around her mother who hugged her back.

'I'm sorry,' Meisa said, 'it was so hard for us to know what to do.'

Star looked into her mother's watery eyes. 'I get that but you've always gone on about being honest. Now I find out you've been lying to me all these orbitals.'

'How could I tell an eighteen-orbital-old girl that a being had robbed her father of his life? We don't have to think about that happening on our planet, do we? Yet somehow I had to find a way to tell you that there were beings out there so full of hatred they had killed your father,' she said tears, rolling down her face. 'I didn't know what to do,' she sobbed.

'It's all right, Mum. I understand.' Star held her mother's head and stroked her hair.

'My head was in pieces; I couldn't believe he was gone.' Meisa wept quietly as the two held each other.

'What happened the day he left?' Star said eventually. 'Can you tell me everything?'

Meisa nodded and wiped her tears. 'There's not much to tell really. As you know, your dad was a general within the Committee so we were used to him travelling to Earth. The day he left …' she smiled before continuing, 'he gave us the biggest hug ever and said he had some really exciting news to tell us when he returned home in ten sunrises time. He walked away but kept looking back at us and waving, beaming from ear to ear. He was so happy.' Meisa broke down in tears so Rhea took up the story.

'Four sunrises later, when I got back from bathing you at the river, we found Eridamus here, her arms around your mum. Tears were pouring down her face. I remember wanting to turn around and go back to the river, to never hear what she was being told. I picked you up and you wrapped your little arms around my neck so tightly it was as if you knew something was wrong. We sat and listened as Eridamus told us there'd been an ambush. Leo hadn't been given permission to land in the compound. They'd said there was a fault with the space compound's door, and he had been guided to a clearing in some woods not too far away. He'd landed and the crew were disembarking when humans emerged from the forest, their guns pointed at Leo and the crew. Your dad telepathically communicated with them to get back on the craft, that he would talk to the humans and explain there had clearly been some kind of mix-up. It was never your dad's strongest subject so it took a while for them to understand what he was communicating to them. When the last Celestian was on board he edged back to the craft when a bullet hit him. The crew heard him cry out and fall to the ground. They took off immediately and came straight back to tell us the news,'

Rhea said.

'Why would humans want to cause us harm, Granny?' Star asked, her eyes glistening with tears.

'Not every being in the galaxy realises how we're all so deeply connected, darling.'

'I'd never have left my friends,' Star said angrily.

'You mustn't blame them,' Rhea said. 'It's protocol – if something like that happens the priority is to keep the craft safe. Without the craft, there's no way of returning home – unless we can locate one of the wormholes on Earth. It's also vital that no human boards our craft. It would automatically return to Celestia, bringing the human with it. No one wants to lose a Celestian but it's much better to lose a Celestian on planet Earth than to bring a human to Celestia.' She shuddered at the thought.

Meisa gulped back her tears and took Star's hand in hers. 'Sabik came to see me the next sunrise,' she said quietly. 'He said that Leo had confided in him, told him this was going to be his last time on Earth.' At this point Meisa gulped back tears before saying, 'He was resigning from his job to be with us!'

'Oh, Mum!' she said, tears running down her face.

Meisa sniffed loudly and in between gulps said, 'Your dad only ever wanted to keep the galaxy free from conflict and war. To make sure all humans had access to organic food, clean water, a roof over their heads. He wanted to help bridge the gap between the rich and the poor. Now those selfish Aldorians are having more influence over the Committee, his plans for Earth aren't ever going to happen.'

The three females sat in pensive silence, Meisa emitting little sobs every now and again.

'Do you dream about him, Mum?' Star said, bringing Meisa back to the present.

'All the time. He's always calling for me, it's so distressing. I follow his voice but whenever I get close a gate comes crashing down in front of me and I wake up. It's horrible!'

'He comes to me too.' Star looked at her mother. 'He tells me how proud I make him, how we'll meet one day. I always thought he meant when I died, but now I'm wondering whether ...' she paused for a moment before continuing, 'he's still alive and living on planet Earth?'

'Don't get your hopes up; if he was alive, he would've been back by now.'

'Not if they're stopping him.'

'But if they're stopping him then it's too dangerous for you to go there!' she wailed.

'If it's that dangerous, the generals won't let them take Further Human Studies,' Rhea interjected.

'Mum, I can't carry on life wondering if he's out there. I have to travel to Earth more than ever now. You see that, don't you?' Star said.

Meisa nodded. 'I wish I could go with you. I loved Human Studies too but I chose to finish when I fell pregnant with you.'

'Do you wish you'd carried on?'

Meisa looked at her daughter, a stunned expression on her face, her eyelids wet from tears. 'Of course not! That would've meant being away from you and I don't care how fascinating humans are, not one of them was half as fascinating as my gorgeous baby female! I wouldn't have wanted to be anywhere else.' They looked at each other and smiled. 'Come here, you,' she said and pulled Star into her embrace, breathing in the smell of her hair.

'Anyway, Mum, you've got no need to worry about me because Lacarta and Alhena are coming with me,' Star said with her head nestled into her mother's chest.

CHAPTER THIRTY-SIX

WHEN THE CLOCK FLICKED OVER to read 17:00 Orion raced to the lift so he was one of the first there. He saw Robert and Mary pointedly head to the one furthest from him and barged through the gathering numbers of people. Robert saw him coming and turned Mary away from Orion, his arm placed protectively round her shoulders.

'I'm sorry!' Orion said, trying to grab Mary's wrist.

'Leave her alone,' Robert said, holding Mary tighter.

Orion grabbed Robert's wrist and pulled him so close he was able to whisper in his ear, 'Read the note,' as he shoved a crinkled-up piece of paper into Robert's palm and curled his fingers over.

'What?' Robert said, confused.

'I said, don't be such a dope,' Orion said, pushing him away, but he knew Robert had heard.

'Leave us alone,' a red-eyed Mary said and turned to squeeze into the crammed lift. Orion stared at them as the doors closed and saw Robert lean down and whisper something into Mary's ear.

The plan was starting to take shape, but could they forgive him enough to meet tonight after what he'd put them through? The note read, 'Meet me at Sam's place 8 p.m. tonight – both of you. Please forgive me. I love you both.'

He returned to the compound and lay on his bed staring up at the ceiling. How many more nights would he have here, he wondered? One, two? It all depended on how quickly Mary felt she could act. He was ready to go; he'd said all the goodbyes he needed to.

As he sat on the driver-less train to the city, beads of sweat trickled down his brow. He half expected Melantho to appear any moment and arrest him for deserting his role. Passengers' eyes darted nervously his way and they edged away from him, fiddling with their masks, making sure they covered their mouths and noses. By the time Orion got to the bar his hands were shaking and he was visibly sweating. He stood in front of the facial recognition pad while it scanned him. A red light lit up. 'Temperature 39.4 degrees' it read. 'ACCESS DENIED. PLEASE MAKE YOUR WAY TO THE NEAREST TESTING UNIT SHOWN ON THE MAP.' He looked around him and was relieved there was no one about. He lifted his hands and let them hover over the screen for a moment. The red light changed to green and the screen read, 'Welcome to Sam's Place! Have a lovely evening.' He hadn't wanted to rely on any of his Celestian powers but this was too important a night to have ruined by a false temperature reading. He ordered a fruit juice and found the darkest corner to wait for them. When Robert and Mary walked through the door he wanted to run up and hug them, nearly forgetting how incredibly angry they were with him. They spotted him and glared in his direction, but then went to the bar and stood there for ages waiting to be served.

'Hey,' he said sheepishly when they finally sat down opposite him. He began talking, saying he wanted to be friends, didn't want to leave on a bad note and as he spoke, he got out his mobile phone and held it on the table to show them what he was doing. He went into settings and shut off all access to the microphone, camera and location services. He nodded at them both to do the same with theirs. Even though this bar had no mobile signal he still wanted to take all the precautions he could. When their phones were shut down, he breathed out noisily, releasing some of his inner tension.

Mary sat there, not looking at Orion, wringing her hands in front of her. Robert glared at Orion with his arms folded. 'You going to tell us what the hell is going on?'

Orion reached out to take Mary's hand but she pulled it away. 'I'm sorry, Mary. I had to; I had no choice. I'm being heavily monitored; every conversation I have is being scrutinised. I'm involved in the surveillance team within the city – sifting out people who are questioning the system.'

'What are you talking about?' she said angrily and finally he was able to tell Mary everything; from the first time he set eyes on her in the surveillance room to how he'd made out she needed monitoring which got him the job in her office. The rest was history. Mary's face was a mixture of shock, repulsion and embarrassment.

'It's disgusting you can watch us like that,' she scowled. 'Were you and your colleagues perving over me?' she said, giving him a hard stare.

'No!' he said. 'I'm not like that!' Her face softened and he reached for her hand which she let him hold this time. 'You were so different – you are so different to everyone else.' He turned to Robert and said, 'You're different too. I'm lucky to have met you.'

Robert nodded and puffed out his chest in pride.

Orion took a deep breath and said, 'Mary, I want you to run away with me.'

Mary's brow furrowed, 'This afternoon you break my heart and now you …'

'Did I really?' Orion interrupted. 'Did I really break your heart?'

'Maybe,' she said shyly.

'That tells you everything you need to know, then, doesn't it?'

'How so?' she asked.

'Your heart is saying life isn't complete without me,' Orion said with triumph.

'Never took you as a big head,' she replied.

'I don't mean to sound arrogant …'

Robert laughed. 'Well, you do!'

'Yes, sorry. It's just that where I'm from we always follow our heart.'

Mary raised her eyebrow and said, 'If you expect me to run away with you then maybe it's about time you started being really honest with us.'

'What do you mean?' Orion asked, looking between the pair.

Robert leant in and whispered, 'Tell us where you're really from.' He raised his eyes to the ceiling and pointed upwards whilst emitting strange beeping and whirring noises.

'What was that?' Orion asked, frowning.

'It was meant to sound like a spacecraft taking off.'

'It sounded nothing like a spacecraft taking off,' Orion scoffed.

'See!' Robert said pointing at him. 'You're not from here!'

Orion looked about, checked no one was listening then nodded his head. Mary and Robert high-fived each other. 'Told you!' Robert said to Mary. 'You're way too in touch with your feelings. Total give away!'

'But if you knew, why didn't either of you say anything?' he asked.

'When did you expect us to mention it? Hey, Mum and Dad, here's my new boyfriend, Tommy. He's an alien,' Mary said, smiling.

Robert snorted and said, 'Yeah, hey, Tommy – fancy a cup of tea? By the way, did I hear you're from some far-off galaxy? Pass the biscuits, would you?'

'OK, OK, maybe there wasn't a good time to bring it up.'

'Too right,' Robert said.

'I was kind of hoping to hear it from the horse's mouth too,' Mary said softly.

A look of confusion passed over Orion's face. 'Why would you want to hear it from a horse?'

Robert leant across to Orion and touched his arm. 'It's a phrase we use. It means she'd rather have heard it from you.'

'Oh yeah, of course,' Orion said, looking embarrassed. 'I didn't think you'd be interested in me if you found out I wasn't from here, I thought it'd scare you off.'

'Scare us off? No way!' Robert said.

'We found you intriguing! No one in that office ever made me a cup of tea and no one had ever really got to know Robert. The people there just dismiss him, think he's too in your face. I knew something was different about you the moment we met. For one thing, your chat-up line was shocking but turns out you can actually talk to girls – something guys on Earth gave up doing years ago. It's only because of you that me and Robert have formed a strong friendship. We both have good taste,' she said, squeezing Orion's hand, who was at a loss as to what to say. 'And if you're wanting to run away with me and escape this shitty city then it's a big yes from me!' she said, rendering Orion speechless one more time.

CHAPTER THIRTY-SEVEN

'How long have you known?' he asked, stunned that they had worked him out.

'Pretty much from day one,' Robert said, looking very pleased with himself. 'It took you a bit longer, but you got there in the end, didn't you?' he said to Mary.

'Yes, but once I got to know you it didn't really matter where you came from,' she said, smiling softly at Orion. 'You're so different to anyone I've ever met before.'

Robert interjected. 'The guys from the compound treat us like we're idiots but we see it all. There's no office like ours round here, people coming and going for a week or two here and there. They stand out like a sore thumb! They look completely uncomfortable in their suits, don't seem to have a clue how to operate our system even though everyone on the floor is meant to have had loads of training. And if they ever come out with us, they never drink alcohol. I mean, who doesn't drink alcohol?' Robert said, taking a sip of Orion's non-alcoholic drink and nodding. 'Just as I thought. I've tried talking to them but apart from you, they're pretty much incommunicado.'

'But seeing the odd person who doesn't fit in and doesn't drink alcohol doesn't make everyone jump to the assumption they're from another planet, does it?' Orion asked.

'No, but me and Robert spend hours on the dark web research-ing,' Mary said. 'It's all there, how ETs mix with us in the city, trying to learn from us. It's fascinating! When me and Robert started chatting, he was able to enlighten me even more.' Mary took a sip of her drink and nodded at Robert to take up the story.

'You see I was brought up in a ...' Robert paused trying to find the right words, 'complex household. Dad workaholic, Mum at home with me when I wasn't at nursery, of course. Dad would be away for days on end and not tell Mum where he'd been. Said work was full-on and told her not to be so intrusive when she asked him more questions. One day she followed him, had to take me with her 'cause I was ill that day. I was only four but I remember it vividly. She thought she was going to catch him with another woman. We followed him into the dodgy part of town. It was deserted so we had to hide in doorways. Kept having to put her hand over my mouth – I was a chatty little bugger, even at that age. We saw him go into this really seedy shop, had pictures of scantily clad women on the outside. I remember her saying, 'I've got you now.' We gave it a minute or two then followed him inside. It was pitch dark apart from a light above a door. We opened it so slowly, wondering what the hell we were going to see. Turns out, there weren't any semi-naked women.'

'What was there?' Orion asked, on the edge of his seat.

'A secret train station. We both stood there in shock – I'd never seen people not wearing masks on a train before! The door slammed shut behind us and one of the people on the platform shouted, 'Civilians!' An alarm went off. We tried getting back through the door but it was locked. Two men in black suits came and grabbed us. I was screaming, begging them to let us go. I only wanted to see my dad.'

'You must have been terrified!' Mary said.

Robert nodded. 'What was worse was I clocked Dad watching the whole thing. He sat on the train and did nothing. I'll never forget the look on his face – completely devoid of any emotion.' He shivered.

'Where did they take you?' Mary asked him.

'They were really nice to me. Handed me over to a couple of ladies who drove me back to the city and dropped me off at my nursery even though I told them I was ill. Told me I'd had a really exciting adventure but not to mention it to anyone as it was super-duper top secret. They said they'd keep an eye on me and if I was a really good boy they'd give me a job when I was older but if I told anyone what I'd seen then really bad things would happen. Struck the fear of god into me so I never mentioned a word to anyone.'

'What about your Mum?' Orion asked.

Robert looked down at his hands. 'I never saw her again. Dad picked me up from nursery that evening. I asked where she was but he put his hand up to silence me. He was fuming. I can remember looking at him in the car on the way home and watching this vein on his neck pumping so hard I thought it might burst open and spurt blood everywhere. He said I wasn't to mention today ever again. Blamed me and Mum for risking his job, all because we couldn't trust him. From that moment on I loathed every inch of him. My feelings for him haven't softened with age either. He's a complete bastard.'

''Scuse his French,' Mary said, giving Robert the eyeball and nodding towards two security guards who were checking people's ID.

'Oh, thanks,' he said, looking over at the security guards. 'Best not to say anything to alert them unnecessarily,' he said to Orion by way of an explanation. 'Anyway, even though I was only tiny I remember everything. Over the years I kept getting visits from officials. Dad'd let them interview me, ask me loads of questions like can I be trusted to keep secrets. They'd set me tasks and if I completed them, they'd reward me. I loved all the attention they gave me; they made me feel special. The only person who'd ever done that was Mum,' he said, looking down at his hands. 'For the first time in my life, Dad started taking an interest in me. It was great – he seemed to like me for once. My confidence was rock bottom because I thought he hated me so much but the harder the challenges were, the more we bonded. As soon as I was old enough, he got me a job at the compound.'

'Are you still working there? Are you in surveillance too?' Orion asked.

Robert shook his head. 'Nah, I couldn't bear it. Don't get me wrong, there was loads to love about it – meeting and interacting with aliens for a start! I'd be the one kitting them out so they blended in. The two that took over from me are rubbish, such bad dress sense!' he said, touching Orion's t-shirt and scowling.

'Cheers!' Orion said.

'No offence.'

'None taken … I think,' Orion replied.

'I just wanted to fit in with "normal" society,' he said, using his fingers as quotation marks. 'Don't we all when we're growing up? It was the biggest disappointment of my dad's life when I told him I was quitting. Never really spoke to me again after that – apart from to tell me what a useless piece of shit I am, throwing my future away.'

'I'm sorry,' Mary said, touching his arm.

'How did you end up in this job?' Orion asked.

'Dad got it. He knew with a gob like mine I could well end up blabbing state secrets. Maybe one day he'll think I'm responsible enough to find my own way in life but till then I remain under his watchful gaze – while I'm at work, that is. Once I'm out of there he has no idea what I get up to,' he said with a glint in his eye. 'And that's just how I like it!'

'But surveillance is everywhere; he knows exactly what you're up to!' Orion said.

'Not when you have one of these!' he said, waggling his phone at them.

'I don't understand,' Orion said.

'Check out the difference between my two phones,' he said, placing them on the table. He pointed at the one on the left. 'This one's the one Dad and the state monitors. All the usual apps, camera, microphone. Take a look at this one,' he said, pointing at the one on the right. 'Looks exactly the same but no microphone, no camera, no apps, no mobile data. Just a basic phone but it's also encrypted so no one can access it. When I left the compound, I was meant to give it back but I said I'd lost it. They were livid, searched me and everything. Wanted to search our house too, till Dad stepped in. Luckily having a dad like mine means everyone is scared to shit of him. Comes in handy at times! I leave the phone that he can monitor round a mate's house while I head off and do my own thing without Dad being any the wiser. What with my phone and the dark web, pretty much all I do stays under the radar. Means I can get into all sorts of mischief,' he said with a wink.

Mary continued, 'You see, they monitor everything we search on the internet but they've still never worked out how to monitor the dark web. There's loads of dodgy stuff on there but if you search hard enough it's all there … everything. How we're kept trapped in this city and managed by a group of beings called the Committee. How city life is meant to be easy and convenient but keeps our bodies sick and drained of any energy. I never realised till recently that the human body is designed to live until at least a hundred years old. Here, our bodies expire soon after retirement. All seems very convenient … spend our lives saving for our pension only for them to get it because we pop our clogs just after retiring or get taken away into an old people's home never to be seen again.'

'You know nearly as much as me!' Robert said proudly.

'I've heard there are trees the other side of the city, hundreds and hundreds of trees,' she said eagerly to which both Robert and Orion nodded. 'Why don't they let us out there? It doesn't make any sense. We're told the world is over-populated yet there are these incredible woods which could give us more space and freedom.'

'But in the city, you have to buy everything. You can't grow your own food or store your own water or make your own clothes. The whole economy would collapse if we started taking control of our own lives,' Robert said.

'Of course,' Mary nodded as it dawned on her. 'Then we'd be free.'

'Precisely.'

'Everything alright here?' one of the security men asked and the three of them looked up and nodded. 'ID, please?' he said, holding out his hand. Orion looked at the palm of the man and something looked unusual about it. It took a moment before he noticed it had no lines on it. 'ID, please,' the man said louder. Each of them got out their ID. 'Could you come this way?' the man said, reaching and taking Orion by his elbow and pulling him onto his feet.

'What's the problem?' Mary asked, panic rising in her voice as the man gripped harder on Orion's arm and began to lead him away from the table.

'Melantho 6548264, abort mission,' Robert said disinterestedly. The man immediately let go of Orion's arm and the pair walked away from the table.

'What the hell was that all about?' Orion asked, visibly shaken.

'Bots … sorry, robots. Artificial intelligence, they're referred to. I call them dumb-ass intelligence. Useless heaps of junk. Total waste of tax-payers money, but isn't everything?'

'What was that you said? Melantho 654 …? Why did they stop

so quickly?' Orion asked.

Robert winced slightly. 'I did tell you I had friends in high places.'

'He's your friend?' Orion said, horrified that someone like Robert could be friends with that man.

'Not exactly friends …'

'Guys, have we got time for this?' Mary interrupted. 'Can we bring the attention away from you, hard as that may be, Robert, to what's really important? Like the rather small fact that Orion and I are running away together and escaping this godforsaken existence?' Mary said with more than a hint of annoyance.

Orion stared at Robert, wondering what he'd meant about Melantho but Mary was right. They had no time to waste. The evening was already rushing by.

Robert stood up. 'I'll get us all a drink to celebrate. When I get back, we can talk about how the hell we're going to get you out of this place.' He grabbed their empty glasses and headed to the bar.

Mary flung her arms round Orion and kissed him passionately on the lips. 'Now when do we start the rest of our lives?' she asked, taking both his hands in hers.

'Think you can be ready tomorrow morning?' he asked.

Mary looked momentarily shocked but said, 'Definitely.'

Orion beamed back at her. Now he knew exactly how they were going to escape. Robert had given him everything he needed to put the final pieces of the puzzle together.

CHAPTER THIRTY-EIGHT

LATER THAT DAY WHEN STAR, Meisa and Rhea were about to begin their evening mediation, Meisa made her excuses and said she was heading out for an early evening walk instead. She went straight over to Lacarta's hut where she found his mother busy preparing the family's evening meal. 'Vega, I need a word... now!' Meisa whispered, looking around to see whether Lacarta was there.

Vega looked a little startled but placed the pot she was just about to dish up from back onto the stove. 'I'm popping to the river, Sabik. The tea's in the pot.' Sabik poked his head around the entrance of the hut.

'Sure honey, hey ...'

Meisa and Vega put their fingers up to shush him.

'Hey there ... you lovely lemata. Your teatime too, is it?' he said, slowly bending down pretending to feed their friendly animal.

'What's going on?' Vega whispered as Meisa linked her arm and led her to Alhena's hut. She signalled for Vega to stay where she was then leant inside the hut where Alhena's mother, Talita, was busy sweeping.

'Hi, Meisa!' Alhena said from where she lay on her bed, startling Meisa.

'Hi, Alhena!' she said a little too brightly. 'Talita, d'you fancy coming for a walk?'

'Err, yes, I suppose so,' she said. 'Is that alright, Alhena?'

'Yeah, go for it, Mum! I'll tell Dad when he gets back.' Alhena got up from her bed and took the broom off her mother, signalling for her to be off.

The three females walked quickly to the river and found a quiet spot to talk.

'Star's definitely going to Earth,' Meisa began.

'You thought she would, didn't you? I'm so sorry,' Vega said.

'Lacarta and Alhena are going too,' Meisa interrupted.

Vega threw her hands to her face. 'Lacarta hasn't said anything to me!'

'Alhena hasn't said anything to me either. How do you know?' said Talita.

'Star just told me. I came to see you both straight away.'

'What are we going to do?' Vega asked, her voice rising in panic.

'I don't know. I briefly chatted to Star once I got over the shock. She says the three of them are even more passionate about studying humans than ever. I tried to remain calm but she could sense my panic and started getting cross. I didn't want to say anything else so I made my excuses and came to tell you.'

'But Lacarta mustn't go. If he goes then he'll find out about glasses and how much easier his life could be. What if he doesn't want to come back?'

'That's exactly what I was thinking.'

'Sabik isn't going to like this one bit,' Vega said.

The two females chatted over the potential hazards that lay ahead if Lacarta chose to take Human Studies further. They knew how much Lacarta loved Star and of course they'd taken great pleasure in watching their friendship grow from such a young age. It was only natural they'd want to stick together at this time in their lives.

'Do you think he'll see it as Celestia betraying him?' Vega asked her two friends.

Meisa shrugged. 'Maybe. I'm sure Lacarta will understand that just because there are things on Earth that make life easier for humans, doesn't mean those things should come back here too.'

'I know, but this is going to be so hard. His bad sight has made everything so hard for him,' Vega said. 'But how can we tell him not to stick with Star when all his life we've encouraged their friendship?'

'And what about Alhena?' said Talita, a touch of annoyance in her voice. 'Have either of you thought about Alhena's feelings in all of this?' Vega and Meisa turned to her, startled at their friend speaking this way. 'You've all been so wrapped up in the effect it may have on Lacarta. Why are you focusing on all the negatives of him going there? So what if he finds out they have glasses on Earth? We all found out a lot of things when we studied humans, that's the whole point. Yes, his life could have been made easier but it's our duty to remind him that if we allow one thing, where will it end, what else will we want? It's our duty to teach that to our young.' She paused for a moment and sighed. 'It's always the same, you only ever think about Star and Lacarta. You never think about Alhena and how she's going to cope. Maybe following Star on her journey is going to be much harder for Alhena than Lacarta,' she said, frustration rising in her voice.

'What do you mean? Alhena has a steeliness that we've all admired for many sun cycles,' Meisa said.

'That steeliness is only there to stop her from getting hurt,' Hamal said, appearing from the woodlands and making them all jump. 'You're both so wrapped up in your own fledglings you haven't once given any thought to Alhena have you?'

'Hamal, please,' Talita began.

'I'm sorry, Talita. They need to know. She's always clearing up the mess your daughter creates without any thanks,' he said to a shocked Meisa. 'Don't try to deny it,' he said, putting up his hand as she went to open her mouth to say something. Talita got up and walked over to Hamal, taking his arm and trying to lead him away. He shrugged her off and continued, 'For some curious reason and despite knowing how much he adores Star, our beautiful Alhena is absolutely besotted with Lacarta and is going to literally follow him to the Earth and back!'

CHAPTER THIRTY-NINE

WHEN ROBERT CAME BACK FROM the bar the three of them sat hunched together. Robert sketched a little map on the back of a beer mat. He then gave them instructions which they listened to intently. Everything he said concurred with what Orion had picked up when talking to General Arrakis.

'I'm going to miss you both,' Robert said when he'd finished.

'We're going to miss you too. You're the best friend I've ever had,' Mary said, taking his hand. 'I'm gutted we had so little time together.'

'It's my fault. I could've made more of an effort with you, especially when you started posting all that stuff on your pages. I'm sorry, I knew you were on the right path but I didn't have the confidence to stick my head above the parapet at the time. I've changed a lot since then.'

'It's fine; I understand,' she said.

'The best thing you two can do is go and be free, have the best life you possibly can. I'll sit in my office and gaze out of the window picturing you two sleeping under the stars,' he said sighing.

'More like digging bits of twig out of my hair and fishing pine needles out of my knickers!' Mary laughed.

Robert sighed again and said, 'I have to admit, Tommy, when you walked in the office, well,' he started fanning himself, 'it was a fight who could get to you first. I thought you were mine till Mary acted all aloof and won you over.'

'I hate to say it but I'm not ...' Orion began.

Robert put up his hand, 'No need to spell it out. I know ETs don't have labels like we do so I thought I could win you over with my vibrant personality and my brooding good looks,' he said, putting his fingers through his hair and giving them a wink. 'I'm cool with it. I just want you guys to be happy,' he said, reaching over the table and hugging them.

Mary turned to Orion and asked shyly, 'What's your real name?'

'Orion.'

Her face lit up. 'What a beautiful name!'

'Now, you two love birds, when are we going to put the plan in action?' Robert asked.

'Tomorrow morning,' Orion said, 'on our way to work. I've tampered with the buzz words in the surveillance system so it should buy us some time. I'm just hoping no one checks the set-up, though. They'll see what I've been up to if they do.'

'But that's Melantho's baby!' Robert said. 'From my time at the compound I noticed that Melantho spends most of his time in the surveillance room. Apparently he's always tweaking the trigger words.'

'I thought he hardly ever changed them?' Orion said with rising panic.

'That's what he'd have you believe but he likes to be one step ahead of the game. He's incredibly possessive about the system – says it's all about protection of the compound and wheedling out any whistle-blowers that could expose them.'

'How do you know so much if your job was just dressing the ETs coming in?' Orion asked.

'Come on, everyone knows how precious Melantho is about his surveillance system,' he said, taking a sip of his drink, avoiding eye contact with Orion.

Orion turned to Mary who shrugged so he decided to drop it. He had even more reason to leave tomorrow. What if Melantho went there today and realised they'd been tampered with?

'I need to say goodbye to Mum and Dad,' Mary said.

'Will you tell them the truth?' Orion asked her.

Mary nodded. 'Now you've altered the system we'll be able to speak freely for the first time.'

'You sure we aren't monitored in this bar?' Orion said, looking around nervously.

Robert nodded his head. 'You've only got to watch out for the two 'bots. When the authorities found out there was no signal here, they made the owner have them. They couldn't bear seeing young people behave like young people. We'd got so used to being careful about what we said, who to and how close to stand next to someone in case we picked up a bug from each other. It's heavenly not to have to worry about all that!'

'Yeah, but it's taking a lot for people to get used to. Look around,' Mary said, nodding at the carefully spread out groups of young people. 'I bet if you took a measuring stick, they'd all be exactly a metre apart. It's been engrained in us for so long, we don't need a ruler to know how far apart to stand.'

'Watch that lot over there, though,' Robert said, pointing to a group near the bar who were tipping their heads back and laughing. A girl held the hand of the one keeping them entertained. A boy had his arm round a girl, and two others were patting their friend on the back laughing. 'Looks like they've been coming here a while,' he smiled.

'I can't figure out why you humans are so scared of each other,' Orion said, shaking his head.

'Everyone's scared of getting sick nowadays – got to keep your distance!' he laughed.

Mary smiled too. 'This place must bug the hell out of the authorities!'

'I bet!' Robert said, chuckling. 'It's the only bar I ever come to now. It's about the only place where you look about and kind of feel people's happiness.'

Orion turned around to look at the people milling about. Robert was right – they even gave off a relaxed energy.

'This is what it'd be like if we weren't under constant surveillance,' Mary said dreamily. 'Wouldn't it be amazing, Tom ... I mean, Orion?'

Orion nodded. 'It is amazing. You need to know what it's like to live freely, Mary. Free to run around, dance under the moon and swim in the river,' he said, tipping his head back, closing his eyes and inhaling deeply.

'Can I come with you?' Robert said dreamily.

'Do you want to?' Orion said.

Robert took a slow sip of his drink then shook his head. 'I'm more help this side of the wall. But one day I'll join you – wherever you are.'

CHAPTER FORTY

THE NEXT MORNING ORION GATHERED a few belongings into the smallest bag he could find. He put the beer mat with the scribbled map into his trouser pocket but he'd pretty much memorised it. A voice came over his intercom saying, 'Captain Melantho here to see you.'

Orion felt sick. He was the last person he wanted to see. He stuffed the bag under his bed just as he heard the door to his quarters swoosh open. After checking his reflection, he flicked a switch on his desk and a screen lit up showing Melantho sitting in his lounge area, one arm draped over the back of the sofa, his feet outstretched. A chill went down Orion's spine.

'How can I help?' Orion said as he entered the room.

'You've actually split up with her,' Melantho said, getting up and walking towards him.

'Ah, you've been listening to our conversations, then? I don't care what anyone else says, you sure are a hard worker,' he added, smiling.

Melantho couldn't disguise the look of hatred he gave Orion but ignored the dig aimed at him. 'You've broken the poor girl's heart – and Robert's from the sounds of it. That man should have some self-respect, the snivelling little freak.'

'Aah, I think that's how you described me when we first met,' he said.

'What're you really up to, eh?' he said, walking slowly round Orion.

'I don't know what you mean,' Orion replied without batting an eyelid.

'I've seen how you look at her. You don't turn off those feelings overnight – especially you Celestians. You lot follow your heart not your head. What's really going in there?' he said, tapping Orion's head. Orion jerked his head away from the man's repulsive touch.

'I've just returned from home, Captain. Being there made me realise how much I love Celestia, how much I need to be there. I can't live on earth. I love Mary – of course I do – but so what? You humans know only too well that love doesn't conquer all. I can't live on Earth and she can't live on Celestia so what choice have I got? Tell her I love her but can't be with her? What pathetic excuse can I come up with that will convince her of that? Better for her to think I'm a selfish idiot, that I'm no better than any other man. This way she nurses a broken heart for a while till she's able to find another guy to settle down with.'

'A noble story indeed,' he said, tapping his chin with his index finger. He pressed the button on the side of the door and it swooshed open. 'I'm watching you, Orion,' he said and the door swooshed shut.

Orion exhaled noisily. Thank goodness they'd decided to leave today. He dressed for work, grabbed his bag and walked confidently down the corridor and onto the train that took staff to the edges of the city. He disembarked with everyone else, walked up the small flight of stairs and through the door that led him to join the masses all boarding their trains into the city. After a short journey he piled off with all the other commuters and searched the benches for Mary.

They clocked each other and as Orion walked past, she joined him in the sea of people as it carried them up the stairs and out onto the street. Instead of taking a right to go to their office, they took a left then a left again by which time the crowd was starting to thin. They kept the same pace as the other workers until they had all disappeared into their office blocks. Not looking at each other they took the next right and found themselves in the rough part of town. Mary shivered as she saw a group of large, beefy men with sunglasses gathered round a burnt-out car.

'This way,' Orion said, grabbing her hand and turning onto a narrow street. In front of them, at the end of the alleyway, was a shop with flickering neon lights. Pictures of scantily clad girls hung from shop windows, empty cans and cigarette ends littered the road and pavement, fast food wrappers floated across the street as a slight gust of wind from the underground trains wafted through the grates. Orion let go of her hand as he went ahead, checking out the next street. It was empty but stretched for what looked like miles ahead. 'This is the one,' Orion said. They walked down the street, quickening their pace.

'I don't like this,' Mary said nervously. Just then two men appeared some distance behind them wearing dark suits and sunglasses. 'Orion?' she said, tipping her head towards them. Orion turned slowly round, sweat gathering at his temples.

'Halt. Increased temperature detected,' a robotic voice said.

'Run!' Orion grabbed Mary's hand as they ran down the street but the robots were faster, leaping effortlessly over them and halting them in their tracks.

'What do we do now?' Mary pleaded to Orion as lifeless hands gripped their wrists.

'Repeat – Halt. Increased temperature detected. Come with us to a medical unit for further testing,' the robots said in unison. 'If you do not come quietly, we will be forced to taser you in accordance with government guidelines,' the robots said, pulling out a taser gun from their pockets.

'What was it Robert said to them the other night?' he said, looking wide-eyed at Mary. 'Melantho!' The robots instantly paused. 'What was the number, Mary? Think!'

'I don't know!' she shouted. 'It began with a six and a five but I can't remember the rest!'

'6578264, abort mission!' Orion tried.

The robots sprung back into life and they tightened their grip even harder.

'You have the right to remain silent but anything you do say will be written down and used as evidence against you,' the robots said and began dragging the pair back down the street.

'Melantho 6548264, abort mission!' said a voice from behind the robots. Immediately, they released the pair and continued back down the road, revealing Robert who had been running to catch up with them.

'Robert!' Mary said. 'Thank god you were here!'

'Lucky I was! You only got one number wrong. So close. Follow me,' he said, checking there was no one else about. 'I'll show you where you need to go and I won't leave your side until I know you're safe.' They walked a little further down the street until they saw a small door in the wall that read GARBAGE. 'Here's where I leave you. Good luck and be happy!' he said, giving them a hug.

Mary opened the door and a putrid smell hit their nostrils. 'We can't go down there! It stinks!'

Robert raised his eyebrows. 'This is the nice way out! The other way is the drains.'

'Thanks so much,' Orion said. 'I owe you big time.'

'You sure do,' he said, smiling.

'Stop right there!' came a voice from just up the road. They all turned to see Melantho standing with his legs spread, pointing a gun right at them.

Orion and Mary stood frozen to the spot, their hopes of escaping evaporating instantly.

'For god's sake, you ruin everything, don't you!' said Robert, throwing his hands in the air.

Orion and Mary watched in horror as Robert walked towards the pointed gun.

'What are you doing, Robert? He's got a gun!' Orion called out but it was as if Robert hadn't heard them.

'Leave them alone! They're nothing to you,' he continued.

'Get out of the way, Robert. I'm warning you,' Melantho snarled over the loaded weapon.

'Or you'll do what? Kill me like you killed Mum?'

'I never killed her, you fool,' he seethed.

'You never stopped her from being killed, did you? You sat there and did nothing.'

'This isn't the time!' Melantho said, waving his gun at him to move out of the way.

'When is the time? Tonight, over a nice cup of tea?' Robert crossed his arms and put a finger to his lips. 'Sorry, I forgot you can't stand to be in the same room as me because you're such a homophobe. You can't even look at me in case you catch it. Here's a news flash, Dad –they discovered you can't catch being gay about forever ago!'

'It's nothing to do with being gay. Get out of my way!'

'What is it to do with, then?' he said, his voice rising in anger.

Orion and Mary stood stock still, stunned at what they were hearing.

'Don't make me do this, Robert,' Melantho snarled and pulled back the trigger.

'Do it, Dad. Go on, do it – you hate me anyway. What do you care if I live or die?' Behind his back he signalled for the other two to go. Realising it was now or never, they threw themselves into the door and slid down the slippery slope that was littered with rotting fruit, vegetables and fast-food packaging. Mary screamed all the way down until it spat them out onto some soft green grass. They stood up and dusted themselves down. Orion plucked a bit of potato peel from her hair.

'We did it!' Orion said.

'I can't believe it!' she laughed.

Just then they heard a cry and the unmistakable sound of a gun being fired. 'Robert!' Mary screamed but there was nothing either of them could do. Instead they held hands and ran as fast as they could away from everything Mary had ever known.

CHAPTER FORTY-ONE

WHEN THEIR LEGS WERE WORN out from running, they fell into the long grass, panting for breath.

'Do you think he killed Robert?' Mary said, trying to catch her breath.

Orion grimaced. 'I don't know. I had no idea that man was his father! Do you really think he'd have shot his own flesh and blood?'

'If he did nothing to stop his wife being murdered, who's to say he wouldn't kill his own son? Do you think we should go back?' she asked but Robert shook his head.

'You heard him. The best thing we can do is be free.' Orion pulled Mary towards him and kissed her. She put her arms round his neck and kissed him back but tears trickled down her cheeks.

'He was the best friend I ever had and I only met him a few weeks ago,' she said and her voice crumpled as she spoke.

Orion held her while she cried and did a silent prayer to Robert, willing him to be alive. He was finally with Mary but at what cost? Was their freedom really worth losing Robert? 'Come on,' he said, helping Mary to her feet. 'We'd better find somewhere to sleep before it gets dark.'

They walked hand in hand through the long grass until they

came to the woods. Huge conifers stretched above them, so high it was like they were reaching for the clouds.

'It's beautiful!' Mary gasped.

'It's Celestia.' Orion gazed up at the trees and the sky above them. He took his shoes off, tied the laces together and slung them over his shoulder.

The tall grass flicked at their ankles, bees hovered above flowers, and birds squawked and chirruped from the trees. Mary stretched out her hand to try and touch one of the butterflies that fluttered around her. 'I've only ever read about these things,' she said, gazing at them. 'You never see them in the districts.'

Orion watched her face as she marvelled at the nature around her. It was like watching a child discover something for the first time. Mary flung her arms out. 'Have you ever seen anything so beautiful?' she said, closing her eyes and tipping her head back.

Walking through the undergrowth and around the trees was hard, especially whilst holding hands, but the two needed to feel connected to the other at all times. Everything felt so familiar to Orion but it was all so new for Mary. She delighted in seeing the birds fluttering about over her head, a deer poking its head round a tree trunk, a rabbit hopping into the distance. Even though the creatures were unfamiliar to Orion he felt a deep connection with them. The clean air filled his lungs and his veins responded instantaneously. His heart swelled, his brain felt clearer and his body coursed with energy for the first time on Earth.

'Watch this,' he said to Mary as they stood under one of the giant trees. He stared intently at a branch, squatted down then leapt effortlessly onto the first branch. Mary shrieked and clapped her hands in delight as he jumped from branch to branch until he landed gracefully next to her.

'Will you teach me how to do that?' she asked.

'I'll teach you everything. Everything your schoolbooks never taught you.'

The sun flickered between the branches of the trees, dancing on their pale faces. Mary noticed Orion's eyes looked brighter and he smiled in a way that lit up his entire face.

When they were hungry Orion cleared a space in the woods and they sat and had their lunch – some sandwiches Mary's parents had made them that morning.

'How did they take it?' Orion asked once they'd finished eating.

'Pretty badly …' Mary said, looking down at her hands. A tear trickled down her face and Orion wiped it from her cheek.

'I'm sorry, I wish it didn't have to be this way.'

Mary looked at him and shook her head. 'Let me finish, pretty badly … at first.'

'What do you mean?' he asked, looking at her.

'They want me to be free.' She took his hand in hers. 'Because you'd taken the buzz words out of the system, last night we talked openly for the first time ever. They hate their life. They know they're trapped in a system that never allows or wants them to be free. They've known about it for years but never had the guts to escape. They loved you the minute they met you. They want us to be together, even if it means not being able to see me for a while.' She looked into his eyes and he saw that her black eye lashes glistened with tears.

'Possibly ever,' he said.

'I can't think like that. Dad's really ill and the state says he's too old to be eligible for free treatment, especially now he's retired and not contributing to the economy. He's dreading moving to the old people's home as well. The thing is, Mum knows which plants could help him but they can't grow anything in their apartment and they've no access to a garden. And even if she could help him he's not sure he wants her to. He'd rather die than being apart from her.'

'We could try and help,' Orion said.

Mary shook her head, 'We talked about that last night. They

even thought about coming with us. Dad said we stood a better chance of escaping without them. They're so amazing. Mum said they could accept never seeing me again if they knew I was out of the system. I don't know how they're going to cope without me but they insisted I go.'

Orion hugged her and thought about how agonising their last night together must have been, just like it had been for him when he'd said goodbye to his mother.

'Where are we going to sleep tonight?' she asked him.

Orion kissed her head and said, 'Under the stars.' He took her hand as they walked deeper into the woods.

CHAPTER FORTY-TWO

THE TWO FEMALES AT FIRST looked shocked, then ashamed as his words resonated with them. Hamal was right; all this time they'd never given any thought to Alhena. She was such a steady presence in their life, always being there for their fledglings but never needing attention herself.

'I'm so sorry, Hamal and Talita. We had no idea she harboured such deep feelings for him. She hasn't ever worn the Tamarama so I assumed she wasn't ready.'

'She hasn't worn it because she knows there's no point. The only male being she's got any interest in is Lacarta. As he's only got eyes for Star, she simply refuses to wear it,' said Talita.

'Alhena's very mature for her age,' broke in Hamal, 'but hates being the centre of attention. She's the most wonderful Celestian and I'm so proud of her. But now she's prepared to study something that isn't right for her just to look after your son who doesn't even appreciate her! I'm sorry, I'd better go before I say something I regret.' Hamal turned and walked back into the woods towards their village.

The others looked to Talita who looked down at the ground. 'He'll be fine,' she said quietly. 'They're so close, that's all.'

'I'm so sorry, Talita. Why didn't you tell us before?' asked Vega.

Talita shrugged. 'I guess we aren't the best at opening up. We spend so much of our time listening to the plants and taking on their requirements, when we come away from them, we're mentally drained. You see, our knowledge of plants comes from communicating with them, not just from snippets of information passed down from previous generations. The plants tell us what illnesses they can cure, which ones we can take and which ones we mustn't. The stories they tell us,' she said, giggling. Vega and Meisa smiled back at her and nodded, not quite sure what else to do. There was a pause. 'I'm joking! Oh dear, listen to me. It's our odd sense of humour. You can see why we aren't the best at communicating, can't you? She sighed. 'Alhena's a special one. Never underestimate the quiet.' Talita stood up and followed Hamal's retreating figure back to their hut.

'We haven't been very good friends, have we?' Vega asked Meisa who shook her head. 'I've become so protective of Lacarta I've stopped looking out for others.'

'He always was a very special one, wasn't he?' Meisa said, placing her hand gently on Vega's.

Vega had always had an intense bond with her son. When Lacarta was born, Vega thought she was going to lose him. His body and head were so floppy, he didn't have the will or the strength to feed from her. The family had watched as Vega painstakingly fed him one tiny drop of milk at a time, causing her to yell out in pain and desperation many times. Unless he fed from her, she had no milk and if she had no milk, she'd lose him. She'd performed this ritual every day for fourteen sun rotations while Lacarta remained utterly unresponsive. The only sign of life his body showed was the rhythmic rise and fall of his chest but his eyes stayed shut and his body limp. Vega carried him everywhere, tucked deep into her hemp sling, close to her chest so he could hear the beating of her heart. She hoped that holding him this close would increase her milk supply as well as transferring her body warmth to his tiny body.

Finally, just when Vega was starting to believe he wasn't going to survive, Lacarta opened his big almond eyes and stared up at his mother as if thanking her for not giving up on him. Vega let out an animal-like noise and sobbed like a baby. Her daughters and husband ran out of the hut, believing the worst had happened, that Lacarta had passed away. When they realised it was tears of joy, not tears of pain, they wrapped their arms around her and gazed down at their beautiful baby brother.

From that moment on the bond between the two was set. Vega had Lacarta in her sling way beyond other mothers. Some believed her overprotective, telling her that Lacarta was ready to crawl. Vega would bat away their comments, knowing that her son was showing no interest in being mobile. She took it as a sign he was content. Lacarta was a smart one; he would crawl in his own time.

His elder sisters adored him as much as their mother. They loved playing mummy to their little baby brother who stayed baby-like far longer than others his age. Sabik would sit and watch his family and see the effect this little being was having on them. To think he had considered not having a fourth. Without Lacarta their family wouldn't have grown the way it had; he'd brought a richness to it that hadn't been there before. It was only later they realised the reason he wasn't crawling was because his limbs weren't developing in the right way. All his joints were floppier and he could twist his arms and legs effortlessly into positions that looked excruciating to them.

It was around the same time they realised he was unable to see very well. His sisters were the first to pick it up, placing objects in front of him on the ground and instead of looking at the object he would gaze at his sisters faces with a big smile on his face as they offered words of encouragement.

Vega refused to accept it at first, saying they too were too quick to find fault. It was only after they sat down as a family and showed her how he would follow their voices but had no interest in anything they put on the ground in front of him she began to join the dots. It broke Vega's heart for a brief while but she soon began to adjust when she saw how Lacarta's other senses were developing. She'd call him from far away and watch his face light up in recognition. She whispered words to him that others couldn't hear, and he would respond with a big beaming smile, putting his tiny arms up to be held. She didn't care if he took longer to crawl, she could see he was developing other senses way beyond Celestians his age.

When Star lost her dad, it was Lacarta who helped his friend cope with her grief. Whenever he heard Star sobbing, he'd put his arms around her and let her cry while they listened to the glorious sounds of nature all around. The two forged a strong bond and Vega and Meisa watched Star's sadness lessen as she began enjoying life once again.

There was no way she could separate them now and there was no way Alhena was going to be stopped from following them to Earth either. The mothers were all learning a valuable Celestian lesson too – how to let go.

CHAPTER FORTY-THREE

NIGHTS SPENT SLEEPING UNDER THE stars surrounded by nature were starting to reap their rewards. Mary's headaches, which she'd suffered from for as long as she could remember, disappeared. Her skin started to glow, her eyes were brighter and she felt more energised.

'It's because your body's connected to nature,' Orion explained.

Mary loved learning about the natural world around them and Orion wanted to know everything about Mary and her upbringing. They walked deep into the forest, talking all the way. Sometimes they'd stop for a rest until Orion got bored and leapt up into the trees. Mary never tired of watching him move effortlessly from branch to branch. He never stopped looking for food he could forage or pools of water from where they could drink. Mary marvelled at his knowledge of plants; it all came so naturally to him. After grabbing a bite to eat they'd lie down on the forest floor and gaze up at the majestic trees above them.

As they lay there Orion told her what it was like to grow up in a system without money and how Celestia was governed by a group of seniors carefully selected because of their age, experience and wisdom. He told her about their Centre of Learning and how each fledgling was encouraged to find their calling in life. 'When we're thirty-two orbitals of age, that's sixteen years old, we're allowed to study humans. After the first lesson I knew I'd found my calling,' he said.

Mary told Orion about her school days and chatted about her history lessons and all the wars they'd learnt about. She reeled off historical dates and named the last ten presidents, getting angry when she forgot who the one before last had been. She talked about discovering the beauty of the English language, how satisfying it was when she finally understood what a subjunctive clause was. When she finished, she noticed Orion had become very quiet. 'Orion?' she said quietly. Orion lay motionless, his eyes closed and his hands behind his head. She repeated his name a bit louder this time and nudged him in the ribs. 'You're asleep!'

'What?' he said, opening his eyes. 'No, I'm not!'

'Liar!' She crossed her arms and turned her back to him.

He shuffled over to her and put his chin on her shoulder, moving a lock of hair away and kissing the side of her neck. 'I'm sorry,' he said.

'No, I'm sorry. Sorry that my life clearly isn't as interesting as yours!'

Orion chuckled lightly. 'You've got to admit Celestia sounds a bit more exciting than Earth! What the hell were you going on about ... subjunctive ... blah blah blah ...' he said, feigning a yawn. 'Jeez, I've never heard anything so boring in all my life!' he moved round to face her and laughed at her grumpy face. 'Come on, it's no wonder I fell asleep!' He yawned, stretched out his arms and lay back on the ground, a smile on his face.

Mary leapt on top of him, tickling him in the ribs. 'Don't you ever call me boring again!'

'Stop!' Orion laughed and scrunched up his body to try and defend himself. 'Get off me!'

'Promise me you won't ever use that word again?' she said, continuing to tickle him.

'I promise!' he laughed. 'Now stop!'

They lay back in each other's arms and thought about how different their formative years had been. 'Do you know what's really sad?' she asked and Orion shook his head. 'On Earth you hardly ever see someone with grey hair. Celestians seem to hold their older citizens in such high regard whereas here they're sent off to sit in an old people's home away from all their family – if they make it to seventy. Our world seems to glorify youth and look down on the older generation. It's as if we treat them like children, yet we know so little and they know so much.'

'We have this amazing ritual at our ceremonies where you get to ask our Seniors advice. It's so helpful hearing their opinions before having to make a decision that could affect the rest of your life.'

'Did you ask for advice before you decided to run away with me?' she asked. He looked down at his hands and traced a pattern in the dirt with his finger. 'I'll take that as a no, then.'

'I didn't want to hear the answer,' he said.

'Wouldn't they have supported your decision?'

He shook his head, 'I don't think so. You see, if we decide to live here, we can't ever go back.'

Mary's eyes widened in shock. 'You mean, you sacrificed everything to be with me?' Orion nodded. 'But never going home again – ever?' Mary shook her head. 'That's heartbreaking. I don't think I could've done that.'

'But Mary, you can't go home either! If you put one foot in the city, you'll be arrested. You do know that, don't you?'

Mary nodded. 'Of course. But it's not like this is going to be forever, is it? I mean, they'll lift all this surveillance at some point. People are waking up to it, Orion. It may not seem like it to you but people are sick of this nanny state we live in. Robert's convinced there's going to be a revolution and says he's going to be leading it.'

'But Robert is probably dead,' Orion reminded Mary. 'I hate to break the bad news but there's not nearly enough of you. I knew that from my first shift in the surveillance room. I'm really sorry, Mary, but you've seen your family for the last time too.'

CHAPTER FORTY-FOUR

A WEEK LATER THEY WOKE up to the sound of a man and woman chatting merrily away to each other. They stood up very slowly and moved so they were hidden behind a tree. A twig cracked under their feet, alerting the attention of the couple.

'Did you hear that, River?' the woman said.

'Probably a deer, dear. Oooh, that sounds funny, doesn't it? A deer, dear. Hello, dear, look at this deer,' the man said, chuckling at his own joke.

'Shut up!' she said.

'Oops, that's me fully reprimanded! Let's go find that deer, alright, dear?' he laughed.

Orion took Mary's hand and gripped it. The tree they were hiding behind wasn't going to provide them with much cover if the couple got any closer. He poked his head gingerly round the tree trunk and came face to face with the end of a very sharp spear.

'River!' The woman yelled not taking her eyes off Orion. 'Over here!'

River approached his wife, his eyes widening when he saw what she was pointing her spear at. 'Who are you?' he said gruffly, drawing up his bow and arrow. 'You'd better start talking or I'll shoot!'

Orion started talking fast – the man and woman had a very determined look in their eyes. He explained they'd just escaped the city, they loathed their jobs, their lives and wanted to be free from the all the rules and regulations. Orion took Mary's hand and told the couple they'd only recently fallen in love and wanted to live freely.

'Have you finished yet?' River asked, stifling a yawn. 'I didn't want your bloody life history. Summer, put your spear down – they're harmless. The name's River and this is my wife, Summer,' he said, stretching out his hand and shaking theirs.

'Don't mind us, we gotta be careful,' said Summer. 'People go missing all the time here. Don't know why they can't leave us alone. I reckon it's coz they're scared. If everyone in the city knew they'd be free to live their lives here they wouldn't stand for it. Keep us away from the city, you keep the masses enslaved, poor beggars,' she said, shaking her head. 'Come on, you two. Stick with us; we'll keep you safe. Reckon you could both do with a cooked meal inside you and a nice warm cup of nettle tea.'

As they walked, River and Summer told them how they, too, had escaped the confines of the city five years ago. Their names had been Sheila and Graeme and were coming up to retirement. They couldn't bear the thought of only being allowed out at certain times in case they picked up a bug, then ending up in a state-run home where relatives couldn't visit in case they infected the residents with a virus. They'd worked all their lives and wanted to live a little, to be free, they just didn't know how. Summer had overheard someone in the office talking about the dark web. She'd gone home and immediately began researching – it blew her mind what she discovered.

'At first I didn't want to believe her,' River said. 'I wanted her to stop talking – what she was saying was insane! I'd enjoyed my job, pretty much, been paid a decent wage, had a nice flat. What more could a man want?'

'But I wouldn't drop it, would I?' Summer chuckled.

'No, you wouldn't and am I glad you didn't? I'd probably be dead by now. I started getting sick, you see. Doctor said there wasn't anything he could do apart from give me tablets to reduce the symptoms. Thing was, those tablets had nasty side effects, didn't they, dear?'

'They certainly did,' Summer said, wafting her hand in front of her nose.

'Not that!' River said shirtily. 'Gave me stomach ulcers, didn't they? And headaches!'

'Oh yes, sorry, dear. Those ones didn't impact on me quite as much as the terrible wind you produced. Blocking that bloody toilet up countless times too. Kept having to call maintenance, didn't I?'

'Sheila!' River said and she stopped immediately on hearing her old name. Mary and Orion looked at each other, stifling a laugh.

'Was only saying,' she said huffily.

'Well, don't,' he said, giving her the eyeball. 'Anyway, Summer started researching and found out there were some plants that could help with my illness, possibly even halt it for good. Luckily, she found some in the park, just by the edge of the lake there. Within a couple of days of taking it my body started to heal. By day three I was sat up in bed, laptop on my lap, researching. I've never looked back. The minute I was well enough, we escaped.'

'How did you know where to go?' Mary asked.

'We knew a man who knew a man, you know how it goes. Eventually got put onto this guy called Robert. He's some kind of vigilante.'

Orion and Mary were wide-eyed and told the couple how they'd managed to escape and how Robert had been there just as they'd got to the city walls.

'Does he know how to stop the AI?' Summer asked and they

both nodded. 'That'll be the one then. He told us he sees it as his duty to free as many as possible from the system. We offered for him to come with us, but he said it wasn't his time yet. That boy's brave.'

Orion and Mary didn't want to mention the fact that they thought he may be dead, especially as they could now see a number of huts within the forest ahead of them. This was not the time or the place. As they drew closer, they saw people milling about around a fire, sharpening spears, chopping food and sat on a log quietly chatting. It felt so familiar to Orion, a wave of homesickness washed over him.

The chattering stopped as the foursome walked closer and people turned and stared. Some stood up and grabbed a spear, getting ready to point it at the two strangers.

'It's alright, everyone,' Summer said, putting her arms above her head and waving, 'we got some newbies here just escaped from the city.' A cheer rang out and people came and slapped them on their backs, shaking their hands whilst offering words of congratulations.

Hours later, with a full meal in their stomachs and exhausted from meeting so many new people, River and Summer showed them to a small hut. 'You got lucky; previous owner went deeper into the woods about a week ago,' River explained. 'The camp isn't for everyone. We're very laid back here but some people can't handle that after being in the system so long. They need time on their own to adjust.'

'Or they might just want to move on to another village that maybe more suitable for them,' Summer added. 'That's the beauty of the woods; you can do as you please. Now, sleep well, you two. Nice to have fresh faces. Every time we find someone in the woods it gives us hope that one day everyone will be free. Night!' Summer and River headed over to their little hut at the other side of the fire.

'I had no idea we'd find all this!' Mary said when they were on their own.

'I know. It's funny, ever since I got here, I've felt really home-sick. Everything about this place reminds me of home: the huts, the fire, the trees, the smells.'

'I'm sorry,' Mary said.

'It's fine, it's better than fine. I had no idea how wonderful Earth was going to be,' he said kissing, the top of her head.

CHAPTER FORTY-FIVE

THE NEXT FEW MONTHS WERE the most blissful of his life. Every morning he woke with Mary in his arms. He'd make sure no one was looking then shape-shift into a bird and fly high above the treetops, swooping and gliding until he came to the nearby waterfall. Once there he would perch on a rock and shape-shift back, dangling his feet over the edge and letting the roar of the water block out any other noise. His mother would've been told of his disappearance now and he thought of what she must be going through. His heart felt stabs of guilt every time he thought of her, fully aware of the enormous pain he'd caused. Often, he allowed himself to cry; the feeling was too much to bear but the thought of not being with Mary reminded him he'd had no choice but to follow his heart. A bird would occasionally come and sit on a rock next to him, cocking its head to one side as if trying to fathom out whether he was human or animal. When he felt ready, he would amble back to the camp, boil some water and bring a cup of nettle or dandelion tea for Mary as she woke. They'd sit in their hut and gaze outside as the forest woke up.

'I've never felt so at peace before,' Mary said. 'In the city my brain never stopped whirring away. I was always thinking of something: how I should look, what I should wear, what band was popular, which brand of shoes I should save up for, whether I was going to be up for promotion and did I even want it if I got offered it? It was relentless!'

'I could tell that when I studied humans. I'd watch the students at work and it was obvious their minds were hardly ever on what was being taught. We're always taught to be in the present. It's a gift after all, isn't it?'

'Wouldn't it be amazing if more humans were able to live like this?' she sighed. 'I look back at my life in the city and it's madness really, isn't it? This way would be better for Earth too? All they teach us at school is how we have to recycle and buy ethically. It makes no sense.'

'But they aren't telling you not to buy, are they?'

Mary shook her head. 'I guess it's to keep the economy going. You don't hear anything else apart from the economy this and the economy that.'

Orion and Mary thrived in each other's company, learning from and listening to what the other had to say. He told her about his family, his wise and patient mother and his father who he used to watch help build the village huts. When the heat got too much to do any physical labour they'd go and relax in the river for hours on end.

'Did your dad really die in a building accident?' Mary asked him one day.

Orion nodded. 'We deal with death differently to you, though. Mum and I miss him terribly but every time we see one of his huts, we think of him. His energy's always around us. I was never lonely either even though I don't have any brothers or sisters. There was always someone about to play with. It takes a village to raise a child after all.'

'Is it normal for your race to only have one child, like we do?'

'Not at all. They both wanted more but we feed our young for so long there's often a bit of a gap between siblings. Then when I was about five, Mum got involved in the Centre of Learning and was so good at her role they decided it was important for her to focus on that. They were so young it didn't matter, they had plenty of time ahead – or so they thought. The sad thing is I found out that they'd planned to try for another the month Dad died.'

'I'm so sorry,' Mary said.

Mary talked about her childhood in the city: going to school, her activities after school, the friends she had, and how her weekends were spent with her parents after their busy week at work. 'That's our real quality time,' she said, smiling.

'You humans and your quality time,' Orion laughed.

'What do you mean?' she said, nudging him.

'Isn't every day quality time? You lot compartmentalise every-thing: this is my work time, this is my play time, this is my 'me' time.' He laughed as Mary began tickling him. 'And this is my family time! Stop it, will you!'

'Only if YOU stop taking the micky. We can't all be perfect like you Celestians, you know!'

Falling head over heels in love and being surrounded by nature was intoxicating and at first, they felt cheated when they had to share their time with others. After a few weeks they were ready to mingle. They still went everywhere together but it was time to allow others in too.

One morning they walked to the waterfall and saw people bath-ing and chatting, some were washing their clothes. They sat on the rocks and listened to their conversations. One lady took Mary's hand and showed her how to scrub the clothes using a particular stone. A man stood stock still in the water, made a sudden grab for something and lifted up a fish – to everyone's cheers. From the other side of the river, a deer came for a drink, its ears flicking nervously. A fox stealthily crept up behind it but just as it lunged, the deer leapt into the water, racing to the other side, giving them a fright as much as the fox. Birds came and sat in tiny rock pools and washed their feathers. Mary was enchanted.

'Where you guys from, then?' a man who introduced himself as Paul said, sitting down on a rock opposite them.

'District 35,' Mary replied.

'What about you?' he nodded to Orion.

Orion had been so focused on the creatures, he hadn't got his story ready and stammered a reply. 'Same.'

'Right.' His eyes narrowed as he said, 'I've seen you here in the mornings. I've only ever seen one man do that. He certainly wasn't from the city or for that matter anywhere on Earth.'

'What's he talking about? What do you do?' Mary asked, her brow furrowed.

'Nothing, I just like leaping up in the trees, that's all. You know, just like I always do.'

'Hmmm,' the man replied.

Orion pulled Mary to her feet. 'Nice to meet you, Paul. We're gonna go get something to eat.'

'Do you think he knows you're from another planet?' Mary asked when they were out of earshot. 'How could he, though? There's nothing different about you.'

'Who knows. Didn't want to hang around and find out either.'

'What if he's one of those alien hunters!' she said, gripping his arm tightly.

'That's what I thought.'

'Maybe it's too dangerous for you here. I don't want to lose you!'

Orion put his arm around her and kissed the top of her head, 'You're not going to lose me, I promise. Might be a good idea to move on from here, though.'

Mary nodded. 'You've got to be so careful. He's obviously seen you doing something to alert him.'

That evening as they sat outside their hut chatting to River and Summer, they saw Paul arrive with another man who had long hair and a beard.

'We're heading to bed,' Orion said, looking nervously at the two men and pulling Mary to her feet.

'You don't need to worry about them,' Summer said. 'They're here most nights; nice guys.'

'I'm tired anyway,' Orion smiled, taking Mary's hand and walking quickly to their hut.

They hadn't been there long when they heard gruff voices outside.

'Is this where he's living?' they heard a man say and another grunt an affirmative.

'Leave them alone,' Summer said firmly.

'Let me past,' a man said.

'Can't this wait till morning?' River's voice this time.

'Get out of my way,' they heard the man say and Mary edged behind Orion as they saw the silhouettes of two men approaching the entrance to their hut with a light so bright, they had to shield their eyes.

'I know you're in there,' the gruff voice said.

'Do you have to do this now?' Summer asked plaintively.

'For Demeter's sake, leave me alone would you!'

Orion's eyes widened. He'd only ever heard that expression used at home but it couldn't be, could it? He pulled Mary to her feet and nodded to her that it was OK. She gripped his arm tightly as they poked their heads out of the hut. 'It can't be,' he said, holding his arm up to shield his eyes from the light. The brightness disappeared immediately, sucked back into the tip of the man's finger as he took a step forward.

'Tell me your name,' the man said, so close to Orion now he was within this man's energy field.

'Don't say anything!' Mary urged him.

'It's fine, Mary. I think I know him!'

The man let out a sob and pulled Orion close to him. 'Is it really you?' he said, touching Orion's face, his hair and arms.

'Uncle Leo?' Orion asked.

The man nodded. 'It's you, it's really you,' he kept saying. 'I've waited so long, so long,' he said, sobbing and hugging Orion like he never wanted to let him go.

CHAPTER FORTY-SIX

ORION AND LEO TALKED UNTIL daybreak. Mary lay in bed listening while the two handsome men sat chatting round the fire until sleep got the better of her. There was so much to catch up on. Orion told him that Meisa had never stopped believing he was alive. He talked about Star and what a feisty young female she had grown to be. Leo laughed out loud when he heard about some of her antics. His heart melted, hearing how protective Lacarta and Alhena had become of her after his disappearance.

'How was the Committee when you left?' Leo asked eventually.

'Not good. They tell us it's a democracy but General Rastaban's throwing his weight around; the others are petrified of him. Arrakis and Zaurak are the only ones who stand up to him, oh, and General Calearo from Mercury, but the other general from Mercury is totally under his spell.'

Leo shook his head despondently.

'What happened the day you disappeared?' Orion asked and Leo told him everything that had happened that day seven years ago.

The flight had gone without any hitches but they'd found it strange being told they had to land in the woods. Something didn't add up and the moment they'd landed they were surrounded by gunmen. Leo tried to placate them whilst telepathically communicating to the others to board the craft.

'Never was my strong point so it took a while for them to understand me,' he said, tutting.

Just as he was about to step on board, they opened fire. A bullet hit his leg and he fell to the ground; the doors of the craft closed and it flew off immediately. As soon as they were gone, the gunmen relaxed and took off their black helmets.

'Congratulations, Leo,' they said. 'Just a practise drill; all went well.'

He stood up, dazed and confused, and looked at where his leg had been hit. A thin trickle of blood seeped through the material but he could walk – albeit with a limp.

'Sorry, about that, General,' one of them said, coming over to him and putting his hand on his shoulder. 'Just a rubber bullet. Aren't meant to break the skin but looks like you got hit at close range. You'll live,' he said nonchalantly and walked away with his gun slung over his shoulder.

Later that day as he sat in his living quarters, feeling dazed from the morning's events, he got called to an emergency meeting. All the generals were seated at the large round table: the two Martians, two Venusians, two Plutonians, two Celestians, two Mercurians, General Rastaban and General Rigley.

'What the hell's going on?' Rigley began. 'Leo's owed an explanation after what happened to him this morning!'

'Aah, yes, sorry about that,' Rastaban said to Leo, his tones silky smooth. 'Just a drill. No hard feelings?' Leo went to object but Rastaban put up his hand to silence him. 'We've decided to suspend all flights to and from other planets for the time being,' he said with a smile on his face.

'You can't do this!' Leo shouted.

'I can and I will. The government have been informed that one of the craft came under attack today. They agreed with me that it's too risky to grant permission for any flights in the current climate.'

'You just said yourself it was a pre-arranged drill!' shouted General Calearo.

'I may have omitted to tell them that, but then you omit to tell them a lot of things, don't you?' he said.

'Since when did you become the one dictating who can and cannot fly?' Leo asked. His hands gripped the arms of the chair, his legs shook underneath the table but his voice gave away nothing of the sinking feeling of dread seeping through his veins.

'Since I began working with the Committee members to find out how we can improve relations between us. It seems there are plenty who aren't happy here,' he said, looking around at the generals. Most of them refused to make eye contact. 'We felt it important to have some time away from the distractions of home to really try and work out some of the tension that's building here,' Rastaban said. 'I took it upon myself to call an emergency meeting so that we could finally work out these little – shall we call them knots? – that are emerging. We don't want to let bad feelings fester, do we?' he said, looking round the room. Most of the generals kept their heads bowed.

Leo looked around, unsure of what was happening.

'It would appear there's a conflict of interest within the Committee,' Rastaban said.

'What do you mean?' General Calearo asked.

'It has been brought to my attention that there's talk of raising the vibrations of Earth, enabling humans to become "fully conscious", as some of you like to call it,' he said, looking to Leo, Arrakis and a couple of others. 'However, this does not entirely fit with the viewpoint of the other planets.'

'What other planets?' Calearo asked.

'Well …' he said slowly, placing a long finger on his chin, 'oh, yes – our planet Aldor for a start. Oh, and my lovely friends, the Plutonians, not forgetting the Martians and my favourite of all, the Venusians,' he said, smiling at them. 'My race has worked tirelessly to ensure the economy runs smoothly. We finally get it to the point where it all ticks by perfectly and then I find out that some of you are preparing to remove the satellites we spent so long sending out to space which lower their vibrations. To put an end to the economy that took thousands of years to build so that humans can become fully evolved. To remove money from the system so humans are "free". All our hard work and some of you want to destroy it!' he roared.

'May I remind you that was the whole point of the Committee,' began Leo. 'To free humans from their material reality and show them a spiritual truth, one with no money. Come on, Rastaban, you know that's what we all signed up for.'

'No! That's not what we signed up for! You never asked our opinion, did you? You banned two Aldorians from being on the Committee yet it was us that provided Earth with their precious monetary system which they have treasured ever since. Humans don't want to be free! Can't you see that?' he said, slamming his fist on the table.

'Don't talk such nonsense,' Calearo said, getting up to go. 'I can't listen to this anymore.'

'Sit back down!' Rastaban shot him such a dark, penetrating look he had Calearo meekly sitting back on his chair in seconds. 'If you stop humans from purchasing, you stop trade between Aldor, Mars, Pluto and Venus. Look at Earth and Celestia – you can grow food, you have a water supply, you want for nothing. Our planets are so hot nothing can grow; the air is so putrid we have to live underground. Earth needs our metals and our knowledge of the monetary system and we need Earth's precious metals for our survival. The monetary system works well for both of us. If the monetary system collapses, so does our planet, putting the lives of all our race at risk.'

'But trade between Aldor and all the other planets would continue!' General Arrakis interrupted. 'The Galaxy would run on trust, just like it always used to!'

'Don't be so foolish, Arrakis!' Rastaban spat. 'What do Celestians need nickel or steel for? Your climate is warm, you build your own houses from wood. It's Earth and its love of consumerism that needs our metals; without Earth, we have nothing. A trust can be broken, Arrakis. A broken trust would mean starving Aldorians, or Martians, or Venusians to death because we have no way of growing food. We cannot expose ourselves to such a risk, we would not be protecting our races. We keep humans enslaved, we keep the economy going, we keep our races alive,' he said.

'General, you don't understand …' Zaurak began.

'I understand only too well!' he said sharply, pointing his finger at Zaurak. 'How wonderful for Celestians to live on such a planet of plenty. You don't give a damn about those of us who live underground because our air is toxic, our water so fetid we have to filter every single drop that touches our skin. Our children never feel the sun on their cheeks or the wind in their hair, just the metal clanking of the doors that keep them trapped inside away from the soaring heat that will fry them in a nano-second. It was us Aldorians that found all the gold on Earth, gold that each one of us here needs to build our crafts. But more than that, gold's heat resistant properties can improve our living conditions. Yet on the day of its conception the Committee took all the gold we'd collected and hid it from the very race that had spent thousands of years mining it. You watch while we have to live deeper and deeper underground to be away from the heat of our planets' atmospheres and you don't give a damn.'

'The gold was taken so that humans can no longer be tempted

by all it has to offer; it was gold that got them into so much trouble!' Calearo said.

'Give the gold to us, then. Allow us the opportunity to look after it, to build our houses so we can live nearer the sky. Our children don't get to see the stars because you keep it away from us, accusing us of being greedy or manipulative,' he spat.

General Rigley, Calearo, Arrakis and Zaurak looked at each other and shook their heads.

Rastaban threw back his head and laughed. 'See for yourselves everyone! These generals don't want to liberate humans, they want to starve our races to death! But we worked your little ruse out and thank Narcissus we did.' He paused for breath before continuing. 'The economy is essential for the safe running of the Galaxy. We must never allow humans to be fully conscious.'

'We'd better take a vote,' General Calearo said, clearing his voice. 'This is not what the Committee set out to do. I'm sure we'll see the majority feel the same. Everyone in favour of keeping the vibrations lower on Earth.' He looked round the room and breathed a sigh of relief as not one hand went up. 'Aahhh, see, General. I think you'll notice that we're all in agreement …' he paused as first the Plutonians, then the Martians slowly put one hand up and finally the Venusians. 'That still only makes six votes against six, we have to have a majority to have it passed,' he said.

'I think you'll find I didn't vote,' Rastaban said, lifting his hand, making the votes seven versus five.

General Rigley sat with his head bowed feeling utterly helpless.

Zaurak stood up, thumping the table with his fist. 'If you hadn't provided them with wheat and barley, knowing full well their bodies can't tolerate grains, the DNA of humans would never've been altered. They'd never have wanted all the material gains you gave them. They were so connected to their planet till then. You could have just left them alone. Instead you've created this beast called the economy that needs feeding but the more you feed it the hungrier it gets.'

'Just because we offered it doesn't mean they had to take it,' Rastaban spat. 'Vote carried to keep humans enslaved.' He slammed his hand down on the table and looked around at the generals, a sickening smile on his face.

From then on Leo was aware that not only did Rastaban seem to have some kind of hold over most of the generals but he'd also colluded with Melantho to increase surveillance on any Committee member he saw as a threat to the new ethos. Leo realised his phone was being tapped, every conversation he had he heard a beep as the surveillance team tuned in.

Rumours were going around the compound that beings from far off galaxies who'd been visiting Earth freely for centuries were now being lured into the compound under false pretences. They'd be greeted enthusiastically by General Rastaban or one of the Plutonians and ushered into one of the meeting rooms. The generals would tell them to wait whilst they got some refreshments. They'd then lock the doors and a gas would seep in through the ventilation system. Once they were all knocked out, their bodies would be taken deep into the corridors of the compound and locked away to be used for questioning or experimentation. Something was being done to them to take any powers away, prohibiting them from escaping.

He'd yet to witness these things but they came from reliable sources. Leo felt it was too risky to work within the Committee any longer. If he stayed, on the hope that travel bans would be lifted, he could find himself in one of these cells. If he escaped to the woods, he may never make it home again but at least he'd be alive. It seemed the better of the two options – just. When his daughter reached the age she could study humans, he would work out a way to intercept her.

One night, after another arduous Committee meeting, he decided he could take it no more and made his getaway. He'd known about the tunnels for years – he'd been waiting at the train station one day when a grate door had fallen open and a sleeping tramp had rolled out onto the floor. The tramp had begged Leo not to tell on him and had stuffed a map of the tunnels in his hand, saying, 'One day you might need it too,' and ran away back into the dark, fetid tunnel. That day had finally come.

When all the Committee members were in their quarters, he told the surveillance team he needed to head into the city. He was observing a human who'd just left his apartment; he had a hunch he was going to persuade another human to escape, he told them. Raising his palms up to the camera he held them still until the glass smashed into tiny pieces. He opened a grate in the side of the wall using his pocket screwdriver, threw his phone onto the track and following the map, crawled along the tunnels for what felt like an eternity until there was the unmistakable sight of bright sunlight and the smell of grass. He scrambled a little further, took out his screwdriver and released the grate. He was free … for the time being.

'How do we change things?' Orion asked.

Leo shook his head. 'The best thing we can do at the moment is be the change you want to see. It's like ripples in a pond. When I first came to the woods there was barely anyone living here. They'd never open up to you, either. They'd got used to treating all humans with suspicion and had no idea how to trust. I've lived here for nearly five years now and look around – it's Celestia.'

Orion looked at the little huts dotted about in the forest, the fires smouldering away and the noise of the wildlife filling the darkness. 'I may have made Melantho a bit angry.' Orion grimaced as he spoke. 'Just before I left, I tampered with the surveillance system.' Orion updated Leo on what he'd done with the trigger words.

'Oh boy, he's not going to like that when he finds out!' he said, chuckling. 'Let's hope humans make the best of the opportunity. There are signs they're waking up. More people are coming to the woods. There's talk of an insider working at the space compound. Don't suppose you picked up on anything when you were there?'

'Could be Melantho's son, Robert,' Orion said.

'His son? What poor woman fell for his smarm, I wonder?'

'One that found herself dead when she delved a bit too deeply,' Orion said. 'Robert helped us escape but Melantho appeared just as we went down the rubbish chute. Last thing we heard was a gunshot. Robert may well be dead now too,' Orion said, shaking his head.

'How much harm can one man cause?' Leo pondered. 'Don't give up hope. We have a way out; we'll get home, I know it,' he said, his eyes twinkling in the early morning sun. 'I'm so lucky I had this to keep me going,' he said, gazing into the sequente. 'If I hadn't been able to see what Star got up to every day, I think I'd have given up a long time ago.' Orion leant over and saw an image of her, fast asleep in her bed. 'How's your telepathic skills?'

'Not bad,' Orion replied.

'Got to be better than mine. That's why I took the sequente every time I travelled. At least I can see her even if I can't communicate with her. You could use your telepathy to contact Star, tell her to come to Earth. Don't mention me. If our plan doesn't work, she'll face losing me all over again. We have about three weeks before Human Studies begin, by which time everything should be ready.'

'But Leo,' Orion began, 'I'm not going home. My life is here with Mary.'

On hearing her name, Mary's eyes flickered open.

Leo put his arm round Orion. 'I know that's what you believe but you're wrong. For humans, life in the woods is good after what they've been through but for us Celestians, living in the woods is a reminder of how great life is at home. Here, we're at risk of being caught every single day. It's exhausting living off your nerves. If either of us gets taken back to the compound I don't think we'll ever see daylight again. No love is worth sacrificing for that,' he said, patting Orion's back.

Orion turned to look at Mary who quickly shut her eyes. 'But I love her so much.'

'I know you do. I know you do.'

The two men went quiet. The light was getting stronger and they needed to get some sleep. They were emotionally and physically drained. Orion crept into bed and put his arms round Mary, snuggling close to her warm body. He closed his eyes and focused on Leo's hut back at home. He could see Star asleep with Meisa next to her. In his head he repeated the words over and over again, 'Come to Earth, Star. You need to study humans; it's your calling.' He'd never tried communicating with a being on another planet before but he wanted to help Leo any way he could. He'd watched Meisa and Star grieve for Leo; they needed him home. As he lay there, so focused on home, tears rolled down Mary's face. She loved Orion and wanted to be with him but overhearing snippets of their conversation, her future with him suddenly felt very uncertain.

CHAPTER FORTY-SEVEN

A COUPLE OF SUNSETS LATER Star strolled down to her favourite spot by the river and sat with her legs outstretched, leaning back on her arms. She'd always felt this calling to study humans and had put it down to her family history but last night it really felt like someone on Earth was calling her, pleading for her to come. She knew it wasn't some crazy dream like her friends had intonated. She had to get there and find out who it was trying to contact her. It had to be her dad; who else could it be? Lacarta and Alhena may not have been destined to study humans but if their friendship was strong enough, they'd stick with her whether it was their destiny or not. Just then a cascade of cold water fell on her warm feet and she yelled out in shock.

Gamua's familiar face popped up in the shallow water, 'Hey, Star! What's on your mind?'

'You don't want to know.'

He disappeared underwater and slowly reappeared squirting another stream of water right over Star's head and body.

She leapt up. 'For crying out loud! I've had enough of your stupid jokes!' She ran towards Gamua, her hands on her hips.

His tiny ears fell flat against the side of his head. The whites of his big eyes shone, and he put a webbed hand in front of his face, peering at her angry face.

'Why can't you leave me in peace for once? I'm sick of it; I need some space!'

Gamua's scaly face crumpled in shock as Star turned on her heel to leave. An almighty howl of pain came out of his beak-shaped mouth causing the leaves of the trees to shake and the river ripple with the vibrations, creating great big waves that crashed up the beach, drenching Star once more and pulling her down with its force.

Using all her strength she gathered herself up and attempted to march away, whilst Gamua continued to howl. She got as far as the trees and looked around to see him sat with his back to her, his head in his webbed hands, his shoulders shaking as he wailed pitifully over and over again.

Star looked at him and her heart melted. 'I'm so sorry, Gamua. I don't know what's happening to me!' she said, running to him and putting her arms around his large body.

Gamua looked into her eyes, his ears still flat against his head. 'Please don't change, Star. Life wouldn't be the same without your sunny face to squirt water at.'

The two friends looked at each other and laughed at the ridiculous sight of each other.

'I'm sorry. I've been studying humans. I can't stop thinking about them.'

'Those boring things? What's the point of that when you could be out here playing with me? Come on, come and meet my family. It's about time you did. Mum's always asking after you.'

'You know I can't breathe underwater!'

'No, but you have me and that's all you need. Now hop onto my back. If you're studying those pesky humans, you'd better have the decency to come and meet us maguas, we're waaaaayyy more interesting!' Despite all her reservations Star straddled his back and put her arms around his neck, pressing her head against his scaly back and closing her eyes in trepidation. 'Hold tight and feel my breathing, you'll be fine. Enjoy the ride, Star, and don't forget to be polite to Mummy. She's absolutely terrifying!'

Star's eyes sprang open. She went to object but her protestations were drowned out as they dived underwater, Gamua's powerful fins taking them so deep so quickly she was nearly thrown off his back. She panicked and clung even tighter to him, until Gamua signalled for her to let go as she was choking him. It didn't take long for her to realise that as long as she held onto her friend and didn't open her mouth, she was able to breathe underwater. The water became colder and darker. Unusual river creatures Star had never seen before swam over to examine this new creature riding on Gamua's back. He greeted them all with a friendly wave.

In the distance Star saw a dim light that grew stronger the deeper they went. As they drew closer Star could see that it wasn't one light but lots of tiny lights emanating from many little domes on the bottom of the riverbed. Star watched in fascination as she realised that there was no water inside the domes and each one held families of maguas going about their daily business. The two carried on until they hovered over one which Gamua proudly announced was his home. Star watched his family look up to see what the cause of the dark shadow over their home was. At first they waved but when they spotted he had a guest on his back, their faces turned to shock and they began racing round, frantically moving pots from the draining board and grabbing clothes from the washing lines that hung in each room. Muffled yelling could be heard as they rushed about bashing into each other, trying desperately to stuff anything they could in some hidden corner.

Gamua swam down, keeping Star on his back, and came to a stop outside the front door. He pressed a button and the thick, grey door slid downwards into the riverbed. With Star still clutching Gamua around the neck, the pair swam into a small compartment and faced a second closed door. He pressed another button and they waited while the first door glided back up and gradually the water emptied until they stood in a dry room. Star hopped off and Gamua took her hand in his large webbed one. He then knocked on the inner door and waited.

The yelling stopped and for a moment all was silent. Then all of a sudden, the door flung open. A creature twice the size of Gamua, wearing the most unusual red and white apron Star had ever seen, greeted them both with wide-open scaly arms and hands with long, webbed fingers.

'Gamua! You've brought guests and without even telling me!' she said with a forced grin on her face. 'How lovely of you being so spontaneous! Don't just stand there, come on in! You must be Star. We've heard all about you!'

Star looked around in wonder at this beautiful home under the water. The room was quite a mess with pots bubbling away on the stove, seaweed hanging from the ceiling, various plants being dried out and a large selection of food items all stored in bottles that adorned shelves, cupboard tops and tables.

'I've heard so much about you too,' Star said.

Mrs Gamua's scales flushed a deep red. 'Now, do call me Mummy, all his friends do. I'm so glad he's finally brought you here. I simply love having visitors.' She saw the bemused faces of her children and tutted, 'Got something to say?'

Her children looked at each other, shrugged and shook their heads.

'Maybe I've become a little agoraphobic down here. One can get a little stuck in one's ways, can't one?'

They looked at their mother and raised their eyebrows.

Mummy Gamua turned back to Star and tutted back at them.

'I love your apron … er, Mummy,' she said, struggling to think of anything to say and feeling remarkably awkward at having to call a stranger 'Mummy'.

'What, this old thing? It's just something I threw on when I got out of bed this morning,' she said, stroking the material, trying to get the creases out of it.

'I've never seen anything so colourful before. Where did you get it from?'

'Oh, err, well, I err … I made it?' she said hopefully.

Behind her, Gamua's sister muffled a laugh. 'What a liar! You nicked it!'

Mummy Gamua gave her daughter a swipe with her webbed hand but missed as her daughter ducked out of the way. 'How dare you, Fatimaua, accusing your mother of such things!'

Gamua interjected, 'This is from a human, Star. Mummy likes pretty things, you see, and one day she found it lying on the river beach. She felt that something so beautiful should never be left alone so she very kindly took it and it's been with us ever since.'

Mummy Gamua's scales flushed red again.

'What do you mean, it's from a human?' Star said in shock. 'We've always been taught that if just one thing from Earth comes here then it'll infect Celestia!'

'That's why Mummy takes them and keeps them down here.'

'I don't get it?'

'There's always one who wants a memory of their time there and smuggles something onto the craft. They tend to come to the river to admire their treasures in private, then either go for a swim or doze off. Mummy sees it as her duty to gather up the offending items.'

'They'd be in so much trouble if they got found out,' Mummy said defensively.

'Can I see what you've found?' Star asked, intrigued.

Mummy Gamua's face lit up and she took Star through to a tiny room that was filled from floor to ceiling with items Star had never set eyes on before. Mummy explained what each item did: she was shown watches that told humans the time, a tie that showed humans have a job, rings that showed humans belonged to other humans, fold-out walking sticks that helped humans walk easier, a variety of brightly coloured bracelets, ear-rings, gloves and a mobile phone.

Star picked an item up and turned it over in her hand. 'What are these?' she asked.

'A pair of glasses!' Mummy Gamua replied proudly. She took them off Star and perched them on her scaly nose, making Star laugh at this amusing sight.

'What on earth do they do?'

'Look through them,' she replied.

Star peered through them but threw them off. 'They're horrible! Everything's blurry!' she said.

'Shows you've got good eyesight!' Mummy Gamua replied then explained herself in clearer terms. 'Everything's blurred for you because your eyes work well. My eyes aren't so good but when I put them on, I can see everything perfectly.'

'But how?' Confusion swept over Star's face. 'I don't understand. Something so simple could've ...'

'Quite right, so simple!' Mummy Gamua said, clasping her webbed hands together in delight.

Star stepped back in shock, dropping the glasses as if they were scorching hot. Mummy Gamua looked on in horror as her precious glasses fell slowly to the floor. She ran over and scooped them up, hugging them to her chest before placing them back onto the shelf.

Star's mind was in turmoil. She had to get out of there; she had to see her mother. What had she been thinking, trying to get Lacarta to come with her?

'I have to go. Gamua, take me home.'

'Mummy's just protective about her things,' Gamua said, glaring at his mother.

'It's not that,' Star said with a glazed look on her face.

'What is it?' Gamua cocked his head, his ears lay flat and his eyes were full of concern. Star threw her arms round Gamua and wailed, 'I'm such an idiot! I've ruined everything!'

CHAPTER FORTY-EIGHT

WHEN ORION WOKE LATER THAT day there was no sign of Mary. He asked around the village but no one knew where she was. Trying to ignore the panic rising in his chest, he ran through the woods calling out her name but there was no reply. He leapt into the trees, jumping from branch to branch, fear coursing through his veins and stopped momentarily when he heard laughter coming from nearby. He followed the voices and found her bathing in the waterfall with Summer and River. Catching his breath, he sat in the branches watching while she chatted happily to the couple. When she got out of the water, he leapt down next to her making her jump.

'Don't do that!' Mary pushed him away and fetched her clothes from a rock.

'What's wrong?' he said, trying to grab her hand.

'Leave me alone!' she said and walked into the forest without a backwards glance.

Orion looked over to River and Summer who were sat in the river listening. He shrugged, gave them a wave and headed after Mary.

'I said, leave me alone!' she said as he caught up with her.

'Mary, what have I done? Did we keep you awake last night? It's been years since I saw my uncle, you know that!' he said, getting annoyed.

'It's not that!' she shouted.

'Then what is it?' He reached out and grabbed her hand, but she jerked it away. 'Can you just tell me what I've done wrong, please! I can't read minds, you know ...' he tailed off as he realised that if he concentrated properly, that's exactly what he could do. An idea sprang to mind. 'Sit here for a moment, will you?' He clasped his hands in prayer and she smiled at him.

'Maybe.'

'Give me a minute, alright? I want to understand why you're annoyed with me.'

Mary looked at him. 'I heard you talking about me!'

Orion went over what they'd said but nothing was standing out apart from saying how much he'd loved her. He held his head in his hands and went over the night in his head. He then reached for her hand and looked in her eyes. A picture of him with Leo appeared in his head. They were reminiscing about home but as if he was able to forwards wind to the crucial moment he went over their conversation.

'But, Leo, I'm not going home. My life is here with Mary.'

'I know that's what you believe but you're wrong. No love is worth sacrificing for that.'

'Oh, Mary,' he said.

Mary's face crumpled. 'You're going to leave me!' she cried.

'I'd never leave you! My life is here with you!'

'Why didn't you say something? Why didn't you tell him?'

'I didn't say anything because I knew it wasn't what Leo wanted to hear. I'll tell him in my own time. I'm never leaving you. How could I? I love you,' he said, pulling her legs over his so they rested on his lap.

'You don't have to do this,' she said, putting her arms round his neck and looking into his eyes. 'Life's so dangerous here. I'd rather know you're alive and safe at home than risk everything to be with me.'

'Leo's got a family back home, a daughter he hasn't seen grow up, a life partner who's grieved for him every day. My family is here now,' he said and kissed her.

'Young love,' River said to Summer as they walked past them. 'Come with us,' he called. 'You can find out what an incredible man your Uncle Leo is.'

Orion gave Mary a kiss. 'You alright now?' he asked.

'Mmm. Maybe I overreacted,' she said, standing up and reaching her hand out to help Orion to his feet.

'Overreact? Never!' he said, putting his arm round her.

Mary and Orion followed the older couple as they walked by the river's edge until they saw people dotted about the landscape, deeply engrossed in whatever they were doing. River explained that Leo had been digging a tunnel which would connect to the ancient underground network of tunnels under the city. They'd been disused for years, though some still carried sewage out of the city. Once connected to the main network Leo's tunnel would enable more humans to escape city life without fear of getting arrested.

Leo appeared at the mouth of a large cave and wiped his brow with his sleeve. When he saw Orion, he waved and walked over to where they were stood. 'You here to help?' he asked and they both nodded. 'It's about the hardest physical labour you'll do but if we get it right it could mean we free so many more. Come on in, I'll show you around the place. Working on this has protected me from lunacy,' he said, looking up at the moon's white silhouette in the sunshine. The tunnel was incredible. Firstly, they entered a large natural cave that was shielded by a waterfall. Rows of people stood either side passing boulders to the person at the end of the line who placed them into sacks and headed off into the forest. The team of people involved was immense.

As they walked Leo pointed his finger and a shard of light shot out, illuminating the tunnel. It didn't take long before the tunnel became so narrow, they had to get down on their hands and knees and crawl in single file. Faint noises echoed round the walls: laughter, swearing, a clank, and the constant chip, chip, chip as their tools worked away at breaking up the ancient rock. 'We're nearly at the end,' called Leo from the front. 'Don't disturb them. It's exhausting and they don't take kindly to being interrupted.'

The tunnel bent a little to the right and with the help of Leo's light they were able to take in the scene in front of them. Two men chipped tirelessly away at the rock face, sweat dripping down their shirtless backs. Next to them was a small pot with a tiny flickering light inside. They never even looked up as the others approached and just continued their chip, chip, chipping.

''Scuse me,' one of the men said, crawling down the tunnel towards them.

'There's no room ...' Mary began.

'Move!' he said gruffly. Mary leant as close into the rock wall as possible but the size of the man meant he had to press incredibly close to her as he crawled past. When they came face to face the man stopped and stared at her. She could feel his breath on her face and tried turning away; she was sure it was laced with alcohol. His tongue darted out of his mouth and he licked his lips. 'Let's hope we meet somewhere nicer next time.'

Mary smiled nervously but didn't reply.

'You alright back there?' Leo called from the front.

The man grunted and continued past the group, dragging a heavy bag of stones behind him.

'Who's that?' Orion whispered to his uncle.

'Russell. He's new to the woods. Not exactly the friendliest bloke. Keeps himself to himself but he's a damn good worker. We can't leave any trace of our work,' continued Leo. 'If anyone official finds out it'll be over for all of us as well as the humans stuck in the city.'

'What do you do with all the rocks?' Orion asked.

'They're used back at one of the camps to build a home or scattered in the woods or river.'

'Why don't they search the woods if they know people live here?' asked Mary.

'The forest gives us protection from their drones. They can't fly underneath the canopy and even if they could it's too thick with trees for them to get very far. They're expensive bits of equipment so you'd be sacked if you wasted one of them "for some rebels" is what they'd think. The problem is that here by the river we're incredibly exposed. Luckily they've only ever made it this far using a dinghy with an outboard motor.' He chuckled and said, 'All that money invested in AI and they still haven't got anything better on a river than those little dinghies. We can hear their engines from miles away. Gives us plenty of time to get out of here. As long as we leave no debris and everything looks natural, they're none the wiser. I'm doing all this for Star and her mother,' he said, bringing the sequente out and placing it in his hand. A tiny image of his daughter appeared inside it. She was sat combing her hair whilst talking to Meisa and Rhea.

Mary gasped in delight. 'They're going to be blown away when they find out what you've been up to,' Mary said, touching him on the arm. He placed his hand on hers and his eyes welled up with tears.

'Thank you. They mean everything to me,' he said as he placed the sphere back into his pocket.

Orion and Mary grabbed a hessian bag from the side and took a load of rocks back with them, leaving Leo chatting with the miners.

It didn't take long for them to find their own jobs within this vast operation. Unfortunately, it meant frequently crossing paths with Russ. Every time he passed Mary, he either ignored her or stared at her in a way that gave her the creeps. Mary would walk upriver to scatter the smaller debris and Orion would leap into the trees with the larger ones, taking them back to the camp in record time. Large boulders were gratefully received for many of the building projects going on within the community.

After a few hours they were exhausted. There was a never-ending stream of people wanting to help and when the ones who'd worked all day were finished, others arrived to begin the night shift.

That evening back at the camp Leo came over to them, keen to hear what they'd thought of the operation.

'There are so many involved! It's amazing!' Orion said.

'The best thing is everyone's just as dedicated as me,' Leo said. 'We all want humans to be free. It means so much to each and every one of us. Some of them have families in the city.'

'That Russ guy gives me the creeps,' Mary said.

'Yeah, I don't think he's very popular with the ladies round here,' Leo said. 'The problem is if we start dictating who can or can't work here, we become as bad as they are in the city. He's a grafter though and that's what we need. I'll do what I can to make sure your paths don't cross.'

'Thanks,' Mary said. 'Do you think humans want to be free?'

Leo shrugged. 'Who knows. All I can do is provide them with their escape.' He grabbed an apple from the table, threw it in the air and caught it with his other hand which was behind his back. 'Night, you two,' he said, taking a bite and heading to his hut.

The village provided food for all the workers and Orion and Mary went to bed with full stomachs, utterly exhausted. Every muscle ached, their fingernails were black, their faces filthy and their hair full of dust but they'd contributed to something wonderful. Orion cuddled up to her and closed his eyes. He pictured Star, back home, and repeated the words over and over again in his head, 'You have to study humans; you have to come to Earth.' He had no real idea if it was working but he knew how powerful the mind was. For the time being it was all he could do.

CHAPTER FORTY-NINE

'DON'T TELL ME YOU'VE PERSUADED Lacarta to study humans?' Gamua asked.

The look on Star's face confirmed that was exactly what she'd done.

Gamua let out an almighty howl and dropped his head dramatically into his hands. 'He's never going to understand why he can't have them! Celestia mustn't become infected like Earth. What have you done?' he said and began howling once again.

'You've risked everything just because YOU wanted him with you!' Mummy Gamua wagged her finger angrily at Star who promptly burst into tears.

'What should I do?' Star wailed.

'Talk to him. Don't say anything about the glasses. Find out if he really wants to study them or if he's doing it for you,' Mummy Gamua said.

'And if he doesn't change his mind?'

A visible shiver went down her spine. 'You'll have to cross that one when you get to it.'

As Star walked home that sunset, she thought about what she'd discovered. Maybe Lacarta wouldn't notice humans wore glasses –

he was short sighted after all. Maybe she was worrying over nothing. A nervous fluttering was gathering pace in her tummy. She knew that studying FHS may not be Lacarta's path but she also knew how stubborn he was. Once he'd made a decision there was rarely any going back, particularly if that decision included plans with herself.

Rhea was outside their hut, fussing over a few lematas and giving them some vegetable peelings. Meisa was cooking tea over the fire, the glazed look on her face giving away the fact that her mind was not on the food.

The three females sat and had their tea in silence, savouring each mouthful of the piping hot casserole. Meisa was keen to find out how Star's day had been so was relieved when Rhea headed off to see friends and they could be alone. Gradually Star opened up, telling her mother about her visit to Gamua's underwater home which lead to the discovery of all their hidden human trinkets. Meisa laughed at the image of Mummy Gamua with her brightly coloured apron but her face changed when Star mentioned the glasses.

'His mum and dad haven't told him about all the tempting things Earth has to offer. We all know about them, it's just that they never really expected him to go to Earth. He's doing it for you, you know?' she said softly.

Star looked at the ground. 'I wanted to have an adventure with my best friends.'

'You know we mustn't intervene with other beings' journeys.'

'Maybe this is his journey? You know how much he loves being with me. Maybe he should find out about these things. I can't see what's so bad about him having them anyway.'

'Lacarta's poor eyesight enhances his hearing and his sense of smell. If he'd had glasses who knows how it would have changed him?'

Star turned to look at her mother. 'They might have changed

him for the better. How would you feel knowing that your life could've been made so much easier but your planet colluded to keep it from you?'

Meisa took a deep breath. 'You make it sound dirty.'

'Maybe that's because it is.'

'Human Studies brings up something for everyone. All our lives could be made easier at some point by accessing things on earth.'

'But glasses, Mum? I mean, that's life-changing stuff! All he had to do was put something on his face and he could see! How can any of you justify not allowing them here?'

'It sounds so simple doesn't it? But we know where it leads, always wanting something else.'

'Our race isn't like that!' Star said, getting up and standing over Meisa. 'We're not humans – don't treat us like we are!'

Meisa stood up and faced her daughter. 'We know that but we also know how similar to humans we can be if a couple of changes were made to how we live. We've lost Celestians to Earth because they think it's so incredible! They find out their bad eyesight could have been sorted; their hearing problem could be treated. They discover they don't have to make their own clothes, build their own houses, make their own food. The times I would love to go to a café instead of cooking! The nights I've sat up late sewing our dresses, wishing I could just run to a shop and buy a new one! See, even I'm impressed with what Earth has to offer, just imagine how Lacarta's going to feel! Why would he come back when he knows how one simple thing could change the rest of his life?'

'Let him have them, then! You know Lacarta wouldn't want anything else.'

'You're missing the point. It's not just him we'd be worried about. If he comes back with them everyone's going to ask him about them, be impressed by them and find out what else they could have from Earth. They'll decide to study HS for the wrong reasons and miss their own path they were meant to travel. Someone else will want glasses; another being will want a hearing aid. Then others will feel aggrieved that they didn't get something. They might want a lighter for their fire, a pair of shoes to protect their feet, a soft blanket for their bed.'

'For Demeter's sake, who cares? They're all simple things. No-one's being greedy!'

'Don't get so angry, Star! I'm just trying to show you why it has to be this way!'

'You're not doing a very good job, then. As far as I can see it doesn't have to be this way at all. Maybe it's time to start trusting Celestians and allow us to have things that help us with our day-to-day lives. Maybe humans have it right after all?'

Meisa took a step closer to Star and held her shoulders. 'I remember what it feels to be your age. I thought I knew everything too.'

Star pulled her hands up, forcing Meisa to let go. 'Maybe we should listen to the younger ones here and not just take orders from the Seniors.'

Meisa gasped and clasped her hands to her chest. 'We don't take orders from anyone! They advise us! How can you say that?'

'They're dictating what we can and can't have! How can any of you think it's OK not to allow something so simple here? It's crazy!'

'It might sound crazy to you but it works. No one is treated any differently here. Our lives are a gift, whatever package we're wrapped up in. Our journey is to see how we use our gift to help others during our time here. We don't tamper with that gift because we were given it for a reason. Humans change everything about themselves: their hair colour, their nails, they wear shoes that make them look taller, wear clothes that make them look older. They smear chemicals over their faces to make it darker or lighter, they pump fat into their lips to make them bigger, put plastic in their boobs to make them bigger …' she said, clutching her chest.

'Boobs?' Star nearly laughed out loud. 'I've never heard them called that before!'

Meisa looked down at her chest and laughed too.

'What did you say they do to them?'

'They make them bigger!'

Star started giggling. 'Why would they do that? They wouldn't be able to run and jump!'

It was Meisa's turn to laugh now. 'Most humans have no need to run and jump like we do.'

Star peered down her top. 'Do you think mine are big enough, Mum?'

'Are you serious?'

'Look at them! I've never really thought about them in terms of size before. What do you think?' she said, pushing them together.

Meisa couldn't help but giggle.

Star stood there for a moment, her hands still on her chest.

'Do you know how ridiculous you look?' her mother said.

Star looked down and began laughing too. Their laughter grew until tears appeared in their eyes and they were clutching their stomachs so hard they had to sit down.

When their laughter subsided, they sat and stared at the glowing embers of the fire.

Star looked down at her hands and arms. 'Look, I've got new markings!' She held them out to show her the faint lines appearing.

'These last few sun rotations you've experienced new emotions: guilt, deceit, shame. Your marks are reflecting this growth.'

'It doesn't feel much like growth to me,' Star replied.

'It might feel like that at the moment. Don't dwell on those negative emotions. They've got no place in your long-term happiness but it's good to recognise how they make you feel. That's why it's so important to make sure Human Studies is your path and not someone else's. It'll always bring up something and you need to have the coping mechanisms to deal with whatever does arise.'

CHAPTER FIFTY

FOUR MOONS LATER THE GROUP of friends were back in the viewing room at the Centre of Learning for another lesson in Human Studies. Only six students remained.

'Morning, everyone,' said Eridamus, looking around at the small group. 'It's no surprise to see so few of you returning. I could see the last lesson had unsettled quite a lot of the class. They've made the right decision not to go any further. This lesson we'll be studying humans at work. As you know, this is something humans do between five and six days a week.' Elder Eridamus placed the pyramid on the floor and said the word, 'Work'. Images flicked by: towering office blocks crowded together in the city, masked and suited humans, wearing masks, crammed into busy train carriages, others standing in front of facial recognition stations, more dressed in dark suits sitting hunched over their desks, others in bland meeting rooms sat around large tables listening to someone at the head of the table, a drone outside washing the windows, endless queues of humans on their lunchbreak at the fast-food joints. As the class watched the images flash by, their elder explained what city life entailed. 'Humans have a variety of interesting jobs available to them such as working in office blocks, running a team of people in the office blocks, cleaning the office blocks, catering for the staff who work in the office blocks and maintaining the office blocks.'

'How can anyone tell them apart?' Alhena asked, not taking her eyes off the holographic images. 'I mean, look at them. They even wear the same clothes!'

'It's called a uniform,' Star said confidently.

Eridamus coughed. 'Not exactly, Star. Some of them wear uniforms. Look,' she said, halting the flickering images. A holographic image appeared of a room filled with women and men wearing white clothes, blue hair nets, blue plastic gloves on their hands and masks over their mouths and noses. 'These are the kitchen staff; they all have to wear an identical uniform but the office workers are able to choose what they wear.'

Star scoffed. 'No one would choose to wear that!'

'It's considered respectful to wear a suit to work and they tend to come in dark colours,' Eridamus explained patiently. She clicked her fingers and the images continued on their slide show.

'Look!' shouted out Lacarta but the image flashed past before anyone could tell what he was looking at. 'Go back, Eridamus!'

Eridamus pointed her finger and as if reading the pages of a book, she flicked her finger until she got to the image he was after.

'Look, there!' he said, standing up and pointing to the frozen image of a man striding down the street, a flash of red poking out from underneath his dark jacket. 'He's wearing something different to the others!'

Eridamus smiled. 'Aah, yes, you see the odd rebel.' She flicked her finger and the image came to life again. They followed the man as he walked or almost bounced down the street, whistling as he did. He looked around at the mostly masked people rushing past him. He shook his head at those who were engrossed in their phones and smiled at others who caught his eye. Some returned his smile, others looked away as if unsure of how to react.

'What did you call him?' Star asked.

'A rebel. He's considered different to the others, more "awake" shall we say.'

'What you mean the others are asleep? They look pretty awake to me,' Star said.

'It's a term coined by humans themselves over a hundred years ago. There are those who continue life, keeping their heads down and doing whatever the government tells them to do. Then there are others, the rebels. They're easy to spot as you've just demonstrated. A rebel tends to wear more colour, they tend to walk differently, they find it easier to connect with people.'

'How many rebels are there?' Lacarta asked.

'Not many, not yet. I'd like to see more but it's hard as humans just don't seem to want to wake up. For the time being, the Committee monitors these rebels quite rigidly as they are considered a threat to the system.'

'What do you mean, monitor?' Alhena asked.

'A rebel would have all their phone conversations recorded, followed by the AI team, cameras on alert in case they start listening to music that isn't played on the radio or TV, computer hacked to make sure they know what websites they're looking at. All that sort of thing.'

'That sounds awful!' Lacarta said.

'I know! You wouldn't want to be a rebel on Earth, would you?' Eridamus said. 'If there are more rebels then the whole system will collapse, causing a lot of businesses to fold. The job losses of the non-rebels will be huge! Waking up humans needs to be done very gently. They need to choose that path for themselves. We can't force it on them. The man you see here will have a ripple effect on those around him and that ripple will continue through them so that one day everyone will be awakened. When that happens there won't be anyone wanting to work in these places.'

'How many years do they work in the office blocks, Elder?' Lacarta asked, not taking his eyes away from the man as he continued walking jovially down the street.

'Between forty and fifty years,' Elder Eridamus said matter-of-factly.

The group gasped in shock.

Alhena put her hand up. 'Elder, you made a mistake. You said forty to fifty.'

Eridamus looked blankly at her.

Alhena coughed. 'You meant to say four to five.'

Eridamus laughed. 'No, Alhena, no mistake. It might sound a long time to you but humans are quite happy with this arrangement.'

'What age do humans die?' Star asked.

'The average age for a human is sixty-eight years old.'

Star and Lacarta counted on their fingers but Alhena was quicker than them.

'But that means they've only just stopped working when they die!' she blurted out.

'It may seem hard for you to understand but this way it keeps humans busy, out of mischief shall we say. Humans like … things. These "things" cost the planet an awful lot in terms of resources. As you get to know humans you'll see that the only way of protecting Earth, and therefore the galaxy and everything in it,' she looked around pointedly as if to say and that means you, 'is to keep humans busy. When we come away from the cities, you'll see the beauty of Earth, the wonderful creatures that roam the planet, the seas filled with huge mammals larger than anything you've ever seen here. It's truly wonderful. Earth is an incredible planet and she has to be protected – at all costs.'

A silence descended over the students.

Eridamus sighed. This bit was always hard for her students to comprehend. 'Before you feel too sorry for humans you have to realise how bad things got for Mother Earth. She was dying! Once humans were sold the idea of materialism, they thought that happiness could be bought.' She clicked her fingers and pictures flashed up of humans shopping: long queues of people outside a mobile phone shop, young children buying the latest gadget then pictures of them sat at home staring at a screen, bashing on a remote they held in their hands, groups of women in shoe shops, teenagers queuing for a pair of trainers outside a sports shop, inside a hair salon, a nail salon, jewellery shops, chocolate shops, music shops. 'They forgot the most important thing – and one that every being in the cosmos knows – is to protect the planet they live on.' She clicked her fingers again and the images changed. She explained what they were seeing as the images flashed by: pictures of factories pumping out smoke, trees being cut down and replaced by palm trees or cattle, huge swathes of discoloured land that was left dead after mining for precious metals, thousands of animals in tiny cages being used for medical experiments, plastic bags floating in the seas and numerous animals lying dead with something over their mouths or noses. 'Whilst all this went on, the economy was thriving. They kept feeding this deadly beast and ignored the cost it had on the planet and her resources. The really sad thing is most of these humans had no idea they were causing so much harm; they did it without even bothering to find out,' she sighed again.

'But I don't get it – humans are still buying! Nothing's changed!' a boy called Reanou said.

'Yes, but there's less of them now, much less. Populations have been reduced and it's incredibly hard for a human to reproduce so they only tend to have one child per couple. Most of them don't have large houses so space is restricted. Now each family is able to purchase whatever they want ensuring the economy survives, which is incredibly important to them, but allows the planet to thrive which is incredibly important to us. Do you understand?' A few murmurs went round the room. 'Are you all happy to continue with the next lesson?'

The six remaining students looked at each other and smiled before shouting, 'Yes!'

'Wonderful. Let's begin – Work,' she stated firmly. The pyramid remained lifeless on the ground. 'Work!' Elder Eridamus said again and a grainy image struggled to emerge from the unit. 'General Rigley!' she said and the kindly face of the General appeared, leaning back in his chair.

'Aahhh, the lovely Elder Eridamus. How wonderful to see you. You've brightened up my day no end. What can I do you for?'

'I'm with my students,' she said, coughing nervously.

The General's eyes widened in alarm and he sat bolt upright, straightening his jacket as he did so. 'Yes, of course you are. I do apologise. Had a bit of paperwork to catch up on.'

'There seems to be a problem with gaining access to the live footage of humans at work.'

'Is there? OK don't worry, I'll sort it. We've been having a few technical issues lately. I'll see what I can do. Back in a jiffy!' The group tittered at hearing a human use one of their funny expressions. A jiffy later and his image returned to the room. 'All sorted. I'm sorry but the footage is pre-recorded. We can't seem to fix the fault – every day at work is pretty much the same so it won't make any difference. As it's not live, you won't be able to use your honing-in techniques. I hope it doesn't spoil your enjoyment.'

The general disappeared and the group watched, wide-eyed, as the holographic image of a city appeared. Humans rushed about on pavements or sat squashed together in train carriages, virtually all of them stared at a mobile phone in their hands and wore masks. Driverless cars glided soundlessly along the streets, dropping off their clients at the office doors. Trams noiselessly travelled up and down the centre of the roads, picking up and dropping off humans at various destinations. Automated food outlets served 'Vegan Bacon Butties – meat options available' by stationary human-looking robots. As the clocks flipped over to read 08:55 virtually all of the people disappeared into the huge office blocks leaving the streets practically dead.

The fledglings followed them as the masses passed through facial recognition stations, removing their masks as they did so, then replaced their masks as they crammed into various lifts that glided noiselessly up the sides of the office blocks, stopping at each floor and spitting a few workers out, before continuing further up the building. Each human knew exactly where to go and were sat at their own desks as the clocks flipped noisily over to read 09:00.

Almost immediately, phones started to ring and a constant pinging could be heard as emails or text messages came through on their computers and phones. Half of the humans had a headset which they spoke into, talking so quickly Star couldn't make out a word they were saying. The other half sat with their heads bent, typing frantically into their computer. They remained like this for most of the morning.

Eridamus stifled a yawn and used her finger to flick through the images which wound forwards at a frantic pace. She pointed her finger in the air as if punching a full stop and the picture stopped and the image came to life again. The clock read 11.15 and a tall dark-haired man, wearing a red shirt, swaggered down the corridor and pushed a door open that said STAFFROOM.

'That's the guy I saw!' Lacarta shouted.

'Sshhhhh,' Eridamus said, putting a finger to her pursed lips.

'But!'

'I know,' she mouthed, winking at him.

They watched as another man got up from his desk and followed him. As he walked past the row of desks a girl looked up and smiled at him but he didn't see her. She followed him with her eyes until he got to the staffroom then turned back to her screen, a disappointed look on her face. The minute she'd turned her back on him he glanced back at her. Seeing the back of her head, he shrugged then opened the door to the staffroom.

'They like each other!' Star thought. Something about him seemed different to the others. His suit looked unnatural on him and his eyes were the most piercing blue eyes she'd seen on a human. A few moments later he re-appeared from the staffroom with a mug of tea in his hands. As he walked up to the girl, he stopped and placed it on her desk. Her cheeks reddened slightly as she said thanks, wrapped her hands around the cup and followed him with her eyes as he returned to his desk. As he sat down, he turned and they caught each other's eyes and smiled.

When the clocks flicked over to read 13:00 everyone took their headsets off and headed to the lift. Once outside, the streets became alive again. Bright neon signs described what food was on offer, Best Kebabs, Best Burgers, Best Hot Dogs, Best Ice Cream Ever, they declared. Underneath each one said, Meat options available, please ask. Humans sat in the park, their masks underneath their chins, chatting and eating their lunches, others sat on benches on their phones, and joggers ran around the outer limits of the park. Before long they gathered their things and returned to their offices just as the clocks read 14:00. Star scanned the room for the couple she'd spotted earlier but both had their heads down, engrossed in their work. A quick fifteen-minute break broke up the afternoon, during which everyone filed to the unisex toilets, then grabbed a drink of water before returning to their desks. When the clocks flicked over to read 17:00 Star saw the man leap up from his desk and almost run to the lift. The girl was there with another man who had one arm placed protectively around her and was gesturing angrily with the other to leave them alone. Star was desperate to find out what had changed between them since that morning but the holographic image flickered before being sucked back into the pyramid, plunging the room back into darkness. Elder Eridamus opened the door and led them back to the main hut. She got the students to sit cross-legged and asked them all to shut their eyes, inhale and exhale until all the stresses of the city had left their bodies.

'Is this really the best it can be for humans?' Lacarta asked.

'Not at all!' she exclaimed. 'Life could be absolutely wonderful as soon as they stop protecting the economy and start developing their own inner spirit. Many are rejecting their modern apartments and all their "things" for a simpler life in the woods which is very encouraging! I long for the day when they look up from their desks and realise that most of their colleagues have left. I'm hopeful that'll happen in my lifetime.'

'But what would happen to the companies they work for? Surely there'd be chaos if less and less people turned up for work?'

Eridamus shook her head vigorously. 'Not at all! How should I put this?' She paused for a moment, her finger on her chin and her arms crossed, 'Every phone call they answer, every email they receive, every text message that pops up in their phone are all pre-programmed. They're answering computer-generated enquiries, complaints or sales. They believe they're dealing with a fellow human but in reality, they're replying to a computer.'

The class gasped in shock.

'You mean they aren't actually doing anything constructive?' said Alhena.

'No! But they all believe they're contributing to the economy which is so important to them.'

'But that's lunacy!' Star said.

'Fantastic, Star! Well done for bringing in your ancient astrology knowledge! It is indeed lunacy in action,' the Elder agreed. 'The thing is, money's only typed into a computer so it's totally meaningless. No one deals with cash like they used to. Of course, there are some jobs that are real: food continues to be packaged up and distributed, water companies have a huge job to do as no one is allowed to store their own, as well as a few factories for the clothes and gadgets that continue to be made – though they do have strict upcycling and recycling laws to adhere to. However, that still leaves an awful lot of humans with nothing to do so this is the perfect way of keeping them occupied. They believe they have to work in jobs like this in order to be fulfilled.' The group sat in stunned silence. 'Tell you what, let's have a break. You've absorbed a lot of information. Take some time to reflect. Find a tree to meditate under or talk to your friends and return here when the sun is at its highest.'

The subdued group walked quietly out of the Centre of Learning. Every lesson of Human Studies seemed to get more complicated. For some it was proving hard to work out whether it was worth studying humans who, it turned out, had no idea that all their hard work was utterly meaningless.

CHAPTER FIFTY-ONE

AFTER FIVE MONTHS OF LIVING in the forest Mary could barely reconcile the new her with the old one who'd loved all her home comforts. Every day Orion would climb to the top of the trees, his bare feet propelling him upwards. He'd leap from branch to branch, showering Mary with the fruits or nuts growing from them.

Their days were spent with Leo and the other wood dwellers helping to build the tunnel. Thankfully, Leo had altered the shift patterns ensuring Mary hardly ever saw Russ. They became valued members of the team and well-liked by everyone.

As they got to know more people, they found out that some of the men and women lived by themselves in houses they'd built using wood and soil. Others preferred living in a group since it gave them the community they'd longed for but lacked in the city. Often that group had helped build the houses, ensuring each couple or family got a suitably sized house for their needs.

Leo's happiness was increasing by the day. He'd been observing Star and Meisa in his sequente and heard Star tell her mother that she was looking forwards to studying humans. 'Won't be long now!' he said to Orion, clapping him on the back. 'With the numbers we've got working on the tunnel we're way ahead of schedule. It should give me time to do a few practise runs, get to know the tunnels and work out how to get to the space compound. We're going home, Orion. I can feel it in my bones!' he said, beaming.

'Leo, it's only you going home, not me. I'm just helping you get there, that's all,' Orion said, noticing the worried look on Mary's face. 'My life is here,' he said, putting his arm round her.

Leo raised his eyebrows and continued with his work.

The tunnel was so close to being finished and the team were working flat out to complete it. Some were sleeping there too; it had become a passion that was all-consuming and food supplies were brought in daily to keep their energy levels up.

'I'm coming to see you, Star,

I won't need a car.

When I see Meisa,

I'm going to kiss her!' Leo sang at the top of his lungs.

His excitement was infectious and gave the group a boost for the final slog.

Mary and Orion continued transporting rocks from the tunnel to the woods but with so many rocks to scatter, finding the right places to put them was proving hard especially at the quickening pace of the men digging.

'Let's go this way for a change,' Leo said one day, pointing downstream. The sun was shining and the cool water looked incredibly tempting after working in the midday heat.

'Aren't we meant to stay upstream?' Mary asked.

'Where's your sense of adventure?' he laughed.

They slung the heavy bags, laden with rocks, over their shoulders, their brows covered in sweat. Mary dipped her feet in the water and sighed in delight as they were immersed by the cool, twinkling water. Orion took Mary's hand and paddled in the shallow water at the river's edge. He bent down and splashed some water over Mary making her cry out in shock. 'Wasn't me!' Orion laughed.

'Who was it then?' she said, laughing back.

'Your guess is as good as mine,' he grinned.

The gentle swooshing noise of a flock of birds flying overhead distracted them and they stood and watched them sweep and swirl above them.

'It's so beautiful here,' Mary said. A fish darted between her feet and nibbled at her ankles making her jump in fright. 'It just bit me!' she cried, watching two tiny dots of blood appear on her ankle.

Orion took her hand. 'Just giving you a little nibble, see if you're tasty enough,' he laughed, wading deeper into the cool water. The river began to widen and the current was stronger, making it harder for them to walk.

'Do you think we should go back?' she asked.

Orion nodded. 'Here's fine to unload,' he said, lowering the bag into the water and taking out the rocks.

As Mary went to swing the bag round, she slipped, letting go of the bag at the same time. Without the added weight from the rocks the strong current dragged Mary downstream before Orion could reach out to grab her. Had she held onto the bag she may not have drifted so quickly but she'd have plenty of time to relive that moment over and over in her head.

Orion abandoned his bag and waded out towards her as she tried to swim against the force of the water. 'Take my hand!' he said, reaching out for her.

'I can't!' she shouted as she drifted further downstream. 'It's too strong!'

Orion dived under the water and swam towards her but the current was gaining strength as the river grew wider. 'Grab onto that branch!' he called out to her.

'What branch?' Mary said, turning around.

'That one!' Orion shouted but it was too late. She hurtled face first into the branch, yelling out in shock. Her hair got tangled up in the branches and leaves, delaying her momentarily. Mary's spluttered and gasped for air. Her hair covered her face but she reached out and blindly grabbed at the branch before disappearing underwater. 'Mary!' Orion called out. Her bedraggled head emerged, clutching onto the branch with all her might as the river clawed at her, beckoning her to carry on their game. Orion let the current push him towards her and grabbed at her waist. 'Let's get you out of here,' he said breathlessly. With her arms wrapped around his neck Orion swam back to the safety of the shore where they sat catching their breath.

'Put your hands in the air!' a voice said. Standing on a boat two yards from where they sat were two police officers. One held a gun pointed directly at them; the other was hastily fastening a rope around a low-hanging branch, securing the boat.

Orion and Mary froze.

At that exact moment an otter poked his head up by the boat.

'Holy cow!' the officer holding the rope said, nearly falling backwards as he spoke.

Orion chose that second to pull Mary to her feet and push her behind a tree. A shot rang out but it wasn't even close.

'You bloody idiot, Carl!' they heard one of the men say.

'It was that ruddy otter!' the other said.

'Wasn't she a beaut?' Carl said, whistling in admiration.

'Sure was. Told you getting posted here was the best shift.'

A robotic voice came from the boat, 'Weapon activated. Explanation required.'

'Wood-dwellers spotted, now disappeared into forest.'

There was a click then a human voice screeched, 'Get after them immediately! We've got your location; reinforcements will be with you shortly.' The voice cut out and the officer scowled at his colleague.

'Why the hell did you have to fire at them, Dean?' Carl asked.

'You know they monitor every shot. Once they've found them there'll be no need for us to be out here. We'll be back at our desks in that pokey, windowless office in no time.'

'Sorry,' Dean said sheepishly. 'It was an accident.'

Carl tutted. 'You line yourself up for a summer of sun and fishing and you go and spoil it two days in. Should never've requested for you to come on this shift.'

'Why don't we make out we saw loads of them. They'll give us weeks to find them,' Dean offered.

Carl shook his head. 'Too late for that. The military will be involved now; we won't get a look in. What a plonker,' he said, tutting. 'Come on, better look like we want to catch these poor beggars. Can't see what harm they do living here, if you ask me – not that anyone ever does.' The two police officers tied the boat to the tree and ran into the woods after Orion and Mary.

'What have we done?' Mary gasped as they leapt from branch to branch back towards the tunnel, her arms gripped tightly round Orion's neck.

As soon as they got there, they ran over to the first workman they saw, a friend of theirs called Harry, and explained that police were on their way into the woods.

'How the hell did they find out?' Harry said as he quickly gathered his tools.

Mary looked at her feet.

'I slipped in the water; they must've heard the splash,' Orion said before she could object.

'You should never have been in the water, bloody fools. You've spoilt everything, you two,' he said, jabbing his finger at them. 'Go, before anyone catches you. It won't just be the military that'll be after you when everyone finds out who's responsible for this. Just think yourself lucky I've got to save my own skin. If not, I'd be wringing your necks with my own bare hands,' he growled.

'Is Leo in there?' Orion asked quickly.

'I don't know. I think so. The men inside won't get discovered – so long as they stay there. Now get the hell out of here!' he said and ran as fast as he could away from them.

Orion grabbed Mary round the waist and jumped up into the trees, leaping from branch to branch as far away from the tunnel as possible. They headed back to the village where word had already spread. People were grabbing their belongings, destroying as much evidence as possible of anyone living there and running deep into the woods.

'Summer! River!' Mary called out. The couple turned to them, their faces clouded in anger and hurt. River drew his bow and arrow and pointed it right at them.

'Don't!' shouted Summer. 'We've got enough to worry about.'

'You've spoilt everything,' River spat. 'We were settled here. First time in ages they've not bothered us and now you've come along and ruined everything. If I ever see you again, I'll …'

'I said, leave them!' Summer grabbed her partner and dragged him away.

'On no!' wailed Mary, burying her head in her hands. 'I've messed everything up!'

Spotting a loaf of bread, Orion placed it in a hessian bag along with the few items they'd gathered over the past few months. Mary put her arms around his neck and he leapt up into the trees, clambering high into the branches out of sight, their hearts pounding hard in their chests. Finding a branch large enough to take their weight they sat and kept lookout. Hours later as the black cloak of night enveloped them, they saw the flicker of torchlight far below accompanied by angry voices.

'Wait here,' Orion said to Mary as he quietly descended the tree. Resting on a branch thick with leaves, he watched a group of men walking through the undergrowth. Four at the front wore military uniform. They were followed by two who were handcuffed together. Two men followed behind them, their guns pointed at the two men in front of them. Orion nearly fell off the branch when he realised one of the handcuffed men was Leo. The sudden movement from above made Leo look up. He looked shocked but smiled momentarily. Orion watched as he slowly reached into his pocket with his free hand. He grabbed the sequente and flicked it effortlessly into the air. The gunmen didn't even notice. Orion reached out and grabbed it as it came hurtling past his head. He raced back to Mary and showed her the tiny sphere.

'What good's that to us now?' she cried.

'The sequente holds the last movements of its previous owner,' Orion explained. 'It'll show us what happened to Leo!'

Mary and Orion peered into the globe and watched with horror as the recent events unfolded before their eyes. The original policemen had been pretty hopeless in the woods, making incredibly slow progress. The boat that arrived with reinforcements contained military men who were much more proficient in the ways of the forest. They had quickly picked up that stones which were normally by rivers were dotted about in the woods and returned to the river to find out more. They walked past the cave and poked their heads inside. When they didn't see anything of interest, they turned to continue further upriver. They watched in agony as the sequente showed Leo and a man they knew as Ben put down their tools and begin walking to the entrance of the cave. She could hear them whistling and willed them to be quiet … if only they'd been quiet. The picture returned to the soldiers who heard the noise and turned back to where they'd just been, holding up their guns just as Leo and Ben emerged from the tunnel. The pair slowly raised their arms above their heads, explaining that they'd just been cooling off after a swim. The soldiers handcuffed them together and frogmarched them back upstream to where they were now.

'It doesn't look like they found the tunnel,' she said hopefully.

'What use is the tunnel if they've got Leo?' Orion asked.

'It means all his efforts won't have been in vain. If we can free humans, we can free Leo.'

He put his hand on her cheek and looked into her eyes. 'Ever the optimist. It's why I love you so much,' he said, kissing her.

But Mary hated herself. It was her fault Leo had been caught; she'd ruined everything. She had no idea how she was going to live with herself now she'd put so many lives at jeopardy.

CHAPTER FIFTY-TWO

THE NEXT FEW NIGHTS WERE incredibly tough. Orion was on watch until the dawn light flickered through the trees then Mary would take over so he could sleep. They tried to spend most of their time in the trees, only coming down when they really needed to. Living on their nerves was exhausting. They didn't feel safe anywhere since they knew it wasn't just the military looking for them but the wood dwellers too.

Mary took the fact that they'd caused so much hurt and upset incredibly badly; the guilt ate away at her and she cried herself to sleep every night. Orion could say nothing to console her.

'I don't belong here,' she wailed one night as they sat cuddled up on a branch. 'I'm not brave like the people here. I could've cost people their lives!'

'Mary, it was an accident! How were you to know there were police officers around the corner?'

'I told you we should never have gone that way. Why didn't you listen to me?' She turned to him with tears in her eyes.

'There you go, it's my fault too.'

'So why do I feel so rotten when it doesn't bother you one bit? I can't live with this guilt eating away at me. We've got no one to talk to now and I loved them all!' Mary silently cried into her hands whilst Orion rubbed her back, at a loss as to what else he could say or do. Straightening up and wiping the tears from her cheeks she said, 'I'm going to hand myself into the authorities tomorrow. I'll feel safer with them, anyway. I dread to think what River would do to us if he caught us.'

He grabbed her by the shoulders. 'Mary, this isn't helping. We made a mistake! Yes, we've spoilt everything for so many people here but it's done now. We can't be the only ones who've messed up. We can't go back. If you let this consume you then you'll be no good to either of us.'

'Is that how you feel about me? That I'm no good to you?' she shouted, tears returning to her eyes.

'Stop this, Mary, stop it now!' he said, shaking her. 'I love you! I'd rather be with you than anywhere else in the galaxy. You've got to accept what's happened and move on.' He broke off momentarily, a thought gathering pace in his mind. 'How about we finish what Leo started?'

'What do you mean?'

'How about we get back to the tunnel and finish his dream? That way we turn all this negative energy into something positive!'

Mary stopped crying and wiped her nose with the back of her hand. 'What if there are other villagers already there? What'll happen if they see us?'

'There's only one way to find out, isn't there? Let's go there now, keep watch for a while and if no one emerges it probably means it's been abandoned.'

Orion held Mary round the waist and leapt from tree to tree, heading all the way back the tunnel. Finding a place in the trees that gave them a good view of the entrance they sat and waited. By night fall no one had visited. They climbed down the tree and bathed in the cool, refreshing water. It was the first wash they'd had in days.

They filled their water carriers, foraged some berries and found a large branch in a nearby tree which was big enough for one of them to curl up and sleep while the other kept a lookout. Orion as always took the night shift and Mary took over as it got light.

The next sunrise, as she sat high in the trees, her thoughts drifted to her parents. She'd watched Orion mouth words over and over again when he tried communicating with Star and decided to try the same technique. Did it work with humans too? She focused on her parents and mouthed the words, 'Are you OK? Are you happy for me?' over and over again. A vivid image of her father appeared in her mind. He was sat in his chair talking to her mother and they were laughing. Laughing as if they didn't have a care in the world. Her mother wrapped her arms around her dad's neck and snuggled into him.

'Our girl did it,' she said and kissed Adam on the lips.

'She sure did,' he beamed. 'She's free, just like we always wanted her to be.'

Mary's eyes fluttered open and a heavy weight lifted from her chest. She may have imagined it, may have seen what she wanted to see, but it felt more than that. She looked around the forest as it came alive with the morning sun. The birds chirruped, the leaves rustled, delicate droplets of dew glistened on the leaves. She looked over at Orion as he slept, held her arms out wide and breathed in the clean forest air. No matter what had happened she was free and she was in love. Orion was right, she couldn't let the guilt eat away at her. She needed to do something positive, something that would prove to all the wood dwellers how much she cared. The tunnel had to be completed; they owed it to them and to Leo. She took a swig from her water carrier but it was bone dry. She checked the bottle. It had been full last night. Giving it a good shake, she noticed something glistening on its side. 'Damn it,' she thought, 'that hole wasn't there yesterday.' She looked over to Orion who was lying on his side, his water bottle trapped underneath him. She tried moving it but Orion didn't stir. He hadn't been asleep long; there was no way she wanted to wake him, so she decided to fill her water bottle herself.

She climbed down the tree, marvelling as she always did, that she was able to do things like this so effortlessly. In the city climbing trees was banned for health and safety reasons. The river was so close, she'd be able to see their tree from the bank. She paddled in the sparkling water and scooped some into her hands, drinking the water before it escaped. Water in the city never tasted this good even though it went through some high-tech purification process. This tasted far purer, untampered with.

She knelt down to fill her water bottle and watched the glistening liquid cascade into her carrier. A little fish got caught up in the strong current so she tipped it out, watching as it swam away. Realising she needed to fix the hole first, she walked along the riverbank looking for some clay that Orion had told her was good for sealing leaks.

It didn't take long to find what she was looking for, just where the trees met the riverbank. She knelt down and began smoothing the grey clay onto the outer bottle and placed it in the sun to dry. It wasn't perfect but it would do for the time being. The feeling of the slippery mud between her fingers was glorious and she marvelled again at how much she'd changed. Just then she heard a rustling in the trees. She looked up and saw the rear of a roe deer bounding off into the distance. 'Must have startled her,' she thought. Just then a large, hairy hand covered her mouth and a knife was pressed against her throat.

'Don't make a sound,' the owner of the hand said as he dragged her into the forest and away from the stirring body of the man she loved.

CHAPTER FIFTY-THREE

THE NOISE OF A DEER bounding through the forest woke Orion that morning. He sat up, expecting to see Mary keeping watch but there was no sign of her. A tightness gripped his stomach. He leapt down from the tree and headed to the river, hoping to see her there filling her water carrier or taking a wash but there was no sign of her. His heart pounded and adrenalin coursed through his veins as he searched the river, then jumped from tree to tree willing himself to see a flash of her hair as she wandered through the forest, but it was like she'd disappeared into thin air. Panic rose from deep within him and tears began their descent, blurring his vision as he searched desperately for anything that would prove she was close by, that she hadn't left him. He thought back to their last conversation. They'd had such a positive evening working in the tunnel. She'd said she was going to hand herself into the authorities earlier in the day but he'd persuaded her out of it – hadn't he? His stomach muscles tightened as the possibility that she wasn't coming back took hold. Within an instant he'd transformed into an eagle. He glided gracefully over vast swathes of the forest. Now and again he'd see dwellers he recognised building new shelters but he knew he'd never be able to ask any of them if they'd seen her. He saw Summer and

River building a shelter and heard River muttering about what he'd do if he ever set eyes on those youngsters again. Summer tutted and told him to 'quit your moaning'. He went all the way to the edge of the forest where he could see the high-rise buildings beyond the outer walls. He pictured her walking back into the city and giving herself in to the authorities, her hands above her head as they pointed their guns at her.

By dusk he had no choice but to give up, there was nowhere else to look. He flew back to the tunnel, utterly bereft. Shape-shifting back to his human form he curled into a ball and sobbed huge, wracking sobs. He longed to hold her in his arms, snuggle up to her and breathe in the smell of her hair. He thought of Melantho and pictured the look on his smug face if he could see Orion now. The thought of that vile man ignited a fire in his belly. He had to find Leo, get him home and he had to find Mary too – hear the real reason she left him.

Now he knew the others were settling much further down the river he felt a little safer in the tunnel. He had no idea where life was taking him, but he had to complete Leo's wishes and if Mary came back this would be the first place she'd look. Living in the tunnel and finishing the job was the only thing he could do.

CHAPTER FIFTY-FOUR

'YOU SAY ONE WORD, I'LL kill you,' the man said. 'Understand?'
Mary nodded frantically. He dragged Mary to a tree, sat down with
her back pressed against his chest and removed his hand from over
her mouth. He stuffed a rag in her mouth, wrapped another piece of
cloth over the rag and tied it behind her head. He then pulled her
roughly to her feet and turned her round so she could see him. Her
eyes widened in horror as she discovered that her captor was Russ.
'Lovely young girl like you shouldn't be wandering round these
woods alone. Never know who might be stalking you.' He laughed
crudely at his own joke. 'I'll keep you safe from those nutters,' he
said, jerking his head at the forest. 'They're all after you. You got
lucky a nice guy like me found you.' The way his voice dripped with
sarcasm meant his words offered little comfort.

As if Mary were a bag of feathers, he threw her over his shoulders and strode into the forest. She tried to wriggle free but his
muscled arms meant all her struggling was in vain. She had no
choice but to give up fighting and wait until they stopped. Maybe
then she could reason with him? She'd read about victims of
kidnappers becoming friends with their captors, working out what
made them tick and then appealing to that gentle bit inside of them

that had been shut off for years. Getting to find out more about him, listening to him and making him believe she respected him would be essential if she wanted to get away from this madman.

Finally, they stopped walking and he threw her to the ground. She tried to stand but he pulled on her arm, causing her feet to slip from underneath her. He looked around, made sure there was no one about then lifted a branch, ducked his head down and shoved Mary inside. 'Home sweet home, honey!' he laughed. Mary looked around at the tiny earthen house. There were no windows but small shards of light reached in from the well-camouflaged door made with branches and leaves. A fire smouldered away in the corner and a dead rabbit hung from the ceiling. Bones littered the floor. Russ tipped his water onto the embers and they sizzled frantically. 'Can't have any smoke coming out now I've got guests. Don't want to get caught, do we?' he said, coming closer to Mary, a knife in his hand. He leant over her and stroked her arm. 'Only place we can get any privacy.' A feeling of utter revulsion filled Mary's body and she squirmed from his touch. His face clouded over and he lifted his arm to strike her but then lowered it as if he'd had second thoughts. 'I bet you taste real nice,' he said, licking his lips, exposing empty black spaces where there should have been teeth. She scrunched up her nose and looked away. 'Had that effect on my missus too,' he laughed. He pushed a lock of hair away from her face and traced his finger down her cheek and onto her chin. Mary jerked her head away and shuffled into the corner of the hut. He came closer to her again and reached round the back of her head. 'You scream or shout, and I'll kill you,' He waited for Mary to nod then placed his knife in between his teeth while he untied her.

As soon as the cloth was out, she coughed great hacking coughs, her mouth was so dry. Ross grabbed his carrier, tipped her head back and poured some water down her throat. It sprayed all over her face but some landed in her mouth. Eventually she felt able to speak, though her voice was course and her throat scratchy. 'What do you want from me?' she asked, her eyes wide with terror.

'Revenge.'

'I'm sorry!' she cried. 'I didn't mean to blow your cover. I slipped and fell.'

'Thought it was your boyfriend who slipped? I'll be looking for him next. Where is he?' he said, coming so close to her she could see the black hairs peeping out of his nostrils.

'Leave Leo alone. It was me who slipped.'

'How noble of you, protecting him. Thought it was meant to be the other way round or are you young people too PC for that?'

'I'm not protecting him. We split up – he's long gone.'

'What do you mean, split up? You two was loved up. Just like me and my missus,' he sneered.

'Your wife! Where is she?' Mary asked, relief flooding over. Maybe his wife would come and find them, make sure Russ let her go.

'Dead.' Russ smiled and turned the knife over in his hand, admiring it.

Mary's heart sank. 'I'm so sorry. You must miss her,' she said, trying to appeal to this huge bulk of a man. There had to be something kind in there, no matter how tough he looked.

'Not really. Couldn't stand her going on at me all the time ... yap, yap, yap,' he said, using his hand as a puppet next to his ear.

'It must've been hard when she died though? What did she die of?' she asked, desperate to keep the conversation going.

He pulled the knife up to his mouth and drew it very slowly across his tongue. 'Stupid bitch went and got herself murdered, didn't she?' he grinned. 'That taught her to stop yapping.'

CHAPTER FIFTY-FIVE

'NOW WE'VE HAD OUR FINAL lesson in Human Studies you need to decide whether you want to take Further Human Studies which, as you're all aware, entails a trip to planet Earth. You have to be certain this is your calling and you're not doing it for anyone else.' She looked pointedly at Lacarta and Alhena who avoided her gaze. 'Your loyalty is towards Celestia and your own path, not to any other being. Is that understood?' The group nodded back. 'Sleep on it. Talk to your parents when you get home. Some of them studied humans. They'll be able to help you. Going to planet Earth can, ahem … un-Earth,' and at this point, she let out a little chuckle at her own joke, 'some complex emotions.'

The following sunrise Star woke to hear Elder Eridamus talking to her mother and grandmother outside her hut. Pretending to be asleep she listened in on what they were saying.

'Any word from your lovely boy yet?' Rhea said.

'Nothing yet. He did say it was going to be hard to contact me while he was away.'

'You must be so proud of him,' Meisa said. 'Not many get to go on such important assignments at such a young age!'

'I certainly am,' Eridamus said with a little tension in her voice.

'Enough about me. I'm here because we need to bring the trip to Earth forwards by a few sun rotations.'

'When are you talking about?' Meisa asked.

'Next sunrise.'

The two females gasped in surprise.

Star inwardly gasped too. She reached for the little spoon that lay under her pillow and gazed at the detail on the handle. She wouldn't be able to meet Procyon now! Maybe he'd forget about her completely if he thought she'd stood him up.

'I think she's awake,' Rhea said to the females, sensing Star was listening.

'Elder Eridamus has some news, darling,' Meisa called.

'I heard,' Star said, coming out of the hut. 'We leave next sunrise?'

'That's correct. Weather conditions are changing. We've been advised it's better to travel sooner rather than later. If you decide to take Further Human Studies you won't need to bring much. All food and clothing are provided so just a water carrier and whatever else you'd like to bring for the journey. The craft needs to travel at optimum speeds; any extra weight will slow it down so pack lightly. See you next sunrise, Star – if you decide this is your path.' She waved at them and headed over to Lacarta's hut.

After breakfast Star made her way over to Alhena's where she updated her on what she'd seen in the little dome at the bottom of the riverbed. Alhena gasped in shock upon hearing about the glasses that could have changed Lacarta's life all these orbitals. 'What are we going to do? How on planet Mars are we ever going to persuade him out of taking FHS?'

'Mum went round after we spoke and talked to Sabik and Vega. They're worried but feel he's come too far to turn back. They think he'll resent them if they stop him from going. They're going to try talking to him one more time. The one thing they've asked if he does go is that it's one of us who tells him about the glasses – or Eridamus.'

Alhena nodded. 'I'd really like to, if that's OK?'

'You sure you're alright with that? I really didn't fancy telling him. I'm pretty angry he isn't allowed them, to be honest.'

'After everything we've been taught? You know why we can't take anything from Earth! Where will it stop and will we need to introduce money if we start bringing in things we can't make? How can we possibly barter with something that is so incredibly special?'

'You sound like Mum,' Star said, looking at the ground.

'I'm serious, Star! You've got no reason to be angry. Anyway, has Lacarta ever suffered? As far as I can tell he's excelled because of his bad eyesight.' She folded her arms and stared at Star.

'Not you as well? I get it – his hearing's better, but so what? If you had a choice, wouldn't you have wanted him to see better? You're meant to be his friend!'

'Lacarta is one of the most important beings to me but the welfare of every being here is also important. If we start changing ourselves or judging what we've been given where will it stop?'

Star looked at her friend and smiled cheekily. 'You'll never believe what Mum told me?'

'What?'

Star moved closer to her and whispered, 'Some humans aren't happy with the size of their chests so they get them enlarged!'

'But why would they do that? I think male chests are lovely, especially Lacarta's,' she said with a wistful look in her eye.

Star laughed out loud. 'Not male chests! Female chests!' Alhena looked puzzled for a moment then peered down the front of her dress.

'These?' She looked shocked as it dawned on her.

Star nodded and said, 'Apparently they think bigger ones are better!'

'But how can you run and jump with bigger ones?'

'That's exactly what I said!' laughed Star. She looked at the ground and traced a pattern in the dirt with her big toe. 'I guess I can see why they don't allow anything back here.'

'If I show him them at least I can put it in a way that'll make him understand why they can't come back.'

'He can get mighty stubborn, though, can't he?' Star said and they both smiled.

Up until now Alhena hadn't been sure that she was doing the right thing, following her best friend to Earth. However, that sunrise she made the decision that if Lacarta wasn't going to be persuaded out of taking FHS then she'd be with him every step of the way. She hadn't found her calling yet so taking FHS may well lead her to it. Maybe this was her time to discover if there was something else out there for her. If she didn't study humans now, she'd never get the opportunity again. She looked back at her time on Celestia and the moments that stood out were the ones when she'd helped another being. Her calling was caring for and looking after others, it always had been. Her feelings towards Lacarta made it impossible to leave him.

CHAPTER FIFTY-SIX

ORION HAD BEEN LIVING IN the tunnel for two weeks. He'd collected some moss and leaves to use as bedding but they offered little comfort from the cold, hard floor.

'Evening!' Veruna said, appearing from nowhere, Tabitha at this side.

'Got you some lovely big walnuts,' she said, slinging her heavy bag in front of Orion's feet. 'Ooooh, and some nice juicy apples. And look at this!' she said, holding up a lovely shiny blackberry. 'Veruna's got more, haven't you?'

'Certainly have. Got to keep our boy's strength up, haven't we?' he said with a chuckle.

'He's not our boy!' Tabitha said. As an aside she said to Orion, 'He's desperate for children. Seems to think of you as our adopted son!'

'We make a very unusual looking family, don't we?' Orion laughed.

'Is it time yet?' Veruna asked excitedly.

Tabitha clasped her hands in prayer and closed her eyes. 'Please say yes. Please say yes. Please say yes,' she repeated.

'Go on, then,' Orion said, digging into his bag.

'Yesss!!!' they both squealed in delight.

Orion got the sequente out and placed it on a large stone in front of them. Veruna grabbed a bit of moss and puffed it up, placing it behind Tabitha's back which she wriggled against until she was comfortable. Veruna sat down next to her, putting his arm protectively round her shoulders.

'Ready?' Orion asked.

'Water?' Tabitha said, searching round looking for her carrier which Veruna waggled in front of her face. 'Nuts?' He got out a few walnuts from his bag and placed them in front of her. 'Crackers?' He pulled out a stone and placed it next to the nut. 'Aannnnnddddd …' she said, dragging it out.

'For crying out loud, what else do you want?' Veruna shouted.

'A kiss,' she said, puckering up her tiny little lips.

Veruna's face softened as he gave Tabitha a delicate kiss.

'Ready now?' Orion laughed.

'Ready,' Tabitha said contentedly as she leant her head on Veruna's shoulder.

Orion placed the sequente on the floor and they all peered closer to watch Eridamus wander round the forest full of rich greens and browns. A brightly coloured creature flew by her side. They sat transfixed as his mother lay on the ground, gazing up at the sky then bathed in the waterfall to cool off. This was their favourite part of the day and Tabitha in particular loved looking at the tiny images of this glorious-looking race. After a while Veruna began to snore so Tabitha gave him a jab in the ribs.

'Sorry, love!' he said, waking up with a jolt.

'I think it's time you two went,' Orion said kindly.

They packed up their things, gave him a little wave and with a click of their fingers disappeared to their homes somewhere beneath him.

Just then he heard voices echoing around the cave. He crawled down the tunnel and saw a group of three men sat round a fire, chatting.

'Can't believe we made it out,' one of them said breathlessly. 'Thank god Robert gave us this map.' he said, folding a tattered bit of paper and placing it into his bag.

Orion's eyes widened. Robert was alive!

'You'd never think he was related to Melantho, would you? The two couldn't get more different,' an orange-haired man said.

'Gives you hope, doesn't it? That the next generation are waking up. Surely, they can see it now. Melantho's a psychopath. He's slipping up. He's going to be the downfall of the whole operation. Humans will never be able to justify being under such heavy surveillance now they see what it was really set up for and not for "your protection",' he said, putting on an authoritarian voice.

One of the men shook his head. 'I wish I shared your optimism. That darned machine is so effective – using all those channels to programme them. Am I glad all the other planets banned televisions.'

'Yes but 21 million less mobile phone users now, Hengha. That's got to give you hope?'

'I'm sorry, Adhil, when you've witnessed what I have it's hard to feel optimistic.'

The third man reached across and patted Hengha on the back. 'It's over now, mate. We're away from that place. We're free.'

'But they aren't, are they?'

The men shook their heads despondently.

'That one from Celestia, you know – Leo,' Hengha said and the other two nodded. 'Melantho's got it in for him. He's in a really bad way, said he'd given up all hope of ever seeing his life partner and daughter again. I wish I could've helped him but there was nothing I could do.' He buried his head in his hands.

'You did what you could. He's still alive, isn't he?' Adhil asked.

The man nodded.

'There you go. He would've been long gone if you hadn't been there giving him food and water, trying to make sure Melantho didn't get much time alone with him. You got any idea what he's got against him, Jatropha?'

'Who knows. We mustn't give up though. Melantho's got no idea how clever some of us are,' Jatropha said.

Hengha tutted. 'As if a human like that could out smart our race.'

'But he's still got a hold over us; we're stuck here after all. While we've got these things under our skin, we're essentially helpless,' Adhil said, pinching at his wrist.

'Hengha, think you can get these out?' Jatropha asked.

Hengha shook his head. 'I've been trying for weeks now. I don't get why they're putting them in all of us.'

Jatropha laughed. 'You serious? They're taking our powers away! Think of the numbers of beings they've put these implants in!'

Adhil continued, 'With us out of their way they'll be able to control the galaxy. We won't be able to use any of our powers against them.'

'We have to get these things out. I hate it; it's like I'm not really me.' Hengha withdrew a knife and slowly cut into his skin. He took an intake of breath but continued pushing the blade deeper into his arm.

'Hengha!' they both cried but neither tried to stop him.

Hengha grimaced. 'I'm nearly there.' Just then a small rectangle glowed red underneath his skin. 'I've got you,' he said, focusing on the glowing light.

The two other men sat transfixed.

Hengha was just about to flick it out when the light moved further up his arm, as if alive. 'Damn you!' he yelled, throwing the knife to the ground.

Adhil reached out and touched his arm. 'You'll get it.'

'I want it out of me,' Hengha growled.

'We all do,' Adhil replied.

'Think of the chaos we'll create if we can get these things out of us,' Hengha said with a chuckle.

Jatropha laughed too. 'One day. Night, guys, and well done for today. Never thought we'd be sat chatting like this tonight.' He lay down on the floor, using his bag for a pillow. The others did the same and before long all three were fast asleep.

Orion felt a flicker of hope in his heart for the first time since Mary had left. Robert and Leo were both alive! He couldn't wait to tell Tabitha and Veruna. Tomorrow the tunnel was going to be finished and he'd have access to the network of tunnels underneath the city. If these beings had found a way out of the compound then he'd find a way in. As they slept, he crept over to where they lay, reached into Hengha's bag and eased out the map. He hurried back to his cramped tunnel and used his index finger to shine a light on it. He nearly punched the air in delight. The title of the map read, 'Underground Tunnel System.'

The next day Orion chipped away until instead of hard, solid rock, his axe glided effortlessly into thin air. He chipped with his axe and scrambled and clambered at the rock with his fingers until he'd created a hole big enough for him to crawl though. The tunnel was so different to the one he'd been living in. A smooth concrete cylinder with plenty of room to stand up. Somehow, he had to work out whereabouts he was in relation to the map. The only way of doing that was to walk up and down the tunnels until he'd worked out the pattern and matched it up to the map. It was going to be a painstaking task but there was no other choice. He grabbed his water carrier and began walking. That night he'd try and find Mary but for now, going to see Leo every evening was as much as his body could take.

Hours later, his legs aching from all the walking, he sat munching on some nuts the pixies had left him. He reached for the sequente, placed it in the palm of his hand and watched as the picture of his mother emerged. In a flash, Talitha and Veruna appeared at his side.

'You starting without us?' she said angrily.

'I was just about to call for you.' Orion told them both about what he'd overheard the previous night.

'Poor Leo. What have they done to him?' Talitha said sadly.

Orion placed the globe on the floor and all of them gathered round to watch the reassuring images appear of Celestia. A picture of Eridamus emerged with a row of students in front of her.

'There's Star!' Orion pointed at the long pink hair of one of the students listening intently to her elder. They heard Eridamus explaining to the small group that the next lesson entailed a trip to Earth and to think carefully before committing to it.

The next day Orion stretched out his index finger to light up the tunnel and began another day of walking the network of tunnels. It hadn't been too hard to make sense of the map. There were a number of ladders that led to manholes which were also marked on the piece of paper. When he could tell the street above was quiet, he poked his head up from one of them and nearly cried in jubilation when he saw the building he'd worked in. There was a strong possibility they'd use that office for the fledgling's day of work experience. He then walked the length of that tunnel trying to retrace his footsteps, as if on the street above, from the office to the train station. As the rumble of the trains grew increasingly louder, he knew he was on the right tracks. By the end of the day he had a better idea of the layout, but he was glad he had time to have a couple of practise runs before they came to Earth – there was going to be no room for mistakes.

When he returned to his bed that night, he pulled out the sequente and placed it on the rock in front of him – "the sequente stand" they had begun calling it. Veruna and Talitha appeared at his side with a few fresh plums, some nuts and more water.

As they watched the images from Celestia, Tabitha got comfy with the help of Veruna and her cushion made of moss. 'Pass me the nuts,' Tabitha said, holding out her hand. Veruna grabbed one from Orion's pile, giving him a sheepish look as he did so.

'Weren't they for me?' Orion asked but he couldn't bring himself to be angry at these tiny little friends of his. Instead he sank his teeth into a plum and leant against the tunnel wall, the pixies either side of him. Seconds later the plum came flying out of his mouth as he heard Elder Eridamus say that Further Human Studies had been brought forwards and was starting the very next sunrise.

CHAPTER FIFTY-SEVEN

THE SUN ROSE OVER THE treetops and the sounds of the forest echoed around the village. The ghuafa's chirped and cawed, hunicha squealed and yelped and the parnictas yawned, one eye opening then closing as it began its lengthy wake-up ritual. Cornichis darted about the treetops spreading the news that it was the day the fledglings were going to planet Earth.

Meisa watched Star leap out of bed, putting on her favourite hemp dress, the one she'd been saving for this day. She looked at her wonderful, passionate daughter who had all the drive and morals of her father.

'I know Dad's alive, Mum. I just know it. He's been coming to me in my dreams. He keeps telling me he's so close to me, that he's so proud of me.'

'He's been coming to me too but it's like he's stuck somewhere. He's calling for me, reaching for me but I can't get close to him. I haven't told you 'cause I didn't want to upset you.' She took her daughter's hands in hers. 'Be careful, darling. I couldn't bear it if something happened to you as well.'

Star looked into her mother's eyes. 'I'm going to find him.' She wrapped her arms around her mother's neck. 'I love you.'

'I love you too.'

After sitting quietly with her grandmother and mother whilst they had their gisenfa tea, Star gathered together the few items she was taking to planet Earth. She lifted her pillow and found the ornate spoon Procyon had given her, wrapped it up in a piece of bamboo and placed it in her bag. Slinging the bag over her shoulder she waved goodbye to her family and did an inwards, 'Yessss!' when she spotted Lacarta and Alhena standing outside the Centre of Learning. They beamed at her when she arrived. None of the other students who'd attended the previous lesson emerged. It was just going to be the three of them.

Elder Eridamus had barely slept either, which was most unlike her. She felt as eager as the students to get there but for very different reasons. Finally, she'd be able to talk in private to Rigley, find out exactly what he knew and how they could free Leo and hopefully find her son and bring him home.

'My wonderful fledglings, it's finally here – your chance to travel to planet Earth. The journey's going to take two sun rises – a day in human terms. We'll have seven nights in human times there before arriving home in fourteen sunrises. You'll have the opportunity to mix freely with them, though you'll be watched at all times – for your own safety. Humans have a fascination with Extra Terrestrials, as they call us. Space travel is kept top secret but there are always some that are determined to expose us and who knows what they'd do with us if they found out we were aliens.'

'But that's why learning to shape-shift would have been so helpful to us!' Star said. 'We'd be able to escape from anyone who caught us.'

'Of course, but you are also far more likely to reveal yourselves once you've been taught how to shape-shift.'

'How fast can we really be, though? I still think it's better to learn it before we go,' Lacarta said huffily.

'Shape-shifting works better when your body is running on adrenalin – when your fight or flight instinct has kicked in. While you are on Earth your bodies will be filled with adrenalin, making it incredibly easy for you to transform into any animal. Your father, in particular, Star, was incredibly skilled at it, transforming into any animal before you could click your fingers.'

'So what? Other humans would never believe them if they said they'd seen someone transform from a human to an animal,' Alhena said.

Eridamus laughed. 'You're forgetting that every human carries their mobile phone at all times. They'll have a picture of your transformation plastered over social media within seconds.'

The three of them nodded slowly as the implications dawned on them.

'I know it's disappointing for you but once you get back, you'll be able to learn it. Just not now, that's all. You still want to go ahead or would you rather stay and learn shape-shifting?'

Lacarta looked at Star and Alhena and raised his eyebrow questioningly.

Star shook her head. 'No, I definitely still want to go. I won't get this opportunity again but I'll always be able to learn shape-shifting.'

'What about you two?' Eridamus asked.

'I'm the same as Star,' Alhena said. 'I'm desperate to learn how to shape-shift but I've come too far to turn back now.'

'You can always turn back,' Eridamus said. 'What is your heart saying?'

Alhena shook her head and looked at the floor. 'I don't know anymore! I can't read it. I think it's telling me to go to Earth but maybe that's my head talking? How am I meant to work out which one it is?' she said, pressing her fingertips on the side of her forehead and making small circular movements.

Eridamus put her hand on Alhena's back. 'Maybe this isn't for you? If you're so confused, I think your heart is telling you something but you're not listening?'

'Well, I'm still going,' Lacarta said and Star reached for his hand and squeezed it.

Alhena watched this small intimate gesture and felt a small stab in her stomach. 'Me too,' she said, quickly recovering.

'Are you sure this is what you want?' Eridamus asked.

Alhena sniffed, 'Definitely. I am listening to my heart and my heart knows I have to go too.'

'It's your decision,' Eridamus said, moving away from her. 'I can only guide you. It looks like we're all going to planet Earth, then.'

They gathered into the Centre of Learning and sat cross-legged whilst she ran through the safety aspects of being on the craft such as staying seated as they left Celestia's stratosphere and when they entered the Earth's. Once the craft was through them, they'd be able to walk about. Eridamus then explained that when they landed on Earth, they'd arrive at the space compound which would be their base during their time there. Driverless trains would take them to the outer parts of the city where they'd be able to join real live humans. There was a chance they'd also be able to have a day in an office block or visit a school.

'How are we going to go unnoticed? We look so different to humans; they'll spot us instantly,' Alhena asked.

'This is where things get interesting. As you know, Celestia runs on higher vibrations than Earth. As you enter the Earth's stratosphere your bodies will undergo various shifts; your bodies will elongate and become plumper. Your noses will become a little longer, your ears more rounded, your beautiful colourings will fade and your markings will disappear. Your hair will change to the colour of human hair. Once you're fully transformed you can get dressed into standard human clothes.'

The fledglings looked at each other with a mixture of excitement and terror etched on their faces. 'We're kind of shape-shifting after all!' Lacarta said.

Eridamus nodded. 'Exactly. Not many get to shape-shift into humans either! I shouldn't really say so myself but,' here Elder Eridamus coughed gently into her curled-up hand with a smile on her lips, 'I make quite an attractive one.'

'I wonder what Lacarta will look like?' Alhena asked dreamily. 'No doubt just as handsome as he is here.' She looked around the hut. Had she said that out loud? Seeing her friends' wide eyes, she realised she had and instantly looked down wanting the ground to envelop her immediately.

Lacarta looked at Alhena and smiled back at her wondering exactly the same – how would he look like as a human?

'You can have lunch here,' Eridamus said, returning to the moment in hand. 'Tuck in. The food on Earth will make you feel bloated, lethargic and heavy. Toxin-free food isn't available so you'll have to eat it and de-tox when you get back. We've still yet to master transporting our food there without it turning rock hard. I'll see you back here after you've said your farewells to your families. It's an emotional time for them.' Elder Eridamus looked at her excited students. She sighed and hoped this was going to turn out all right. In all the orbitals she'd taught FHS she'd never had such a tight-knit group and she'd never flown into such uncertain territory either.

After lunch, during which they gorged themselves on kiwi fruits, nectarines, mangos, almonds, hazelnuts, jack fruit and dates, the group were able to return to their huts to say a final farewell to their families.

Meisa hugged her daughter with all her might and wished her luck. 'I'm going to miss you.'

'I'm going to miss you, too.' Star closed her eyes and hugged her mother back. 'I'm going to find him, Mum.'

'I know.'

'More importantly, enjoy every minute of it,' her granny inter-jected.

Star turned to Rhea and beckoned for her to come over and join the two of them in their hug. Tears trickled down Rhea's face and onto Star's hair, making Meisa cry too. Eventually Star pulled away and returned to the Centre of Learning, waving but not daring to turn around in case she burst into tears too.

Over at Lacarta's hut, Vega was in floods of tears at the thought of being separated from her son.

'I'm going to be fine, Mum! I've got Star with me!' he said.

'And Alhena,' his father said pointedly.

'Yeah, and Alhena. We'll be fine, I promise. Please don't cry!' he pleaded gently, putting his arm around her.

'I know you will,' she said between great big hacking sobs. 'I've just never been apart from you for more than one sun rotation.'

Lacarta leant over and gave his mum a hug. 'I love you, Mum.'

'I love you too – my wonderful son,' she said, clutching at his neck. 'I'm so proud of everything you've achieved.' She released her grip and tried to pull herself together. 'Now, go and enjoy the trip to Earth but be safe and don't let Star lead you astray!' she said, hoping she sounded a little lighter than she felt.

Lacarta's sisters and father came and hugged him one by one, offering words of love and advice. Sabik held his son's head in his hands and gazed into his eyes. 'I love you, son,' he said, giving him a kiss.

'I love you too, Dad,' he replied. He waved his family goodbye and headed back to the Centre of Learning.

Alhena's father, Hamal, stood watching his daughter with tears in his eyes while she did some last-minute tidying of her area of the hut, ready for her return. Words always failed him at times like these. Each one of her family came and hugged her before she headed off back to the Centre of Learning. She turned and waved, blowing them all a kiss as they waved back from their hut.

Elder Eridamus watched the three fledglings walk towards the Centre of Learning for their final journey and guided them into the small dark room in the woods. She placed the pyramid on the floor and said, 'Flight deck three'.

An image shot out of the pyramid and a striking female came into view. She had a clean-cut, straight black bob and pale green eyes. The markings on her face swept delicately around her eyes and cheeks then snaked down her neck and onto her upper arms.

'Ready for lift-off, Mirienne?'

'Ready and waiting, Eridamus. A little earlier than planned, too! You like to keep us on our toes. We've had confirmation that weather conditions are good. Once you've spoken to General Rigley, we're off.'

The image disappeared and Elder Eridamus uttered the words she looked forwards to saying every sun cycle, 'Celestian students embarking on Further Human Studies. Is Earth ready for their arrival in twenty-four hours' time?'

His familiar image came to life in front of her.

'Affirmative, Elder Eridamus,' he said, smiling at her and turning to see the fledglings.

'Congratulations, Star, Lacarta and Alhena on deciding to take Further Human Studies. We can't wait to meet you.' He gave a nod to the group, then disappeared.

'Let's go and board the craft,' Eridamus said to them.

The three looked at each other, each one bursting with anticipation.

Elder Eridamus turned to the side of the hut, pressed a hidden lever in the wall and a very well-concealed door opened up in the floor just near to where they stood. A dirty head with a mass of thick, brown curls poked up into the hut, beaming at them all.

'Hi, guys. My name's Altair! I'll be taking you to your craft. Take it steady coming down here! Once you get past these steps you'll enter a well-lit tunnel.'

Elder Eridamus beckoned for the group to start making their descent, ensuring that Lacarta wasn't the first one and that she was the last. A few steps down she leant into the wall and fumbled around until she found what she was after. She pulled on a lever and the door above her shut, leaving the room in silence once more.

'Only a few more steps,' the friendly-faced Altair called out.

The students followed, holding tightly onto the ladder. As they reached the bottom rung a low humming noise could be heard in the distance.

'Hold on to the rail here. Not long till we reach the craft now,' he called out. They scrambled around in the dark until they felt a cold hard rail. The darkness was replaced by artificial dull orange lighting and the low humming noise grew steadily louder as they walked along the tunnel. A light in the distance grew brighter and brighter until they reached the end of the tunnel which then opened up into a huge concourse where three dome-shaped spacecraft with saucer-like bases hovered. The place was alive with beings hastily rushing here and there.

'Holy Demeter!' Star said. 'What is all this?'

'Are they our craft?' Lacarta asked, squinting his eyes to try and see better.

'Lacarta, they're incredible!' Star took an intake of breath.

'It's the most mind-blowing thing I've ever seen in my entire life,' Alhena said to Lacarta. 'They're round and silver with tiny blue lights going all the way around the base of them. They're hovering in mid-air!' she cried and clapped her hands in delight.

The noises in the hangar were like nothing any of them had ever experienced before. Metal screeched, drills whirred, moving objects beeped and the craft gently hummed as they hovered above the ground.

'Stay close – we don't want to get in any being's way. It's very stressful getting the crafts ready. The one you'll be on is over there,' Altair said, pointing at the central one.

Star looked at her friends' faces, open-mouthed in awe, and knew they'd made the right decision to take Further Human Studies. This was, without a doubt, the greatest day of their whole lives.

CHAPTER FIFTY-EIGHT

ALTAIR WALKED WITH HIS HEAD held high across the concourse, stopping underneath the central spaceship. 'Welcome to your craft,' he said, bowing slightly and gesturing with his hand for them to board. As he did so a set of silver stairs appeared as if from nowhere, leading up to a small hatch in the bottom of the craft. 'Have an incredible time!'

They looked up as the hatch glided open and the female they'd seen earlier as a holographic image waved down at them.

'Welcome to Craft 612, fledglings. I'll be your pilot for both journeys. This wonderful machine has served me well over the years but that's due to the fact I respect it and treat it well. I expect you to do the same. I can see you're all desperate to get there so come on up. Find yourselves a seat and enjoy the ride. It will be utterly mesmerising.' Elder Mirienne stood aside as one by one they reached the top of the steps and she welcomed each of them onto the craft.

Star looked at Lacarta and Alhena who smiled back at her, their eyes wide and bright, just like hers. She tried to take in every detail of the craft and Elder Mirienne but there was so much to absorb. Their pilot exuded an air of warmth combined with great intellect.

Star instantly felt in awe.

Inside, the craft felt a lot smaller than it looked from the outside but there was still plenty to take in. A soft pale-blue light came from the outer edges of the floor and ceiling. The floor was a very pale grey and their feet sunk into the unusual material as they walked towards the small row of white seats. At the very front of the craft were two larger white chairs which faced a large silver screen and a panel that covered the front of the craft with various dials, buttons and handles.

'Can you believe this?' Star said, trying hard to keep her emotions under control.

'It's totally awesome!' Alhena said, stroking the fabric of the chairs. 'Have you ever felt anything so soft before?' She laughed at the pure joy of touching something so foreign to her.

Lacarta grabbed a hand of both girls and squeezed them in excitement. Just then they heard a faint hissing noise as the stairs disappeared as if by magic into the base of the craft and the hatch doors closed.

'We're travelling in convoy today,' whispered Mirienne to Eridamus as they walked to their seats.

Eridamus looked at her in alarm.

'They want to make sure we get there safely. Something strange is going on.' Mirienne sat down and spun her chair round to face the three eager students. 'Enjoy the flight, everyone. Get some sleep if you can. I know it's going to be awesome going to space for the first time but you do need your rest. Your studies are incredibly important.'

Elder Eridamus and Elder Mirienne pressed a button on their chairs and they spun round so they faced the large, silver screen. Mirienne flicked various switches and the front of the craft came to life in a display of lights, whirring and beeping. The screen began moving upwards, out of sight. This had hidden a large window so the group was now able to see all the action going on outside the craft.

Star placed her hands on the soft armrests of her chair. Just as she did so a belt slid across her lap, wound its way between her legs and clinked gently into a socket at the base of the seat.

'Ready for launch?' A voice came through the craft.

'Affirmative,' Mirienne replied, continuing to press numerous buttons and switches.

'Lift off after three. Three … two … one … lift off …'

Star felt the craft shift as the magnetic force holding it to its base was released. It hovered for a couple of moments then began edging forwards very slowly towards a long, dark tunnel, gathering pace as it did so.

'Hold tight!' their pilot called out as she pulled back on a lever. The students gripped the arm rests and the craft accelerated down the widening tunnel. Then suddenly they were out, flying over Celestia and her setting sun.

In no time at all their planet faded out of sight and the great expanse of her sky, then space, enveloped them in a way they'd only dreamt of. The stars twinkled so brightly and the planets shone like jewels. Star had never seen anything so stunning. Despite the knowledge that they were travelling at such high speeds, it felt effortless. Occasionally they'd experience a little bump or jolt but generally it felt as if they were floating on a calm sea.

'Enjoy the view,' Mirienne said, turning to them. 'You might spot other planetary beings travelling to or from Earth. It's peak season now spring is here.'

The expanse of the galaxy had them all awestruck. Star pointed at a black hole which she remembered from her studies, had died millions of orbitals ago. Lacarta pointed to a fireball; Mirienne explained they were witnessing the birth of a star. Alhena spotted the faint lights of another craft far off in the distance.

After a while the students grew tired. They grabbed a bite to eat, chatted about the incredible day they'd had, then asked the two Elders if they could turn in for the night. Eridamus gave them each a blanket and pressed a button which tipped their chairs back and extended their footrests, turning from a chair into a comfy bed. They pulled the blankets up to their chins, snuggled into the spongy mattress and before long the three of them were fast asleep.

Eridamus leant over to Mirienne. 'What's with the convoy then?'

'Orders from Rigley,' she said, raising her eyebrows. 'I've got a feeling he's got a bit of a crush on you.'

The Elder laughed nervously. 'I don't think so. Relationships between our races never work out.'

'You mustn't dismiss him just because it hasn't worked for others. It's about time you had some romance in your life.'

The women sat in silence, watching the beauty of space and all its miracles play out in front of them.

'Any word from him yet?' Mirienne said, breaking the silence.

Eridamus shook her head despondently.

'I'm sorry.'

The two women gazed out at the wonderful sight in front of them.

'Makes you feel so small doesn't it?' Eridamus said.

'It certainly does.' She paused before saying quietly, 'And that's exactly the way it should be.'

Eridamus pulled a blanket over herself and curled up in her seat while Mirienne flew the craft steadily through the galaxy towards Earth.

CHAPTER FIFTY-NINE

'COME TO EARTH, STAR. COME to Earth, Star,' the voice repeated over and over again. She tried searching for him but there was nothing to see, just a hollow space filled only with the echoes of his voice. 'Come to Earth, Star. Come to Earth.' She tossed her head from side to side searching for him. The voice faded away as another clearer voice could be heard.

'Earth to Star. Earth to Star!' Alhena said, shaking Star.

'Argh!' Star sat bolt upright. 'Are we here?' she asked, rubbing her eyes.

Alhena laughed. 'No, sorry, I couldn't resist saying that! Look outside.'

Star looked out of the side circular windows to see another craft, the shape of an enormous egg. Inside she could see grey, thin beings with huge almond eyes staring right at them. 'Wow! Don't they look funny!'

'They're probably thinking exactly the same!' giggled Alhena.

The girls waved but their greeting wasn't returned. Instead the funny-looking beings continued to stare back – their faces devoid of any emotion.

'Just the Martians,' Mirienne called back. 'Nothing to worry about. They like to play the scary alien role but they're as soft as our lemetas when you get to know them.'

The three craft flew in a triangular formation, staying equal distance apart from each other the whole time. Apart from the odd storm it was an incredibly peaceful flight.

The fledglings got up a couple of times and stretched their legs. Alhena and Star kept Lacarta informed as to everything going on outside but eventually he asked for a bit of silence so he could rest.

They passed planets, shooting stars, comets, meteorites, entrances to other galaxies, deceased planets and stars making their final journey to black holes. Everything they'd studied in Astronomy, they witnessed first-hand; it was utterly incredible.

Then gradually something came into sight and Star sat up straight, staring intently out of the window. What she saw was so beautiful she had no idea how she'd ever find the words to describe it. A planet was coming into sight that was made up of deep blues, rich greens, dark yellows and wonderful light browns covered by swirls of the purest white. It was in such contrast to the other planets, which had been generally various shades of one single colour – purple, red, yellow or grey.

Elder Eridamus turned round to watch their faces. 'Isn't she the most beautiful thing you've ever seen? Time to put your human clothes on,' she said, pulling out a case and handing each of them an army-green overall. They placed their Celestian clothes in the bag and stepped into their new clothes which hung off them.

'Take your seats. Shape-shifting about to commence,' Mirienne said, just as they felt the craft jolt. 'We're now entering the Earth's stratosphere. The vibrations are lowering,' she called out.

Star looked at Elder Eridamus whose hair was shrinking, losing the glossy silver colour it had and turning a pale grey. Her nose grew longer, her ears grew shorter, her markings faded and her body began lengthening. Star was transfixed until she realised this was happening to her too. She looked down at her hands as the markings disappeared from sight. Her long thin fingers shrank, her skin changed from a very pale pink to a soft brown. She looked down at her legs as they grew longer then gripped her chest in shock as she realised she was growing there too. She looked at Lacarta who was also looking down at his body in alarm. His brown skin became a little paler but he didn't appear to be growing much taller, though his body was becoming plumper and his legs and arms were thickening. His eyelids became a little heavier, his eyes slanted a little towards his ears which had dropped down nearer his cheek. His glorious bright red hair was now a rich dark brown.

Alhena's long blue hair was also a very dark brown and finished at her shoulders in an immaculate bob. She'd grown a few inches in height, gained a few extra pounds all over but her fingers were smaller and stubbier. Her skin that had only had a hint of brown had turned darker, her eyes changed from piercing blue to hazel and she now had a slim, pointed nose.

'What's happening to me?' Lacarta asked, staring at his hands, frustrated by the blurry images.

'You look so handsome!' Alhena exclaimed.

'All our markings have gone!' Star said.

'Not just that but look at the size of all of us! We're taller and bigger! Look at our hair!'

Star and Alhena kept squealing every time they looked at their bodies and poking each other, examining the other's nose, ears and eyes.

'We look exactly like the humans we saw in school!' Alhena said, loving every minute of their transformation. She peered down the top of her overalls. 'What the … they're massive! Why would humans want anything bigger!' she laughed.

The craft flew effortlessly through the clouds until suddenly Earth was right underneath them. They hovered over the ocean whilst Elder Mirienne tapped in something on the dashboard. 'I can take it from here,' she said into a little microphone.

They looked outside and saw the other two craft perform a little lightshow before disappearing back into the clouds. Their craft then flew to the right, covering the giant ocean within seconds.

'Permission to land, General?' Elder Mirienne said.

'Permission granted. Pleasure to have you back.' The voice exuded authority.

The craft flew over a huge expanse of golden desert and headed towards a sandy mountain range. The scenery was desolate and even the mountains ahead didn't break up the bleak picture. As they drew closer a door hidden in the side of one of the mountains began opening. Mirienne gripped a wheel and the craft tipped slightly from side to side. She manoeuvred it so they were in line with a thin strip of lights, leading up to and inside the mountain. Very slowly she eased the craft inside until it glided smoothly to a standstill. The giant doorway gently closed after them.

Star couldn't take her eyes off the scene outside the craft. Where there'd just been desert, they were now inside a building not entirely different to the one back on Celestia. From where she sat Star could see humans in overalls, similar to the ones they were wearing, dashing about. A monotone voice said, 'Celestian crafts have landed. I repeat, Celestian crafts have landed.'

'Congratulations on completing your first flight to planet Earth,' Elder Mirienne said as she spun her seat around to face them. 'You've excelled yourselves. Enjoy your week of FHS and I look forward to taking you back to Celestia in fourteen sunrises time – I mean, seven days' time. Got to use the Earth lingo now, right?'

Star reached across and grabbed Lacarta and Alhena's hands. 'We've done it, guys! We're actually here!'

CHAPTER SIXTY

THE GROUP OF STUDENTS PILED off Craft 612 and stepped cautiously onto planet Earth for the very first time. Eridamus's face lit up when she saw General Rigley stood at the bottom of the steps waiting to greet them all. He smiled back at her and her heart performed a tiny somersault. She looked at her students and remembered how she'd felt when she'd taken her first step on Earth all those orbitals ago. Thank Demeter they hadn't learnt shape-shifting just yet. With the amount of adrenalin coursing through their veins they could have already changed into numerous different animals without knowing how to keep it under control. It took many moons to learn that technique.

'Welcome back, Elder Eridamus,' General Rigley said, holding out his hand for her to shake as she stepped lightly off the bottom step.

'Many thanks, General Rigley. It's good to see you again,' she replied, extending her pale, slim hand and placing it in his.

'It's good to see you too, Eridamus,' he said, seeking eye contact with her. 'I mean, Elder Eridamus,' he said apologetically then turned to the students. 'Welcome, Lacarta, Star, Alhena, and congratulations on studying FHS. We've got an early start tomorrow so you might want to have an early night.'

The three of them all hastily shook their heads and he roared with laughter. 'You've got plenty of time here, don't worry. First thing tomorrow you'll be back on board your craft for a flight round Earth. Then you've got a "night on the town" as we call it. We're currently sorting work permits out for you so you can spend a few days in one of the offices mixing with the workers. I'm also hoping to get you into one of the schools for your last day. Use tonight to relax, it'll be the only chance you get. It'll also give you time to adjust to your new human selves. What a striking bunch you make,' he said, looking around at each of them. When he got to Lacarta he did a double-take, an expression of confusion clouding his features.

'Something wrong?' Elder Eridamus asked.

'Please excuse us one moment. I need a word with your elder,' he said, taking her arm and leading her round the back of the craft.

'What's going on?' she asked as he looked both ways to check no one was in earshot.

'Haven't you noticed?'

'Noticed what?'

'About Lacarta? Surely, it's as obvious to me as it is to you – though it's been so long even I wouldn't know for certain,' he said pensively.

'What? What's so obvious?' she said, looking back towards Lacarta and then it dawned on her.

'Oh my!' The words fell out of her mouth.

'You see it now?'

'Oh, I see it alright. Has this ever happened before?' she asked.

'Not in my time. Trisomy 21 was eradicated years ago. Melantho's not going to like this one bit!' he said raising his eyebrows.

Eridamus tutted. 'Maybe this is exactly what Earth needs. It's not right babies like him aren't born here.'

'I didn't make the rules, as well you know.'

'It's about time those rules were changed,' she said, crossing her arms and glaring at him.

'My sentiments exactly but I'm not like most humans and I'm nothing like Melantho. Everyone here thinks he can do no wrong. Be interesting to see if he exposes his true colours.' He lowered his voice and went to touch her arm. 'I've missed you.'

'Not now,' she said, pulling her arm out of his reach.

The two of them walked back to the bottom of the craft where the fledglings stood transfixed as they watched all the workmen hurry about the hangar. Their faces lit up when they saw Eridamus.

'Sorry about that,' she said. 'Follow us while we take you to your quarters. I hope you like them. Food and drink will be provided once you've settled in. You must be very hungry.' Then as an aside to Rigley, 'Not that human food has any kind of nutrition in it.'

Rigley nodded and smiled back.

The general guided them around the craft, up a steep set of metal steps and through a door that had the word EXIT written in red. It slammed shut behind them and the noise of the hangar disappeared instantly. They now stood in a white, narrow, brightly lit corridor.

'Not far now,' he said, leading the way.

Elder Eridamus walked alongside him and Star watched as they chatted animatedly. Star had never seen her elder like this before.

After a number of sharp turns by which time the fledglings felt totally disorientated, they came to a halt outside a door which had the words, CELESTIAN QUARTERS.

The general pressed a round, silver button and the door glided open revealing a small cosy room filled with brightly coloured furniture. The sofa was a lovely mustard yellow with bright blue cushions dotted about. In front of it was a small table with three mobile phones on it. A television screen filled the wall in front of the sofa and the fledglings were hit with their first blast of images and sounds from this machine they'd heard so much about.

'Turn that thing off, will you, General?' Elder Eridamus snapped. 'I can't hear myself speak!'

'I can't. I can turn it down though,' he said, finding the remote on the table and turning it to mute. 'As I said earlier, you might notice a few differences this year. Nothing to be alarmed about,' he said to her in a way that meant the exact opposite.

'I see.'

'Your lot won't be bothered too much by the TV, I'm sure,' he said, placing his hand on her arm.

'Don't be so ridiculous,' Eridamus said. 'You know how addictive it is!'

'Excuse me, Elder,' Alhena said, sitting down and signalling at her to move aside so she could see the screen.

'See what I mean?' Eridamus clicked her fingers in front of Alhena's eyes, snapping her out of her trance. Alhena looked huffily at her elder, then back to the screen where a family of funny yellow creatures were getting up to some crazy antics.

'Come and have a look at your bedroom,' the general said, pressing a glowing button on the wall. The students reluctantly dragged themselves away from the television as the door glided silently open revealing a softly lit room containing three large beds, two on one side, the other opposite them. The beds looked the most wonderful objects they'd ever set eyes on: crisp white sheets, large inviting pillows, brightly coloured cushions in front of the pillows with matching throws.

'We colour coordinated each bed to match your natural hair colours back home,' Rigley said smiling at them.

'Holy Demeter!' Star said, spotting her bed with its pink pillow and throw and leaping onto it. 'Come on!' she said, rolling around and laughing. 'It's divine!'

Alhena went first, sitting on the edge softly bouncing.

'It's OK,' Rigley said. 'Enjoy it.'

Lacarta's eyes could easily make out the bright red of his throw so he walked carefully to his bed and stood at the bottom of it, gazing at it for a moment. He then held his hands in the air and shouted, 'Weeee!' before throwing himself face down onto the sumptuous duvet and pillows.

Everyone looked over at him and laughed.

'It's amazing!'

Alhena chuckled and lay down, placing her hands on her stomach and closing her eyes, a big smile on her face.

Star, whose bed was opposite the other two, got up and drew her index finger up to her lips. She crept over to Alhena's bed and leapt on top of her, putting her arms around her and rolling round on the bed together. 'This is what you need to do,' she said, laughing as Alhena squealed with shock.

'I remember what it was like the first time I laid on one,' Eridamus said to Rigley as they watched the students.

'I wish I'd been there for that moment,' he said, winking at her.

A bit of colour went to her cheeks and she smiled at him. 'Cheeky.'

'Look, we've got our own screens here too!' Star said, pulling at a long metal arm that swung round over their beds. Elder Eridamus tutted noisily and raised her eyebrows to the general who nodded back knowingly.

'You've got everything you need for a comfortable night's sleep. Nightwear is underneath your pillows. The screens turn off at 11 p.m. so you can get a good night's sleep. Ready to see the kitchen?' Rigley asked.

The three of them leapt off their beds and Rigley took them to the small brightly lit room. The gleaming white cupboards were a stark contrast to the black shiny worktop.

'Where do we eat?' they asked, looking around.

'Through there,' he said, pointing towards the sofas.

'But they can't eat in front of the television!' Eridamus said. 'Their bodies won't even know they've eaten anything.'

Rigley looked a bit sheepish. 'You don't need to have every meal there. We have our own canteen on the compound that you're welcome to use as well. It's just that some nights you might fancy grabbing a pizza and curling up in front of the TV.'

Eridamus looked utterly horrified. 'Are you advising my students to not only eat rubbish but watch it too?'

Rigley looked deeply uncomfortable. 'I'm not advising your students to do anything they don't want to do. I'm merely passing on suggestions, that's all. Feel free to make your own minds up.' Eridamus folded her arms and glared at him. Rigley held out his hands and shrugged. 'It's just a suggestion.'

'What's this?' Lacarta asked, jabbing at some buttons on a wall, springing a machine into life.

'That's a microwave,' Rigley said, pressing the largest button which stopped the whirring immediately. 'You can cook your food in there if you're short of time.'

'You can certainly not cook your food in there!' Eridamus retorted. 'If you do, it won't be food when it comes out. How can you even suggest they use this thing? It'll not only poison the food but it'll poison their bodies too! Tell us where the oven is so they can cook proper food.'

Rigley shook his head. 'I'm sorry, this is it. All the ovens were taken out a few months ago.'

'Then you won't be cooking in here, then,' she said decisively. 'Your bodies aren't designed to eat toxic food like this. Nor, for that matter, are humans,' she said, giving Rigley the eyeball.

'Looks like we'll be seeing you at the canteen, then,' Rigley said, moving another protruding TV screen out of his way as he guided them back into the lounge. Images of products flashed up on the screen and the students sat down on the comfy sofa, instantly transfixed.

'Try and get a good night's sleep before our busy day tomorrow,' Eridamus said.

'Your elder is sleeping in the next room along so rest assured she's close by if you need her. Is that OK?' He looked around the room but no one bothered answering him. 'We have a spot of business to attend to before we finish for the day,' he said a bit louder.

Star waved nonchalantly at him. 'Bye, guys.'

'Bye,' Lacarta said, grabbing at some nuts that were in the bowl in front of them.

'See what I mean?' Eridamus said.

'Come on, let's get out of here. We need to talk,' he said, leading a disgruntled Eridamus out of the room.

As they closed the door a man in uniform rushed past them. 'Slow down, officer!' cried out Rigley.

The man stopped and turned. 'General Rigley, it's Rastaban. He's in a bad mood again,' the man replied, beads of sweat on his brow. He turned and continued running down the corridor.

'Looks like we'd better catch up tomorrow,' Rigley said to her and followed the man's retreating figure.

CHAPTER SIXTY-ONE

THE NEXT DAY, AS STAR eased her eyes open, she felt momentarily disorientated. Where were the sun's rays kissing her cheek and where was the lemata that playfully tugged at her blanket? Then it all came flooding back, she was on planet Earth. The air-conditioned room felt clinically cool and she pulled the crisp white sheets over her shoulders. She didn't feel her usual urge to leap out of bed so she lay there for a few minutes in quiet contemplation. Propping her head on her hand she looked over to see if Alhena or Lacarta were awake but neither seemed to be stirring. One of Alhena's eyes was slightly open so Star followed her gaze and realised she was staring at Lacarta as he slept.

'Alhena?' Star said, making Alhena jump.

'Yeah?'

'You OK?'

'Fine, thanks. You?' she said absent-mindedly.

'Feels weird, doesn't it? Waking up here and not back home.'

'Yeah, but I'm loving it,' she said, her gaze fixed on Lacarta's sleeping body.

Star 'Mmmm'd' an agreement but something about Alhena's manner troubled her. 'Lucky we haven't seen anyone wearing glasses yet.'

'You'll let me be the one to show them to him, won't you?' Alhena said, sitting upright and staring at Star.

'Of course, you're much better at that sort of stuff than me. When you gonna tell him?'

'I'm not sure. I was kind of hoping it might just happen naturally.'

Just then they heard a click and a monotone voice came over the speaker system. 'Morning, fledglings. We hope you slept well. You have an hour to get yourselves ready for the flight around planet Earth. Wear the uniform you arrived in. Breakfast is being served in the canteen. Someone will come and fetch you at 10:00 hours.' Another click and the voice cut out.

Once they were dressed, they headed to the canteen; the delicious smells of baking bread hitting them long before they'd reached the room. A few uniformed men and women sat eating in silence at separate tables.

Eridamus sat with Rigley and waved as they entered the room. 'Help yourself to some fruit then come and join us,' she called out.

The three students walked to the buffet area, passing row upon row of delicious looking items until they got to the tiny selection of unappetising fruit at the end of the table. Each of them tentatively placed a couple of items on their plates and went over to see the other two.

'Can we eat some of the other food tomorrow?' Lacarta asked as he took a bite into his browning banana which promptly collapsed in two in his hand.

'You can hardly describe that stuff as food. Best to stick to the fruit,' Eridamus said, chewing awkwardly on an apple. 'Tuck in. It's delicious, just like home.' She took another bite and tried smiling but instead it turned into a grimace. 'Mmmm, delicious!'

At 09.45 the group were back at their quarters, their stomachs growling after their paltry breakfast. 'You've got fifteen minutes before we need to leave,' Eridamus said. 'We'll wait here while you make your beds and brush your teeth.'

As soon as Star, Lacarta and Alhena were in their bedroom, Rigley closed the adjoining door and beckoned Eridamus over to the kitchen. 'You still hungry?' he asked, searching the cupboards.

'A little,' she said sheepishly.

He found a tin of beans, tipped the contents into a bowl and put it in the microwave. Eridamus scrunched up her nose. He placed his phone underneath the machine and turned it on. The microwave whirred away. 'There's not meant to be any surveillance cameras in here but I can't be too sure anymore,' he whispered. 'They won't be able to hear a thing while that's running, gives dreadful interference on the mobile network.'

'What's going on?' Eridamus said.

'Melantho's behind all this: the extra screens, taking the ovens out, the poor choice of fruit.'

'I thought that apple was rotten!'

'He's pushing every being on the committee to eat junk food by making the stuff they want to eat look so unappetising.'

'But alien bodies can't take processed food! It's poisonous!'

'And highly addictive. You wouldn't believe the scramble in the canteen over the pizzas, burgers and hot dogs. I tried complaining but they won't listen to me, Zaurak or Arrakis, anymore.' Rigley watched as the beans bubbled away. He pressed the timer, adding another two minutes to the cooking time.

'Have they forgotten the reason we allow our young to take Human Studies is to remind the galaxy how NOT to run your planet?' Eridamus gripped the edge of the worktop.

'Melantho and Rastaban make a bloody convincing double act. They've been telling them the compound is raising funds by branching out into fake meat. He's then getting them to offer advice on the products so they can find something everyone's happy with.

Rastaban says he's heavily involved in production to ensure it remains sugar, grain and chemical free. You only have to take one bite to know he's lying.'

'But that'll tamper with their DNA!' Eridamus said, bringing her hand up to her mouth.

'It's already happening. Their minds are being altered and it's calcifying their pineal glands. It's changing the way they view humans and they're beginning to wonder whether humans have had it right all along. They're now saying every being should be free to choose what they want to eat – just like humans. Rastaban says it's being "foodist" not to allow it.'

Eridamus nearly burst out laughing.

'I'm not joking! They actually believe him! He's brainwashing them by using food and fear to lower their vibrations. It's so clever,' he said, shaking his head.

'Don't you ever use that word to describe him!' she said, waggling her finger. 'He's evil, that's what he is. The last thing we want is to have more races operating within fear vibrations. It's bad enough watching humans. The whole object of the Committee was to raise Earth's vibrations so humans can see how destructive the economy is and stop protecting it. What are they thinking making other races eat food that lowers their own high vibrations? It doesn't make any sense.'

'That's what I thought. Until I overheard Rastaban and Melantho talking one day. The reason the economy works for Aldor is because their planet's toxic and they have to buy everything in – it suits them to have a currency. Celestians and Mercurians operate by bartering but your system's based on trust. Rastaban says if we get rid of the economy on Earth, there's nothing to stop your planets from breaking that trust and leaving their race to starve to death. I don't know how we can raise the vibrations of Earth and keep all the planets happy. It just doesn't seem possible,' he said, rubbing his forehead.

'But they'll learn to trust; it doesn't happen overnight! We can't leave humans enslaved forever just because the Aldorians find it hard to trust. It's not right!'

'What choice do we have?' He held out his hands and shrugged.

'You can't give in to them so easily. The Committee can draw up an inter-galactic bartering contract that we all agree to. How hard can it be?'

Rigley grimaced. 'That involves reasoning with them but you know what they're like. It's impossible. They'll find some way of dismissing it. It's like they don't want anything to make sense. I'm beginning to think it's more about something else than the whole trust issue.'

'What else could it be?' Eridamus asked. The microwave pinged making them both jump. The door sprung open and the beans smouldered away inside. Rigley pushed the door shut and put another two minutes on the clock. What was left of the beans crackled away.

'Rastaban's started asking questions about the gold that was hidden a hundred years ago.' He waited a moment as Eridamus took in what he said. Her bulging eyes confirmed she'd realised the enormity of what this meant. 'He reckons it's planet Aldor's right to have it as they were the ones who'd spent thousands of years mining it. The gold would mean they could build their houses closer to the surface. They say it'll mean their children can see the sky for the first time in their history. They're pulling on all the heart strings of the generals and making them question the whole ethos of the Committee.'

'But they mustn't ever find the gold. That's what started this in the first place,' she said.

'He's telling everyone that Celestians look down on them and they're the ones who've purposefully kept it hidden from the planets that need it. Only the generals from Mercury see through his plan.

Rastaban started to panic when we decided to push ahead with plans to raise the vibrations here. He thinks if they find the gold it'll protect them from the inevitable collapse of the global economy. That's why they've become so obsessed with locating it. Whilst humans continue feeding the economy, the galaxy remains safe.' He reached out and gently touched her face. 'I'd hate to see beings like you enslaved. Humans don't know any different.'

'But I want you to be free!' she said, putting her hand over his. 'Then we can be together properly. I get sick if I stay here too long and you aren't ever allowed to live on Celestia! I've lost my husband, my son and I can't be with you either!' Tears threatened to spill over her eyelids.

'What choice have we got? At least we'll get to see each other every time you teach FHS students. If we rock the boat there's a chance they'll stop inter-planet travel completely.'

'But this isn't a relationship, Henry! This isn't what I want for my life!'

'It's not what I want either, is it?' he said, gripping her tightly by the shoulders and staring deep into her eyes. 'I love you but what choice have we got?'

Eridamus turned her head away from him and tried to wriggle free from his grasp but he wouldn't let her go.

'They've started searching for the gold already – it's only a matter of time before they find it,' he said and Eridamus slowly turned back to him, a look of horror on her face. 'That's why they're hardly letting any craft in. If no one else is flying they've got the whole galaxy to themselves while they work out where it's been hidden. Just think what they'd do if they got their hands on it. They'd be able to create a galaxy economy with planets trading with each other. A global economy is no longer enough for them!'

'But then we'll all be enslaved!'

'That's exactly what they want! And if they carry on charming the generals from the other planets, they'll also gain access to immortality.'

Eridamus took an intake of breath.

'And I can guarantee they won't be sharing that with the likes of you or me.'

'But the gold was hidden by the original Committee members; they'll never find it.' Her voice was rising in panic, her eyes searching his. 'Only a few beings were given the knowledge of its whereabouts and even I don't know who they are!'

'But think about it, they've got Leo, haven't they?' he said, raising his eyebrows.

Eridamus stood there in shock as it dawned on her. 'You think he knows?'

'It's the only thing I can think of.'

'He'll never tell them.'

Rigley grimaced. 'Let's hope not but he's in bad way, really bad from what I can tell. I don't know how much more he'll be able to take. It's only a matter of time before he either tells them or they kill him.'

'We have to get him out of there,' she said.

'I've got an idea.' The microwave pinged. Its door flung open just as Melantho walked in.

'Breakfast time, Rigley?' Melantho said, peering into the bowl. All that remained of the baked beans was a tiny bit of red fluid that sizzled away. 'Mmmm, tempting,' he said, smiling.

'Funny – my appetite's gone anyway,' Rigley replied.

'Cooking's never been your strong point, has it? Greetings, Elder Eridamus.' He held out a limp hand which Eridamus reluctantly shook. 'Everything to your liking?'

She opened her mouth to say something, saw the look on Rigley's face and closed it. He smiled and said, 'I'll take that as yes. Wonderful.'

The door from the bedroom quarters opened and in walked the three fledglings, chattering away. Their excitement ground to a halt when they saw Melantho, a crooked smile on his face. 'Ahhh, how lovely to meet you,' he said, offering his hand for each of them to shake. Star went first, then Alhena. Melantho 'mmm'd' after each handshake and held their hands and their gaze a moment longer than was necessary. He withdrew his hand reluctantly from Alhena's – giving her a lingering look – and moved onto Lacarta who had his hand held out expectantly but just as Melantho was about to shake it, he recoiled in horror. 'How can this be?' he asked, looking from Lacarta to Rigley.

Lacarta's hand remained outstretched but he turned to Star, confusion clouding his face.

'It's alright.' Star placed his hand down at his side and said to Melantho by way of an explanation, 'Lacarta can't see very well,' she said brightly.

Alhena began, 'Yes, Lacarta, we've been meaning to tell you ...'

Melantho held up his hand to silence her and she shrank away from his cold, hard stare. 'Explain yourself, Eridamus,' he demanded as the fledglings looked on in mounting confusion and horror.

'I don't know what you mean,' Eridamus said curtly.

'Explain why you've allowed this one here.'

'What do you mean "this one"? How dare you speak to him like that!' Alhena stood with her hands on her hips, glaring at Melantho.

Melantho swiftly turned to Alhena, stooping to her level so quickly she stumbled back in shock. 'Get away from me,' he hissed.

Star pulled Alhena to her and put her arms around both her friends.

Rigley stepped in front of Eridamus and signalled for her to move behind him.

'I don't think the Committee will see this as a problem,' Rigley said as calmly as possible. 'No one will think anything when they see

Lacarta; he's just the same as the other two.'

As quick as lightning Melantho turned from Alhena to Rigley. 'I'm sorry if I don't share your optimism. Humans haven't forgotten about it that quickly.'

'Forgotten about what?' Alhena shouted, breaking free from Star so she could face Melantho. 'What are you talking about?'

Melantho turned back to Alhena, his eyes as black as coals. 'Don't you dare speak to me like that, you silly little girl. Get away from me before I call security,' he said, batting her away. He leant down so his face was level with Lacarta's and narrowed his eyes. 'It's quite extraordinary when you get close, isn't it? How similar you are yet so different. It's no good though,' he said, straightening his back. 'We can't allow this. You'll have to send him back.'

Lacarta's eyes filled up with tears and he looked to his elder. 'What does he mean? I don't understand!'

Eridamus walked to Lacarta and took his arm, leading him to the bedroom. She turned to Rigley and said, 'Deal with it. Lacarta isn't going home. He's got every right to be here, just like all of us.' The door swooshed shut behind them.

The two girls stood there still holding onto each other and watched as Melantho faced Rigley. 'Whatever hold that one has over you, that boy is not staying here.'

'She doesn't have a hold over me.'

'Don't treat me like an idiot,' Melantho scoffed. 'I've seen what a little lap dog you are around her. You're the laughing stock of the Committee,' he smirked as Rigley flinched. 'Now get this one back on the craft before I send them all back. Can't have the likes of him wandering around the city.' He walked to the door and went to press the button to open it.

'I wouldn't be quite so hasty,' Rigley began, not having a clue as to what he was about to say.

Melantho's hand hovered for a moment before placing it back

by his side. He turned to face the general. 'And why not?'

'The last thing we want right now is another craft out there. Isn't Rastaban after a no-fly zone for the next twenty-four hours? He had a bad day by all accounts yesterday. You'd hate to give him a worse one today I'm sure.'

A nerve twitched in Melantho's right eye.

'What's he going to think when you go against his decision. He's had this planned for weeks, hasn't he?' Melantho muttered something under his breath. 'What was that, General?' Rigley asked, knowing he'd cornered Melantho.

'What do you suggest?' Melantho muttered.

'That we carry on as we were. As far as I can see, nothing's changed.'

'How can you say that? Everything's changed now that one's here!'

'It's been years. No one's going to spot it,' Rigley said.

'But what if they do? How the hell are we going to explain that down syndrome children can do everything a normal child can when we've been terminating all "at risk" pregnancies for decades? There's going to be a riot if they find out.'

'Trisomy 21, General. They stopped calling it that years ago.'

'Stop with the detail!' he said, lashing his hand out. 'Who gives a toss what it's called? We can't have him out there. It's too risky.'

'Who actually looks at anyone nowadays? You know – the way we're trained to,' Rigley began calmly. 'They're all too busy on their phones. Even if they spot something, no one's going to ask outright, are they? They'd be way too worried about being accused of offending him.'

Melantho's face softened a little.

'Tell you what, if we get wind of anyone giving him funny looks, we'll call him back to base. That sound alright?'

'Hmm,' Melantho scratched his chin. 'If he stays, he mustn't go anywhere near the city.'

'But then we'd have to find someone to supervise him at all times. I'm not sure we've got the staff to cope with that, have we? Anyway, who can we possibly ask to keep an eye on him? They'd be more likely to be the ones to notice than if he were a face in the crowd.'

'Maybe,' Melantho pondered. 'If he gets found out it's your neck on the line. I never met him. Right?'

Rigley nodded.

'Good. Did I hear he has bad eyes?'

'Yes, General!' Star butted in, relieved that he was able to stay. 'He's so short-sighted.' Alhena jabbed her in the ribs.

'What?' Star said in annoyance. The look Alhena gave Star silenced her immediately.

'Bless him. We'll have to see what we can do about that,' he said under his breath. The door swooshed open and he walked out of the room.

In the bedroom Lacarta turned to both Eridamus, tears in his eyes. 'What does he mean, he'll have to send me back?'

'The man's an imbecile,' Eridamus said then paused knowing Lacarta needed to hear the truth. 'Humans like Melantho have a tendency to put everything in boxes, compartmentalise things. You saw it in their schools – this child's clever, this one's got ADHD, this one gets bored so he's naughty.'

'But how does that relate to me?' he shouted.

'It turns out you also have a label on you – it's called Trisomy 21. This label, just as all labels humans put on themselves, means nothing. Many years ago some very influential humans perceived it as a drain to their precious economy and after years of effective pre-natal testing, they managed to eradicate Trisomy 21 nearly a century ago.' She squeezed his hand as she said this, hating to give him this information.

'You mean I wouldn't have been allowed to live?' he said, stunned.

She shook her head. 'It's their loss. How would we learn and grow if everyone were the same?' She pulled Lacarta to her and hugged him.

They stood there a moment until they heard the door open and Alhena's head poked round. 'You alright?' she asked. Lacarta nodded. 'He's gone now.' She took his hand and led him back into the living room.

Eridamus joined them. 'Don't worry about that awful man. He's everything I despise in a human. This is what I'd do if I got my hands on him,' she said as she crouched down, did a vicious chop with one hand and a kick with her foot. She twirled around looking menacingly at the group, leapt into the air, performed another chop and a kick whilst emitting a screeching, 'Hiiiiiii ya!' at the top of her voice, making the group howl with laughter.

To Eridamus's horror the door swooshed open again just as she was mid pose and Melantho appeared, holding something in his hand.

'Another busy day, Eridamus?' he asked with one eyebrow raised. He walked towards Lacarta with a patronising look on his face. 'Allow me to apologise for my behaviour earlier. It was most ungracious. I'd like to try and make it up to you, to show you I'm not the sort of man your elder would have you believe. Here, take these as a gesture of good will.'

The rest of the group watched in horror as Melantho carefully unfolded a pair of glasses and drew his hand up to place them on Lacarta's nose, hooking the arms swiftly over his ears.

'What are they?' Lacarta asked. Then as he looked through them his whole face changed. 'I can see!' he said, turning to see Alhena and Star staring at him, a look of horror etched on their faces. 'I can see!' he said, turning to Elder Eridamus and General Rigley who stood frozen in shock. 'What's wrong?' he asked, concern growing in his voice.

Elder Eridamus composed herself and managed to force a smile. 'Nothing! Everything's fine. It's wonderful,' she said brightly.

'What your elder's struggling to explain is that she didn't expect or want me to give you these items. Isn't that right?' He looked at her but continued without waiting for a response. 'She wanted you to continue to suffer, just as you've always done. She never wanted you to find out about these wonderful items that can change your life for the better. Something so commonly used on Earth yet your planet has purposefully kept them from you.' He folded his arms, a look of pure pleasure plastered on his face.

'Is this true? Have you known about these all along?' Lacarta turned to Eridamus, anger rising from deep within him.

'This isn't the time or place, Lacarta.' General Rigley stepped in, taking his arm.

'Get your hands off me,' Lacarta yelled, pulling his arm away.

Rigley stepped back.

'Is what he's saying true?' Lacarta's eyes searched his elder's for answers.

'Partly. We did want you to have them while you were here but you know they can't come back with you.'

'But why? For the first time in my life I can see properly! Why would Celestia stop me from having these?'

'Just leave him alone!' Alhena yelled, pushing Eridamus away and grabbing Lacarta's hand. 'It was meant to be me that told him!'

'You knew as well? And you didn't tell me?' he said, staring at her, anger and hurt etched across his face. 'What about you?' he said, turning to Star who nodded and looked down at the ground. He let go of Alhena's hand and turned to Eridamus who took his hand and led him to the sofa. He listened intently while she explained how they'd been very keen on Lacarta accessing them while he was here. She had just been choosing her moment to tell him, that was all. She told him of the dangers of bringing such items back and the ramifications to every being if they realised Earth held such tempting items. It could lure fledglings to study humans for the wrong reasons, possibly even mean they chose to live here just to access things their planet couldn't make. She reminded him of the ancient rule on Earth of divide and conquer and explained this was what Melantho was up to. His eyes that had been brimming with tears softened. He looked down but then threw himself forwards, wrapping his arms around her and burying his face into her dress. Elder Eridamus put her arms around him. 'I'm so sorry. I'm so sorry,' she whispered. At that very moment, from behind them, they heard a roar followed by the noise of glass smashing on the floor.

CHAPTER SIXTY-TWO

'AAAAARRRGHHHHHHHHH!' ALHENA SCREAMED AS SHE flung herself at Melantho grabbing at anything she could use to hit him with. 'I hate you, I hate you, I hate you!' she screamed as she bared her teeth and lashed out over and over again. 'You leave my Lacarta alone! You've ruined everything!' Rigley tried to pull her away but she was too strong. She clawed and scratched at Melantho's face and red marks appeared as she drew blood. She grabbed his fringe and pulled it hard making him yell out in pain. He drew his hand up to hit her and held her back with his other.

'Get away from me!' he roared. Like a crazed animal Alhena continued to lash out, the others doing their best to restrain her. Melantho brought the back of his hand down and as if using her like a tennis ball, smacked her across the side of her face with all his might, hurling her into the corner of the room. 'Eridamus,' he spat as a stunned Alhena sat in a crumpled heap in the corner with blood oozing out of her nose, 'this class are your lowest yet. I've put myself out for your planet for too long but no more. This visit will be your last.'

'You can't do that, Captain Melantho; you need us!' Eridamus shouted.

'General Melantho!' he screeched.

'General! The galaxy needs us to have good relations; it's how it's been for orbitals!'

'I'm so sorry!' wailed Alhena from the corner of the room. 'I'm so sorry!'

'You should've thought about that before you lost control of yourself, young lady,' he said, his chest heaving. 'I won't tolerate this behaviour. You think yourselves better than us but you've clearly got no idea how to conduct yourselves. This does not reflect well on Celestia and its role within the Committee needs to be put under scrutiny. Celestia is meant to be all "peace and love"' he said, making V's with his fingers, 'but look at you. You're pathetic,' he spat. 'Get out of my sight. Enjoy your new-found vision, young man – they're yours to keep – forever,' he said pointedly. At that, he turned on his heel and left.

The group stood there shell-shocked, trying to take in everything that had happened. Alhena crawled to the sofa, sobbing hysterically. Eridamus crouched down next to her and rubbed her back. 'You can't let humans get to you like that. Maybe Further Human Studies is too much for you,' she said and glared at Star who averted her eyes.

'Here, have this,' Rigley said, offering Alhena a wet cloth to put on her cut.

Once the blood had begun to clot and Alhena felt up to walking, Rigley said, 'I think it'll be good to have a change of scenery. Come on, let's go on that trip round Earth.'

'Good idea,' Eridamus replied. 'What's the betting Melantho changes his mind by the end of the day,' she said doubtfully.

They made their very subdued way through the corridors until they got to a thick door which read NO ENTRY. AUTHORISED PERSONNEL ONLY. General Rigley spoke into a little device on the collar of his uniform and a small window at the top of the door opened then slammed shut. After a series of clicks the door opened. The officers saluted as they filed past him and into the hangar holding their craft.

Today there was even more activity. Various different types of craft were in the building being cleaned by large machines that had long metal arms with hoses attached to them. The door to one of the spaceships was open showing a group of humans inside hoovering and dusting. Workmen with toolkits were going over every nut and bolt, making sure they were secure. The noise in the hangar was so loud Lacarta had to cover his ears. Carts beeped as they reversed, jets squirted water out, men called instructions to each other and engines revved as checks were being made. Electricians were busy working on their own craft, running tests. The craft emitted soft beeps as a circle of lights around its middle completed a circuit. The men wore black visors over their faces to protect their eyes from the bright lights. Another craft, the one from Mars they remembered, resembled a large chicken's egg and had a lovely translucent outer shell. The doorway to it was halfway up and the fledglings watched as workmen and cleaners hurried about inside it making their checks.

The third craft was shaped like a long thin rocket, encased by a grey, outer shell. Small windows went all the way along the craft, a door was positioned halfway down its body and a row of lights beneath the windows were again being cleaned and checked. A little shiver went down Star's spine.

'That one's from planet Aldor,' a voice beside her whispered and she turned to see General Melantho so close to her she could feel his breath on her neck. Alhena's nails had left angry red marks on his cheeks. She faked a smile and turned back to look at the rocket-shaped craft. Fewer humans seemed to be working on this one. Some went to clean it but were stopped at the bottom of the stairs and ushered away. Star could see the silhouette of someone on board walking slowly towards the door. When he got to the doorway he turned, put his hands on his hips and looked down at the scene below him. He was dressed from head to foot in black, a black mask covered his nose and mouth so that the only piece of him visible were his eyes. The people working stopped what they were doing and looked up at him. He extended a long finger which he drew slowly across the outside of the craft. He held it in front of his eyes to inspect it then let out an almighty roar. The workmen below shook in terror. Star couldn't take her eyes off them.

'What's going on?' Elder Eridamus asked, looking between the two generals.

'Why don't we wait and see?' Melantho said with snake-like charm that oozed out of every pore in his body.

'Come this way, you three.' Eridamus tried to usher them away but it was too late. A shot of light burst from the man's finger and hit one of the men on the ground who screamed and dropped to the floor, clutching his foot. A trickle of blood seeped onto the concrete below.

Within moments a small vehicle parked up next to him. Two uniformed men got out and swiftly pulled a stretcher from the back which they placed on the floor. Without speaking they lifted the howling man onto it and placed him in the back of the van before closing its doors and speeding off. Seconds later another vehicle screeched to a halt by the little pool of blood. Out stepped a human dressed in the same bland uniform. He picked up the discarded cleaning equipment and continued with the job as if nothing had happened.

'What the hell's he playing at?' General Rigley said through gritted teeth.

'Rastaban must've got out of bed the wrong side – again,' Melantho smiled.

'He can't treat people like this; it's inhumane!' Rigley said, seething with rage.

'You'd better lodge a formal complaint with the Committee, then, hadn't you?' Melantho sneered.

CHAPTER SIXTY-THREE

NO ONE SPOKE AS THE group entered their craft. Elder Mirienne gave Eridamu and Rigley a look before greeting the others with a warm smile. She gave Lacarta a double-take when she saw his glasses. 'Welcome back. You had fun so far?' Her question was met with an awkward silence. 'There's always a lot to take in at first,' she smiled. 'Strap yourselves in for another awesome journey!' As soon as they were seated, she pressed a couple of buttons and the craft began moving slowly towards the opening doors of the mountain. As soon as they were wide enough, she pulled down hard on a lever and within seconds they were out of the hangar. It wasn't long before they were virtually skimming over the silvery waves of the ocean. Out of nowhere a whale leapt into the air, making the fledglings cover their mouths in delight. Eridamus gave them a running commentary of what creatures they were watching and where they were. She pressed a button and whale noises filled the craft along with a translation of what the whale was saying. 'What a beautiful day! Let's put on a show for them.'

They watched the whale disappear then reappear, arching her back as she jumped into the air, showing the group her enormous white tummy. A smaller whale leapt out of the water just behind her.

'Think of what Gamua would say if he saw these beautiful creatures!' Star said to her friends. A shoal of flying fish flew in front of the craft.

'Underneath you we have a family of vaquitas,' Mirienne said as they peered out of the windows. 'Look down!' she said as the floor of the craft slid away, revealing a sheet of glass that meant they were now able to see everything beneath them too. 'These were brought to the edge of extinction by illegal fishing nets. We've worked tirelessly to ensure their endangered days are well and truly over,' Eridamus said, smiling. The ocean gave way to glorious, green fields and then huge, vast mountain ranges. Elder Mirienne glided skilfully in and out of the mountains, making the youngsters gasp in terror at frequent intervals.

'A hundred years ago, due to the effects of deforestation, these mountains barely saw any snow. Now they're snow-covered all year around, just like they used to be.' The mountain ranges gave way to deep ravines and once again she manoeuvred the craft effortlessly in between the rocks. She showed them the Grand Canyon, Victoria Falls, volcanos, the ancient pyramids and Stonehenge.

'Enjoying your glasses, Lacarta?' she asked, calling over her shoulder. He nodded eagerly in response. 'At least you can see the power and awe of Mother Earth.'

'It's incredible to be able to see clearly after all these orbitals,' he said, relieved that someone had finally mentioned them.

'Whilst we're on Earth it's fine to use the things that can improve our lives. We'd be foolish not to,' she said.

Within moments the scenery changed and they were high above the treetops; the canopy was so thick they couldn't see anything underneath the leaves. They followed the contours of a river as it meandered down through the thick jungle. 'Below is the Amazon rainforest. Back in 2021, this was nearly destroyed due to cattle farming for some of the largest corporations on Earth. Industrialised cattle farming was banned a long time ago so it's now able to recover and thrive.'

The craft slowed down so they could get a close look at the forests and rivers beneath them. Eridamus gave a constant commentary, 'Here are the Andes. The tallest mountain in the world, Mauna Kea, which from its base under the ocean is taller than Mount Everest. Victoria Falls the largest waterfall in the world …' Gradually, her voice and the names merged into one and the fledglings felt themselves drifting into a deep sleep.

Rigley leant forwards and whispered, 'I need to talk to you both.'

'I'll put the craft on autopilot.' Elder Mirienne flicked a switch and turned her chair round.

'Have you updated Mirienne?' Eridamus asked.

'We managed a brief chat last night.' Rigley breathed deeply before saying, 'I think I've discovered where Leo's being held.' He watched their faces as the words sank in.

'Is he alive?' Eridamus said, looking over to the sleeping fledglings.

'I don't know. I came across this blank steel door with no entry system. When I checked it against an old map of the compound it was used as a vault to store seeds. I asked a couple of officers where the seed vault was but they pointed me to a different area entirely!'

Mirienne's eyes widened as she tapped her lips with her index finger. 'If they're still storing seeds but not in the seed vault, what are they using the original one for now?'

'That's what I thought. I asked one of the officers why the seed vault had been moved but he said it hadn't. They'd just run out of space and had to expand it. But then he said he'd had to move every single seed from the original one because it needed a good clean before refilling it as it had got a bit damp. The thing was, no one had asked him to put the seeds back and he hadn't been allowed in since. He didn't dare question further as the orders came from Rastaban.

He told me the original seed vault was made up of lots of different cells – like prison cells, he called them. Another thing he couldn't figure out was why he had to seal each one so securely and install a really bright light in each of them when the other seed vault was kept in complete darkness.'

'That has to be where they're keeping him,' Eridamus said.

'I think so. I've got no idea how to get past the door, though. I've looked everywhere but there's no way of opening it.' Rigley crossed his arms and shook his head.

'If you get me there, I'll get us in,' Eridamus said.

'Really?' he asked surprised.

'There's more to me than meets the eye,' she said.

'I don't doubt that one bit,' he replied, taking her hand and smiling.

'Told you he had a thing about you!' Mirienne said.

'Have you not told her yet?' Rigley raised his eyebrows.

'I don't like to broadcast my personal life,' she said, lowering her eyes and smiling at Mirienne. 'We may be "courting", as they say on Earth.'

'Good for you!' Mirienne laughed.

Rigley kissed the back of Eridamus's hand. 'There's never a dull moment with you in my life and this trip is certainly no exception. Make sure you're both ready tomorrow night at midnight. I'm going to give the guards on duty a little something to help them sleep. Then I'll be able to shut off the cameras within the compound. Mirienne, you board the craft and get it ready for us. Eridamus, we'll wake the students then I'll take you to where they're holding Leo. I'd rather get him first but it's too risky in case something goes wrong.'

'You'll be in so much trouble when they find out,' Eridamus said, touching his face.

'There's too much at stake for me to worry about that. If that gold gets in the wrong hands the whole galaxy will be enslaved, not just humans.'

As they plotted Leo's escape, they never noticed that Star had been watching them the whole time.

CHAPTER SIXTY-FOUR

ONCE THEY WERE BACK AT the compound the students were given time for a rest before their "night on the town". Kelly and Ben arrived with a mobile wardrobe stacked with going-out clothes which they wheeled into their bedroom.

When they'd chosen their outfits, they opened the door and Ben whistled in admiration. 'You aliens sure are hot!' he said, fanning himself with his phone.

Star wore a short skirt that showed off her slim, toned legs and a long-sleeved, figure-hugging black top that gave her enough coverage not to feel awkward but also complimented her shape. Alhena wore a brightly coloured long dress that was tight around the chest but fell into an ankle length A-line skirt. Both wore flat, ballet-style shoes. Lacarta wore dark blue denim jeans, a white t-shirt with the word "Levis" written on it and Converse on his feet. He put his glasses on and stared at his reflection in the mirror, a big smile on his face. Alhena beamed at him as he did a twirl.

Kelly added a few accessories to each of them then passed them over to Ben for the finishing touches.

'We've set your phones up on all the social media sites in case anyone looks into you. If you need to pay for anything, it's all done via your phone. Looks like you're ready for your first night on the town!' he said, ushering them out of their room. As Lacarta walked past him Ben did a double take and opened his mouth to say something but Kelly put her finger up to her lips and glared at him.

'What's with the lad?' he asked her as they walked down the corridor, the students in front of them.

'Sshhhh!' she said. Then quieter, 'I'm not quite sure. Something a bit different about him, though, isn't there?'

'Yeah, can't put my finger on what it is.'

'Don't say anything, will you?'

'Moi?' he feigned shock. 'Course not.'

Within an hour they were heading out of the station and into the bright city lights. Star gazed up at the tall buildings above her. Coca-Cola, Pepsi, Subway, Burger King and McDonalds' advertisements beamed from every spare space there was. The streets were busy with young humans milling about, all with masks on.

Lacarta stared at a group walking past them.

'Lacarta!' Star nudged him.

'What?'

'Don't stare!' she whispered.

'I'm sorry,' he whispered back, 'but I don't think I'll ever get used to seeing people with masks on their faces.'

Ben walked quickly and soon they found themselves standing outside a bar called Sam's Place. 'Here we are,' he announced. 'Give me a sec. My mobile phone doesn't get a signal down here so I'll check my messages then be with you.' He walked off with his head bent over his phone.

Kelly tutted. 'Can't live without that damned phone.' They headed down the steps into the noisy room below. 'I'll get the non-alcoholic drinks,' she said pointedly and headed to the bar, signalling for them to go and sit on a large, inviting, red sofa in the corner.

After a few minutes she arrived with a tray of drinks and asked Lacarta to budge up so she could sit down. Each of them took a tentative sip and scrunched their faces up as the foreign-tasting fizzy liquid landed on their taste buds.

'Hey, Kelly!' an attractive man said, plonking himself next to her, giving her a kiss on the cheek.

'Hey, Robert,' she said, beaming at him.

'You on a work night?' he asked, looking at Star, Alhena and Lacarta.

Kelly nodded. 'This is Star, Alhena and Lacarta.'

'Nice to meet you guys,' Robert said, smiling. 'Ben with you?' and she nodded again to which Robert tutted. 'He walks like he's got a bee up his bum,' he said, eyeing Ben as he walked rigidly to the table.

'Robert,' Ben nodded.

'Ben.'

'What do you think of our lovely planet, then?' Robert asked, much to the alarm of the others. 'It's alright! I used to work at the compound. Ben took over from me; think you've still got a bit of learning to do, haven't you?' he said, winking at Kelly who laughed as she sipped her drink.

'I think it's amazing!' Star said. 'It's so noisy but I love it!'

'The last one I met loved it here as well. In fact, he loved it so much, or should I say he loved a human so much, he never went home!'

'That's so romantic!' Alhena said breathlessly, staring at Lacarta.

'He was everything you'd ever want in a man,' Kelly said dreamily. 'Kind, funny, caring. Easy on the eye too.'

'Oy, me and Ben'll get a complex, thank you very much!' Robert said.

'You know you're already all those things, Robert,' she said, nudging him, 'but since you're gay it's not likely I'm going to end up with you, is it?'

'What about Ben here? Isn't he any of those things?' he asked and they all turned to look at Ben who was scrolling through pictures on his phone. The group stared at him for ages expecting him to say something but he was too engrossed to hear them. 'Guess not,' Robert said sighing. Robert glanced at Lacarta and smiled. 'Excuse me, mate, you alright?'

Lacarta looked about, making sure he was the one being spoken to. 'Yes, thanks.'

'It's just you look like something's happened to your face or something,' he said, circling his face with his finger.

Kelly glared at Robert and muttered, 'Shut it,' under her breath.

Robert looked at her confused. 'What? What's the matter? Oh no, did something go wrong when you came to Earth?'

Ben leant over to Robert and said, 'He's Trisomy 21, I've been researching it on my phone.'

Robert tipped his head back and slapped his hand on his thigh, 'This is just brilliant, bloody brilliant. Hi!' he said, reaching his hand across to Lacarta and shaking his firmly. 'Great to meet you. Wow, I bet they never expected this back at the compound. How did they take it?'

'Not good,' Lacarta said. 'I'm not quite sure why it's so bad.'

'Because women aren't allowed to have babies like you, even if they want them,' Robert said.

'I know,' Lacarta replied. 'It's terrible.'

'Too right it is,' Robert said and Lacarta met his eyes. 'Most people aren't bothered about the diagnosis but they're given so many terrifying facts about it they end up feeling like they've got no choice but to terminate the pregnancy.'

'Why would they create so much fear? I'm just the same as Star and Alhena back home. It's only here I've been told I'm different,' Lacarta said.

'Partly because they thrive on spreading messages of fear but also because "they" don't want babies like you born,' he replied.

'Why not?' Alhena asked.

'Who knows? I've got my own theory though,' he said, tapping the side of his nose.

'What's that?' Kelly asked.

'I did a load of research on this. I found out one of the main side effects of Trisomy 21 is that they can be very affectionate, loving people.'

'But that makes no sense?' Alhena said.

Kelly interrupted. 'It does if you look at it from "their" point of view. They want mums and dads at work, kids in nursery from a few months old. If they become too attached to their baby, they find it really hard to go back to work. A trisomy child would need to be looked after longer, therefore increasing the time a mum has to bond with them. If they realise how loving they are they'll never want to leave them. Then the woman becomes a drain on the economy – not contributing to the taxation system.'

'Exactly! Kelly, you've come a long way since we last met!' Robert said, leaning back and crossing his arms. 'I'm impressed!'

'You have that effect on people,' she said, nudging him. 'You wake us up from our slumber.'

Robert smiled at her. 'Let's hope so.' He leant towards the three students and said, 'Hey, we're on a night out, aren't we? Anyone take your fancy?' They looked slowly round the bar. One man was eyeing up a girl who stood with a group of friends, blissfully unaware of his eyes on her.

'Why doesn't he go and talk to her?' Star asked Robert, pointing at them.

Robert laughed. 'He hasn't had anywhere near enough to drink yet!'

'That guy looks nice,' Star said, pointing to a man who seemed to be keeping all his friends doubled up with laughter.

'That's Joel,' he said. 'He works with me. Totally different in the daytime to who he is at night. Won't say boo to a goose at work.'

'He works with geese, does he?' Lacarta asked.

Robert leant over and touched Lacarta's arm. 'It's a phrase, honey. You're just like Orion, he took everything literally too!' he said, leaning back into the sofa and taking a sip of his drink.

'Orion?' the three said in unison, their eyes bulging in surprise.

Robert looked at all of them staring at him and leant forwards. 'Do you know him?'

'He's my cousin! We've been told he's on some space mission to another galaxy and won't be back for another orbital!' Star said.

'Ah, well that would appear to be a lie of sorts,' he said.

Kelly continued the story. 'Orion fell madly in love with the lovely Mary Wright, as she became known at the compound. They made such a great couple. Robert helped get them together, didn't you?'

'Do you mean to tell us Orion's living here – on Earth?' Lacarta asked.

'That's exactly what we're telling you,' Robert said.

'Where is he? Can we see him?' Star said.

'They're living somewhere in the woods together,' Kelly sighed. 'Sleeping under the stars and gazing into each other's eyes, no doubt.'

'His poor mum!' Star said.

'I can't believe she never told us,' Lacarta said, his eyes filling up with tears.

'You know them well?' Kelly asked.

'She's our favourite elder,' Alhena sighed.

'Come on, then,' Robert said, changing the subject, 'are you guys going to give us another love story to dream about when we're back home in our dull apartments?' He looked around at Star, Alhena and Lacarta. Alhena was staring at Lacarta as she took a sip of her drink, a misty-eyed look on her face. 'Oops, didn't realise you were already taken, mate!' he said to Lacarta, nodding his head towards Alhena.

'What?' he said, looking at Alhena and then to Robert. 'Us … a couple …? No, we're just friends.'

'Awwwkwaarrd!' Robert said, grabbing his drink and phone. 'Sorry, Alhena.' He grimaced as she glared back at him.

'Err, Ben?' Kelly said but Ben didn't look up from his phone. 'Ben?' she tried again. 'Ben!' she said, giving him a kick under the table. 'Help me get some more drinks.' She grabbed his hand and dragged him to the bar.

Lacarta turned to Alhena, his brow wrinkled in confusion, 'What did he mean?'

Alhena took a sip of her drink, 'I'm not really sure,' she shrugged.

'Was he right?' Star asked her. 'Do you like him?'

Alhena shrugged again, then said quietly, 'Maybe.'

Lacarta looked down at his hands and then up at Alhena, a grin spreading across his face. 'Really?' he asked and she nodded back. 'For how long?'

'Only for forever. It's always been you,' she whispered. 'Only you.'

'I had no idea.'

'I know. It's fine. I know you love Star.'

Confusion flickered over Lacarta's face, 'Star? I don't love Star! We're best friends! We'd be terrible together, wouldn't we?'

'Alhena, I can't believe you'd think that! We've been best friends for as long as I can remember, nothing more,' Star said.

'I just thought …'

'You thought wrong,' Lacarta said firmly. 'The thing is, I've always liked you too but you're so independent, spending so much time with your plants. I didn't think you had time to think about anything else,' he smiled.

'The reason I spend so much time with them is because they let me prattle on about you!' she said.

Lacarta took her hand in his and kissed it. 'Alhena, would you do me the greatest honour of being my "girlfriend" as they say on Earth?' Alhena nodded and laughed at the same time.

Star sat slightly apart from them, her arms crossed. Jealousy that had initially crept into her outer extremities shrivelled back. She leant forwards and wrapped her arms around the two best friends she'd ever had.

CHAPTER SIXTY-FIVE

THE NEXT DAY THEY WOKE early having slept surprisingly well despite their late night. Alhena and Lacarta, who loved his glasses so much he even slept with them on, couldn't stop looking at each other and giggling.

'Guys, I need to chat to you about yesterday.' Star said after breakfast. Just then the door swooshed open and General Arrakis and General Zaurak walked in.

'Lovely to see you all!' they said, their arms outstretched. 'I'm sorry we haven't been to see you sooner. Have you enjoyed yourselves?'

'It's been incredible,' Lacarta said, gazing at Alhena.

'How wonderful. She's certainly very beautiful, isn't she?' General Arrakis said.

'She sure is,' Lacarta said dreamily.

Star whispered to Lacarta, 'He means planet Earth.'

Lacarta looked at her and frowned, 'I know!'

'Today, fledglings,' began General Zaurak, 'you'll be able to mix with humans going about their daily business. Your uniform is in the drawers underneath your beds. Don't forget to bring your mobile phones which are also there as well as your exemption badges which state you don't need to wear a mask.'

'We went out last night without wearing them!' Star said.

'It's fine. Things are a bit more casual in the evening. All the elderly are either at home or in old people's homes. During the day if you aren't wearing an exemption badge, you'll be expected to wear a mask. You need to keep these on your person at all times. We're hoping you'll be able to have some time in an office but until we gain the correct passes, you'll be free to roam the streets of our city, under constant surveillance, of course. If you ever feel under threat press the red button on your phone and an official will be with you within seconds. Eridamus and Rigley have offered to show you round. Normally we'd like to but we have too much on our plate at the moment. Let's hope things settle down soon,' Arrakis said as an aside to Zaurak.

'They'll be taking you there in thirty minutes. Don't be late. We don't want you to miss all the fun of rush hour,' Zaurak said, smiling.

The fledglings opened their drawers and got dressed into the clothes they'd been given. The girls wore skin-coloured tights, a navy-blue skirt, a white shirt and a matching jacket. They pulled out a pair of black shoes that had a small heel and placed their feet into them, scrunching up their faces in pain as they felt their toes twist into positions they'd never been manoeuvred into before.

Lacarta wore dark trousers with matching jacket and a white shirt with a brightly coloured tie around his neck. On his feet he wore shiny black, pointed shoes that he took an instant dislike to. After breakfast they brushed their teeth and waited for the next set of instructions.

At 8.15 a.m. the door swooshed opened and General Rigley and Elder Eridamus entered the room wearing similar clothes to the fledglings. The door swooshed shut.

'You all look very smart, well done,' said Rigley. 'We'll be with you at all times today so you've got nothing to worry about.'

Eridamus continued, 'Your bodies will find the sights, sounds, smells as well as the electromagnetic fields from all the Wi-Fi and mobiles phones very toxic so you may feel your head pounding at times. When you return here, you'll be able to ground yourselves and rid your bodies of all of them. The space centre is completely protected from all the emissions. If for any reason we get split up then our numbers are in your phones but do not press them against your ear – they're incredibly harmful to your brains. If you must use them, hold them as far away from your body as possible.'

Eridamus pressed the button and the door glided open. Grabbing their bags and slinging them over their shoulders the students followed her and the general down the corridor. Humans walked past them in the corridors, generally uninterested in the small group. As one group walked past, Star made eye contact with a male who stared back at her – his eyes as black as night. He brought his hand up to his face and using two of his long thin fingers he first pointed them at his eyes and then to hers. Star shivered involuntarily. Once he was past her, she couldn't resist turning her head to get another look. As she turned, he was doing the same. Their eyes met and she felt frozen in fear. He opened his mouth and a tiny, forked tongue snaked its way around his lips.

CHAPTER SIXTY-SIX

TIME WAS RUNNING OUT AND Orion still hadn't found Mary. He'd enlisted the help of the two pixies but every search drew a blank. He was starting to give up all hope of ever seeing her again.

He'd searched for her himself by shape-shifting into every animal he could think of in order to cover every inch of the forest. When he gave up looking, he'd eat some of the root, allowing his soul to travel at breakneck speeds to the space centre.

A few days ago, Melantho had stopped beating Leo and Orion felt he could breathe again. The relief was huge. Leo had been given food and water and he'd started to get some colour back in his cheeks. Melantho had been extra friendly to Leo, gently asking him where "it" was but when Leo said he didn't know, he'd let it go and said, 'Not to worry, it'll come to you.' One day they'd even sat there laughing about some of the committee members and how hooked on the 'Me, Myself and I' app they'd become. At one point Orion wondered if he was going to let Leo go. That was until Melantho returned with an array of sickening implements that he carefully extracted, with his black-gloved hands, from his toolbox one by one. As he lay each one on the table he said, 'That one's for Monday, that's for Tuesday, this one's for Wednesday ...' until he'd placed seven items of torture on the table across from where Leo sat.

'Ready to talk yet?' he'd asked when he'd finished.

'What do you mean? That's what we've been doing isn't it?' Leo said, his voice rising in panic.

'I've tried being nice to you, haven't I? Isn't that what I've been doing while you bleat on about the other committee members telling me what you really think about them? I've tried to save you, but you leave me no choice. We start tomorrow. Least you've got your strength up.' He let out a little laugh. 'Monday's particularly nasty. I find my … ahem … "patients" often throw up anything they've got left in their stomachs.'

'Please don't do this,' Leo pleaded. 'You can't want this for either of us.' He paused a moment then said, 'What has Rastaban got over you?'

Melantho paused for a moment. 'What do you mean?'

'We didn't always see eye to eye but is this really what you want? To torture me until I either die or make up whatever it is you want me to tell you? I don't know what you're looking for and I definitely don't know where it is!' For a moment it looked as if he'd got through to Melantho as his eyes softened and his shoulders slumped forwards as if all the fight had gone out of him. 'Come on, neither of us want this. Do we?' Leo said softly.

At that point Melantho reached over, grabbed a short knife from the table and charged at Leo who reeled back in shock. He held the knife to Leo's throat so hard a line of blood seeped over the shiny blade. 'You make me sick,' he seethed. 'You come here, lording over the Committee, expecting everyone to bow down to you.' Leo went to open his mouth but felt the blade sink further into his skin. 'We've had enough. Aldor worked tirelessly for centuries to mine all the gold. They did it for their children! And you lot have taken it and hidden it from them. How sick can you be? None of you lot give a stuff about humans. If you did, you'd let Aldor have the gold.

They'd be at peace.' Melantho slowly removed the knife from Leo's neck and walked back to the table. 'Then they'd liberate humans. They'd never let humans have the gold again; it's too dangerous for them but not for Aldor. It'll save them.'

'Is that what you believe? That once they've got the gold, they'll free everyone?' Leo almost laughed. 'Why didn't they do that when they had access to all of it? Answer me that, eh? They had it for centuries!'

Melantho turned round to face Leo. 'What do you mean?'

'I mean they've already had the chance! Celestians don't have any need for gold. It's never been in our charge, has it? We've never had access to the banks or any of the vaults. He's messing with you, Melantho! Can't you see that?'

Melantho picked the knife up and hurled it towards Leo who moved his head just as it whistled past his ear. 'Rastaban trusts me and I trust him. He's been manipulated and mistreated by the Committee for too long. I promised him I'd help find the gold and I'm a man of my word. Unlike you,' he spat.

'You're playing a dangerous game. Why can't you see that? Aldorians aren't like you or me ...'

'Don't you dare make out we're the same!' Melantho screeched. 'I'm nothing like you. I'm going to fight for my race and for the Aldorians. You don't know anything about Rastaban. He's a kind, decent family man ...'

'A family man? What are you talking about?' Leo shouted.

Melantho pointed at Leo and yelled, 'You say one more word against him and I'll start work on you today, not tomorrow. Understand?'

Leo shrank back in the chair.

'It's you who's playing a dangerous game, Leo. When I come back, you'd better start talking. I'm going to look forwards to working with ... I mean ... on you.' Melantho let out a cruel laugh, turning the bright light off as he left the room, plunging Leo into darkness for eighteen interminably long hours.

Five days into the week of torture and his current method of questioning was placing electrodes on the base of Leo's feet. Melantho would flick a switch which sent shock waves through Leo's body. The vein on Melantho's neck pumped angrily as he watched Leo writhe and scream in agony and at times Orion was sure a smile passed over his lips. Then he'd flick the lever and it would all be over, until his return a couple of hours later. He'd slam the door shut, taking his gloves off as he left, saying he'd go and get some more tips from Rastaban. But still Leo refused to talk. The tap continued to drip from the basin in the corner.

Orion was in turmoil. He'd pinned all his hopes on the pixies finding Mary but their searches had all been in vein. He was starting to accept the fact she must have given herself up to the authorities just as she'd said she would.

He placed the sequente on the floor and called for the pixies. Within a flash they were there. Tabitha had a towel wrapped round her head and body; two tiny slippers adorned her feet. Veruna was in a pair of pants and had foam all over his chin, a razor in his hand.

'What is it?' they both said angrily.

'What are you doing?' Orion asked.

'Getting ready to go out!'

'Have you found Mary yet?' he asked and they both shook their heads. 'Me neither. I can't leave without knowing.'

'It's time to accept she's gone home,' Veruna said, patting Orion's hand gently.

'We've looked everywhere,' Tabitha said.

A tear fell from Orion's face onto the ground, splashing both of the pixies.

Veruna sighed. 'Tell you what, as soon as it's daylight me and Tabitha will head out one last time.'

Orion nodded resignedly. 'I don't think I'm ever going to see her again.'

'I know son, I know,' Veruna said.

That night Orion didn't sleep a wink. Part of him was desperate to find Mary and be with her but the other part knew he had to move forwards with his life. The only way he could do that was by trying to get home now he had potentially the only opportunity available to him. Twice he got up and walked along the tunnel to the grate located by the office block he felt sure Star would be visiting. Both times he checked he could move the heavy lid, becoming paranoid that something would stop him from intercepting her at the last minute. He'd even poked his head out to see whether there were surveillance cameras on the street and was relieved to see they were further down – where the street met the busy road. He tried shape-shifting but his energy levels were so low he had to give up.

His plan was really not that watertight when he thought about it. Yes, he'd been able to communicate with Star telepathically and view her in the sequente but he had no way of communicating with her directly. 'If only I had a mobile phone, it would all be so much easier,' he thought with some irony. The office block, where he'd worked all those months ago, had to be the only place they could visit. There'd been no other offices that he knew of which allowed visits from aliens. If Star came here, he had to hope that, somehow, he was able to intercept her whilst she walked along the street or before she entered the building. There were no guarantees either of those things would happen, though.

When he finally lay down to get some rest it was getting light. As promised, the two pixies appeared a little bleary-eyed after a late night but determined to give the search their best shot.

'Thanks guys. Thanks for everything. I'm going to miss you – if I manage to get home that is,' Orion said, bending down and hugging them.

'Whenever you need us, we're here for you,' Tabitha said with tears in her eyes. 'The underworld will always welcome you. You know that, don't you?'

Orion nodded, 'Thanks so much and good luck. Bye, Veruna; bye Tabitha.' He shook Veruna's tiny hand and gently kissed the back of Tabitha's. With a click of their fingers they were gone to search for Mary one last time.

CHAPTER SIXTY-SEVEN

A TINY SHARD OF SUNLIGHT crept in from one of the few gaps in the mud walls and rested on Mary's cheeks. She opened one eye and felt a wave of nausea hit as she remembered she was still in the hands of this maniac. None of the stories she'd read about befriending your captor had worked. There was nothing more she could do to stay alive. Russ was planning to kill her today, the anniversary of his wife's death. He'd waited all this time for a reason. He'd said he wanted to do it on a special day. A day that meant something to him.

'Then I'll be able to remember you and my missus on the same day every year,' he sneered. 'Not much good with dates so it'll save me celebrating twice.'

Mary had got used to him saying such foul things and knew he got a kick out of it. She now knew to remain devoid of any emotion no matter how sick his comments were. When she'd first started crying, he'd smiled. She thought he was softening so she'd pleaded with him, begged him to let her go. It was only when he grabbed her hair and kissed her roughly on the mouth, she realised how much he enjoyed seeing her beg for mercy.

He'd kept her hands tied the whole time, only loosening the

rope when she needed to go to the toilet. Still he wouldn't take his eyes off her no matter how many times she asked him to look away. When he had to go out to hunt, he tied her so tightly against the pole in the middle of the hut she had no hope of wriggling free. None of the escape tricks she'd seen in the movies worked. In all the days they'd been here she'd never heard one other human walk by and the hut was so well hidden they'd never notice it even if they did. All hope of being found had long gone.

She thought of Orion and how she'd never have the life she'd longed for with him. There were going to be no little Mary and Tommy's running about the place after all. A tear slid down her blackened face and dropped onto the ground below.

She tried to move but Russ had tightened the rope around her hands and feet particularly effectively last night. She looked around and saw Russ sharpening his knife on the stool in the corner. Seeing her awaken he smiled a sickening smile. 'It's time,' he said and came over to where she lay. He drew the knife across her cheek and a tiny trickle of blood appeared.

'I'm going to enjoy you more than my wife,' he said.

Mary felt all fight ebb away from her. There was nothing she could do apart from surrender to her fate. She just prayed he'd make it quick. Just then a stone came hurtling through the hut, smacking Russ square in the eye causing him to yell out in pain. He dropped the knife and pulled his hand up to his face.

'What the?' he managed to mutter before falling headfirst onto the floor, right next to where Mary lay, as shocked as he was. He tried scrabbling to his feet but found himself being hurled back onto the floor, his chin hitting the stool he'd only just sat on.

Mary felt some light feathery fingers undoing the rope that tied her hands and feet together. She pulled herself onto her feet.

'Come here, you,' Russ said, getting onto his feet and reaching out to grab Mary just as his knife came hurtling through the air whizzing past his cheek.

'Run, Mary and don't look back!' Tabitha shouted at the top of her voice. Mary looked around but couldn't see where the voice came from. She ran blindly out of the hut and looked back to see whether Russ was chasing her. Russ was in his hut, hopping this way and that as eight tiny green pixies wound the rope that Mary had just been tied with around his feet. His arms flailed frantically as he lashed out – not sure what he was aiming at since he couldn't see what was doing this to him. He was so disconnected with nature, the mere thought of pixies existing let alone being able to do this to him would have had him falling off his stool with laughter. Sometimes it fitted that humans didn't believe in them. 'Arrrgghhhh!' he cried as a stick whacked him behind his knees making him fall to the ground. He looked up to see the knife he was just about to use on Mary waggling in front of his face as if it were dancing of its own free will. 'What the?' he screamed as a stick came hurtling down on his head, knocking him clean out. The pixies wrapped the rope around his arms and feet and danced on Russ's unconscious body.

Tabitha and Veruna had been discovered the night before, wailing that they'd lost their boy, that they were never going to see him again. When they'd calmed down, the chief pixie, Great Jed, had asked for the full story. He'd been cross at Veruna and Tabitha for keeping Orion a secret, especially when he'd heard about the sequente. Old Jed got a map out of the woods and crossed off all the areas they'd already searched. It didn't take long to discover which areas they'd missed and search parties had been sent out to each location.

'This way!' Veruna and Tabitha said, running in front of Mary as she now followed the tiny creatures through the forest towards the tunnel.

'Who are you?' she called as they ran.

'Friends of Orion!' Veruna shouted. 'He's been looking for you every night. The man hid you so well, it's taken us ages to find you!'

'He was just about to kill me!' Mary panted.

'We'll sort that man out when we've got you safe. The woods will be rid of him soon. I have a feeling the Skriffter is going to be super hungry tonight,' Tabitha said with a chuckle.

They raced through the waterfall, down the long tunnel until it narrowed and Mary had to get down on her hands and knees. The pixies guided her to where it met the city's network.

'He did it!' Mary exclaimed on seeing the gap in the wall.

'We've missed him; it's too late!' Tabitha wailed.

Mary held the little pixies in the palm of her hand while they told her all about Orion and how they'd been looking after him ever since she'd disappeared. They explained to her that he'd made the decision to go home once he'd freed Leo. 'When's he planning to leave?' Mary asked breathlessly.

'Tonight! He's going to try and intercept Star while she's in the city and then meet at the space compound. The tunnel is so long you're never going to make it in time.'

'I've got to try! Thank you so much,' Mary said, waving good-bye. She slipped through the hole in the rock face and onto the concrete tunnel the other side.

CHAPTER SIXTY-EIGHT

GENERAL RIGLEY GUIDED THEM THROUGH the maze of the space centre and finally onto a platform where they waited for a train to arrive. It glided to a standstill in front of them and they hopped onto the empty carriage.

As it headed out into the bright sun and away from the compound, they took in the scenery around them. At first all they could see were enormous fields but gradually the countryside began to change, trees became greener and thicker. At one point they went through a deserted village, its houses stood desolate and dejected having long forgotten what it felt like to have humans living inside. Stray dogs pottered in and out of the houses, chasing cats as they searched for food. Soon the high-rise buildings came into sight.

'That's one of the residential districts,' General Rigley said as he leant over to the three of them and Elder Eridamus sighed sadly.

As they got closer, they could see the buildings were about thirty storeys high with little windows on each floor. Some were open, letting the curtains flap gently in the wind. Each building had huge masts on it which the general explained were for their mobile phones and televisions. The train eventually pulled into the station where they disembarked, walked through a small door and found themselves the first ones on a commuter train into the city.

They thanked their lucky stars they had a seat but that didn't last long as the general made each one get up for either a heavily pregnant lady or an older person. Within minutes they found themselves pressed closely against humans of all shapes and sizes, all wearing face masks. At one point Star found her nose pressed forcibly into a large man's sweaty armpit as the train lurched to a stop. The man neither looked up from his phone nor registered this intrusion of his physical space. When the doors flung open, they piled out of the station where they were instantly blasted with the noise they'd last heard at their Centre of Learning. Sirens whirred, songs blasted out from various shops, billboards flicked through adverts, cranes crunched metal on metal as they built more office blocks around the already very dense space.

'I can't take this noise!' Lacarta cried. Humans close by gave him funny looks.

'Hold hands!' Star said as the two females grabbed a hand each, pulling him through the crowds until they turned a corner into a quieter street. Elder Eridamus and General Rigley were nowhere to be seen.

They watched as hundreds, if not thousands, of humans marched past, all immersed in their own worlds. Then a click as the clocks turned to 08:55 and the streets were deserted as the humans descended into their large office blocks.

'Bloody commuters,' a gruff voice said next to them. They turned to see a scruffy looking man sat on the concrete road, a hat with some bits of food next to him. 'Used to be one of them myself till they closed my bank accounts. Just like that,' he said as he clicked his fingers, 'and I'm deleted from the system, as if I'd never existed.' A police car sounded its siren and the man gathered up the food, shoving it all into one of his deep pockets. He placed the hat on his head and walked away.

'Where did Eridamus go?' asked Star. They poked their heads round the corner of the building and were relieved to see Rigley and her walking towards them. Eridamus's worried face relaxed when she spotted them. She signalled for them to follow her and Rigley. Only a few humans remained on the street. A man swept the pavement, the gentle swooshing sound of the brush on the concrete echoing around the empty streets. A food van arrived and began setting up. He put up his sign offering 'Coffee, Tea. Expressos'. A billboard above them with a strip line underneath broadcast the latest news updates.

They walked until they got to a large open space labelled City Park. A few lonely trees swayed gently to and fro, providing scant shelter for a couple of rickety swings, a rusty slide and a tired-looking roundabout.

The general got out his phone and said clearly, 'Could I have a cup of traditional tea, one cup of black coffee, one white, one expresso and a cup of hot water with lemon in, please?'

Star looked at her two friends in confusion.

'Certainly, sir,' Elder Eridamus replied in an unusual voice. She then proceeded to cup her hands round her mouth and make the most unusual gurgling and hissing noises from her mouth.

'We don't have long,' the general whispered whilst Eridamus made the strange noises. 'We've got to get you home – tonight. I'll explain later.'

'I heard you talking on the craft yesterday,' Star said, interrupting him. 'You've found Dad.'

Rigley put his finger up to his lips. Alhena and Lacarta looked between the pair, their eyes wide and questioning. 'When you get back to the compound you need to act totally normal. Tell whoever asks you're looking forward to working in one of the offices tomorrow. We'll come and get you soon after midnight; you need to be packed and ready to go.'

Elder Eridamus continued making the noises but she knew time was running out. There was only so long five drinks would take to make. 'Here are your drinks, sir,' Elder Eridamus said. She made a little beeping noise, feigning accepting payment, and the conversation was over.

The group split up with the three fledglings wandering around the streets unsure of what to do next. They couldn't go for a drink since that was what they'd just pretended they'd done. They picked up a packet of crisps from a stall but put it back on the shelf until the owner forced them to buy it now that they'd touched it as they were spreading germs. Star pulled out her phone and placed it next to the woman's machine until it confirmed the transaction had been processed. The clocks in the streets clicked noisily as every minute passed and a new digit flipped down, the empty streets carrying the noise further than it would normally go.

Eventually a bell rung out at 13:00 and within minutes the streets were once again alive with humans pushing past them, shoving them this way and that. The kiosks and food outlets filled with people as they queued for their lunch. Vegan chicken burgers, vegan chicken wings, best burgers, meal deal, sandwiches were all on offer – meat options available on request.

Again, Lacarta found the noise overwhelming so they snuck down a back alley to escape. Finding a doorway, they sat down, relieved to be away from all the chaos. They breathed deeply, trying to regain some kind of stability in this chaotic world. Out of nowhere they heard, 'Don't move,' at which point they all turned towards the voice to see where it was coming from. 'I said don't move!' the voice tutted. 'You can tell you're not from here. Now stay quiet or they'll detect you.' The three tried to look around without moving their heads too much. 'I'm underneath you,' the voice said and very carefully, so as not to draw any attention they looked at a small circle in the road with a grate over the top. They leant forwards a fraction and could see a pair of eyes staring back at them.

'Which one of you is Star?'

Star looked startled upon hearing her name but nodded very slightly.

'It's me, Orion!' he whispered and Star's eyes bulged. 'I need to get a message to my mother.'

Moments later they found Elder Eridamus and the general walking together further along the street, their eyes a little misty as they gazed at each other. Star walked quickly past them saying loudly to Lacarta and Alhena, 'Could we just grab another drink please?'

The elder and general looked from Star to each other.

'Another round of tea and coffee maybe?' the general suggested to Eridamus who nodded back.

They turned the corner and headed back to the park where once again Elder Eridamus began making her coffee-making machine noises.

'Orion's here,' began Star, noticing Eridamus's eyes visibly widen in alarm and joy.

'He's where you found us a moment ago.'

'Here are your drinks,' the elder said, mimicking the beep of someone paying.

'Let's head back to the office, shall we? They might have our passes ready now,' the general said loudly, as the group signalled for him to follow them.

They walked back the way they'd come but just as Star was about to point to the manhole they saw two robotic-looking policemen heading their way. The general clutched his stomach and groaned, feigning illness. He looked at Elder Eridamus who put her arm around him, seemingly understanding what he was doing. The policemen walked steadily towards them.

'You feeling alright, General? No need to hurry; we'll sit here till you feel better,' Eridamus said, trying to keep up the act.

'What seems to be the problem?' the robots asked in unison.

'No problem, thanks officers,' Rigley said.

'Why are you littering the streets? The streets are not a place for vagabonds and tramps.'

'He's neither of them, I'll have you know!' Eridamus retorted.

'Don't raise your voice,' they replied.

'I'm not raising my voice!' she said, raising her voice.

'Please come to the station for questioning.' The robots moved to grab an arm each.

'Rigley 874593 – release suspect,' Rigley said.

The robots released Eridamus and moved on further down the road.

'What the hell are you doing?' he whispered.

Eridamus looked a little sheepish, 'Sorry. I can't bear to hear you being spoken to like that.'

Just then they heard a rattle coming from the drain nearby. A pair of eyes peered out from the darkness below. 'Mum!' he said.

Elder Eridamus gasped and reached for his hand but Rigley stopped her.

'I need you to help me, Mum. Can you do that?' His mother ever so slightly nodded. 'Meet me at the compound's station tonight at midnight. I'll make my way there along the drains.' Star could see the tears in her elders' eyes.

'You feeling better now, General?' she said, without giving any emotion away.

'Much better, thanks. Do you mind if we head back? Not sure if I'm up to showing you round the office today,' he said calmly as they walked back to the station.

CHAPTER SIXTY-NINE

WHEN THEY GOT BACK TO the base the group knew they needed to find somewhere they could talk without being overheard. The only place they could do that was aboard the craft. Lacarta made out he'd lost his glasses and could have left them there. The officer on duty waved them through. The building was as busy as ever, humans coming and going on carts, jeeps and trucks with ladders.

A group of humans were milling about at the base of their craft. Rigley showed them his ID and they allowed the group on board. The minute they boarded the craft and closed the door, they knew they only had moments before this action would be registered, possibly sending an alarm to the other generals. Eridamus let out a little sob and fell into Rigley's arms.

He stroked her hair saying, 'It's OK now, Eridamus. It's going to be OK.'

They hurriedly talked through the plan for the evening ahead and disembarked from the craft with moments before the alarm alerting the generals was due to sound.

That night the students were offered pizzas, hot dogs, burgers, crisps, chocolate brownies, cider, and alcopops to have in the comfort of their own quarters. The three of them pretended to eat and drink a few of the items by moving the food from their hands in front of their mouths into a napkin which they placed on their laps under the table.

The plan created by General Rigley on the craft was in motion. The general and Eridamus had explained that everyone was expected to be in their quarters by 22:00. General Melantho never slept on the base so would always leave around 18:00. They had suspicions that he had his own in-built surveillance room at home but hoped he'd be fast asleep by the time they started their escape. Military personnel manned the centre until 22:00 then it was just a couple of officers based in the surveillance room that did the night shift.

General Rigley had checked the names of the two on night duty and was relieved to see that he was on good terms with both. He planned to offer them some tea from his flask, something he'd often done but this time he'd have added a few sleeping pills to it. Once they'd taken effect, he'd get Eridamus and they'd make their way along the drains to where Orion would be waiting for them. The three of them would return to the compound, come and get Star, Lacarta and Alhena and then try and locate Leo. Mirienne was to be on board the craft before they closed the hangar for the night. She was currently working out how to board it without being noticed and planned to remain there for the evening. If anyone asked her questions, she could easily persuade them that she needed to check the craft over. She was well known for her fastidiousness.

Just before Captain Melantho left for the day he visited the group and asked how they were finding their meal. They all told him it was delicious and thanked him for providing such a good spread. As the door closed behind him, they all looked at each other; they couldn't bear being anywhere near the man.

Once the clock flipped over to read 22:00 General Rigley walked to the surveillance room, grabbing a chair and sitting down with the officers on duty. He chatted animatedly about people they were observing whilst pouring them both a cup of tea from his flask. They were too focused on the screens to realise he didn't take a sip. Gradually the tablets began to take effect, their speech became slurred and their heads slumped forwards into a deep sleep.

The general reached over and turned off the cameras that would reveal their movements. He put his phone on airplane mode then returned to where Elder Eridamus sat nervously waiting for him in her quarters. Telling her the coast was clear, they ran along the corridor and to the station. It had been a long time since he'd gained access to the drains but he knew exactly where they were. He'd always wondered if one day he may need these to escape too.

Close to the platform they found a large, grated square in one of the walls. He used a small drill from his pocket to take out each of the corner screws. Then he eased out the cover to reveal Orion's blackened face. 'Mum!' Orion said, falling into her arms.

The two hugged but Rigley knew they didn't have much time before the pills wore off. 'Hurry,' he said quietly.

'They're holding Leo,' Orion said as they walked quickly back into the compound. 'They've implanted something underneath his skin to stop him from using any of his powers.'

'Damn! I knew it,' Rigley said.

'That explains why he's not been able to escape!' said Eridamus.

'It must have something to do with those strange barcodes I saw on the files. I bet they've been doing it to all of them,' Rigley said.

Orion nodded. 'From what I've heard that's exactly what they've been doing. They're disabling the powers of many of the races that have been visiting. Who knows how many they've inserted the implants into.'

'But why Leo? Our powers are nothing compared to some of the other races!' Eridamus said.

'They're convinced Leo knows where the gold's been hidden,'

Orion said.

Rigley and Eridamus exchanged worried looks.

As they passed the surveillance room they could see both offic-ers still slumped on theirdesks. They were about to carry on when Orion stopped suddenly. 'What if they've got cameras where Leo's kept? They'll catch us all on film!'

'Of course!' Rigley said. 'We have to turn them off!'

'But we might wake them,' Eridamus said.

'We have to try. If they wake up, I'll do the talking,' Rigley said. He eased open the door and they crept into the small, dark room. Rigley scrolled through all the cameras; thousands of humans slept in their beds.

'It's no good, I'm never going to find it. If there's cameras in his cell they're going to have them well hidden, aren't they?' he whispered.

Suddenly one of the guards shouted, 'Stop! No, Eddie, stop!' All of them froze, wondering how they were going to explain them-selves but before they had to work out what excuse they were going to use he snorted and fell back to sleep. Orion wiped his brow with the back of his hand.

'Have you ever seen Melantho looking at something he shouldn't?' Eridamus said.

Orion and Rigley raised their eyebrows. 'All the time!' Rigley replied.

'Any idea where he'd be storing these?' she asked.

'Maybe he has a private account?' Rigley said, typing Melantho's name into the keyboard. A notification popped straight up. 'Private Account, please type in password.'

'What the hell could it be?' Rigley asked the other two who looked utterly flummoxed.

Rigley punched a few suggestions in but all were rejected. 'Hmm, I don't suppose it would be ...' he pondered as he typed in

Rastaban. Immediately the screen read 'Access Granted'.

'What's the betting most of them are of attractive women?' Orion said. 'He's a right perv, Mum.'

'Orion!' she said. They turned to watch as Rigley examined the screens in front of them. An array of similar looking, attractive female faces smiled back at them.

'Told you,' Orion said.

At the bottom right of the viewing panel a smaller screen with the sub-heading 'SEED STORAGE' could be seen. Rigley clicked on it and suddenly they were viewing the inside of grey, concrete cells. 'He's here. I just know it,' Rigley said as they flicked through the cameras that were in each cell.

'What are we looking at?' Eridamus asked, screwing up her nose. Then as it dawned on her she gasped and took a step back. 'But there are so many of them!'

'Look!' Orion said, pointing at camera number 343. Rigley zoomed in on the image and they could just make out the image of a body lying in the foetal position on a floor. 'That's him! Now shut the cameras off!'

Rigley flicked a switch and the cameras went black.

'Come on!' Eridamus said, opening the door. They eased out of the room and ran to the student's quarters. The door swooshed open to reveal three very relieved faces.

As they followed the general and Eridamus, Star grabbed the opportunity to talk to Orion. 'It's been you calling me hasn't it?' she asked.

'Yes, I'm so glad you heard me.'

'I thought it might have been my dad,' she said.

'Telepathy wasn't his strong point. After the ambush he never wanted to use it again, said he blamed himself for not seeing it happen before they got off the craft. He's been watching you in this,' he said, pulling out the sequente. 'Every night he watched you; it's what got him through these last seven years. That and building the tunnel.'

'What tunnel?'

'He's spent the last five years, ever since he escaped the compound, digging a tunnel that connected to the city's network. Without the tunnel I wouldn't be here,' he said.

The group turned a corner, went down some steps, turned another corner and there it was – a big steel door with no handles or knobs to open it with. A sign on it said, STRICTLY NO ENTRY. AUTHORISED PERSONNEL ONLY.

'This is it,' Orion said and the general nodded. 'I've been coming through this door every night using adastral projection.'

'It's been used to store seeds for as long as I can remember then all of a sudden it became out of bounds and they put on this steel door that no one had access to. I knew something wasn't right, I had no evidence until recently. I wish I'd probed further.' Rigley scratched his chin. 'How the hell are we going to get inside?'

'Stand aside, gentle males,' Eridamus said with a small smile on her face.

She placed her hands on the door and began chanting. The patches around her hands heated up until the metal was so hot they could see the inner workings of the door. She pushed her hand into the scorching metal and moved the locking system until they heard a satisfying click and the door gently opened. She took her hands away from the door, stopped chanting and gestured for the males to enter.

'You told me there was a lot more to you than meets the eye,' Rigley said in admiration.

'I certainly did. It's been a long time since I've had to use that one,' she said.

They entered the poorly lit corridor that had doors either side as far as the eye could see. The most putrid smell hit their nostrils and they put their hands over their noses to try and block the stench.

As they closed the door behind them Star, Lacarta, Alhena, Orion and Eridamus gradually began turning back into their Celestian form.

'Holy Demeter, the vibrations are different here! They've raised them!' Star cried.

'Of course! That's why Leo's been in his Celestian form!' Orion said. 'I thought it was because he was so weak.'

For the first time since they'd met, Rigley watched as the woman he'd loved all these years transformed into her true form. He gasped and said, 'You're beautiful!' He stroked her hand as the markings appeared, snaking up her arm and towards her neck. Her tired-looking grey hair turned back to the rich silver colour she had on Celestia.

'Thank you,' she said coyly.

'What is this place?' Lacarta said. He peered into one of the little windows and screamed instantly, recoiling in shock. Inside lay a badly beaten alien, curled up into the foetal position.

'What is it?' said Star as she stood on her tip toes.

'Don't look, Star,' Rigley said, but it was too late.

'No!' she cried, turning to her friends, her face ashen. 'It's alive!' Her eyes were wide in shock as the creature moved ever so slightly.

'We have to hurry,' Rigley said, taking her hand. 'Come on.'

The group ran down the corridor to where Orion stood surrounded by identical looking doors. 'He's in one of these; we need to split up.'

All of them began peering into the cells, frantically trying to find which one held Leo. Every single one housed an alien. All were incredibly sick and some were dying, too weak to even lift their heads up off the floor to see what the disturbance was.

'We have to save them!' Eridamus cried.

'We can't,' Rigley said to her. 'There're too many. Our plan's to get Leo. That's what we have to do.'

The three of them carried on opening and closing the windows until finally they found him, barely alive, curled up, his long pale arms wrapped around his body, his tangled, violet hair barely visible amongst the filth and dirt of his cell.

'Leo, it's me. Orion,' he said into the window.

Leo looked up from the floor but his head fell back down, such was the effort it took to lift it. 'Leave me alone. I can't take it anymore,' he said.

'Star's here. She's finally here,' he whispered. 'Open the door, Mum.'

Elder Eridamus put her hands on the door, just as she'd done earlier. They heard the gentle, reassuring click as it opened. 'Stay here with Henry,' she said to the students as herself and Orion went inside the tiny, cramped, fetid cell and knelt down next to the frail body of their friend.

Leo began whimpering, 'Please don't hurt me, General Melantho! Let me be,' he said, trembling in fear.

'It's over, Leo. You're safe now,' Orion said, cradling Leo's head in his hands.

Leo looked up into the faces of the two Celestians and recognition flittered in his eyes. 'Eridamus? Orion?' he said.

'We've missed you so much, Leo,' Eridamus said.

Rigley took his jacket off and passed it to Orion who wrapped it round Leo's body and lifted him up. His form was so slight he carried him effortlessly out of the cell.

'Dad?' Star said with tears in her eyes as Orion walked past her carrying her father's lifeless body. Orion nodded sadly.

Suddenly the doors of the other cells were rattling; yells from the aliens cried out as they realised one of them was being rescued.

'Help us! Save us!' they called out over and over again.

As Alhena walked she covered her ears; it was too much to bear hearing the pain of so many beings.

'I can't leave them!' Eridamus cried.

'You have to, there are too many!' the general pleaded with her.

They got to the door that would lead them back to the concourse, away from the pleas of desperation. Eridamus ushered Orion out first as he held Leo, then the students and then Rigley. Just as she was about to close the door, she took one last look back at all the aliens clambering at their doors and screaming out at her. She lay her hand on the cell door closest to her until she heard the gentle click as it opened. 'Maybe I've helped just one of them,' she thought to herself as she shape-shifted back into her human form.

'Come on, we don't have time to waste,' Elder Eridamus said quickly before the others had time to wonder why she was so far behind them.

They raced down the corridor and into the hangar. The general held the door open for them as they piled passed him. He was about to close the door when a hand grabbed his shoulder. 'Stop right there!' a voice boomed.

CHAPTER SEVENTY

STAR NEARLY BURST INTO TEARS, picturing her mother's face as she was told that not only had she lost her soul mate but now her daughter too. She thought of her friends spending the rest of their lives in one of the dark, fetid cells.

Rigley turned to see Mark, one of the officers from the surveillance room, pointing his gun at them. 'The thing is Mark ...' Rigley began – his mind a complete blank. For a moment the two men just looked at each other before the silence was broken.

'Let them go,' another voice came from behind Mark.

The group turned in amazement to see Robert with a gun in his hand that he was pointing at Mark.

'Robert!' Orion cried with relief.

'What the ...?' Mark began.

'I said, let them go!' he barked, pulling the safety catch back on the gun.

Mark took his hand off the general's shoulder then turned to Robert.

'How the hell are you going to explain this one to your father?' he said.

'That's none of your business,' Robert replied. 'Pass it here and put your hands in the air,' Robert barked and Mark kicked his gun towards him. He leant down and picked it up, keeping his gun aimed at Mark the whole time. 'Looks like you just lost your job, mate.'

'What do you mean?' Mark asked.

'Drinking on duty. You know Dad's a stickler for that. He's not going to like it one bit, as well as falling asleep on the job. Got it all on camera,' he said, pulling out his phone showing a video of Mark and his colleague dancing around the surveillance room without a care in the world, topping each other's mugs up with vodka. Then another shot of them both with their heads slumped over their desks, snoozing contentedly, a little pool of dribble collecting on the desktop.

'But that never happened!' he protested.

Robert gasped. 'Thing is, the camera never lies, does it? Fortunately, I managed to take enough pictures of you both at the Christmas do last year to make a little home movie, shall we call it.'

All the colour from Mark's face drained instantly. 'Please, I beg of you, don't show him that. I'll do anything, your father … Rastaban … I'd hate to be on the wrong side of them.'

'I reckon your life will be a whole lot easier if you just head back to the surveillance room and pretend to be asleep until these lovely beings are safely on their way home. When my father arrives at work, incandescent with rage because these guys have managed to escape, you can explain that you were drugged, slept through the whole thing, only woke up when it was too late. That way you stand a chance of keeping your job. He's going to think you're an imbecile if you had them and let them escape. Any mention of me in this, then he'll be shown the footage of you and your mate having a little tipple. I've even got footage of you next to the bottle in the surveillance room.'

'But he'll never believe you! He can't stand you!' Mark said.

'Which is precisely why it won't be me showing him the footage. I've set up an anonymous account. You make one false move, I'll send the video over to him in an instant. Why don't you allow Zaurak and Arrakis the pleasure of accompanying you back to the surveillance room and get into position before I change my mind and accidentally send this video over right now,' he said as he placed his finger over the send button on his phone.

'I'm going, I'm going!' Mark said whilst being escorted away by Zaurak and Arrakis who emerged from behind Robert.

'Good luck!' they said, waving to the group.

'Aren't they coming with us?' Star said.

Eridamus shook her head. 'They're dedicated to the Committee. They'd never leave.'

The door slammed shut as the group ran down the stairs and into the hangar. Mirienne's face popped out of their craft. The craft lit up and its engine murmured softly as Mirienne started her up.

'Mum, do you think you can carry Leo?' His mother nodded and Orion eased Leo's tiny frame into her outstretched arms. Orion turned to give Robert a hug. 'Robert, what can I say apart from thank you!'

'It's not me you need to thank, Orion,' he said, turning as a figure emerged from the shadows.

'Mary!' Orion cried.

'Russ kidnapped me! Two pixies, Veruna and Tabitha, helped me escape and took me back to the tunnel to find you. You'd already gone, though! I managed to get to the outer limits of the city when I came across two people who'd just escaped the city with the help of Robert. Orion – they were only able to escape because of the tunnel! It's already being used! They showed me how they'd accessed it from the city and there was Robert just about to head back to work. You can't imagine how relieved I was to see him!'

Robert took up the story from there. At home the previous

evening he'd overheard his father on a phone call muttering about three students from Celestia who were on Earth, studying humans. 'He can't bear you lot studying us. He was moaning about why all their names had to be something ridiculous like "Star". It didn't mean anything to me at first. Then I remembered meeting you in the bar and when I saw Mary, she explained how you were trying to reunite Leo with his daughter, Star! That meant you had to be heading to the compound. We ran down the tunnels and came straight here. When you weren't here, but the craft was, I got Mary to hide while I went looking for you. Luckily Zaurak and Arrakis happened to be here and they said they'd make sure no one entered the hangar. They'd cottoned onto your plan and were trying to make sure you got home. I headed back to the surveillance room, noticed that one of the guys wasn't there so I came straight back. Just as I arrived Mark was there, pointing his gun at you lot!'

'I thought I'd missed you!' Mary said to Orion. 'I thought I was going to get here only for it to be too late. I didn't think I was ever going to see you again,' she said, looking into his eyes.

Eridamus gently coughed an, 'Ahem,' behind them and stepped forwards a little, 'Lovely to meet you, Mary. I'm Orion's mother,' she said, extending her hand.

'I've heard so much about you!' Mary said, ignoring her out-stretched hand and wrapping her arms around Eridamus. 'I'm so glad he's going home; he'll be safe now.'

'You're clearly a very special young lady,' she said. 'Thank you for loving my son. Maybe when this is all over he'll be able to return and be with you again.'

'I hope so but I'm just glad I got to say goodbye,' she said, looking up at Orion and kissing him. 'I love you so much.' The pair held each other, not wanting to let go. 'Now go!' Mary said, pushing Orion away.

'Looks like this is where we say goodbye,' Henry said to

Eridamus.

'Doesn't seem to be our time, does it?'

He shook his head. 'Maybe one day.' He stroked her cheek and kissed her. 'Take care.'

'You too. Be careful.'

'I'll be fine,' he said. 'I love you.'

'I love you, too,' she said. 'If the universe wants us to be together, we will.'

'You and your universe,' he smiled. 'Now focus all your attention on getting Leo back home.' He leant forwards, being careful not to harm Leo, and kissed her. 'Good luck. I won't ever stop thinking of you.'

Eridamus turned and walked up the steps and onto the craft, placing Leo gently down on the floor. She waved from where she knelt and Henry blew her a kiss.

The three students followed, waving at Robert and Mary.

'Come on, Orion! We have to go!' his mother called out. Orion turned to his mother and then back to Mary and instantly she knew it, before he'd even said the words. Her hand shot up to her mouth and tears sprung to her eyes.

'I have to do this, Mum,' he shouted. 'You know that don't you? I love her so much.'

Eridamus nodded, unable to speak but knowing exactly why her son had to stay. He had to follow his heart; he'd never be whole if he didn't. He turned to Mary and walked slowly towards her. Her face crumpled and she cried out, 'You can't stay! It's too dangerous!'

'But I can't leave either. My destiny is with you,' he said, pulling her into his arms and kissing her.

'I don't want to lose you,' she said, kissing him back, tears of joy and sadness trickling down her face.

'Looks like I'd better find you two somewhere safe to live. I can assure you that won't be at mine!' Robert said, putting his arms around them both and signalling for them to wave as the craft burst into life. The stairs disappeared into the craft and the door glided shut; lights shone brightly round the middle and its engine whirred into action. Within seconds it was lifting off, speeding down the tunnel as the group made their way back to Celestia.

CHAPTER SEVENTY-ONE

MELANTHO STRETCHED HIS ARMS, RUBBED his eyes and yawned. He looked at his clock which read 00.45. He shivered as the cool air of his apartment embraced him. Grabbing his dressing gown from the back of the door, he walked to the bathroom. On the way there he passed his surveillance room and poked his head around the corner. The screens stared blankly back at him. 'Must have turned them off,' he thought to himself. He noticed Robert's door was open and the bed still made. 'Out on the town again,' he tutted and his stomach tightened as to what he could be up to. How different Robert was to himself as a young man.

As he turned the light on in the bathroom, he scrunched his eyes up from the brightness then looked in the mirror. His bleary-eyed reflection stared back. His finger traced the red scratches on his face. He scratched at one of the scabs which had started to heal. Fresh blood trickled down the side of his face. He wiped it off with his finger, then licked it clean. He was about to go to the toilet when suddenly he was wide awake. His heart pounded as he ran back to the surveillance room. He hadn't turned it off before he'd gone to bed! He began punching at the buttons but none of the cameras were working. Just then the screens went gravelly and burst into life.

It took a few moments for him to register that instead of seeing a huge flying saucer in the hangar, he was staring into a large blank space. Frantically, now, he scrolled across to find the camera he needed, the one that meant everything to him and Rastaban. Finally, he reached it; camera 343 showing what was now an empty cell.

He slammed his fist onto the desk and a pain that had been hidden for many years welled up from deep inside of him, a hurt known only to those who have experienced truly unbearable pain.

The noise that came out of him was so unrecognisable even to himself, it could barely be described as human.

CHAPTER SEVENTY-TWO

MIRIENNE PULLED BACK THE LEVER and pressed down hard on another, causing the craft to go so low they were skimming the tops of the trucks beneath them. From beneath them Robert opened the door to the hangar just as Elder Mirienne pressed a button. The craft accelerated and they were out. They turned back to see the huge door of the hangar draw firmly shut.

'We did it!' they yelled.

They cheered and hugged each other until the craft burst through the Earth's stratosphere and out into the glorious night sky with all its stars and planets twinkling in the distance.

'We're going to get you home,' Eridamus said, stroking Leo's matted hair as her tears dripped onto his filthy face. His breathing was laboured and his eyes badly swollen. She bent her head so she could feel his breath as she stroked his face. He emitted a small grunt. 'It's OK now,' she whispered and his eyelashes fluttered slightly.

'Star? Do you want to come and see your dad?' she asked.

Star had been watching Eridamus tend to her father but had been too shocked to be able to do anything.

'Shape-shifting about to commence!' Mirienne called out. The craft jolted and gradually all of them began returning to their natural form. Alhena and Lacarta gazed at each other as the beings they had fallen in love with began to re-emerge. Lacarta held her hand until her transformation was complete. 'You look so much better as a Celestian,' he said, stroking her face.

'So do you,' she smiled. They turned to look at their friend as she bent down next to her father's body.

'He needs you,' Eridamus said, placing his hand in hers.

Star turned his arm a fraction and there it was, the line that she'd looked at when she was younger, the line that said he had a daughter about thirty-two orbitals old. 'Dad,' she sobbed and lay down next to him, holding her hand in his. Star lay next to her father the whole journey, not wanting to take her eyes off him in case he stopped breathing. She watched the gentle rise and fall of his chest, willing him to live.

A few hours before arriving on Celestia, Leo's breathing worsened. 'He's not breathing properly!' Star cried to Eridamus who came to sit with her, stroking Leo's hand.

His eyes fluttered open and he stared into the big, clear eyes of his precious daughter.

'My lovely Star,' he whispered. 'Tell your mother I love her.' His eyes closed and his chest ceased it's rise and fall.

'No!' screamed Star at the top of her lungs. She shook his body. 'I'm not going to lose you now. I can't lose you!' she cried.

'Move aside, Star,' Elder Eridamus said calmly. 'I'll see what I can do.' She lay her head onto his chest and chanted gently over and over again. Two Celestian crafts flew past, on their way to meet Mirienne's craft on its journey back home, just as General Rigley had requested. Mirienne flashed her lights to get their attention as they shot past her. Moments later they were back, guiding her back in a perfect pyramid, to the safety of Celestia. Eridamus breathed intermittently into Leo's mouth, laying her hands on his chest which remained motionless. She continued regardless, until finally, a beautiful planet came into sight; her rich blues and deep greens stood out against the darkness of space. Before long they were bursting through Celestia's stratosphere and into their own space compound.

'Alhena, go get Meisa,' Eridamus said the moment the craft landed. Alhena ran through the village. Beings were just waking up and having their morning drinks. 'Meisa,' she panted and Meisa turned to her with a look of such terror in her eyes.

'Star!' she cried, dropping her bowl. She ran towards the Centre of Learning, and onto the craft where her daughter sat next to a pile of tatty clothes.

'Mum!' Star said.

'I thought something had happened to you.' Seeing the tears in her daughter's eyes, she took in the scene around her. Her gaze passed over the fabric that lay next to Star, then noticed a hand poking out from underneath them. 'Leo?' Meisa asked.

Star nodded, tears pouring down her face.

Meisa knelt down and touched his face, showering him with kisses. 'Leo. Leo, it's me. It's Meisa,' she said, tears running down her face. She lay her hands on his chest and using every ounce of energy she had she began chanting the same word over and over again. 'Revitaemorum.'

His eyes fluttered and his fingers began moving. The wounds on his face shrank back and his skin took a richer tone. His lips lost their cracked, chipped look as life seeped back into every corner of his body. He felt for her hand and brought it up to his lips. 'My love.'

Meisa burst into tears and lay her head on his chest. Star looked on, her heart ready to burst.

'Thank you,' he said to Star, reaching for her hand. As he took her hand, his inner wrist glowed a very faint red, unseen to both of them. 'Thank you so much.'

CHAPTER SEVENTY-THREE

THE MELODIC NOTES OF "HAR Ji" echoed throughout the trees. The fireflies lit up the trees and the crystals levitated gently, ensuring the music could be heard from all around.

Star and Rhea stood outside their hut waiting for Leo and Meisa to emerge. Meisa helped Leo onto his feet and with the aid of a stick he joined his family as they walked slowly to Eridamus's hut. Eridamus was sat on her own waiting for them. She'd finally been honest with the village and told them the truth about Orion; he wasn't on a dangerous space mission but had fallen in love with a human. It was still so hard for her to accept he was never going to return but it was clear to her how much he loved Mary. A part of her was envious that he'd made the brave decision to be with her. No matter how much she loved Henry her journey was on Celestia, teaching the fledglings at the Centre of Learning. She'd told a little white lie when she said she couldn't live on Earth. She could, she just didn't want to. Maybe her love for him wasn't strong enough, she'd wondered time and time again. She stood up and linked arms with Rhea, resting her head on the older being's shoulder.

The whole village had been shocked at the pitiful sight of the man they'd remembered as being so full of life. The Seniors had called an urgent meeting to try and decide what to do now Earth was in such chaos. Discussions were underway but it wasn't proving easy to find a way forward.

Star waved at Lacarta and Alhena who were hand in hand, followed closely behind by their proud parents. Alhena's dad looked like he couldn't be happier for his daughter. The group exuded love.

Lacarta was still adjusting to life without his glasses, or so they all thought. Little did they know Alhena had sneaked them onto the craft. It was to be their little secret.

Star, Rhea and Meisa watched as Leo began to heal slowly. Meisa's healing abilities, passed down from generations, were strong but he was so frail and so much had happened to him it was going to take a while. They still didn't know if he had the mental capacity to ever truly recover.

Great numbers of Celestians gathered around the Waterfall of Source and lay down, allowing the music and energy float over them.

Later that night when the dancing was in full swing, Star went to sit with Lacarta and Alhena where one of the carpenters was carving an old tree trunk into an intricate stool. Indus hummed a tune whilst strumming his pequinatar quietly as the three of them sat and talked, still piecing together everything that had happened.

'I missed you,' a voice said and there he was.

Star leapt into his embrace. 'Procyon! I missed you too!' she said.

'I heard you found him. Is he going to be alright?' he said, searching her eyes.

She nodded. 'Thanks so much for persuading me to go. He might have died if I hadn't got there.'

'Are you OK?' he said, stroking her hand as she nodded. 'Are you here to stay or are you going to take an apprenticeship?'

'No way. I never want to see another human again,' she said and they both smiled.

'Told you they were dull, didn't I?' he said. He reached out his hand and touched her cheek, pulling her hands up to his lips and kissing them.

The two young beings leant into each other and swayed gently to the beat of the music.

Celestia would look after them now.

A BIT ABOUT THE AUTHOR

Jessica Ammes lives in Suffolk with her husband, four children, three dogs and two cats. With her good friend Kaz they set up Joinavision. The ethos of the group is to break down the lines of division that are so detrimental to society, empower people to make informed decisions on their health and connect local people. Please join us on our journey at www.joinavision.co.uk.

Printed in Poland
by Amazon Fulfillment
Poland Sp. z o.o., Wrocław

65179359R00226